FAITH & FIDELITY

Tere Michaels

Prologue

He wore the navy suit because it was her favorite, the light blue shirt because when he looked down at his cuff, the slender line of color made him remember her eyes. For twenty minutes he tore through the closet trying to find the tie she'd gotten him last Christmas, but his eyes kept filling with tears and he couldn't see a thing.

Someone—maybe his sister-in-law Elena—came to the door and told him the limo was waiting. He didn't turn around, didn't acknowledge what she said. The flare in the middle of his chest terrified him and he couldn't find his voice. Eventually he gave up the search for the tie and settled for a blue one with tiny green leaves. He walked to the mirror, began tying his tie while studiously avoiding looking at his own face. He fixed on a random point—the headboard of their bed—and suddenly fell into a pit he had been avoiding since she'd died.

Less than a week ago, he and Sherri had been lying there together, enjoying a rare moment of quiet "grown-up time." He'd come home late—as usual—and found her already asleep, curled up on his side of the bed. When he'd slid in behind her, he saw she wore his faded USMC T-shirt. And nothing else.

"Mmmm, baby. What did I do to deserve this?" he asked, pressing his mouth to her tousled blonde hair.

She rolled over, rubbing her still-closed eyes, a sleepy smile crossing her face. "You? Oh no, honey, this is *my* reward."

They'd laughed quietly, easily. Taking time to talk over her day, his hands roaming all over her body. She told him a silly story about her misadventures in carpooling that day and ended with, "Don't you agree I deserve something special?"

The mischievous look in her hazel eyes was his undoing, and he leaned in to kiss her deeply. After nearly twenty years of friendship and fifteen of physical passion between them, there weren't many surprises left when they made love. But somehow, the pleasure that came from learned rhythms and unspoken commands more than made up for any mystery that was lacking.

In the end Evan buried his face against her neck, breathing in her scent and breathing out his moans. He felt her stiffening and lifted his head to watch her. She bit her lip and arched against him, silently. Always silently. "Oh God," he whispered, following her quickly. They'd cuddled, whispered their sweet silly sayings back and forth, the ones too intimate to share in the daylight. Evan got up to put his shorts back on, handed Sherri her T-shirt. Went to the kitchen for his ritual glass of "post-coital water," as Sherri drolly put it. When he came back she was curled up again—on her side this time—sleeping soundly. He went to bed, wrapping himself around her.

And three days later…three days later his phone rang at the precinct and she was gone.

* * *

The viewing took six painful hours. Evan spent the entire time sitting in the front row, at least one of his children huddled by his side at all times. They were feverish with grief, restless and dazed from weeping. He knew he should get up and circulate around the crowded room, but his legs would not cooperate. He could barely manage the small talk he was forced to make when someone new arrived.

He watched them kneel at Sherri's coffin, whisper to each other. (He presumed about how she looked so wonderful, so young and beautiful. You'd never have guessed she was thirty-four, the mother of two teenagers, and two not far behind. You'd never have guessed that some asshole with a suspended license had driven his pickup through a stop sign and into the side of the family Explorer, killing her instantly.) Then they'd walk over to the MacGregors—her parents, Phil and Josie, and only sister, Elena—and finally end up in front of Evan, mouthing their condolences and sympathy.

He just wanted them all to go away.

By noon the crowd had thinned a bit. Saturday afternoon meant errands to run, he supposed. Elena took the kids across the street to the diner for lunch. Phil went outside for a smoke. Evan and Josie sat silently next to one another; he was trying to swallow the sobs that were fighting to get out, his mother-in-law was on her fifth novena of the day.

Listening to Josie's earnest mumbling of prayer next to him, Evan thought about his own family. Or lack thereof. His father was long gone, as well as the stepfathers he assumed were dead by now; his mother vegetated in an upstate nursing home, losing another year of her memory every day. He had brought nothing of family history into their marriage—no warm stories, no aunts, uncles, cousins. Just nightmares and demons that Sherri would tenderly soothe away in the dead of night. Everything they had created had been filtered through Sherri, through her happy childhood, through her dreams of a big family.

"Your friends are here Evan," Josie said softly in his ear.

Evan blinked and turned to his mother-in-law. Her face— Sherri's face from somewhere down a timeline that didn't exist anymore—was inches from his. He could barely hear her voice.

"Your friends, dear. From the police force." Josie motioned to the group milling awkwardly around Sherri's casket. Helena Abbott, Vic Wolkowski, Jonah Moses, and Kalee Jensen, all dressed formally, all wearing their ever-present trench coats.

Vic made the sign of the cross and knelt down to say a prayer. Helena rubbed her eyes and took a deep breath before crossing over to where Evan sat with Josie.

Evan stood up and accepted Helena's tight embrace. "Hey partner," she whispered in his ear. "How ya holding up?"

He shrugged, his chin resting on her shoulder. No one except his children had touched him like this in days, and it was very nearly his undoing. "I just wish it was over," he whispered back. *I just wish this never happened*, he thought.

Helena pulled back from the hug, keeping her hands firmly on his arms. "Do you need me to do anything? Anything at all, all you have to do is ask."

He shook his head. "No. I think I'm okay right now. I'll let you know—really." He was grateful she let the lie pass without challenge. "Uh, Helena, this is Sherri's mom, Josie MacGregor.

"Mom, this is Helena Abbot, my partner."

The women shook hands. "Yes, I remember you from the hospital. It's so kind of you to come."

Oh right, the hospital. Running anxiously down the corridor, flashing his badge, trying to get some answers. Helena trailed behind—she'd refused to let him come alone.

"I didn't know Sherri very well, but...I just wanted to say how terribly sorry I am for your loss, Mrs. MacGregor."

Mr. Cerelli? This way.

"Thank you, Miss Abbot."

We made the initial identification from information found at the scene.

"Mrs. MacGregor, this is our captain, Victor Wolkowski."

"Thank you for coming, Captain."

We just need you to verify this is your wife, Sherri Cerelli.

"I know something of what you're going through, Evan, if you need to talk…"

Evan nodded grimly, tightening his grip on Vic's hand. In all the years they'd worked together, he never imagined this was something they'd have in common.

Cold and pale on the metal gurney, a clean sheet placed over her. They'd wiped off most of the blood. The left side of her skull was crushed. All the air left Evan's lungs in a single instant. An ER doctor was quietly telling him…she'd been DOA…probably died on impact.

"Thanks, Vic."

Moses and Jensen hovered quietly in the background until Evan motioned them over.

Another round of introductions. Another round of helpful offers of comfort, camaraderie, assistance. Evan politely thanking them, an unspoken but shared knowledge that he couldn't accept what they offered. The small group lapsed into awkward silence after the usual chitchat was done. Thankfully, the children and Elena returned from lunch and everyone's attention was diverted.

They let him touch her hand and kiss her icy lips. It wasn't Sherri at all, and he felt like he was cheating to be grieving for this corpse.

Helena and Vic stayed for the rest of the viewing, moving to sit behind Evan's right shoulder once the crowds starting swelling again. He wished he could let them know how comforting it was to him.

The closing of the casket was the worst part by far. By the time Sherri's family finished their good-byes, the children had gone quickly from weepy to hysterical. Once the children had each said their painful good-byes, Evan stood there helplessly, knowing there were no more children, no more excuses.

Phil and Josie seemed to sense his bewilderment. They gently led the children away to get their coats and wait in the car for him. Only Elena remained, but she stood outside the door to the viewing room with Father Deckard, leaving Evan his privacy.

He knelt down to finally face his wife. He looked at the pale representation of the strong and vibrant woman he had loved for twenty years. He remembered the first time he saw her, in junior high. He remembered falling so deeply in love with her, so quickly that it bordered on obsession. It would probably surprise people to know he'd never kissed another woman in passion, never felt another woman's body. It had always been he and Sherri, joined at the hip since they were fourteen, joined at the heart for twenty years. The panic set in so fast he didn't realize he was sobbing until his forehead touched Sherri's clasped hands, folded neatly over her prayer book. What was he supposed to do? She was everything.

His friend, his lover, his anchor. She made everything safe for him.

"Oh Jesus, Sherri. Oh baby, I'm so sorry. I should have been home more, I should have done more. Oh I'm sorry. Please forgive me, Sherri." He wept and wept until he felt his entire being split in two. He drowned in the grief and only the distant thought of his children brought him up for air.

Elena was holding him when everything came back into focus. She stroked his hair and made soothing noises close to his ear. "Evan? Honey, just breathe, okay?" He heard her say something to Father Deckard—*Make sure the kids don't come in. They shouldn't see this.*

Oh God.

He pulled himself together one piece at a time. This wasn't him, this wasn't going to help anything. He had his kids to take care of. At some point he'd have to go back to work. *Okay, Evan. This is who you are. Be a man. Sherri's gone but you still have responsibilities. Come on. Get off your knees and say good-bye.*

Gently he shrugged Elena off. He staggered to his feet and leaned over the casket, this time pressing his lips against Sherri's forehead. He prayed for her immortal soul. He asked God to take care of her, because she deserved to have someone watch over her for a change. She'd been the best possible wife and mother, and he loved her so much and he wanted her to be at peace. Amen.

Evan wiped his eyes on his sleeve and moved away from the casket. He didn't look back. He couldn't. Father Deckard made noises in his direction but Evan kept walking. He'd never had much use for organized religion; he and God had an uneasy relationship at best. The children were being raised in the Church for Sherri's sake—that wouldn't change.

He strode out of the viewing room, through the tasteful lobby of the funeral home, and out the door. The kids were huddled together in the backseat of his sedan. Danny and Elizabeth had given in to their exhaustion and the other two girls didn't look like they were going to last too long.

"Thanks, Mom, Dad. I'll see you tomorrow at church."

"Evan, please, we can take the kids to our place…"

"No. I'll see you both tomorrow." He kissed Josie, shook Phil's hand, and got into the car.

As they pulled away, he heard Kathleen's quiet voice from the back seat. "Daddy?"

"Yeah, sweetheart?"

"What are we going…I mean, what's going to happen now?"

The "without Mommy" hung heavy in the air.

Evan took a deep breath and tapped into the last reserve of his strength. "I don't know exactly, Kathleen—I'll be honest with you. But I'm going to do my very best to make sure we're okay. I promise."

This seemed to placate his daughter enough. She laid her head down on Miranda's shoulder and closed her eyes. Evan caught his eldest child's eyes in the rearview mirror. They shared a weary moment then Miranda rested her heavy eyes as well.

Then Evan was alone with his grief.

Chapter One

Matt Haight sat in his car, watching the entrance of the Stag Bar with butterflies in his stomach. Come to think of it, more like a hornet with an Uzi. He could smell all the cops in there from across the street; inside, in that sea of blue, was the place he wanted to be most, and least, in the world. Only Abe Klein's retirement party could bring him to the city, into a room full of detectives and beat cops, reminding Matt over and over of what his life no longer was.

It'd been a long time since he'd hung with cops from Manhattan. Staten Island might well be a leper colony (and he the head leper?) because no one wanted to be there, and no one wanted to admit knowing Matt Haight. Then again, he hadn't been a cop for almost a year so, basically, no one gave a shit in triplicate.

Jesus H. Christ but did he need a drink.

With shakier hands than he would ever admit to, Matt swung his tall, muscled form out of the sedan—he supposed it was some sort of psychological thing that he still drove a detective's car, still dressed like he was on the force. He just couldn't seem to give up the illusion of his former life. They called him Lieutenant Matt at the security firm he worked for, and with a smile that was forced and false, he would laugh at the joke and walk away. He'd gotten very, very good at walking away—a hard lesson learned for Matty but he figured at forty-fucking-two years old, he might as well start acting like an adult.

Or so he liked to tell himself right before he got falling down drunk.

Suddenly, he was inside the bar, taking automatic inventory of the wood paneling, boxing memorabilia, and TVs at either end of the bar playing baseball games—gee, Anybar NYC. Boy, did this place look familiar.

A quick scan told him that he didn't know anyone milling around the main room; he could hear the roars of laughter and raucous buzz of conversation from the back. At some point he'd have to go find Abe in that sea of familiar faces and give him his most sincere congratulations, but first Matt moved to the bar, checked the Yankee score, and waited for the bartender to catch notice of him. He knew there would be whispering and he didn't want to hear it. So he'd wait until he was just a little bit drunk.

The door behind him opened and he turned to see if it was someone he knew. Vic Fucking Wolkowski! A big smile crossed Matt's face.

"Hey Vic!"

The bald captain was taking off his jacket and turned to face the voice. "Matty! What the hell are you doing here?"

It wasn't meant to be a slight but it hurt anyway.

"Couldn't miss Abe's sendoff." The two men shook hands heartily.

"You look good, Matty. They tell me you left the force."

"Yeah, yeah. Time to move on." He shrugged, pretending it was no big deal. Vic kindly played along. "I got a decent job, working for a corporate security firm. We analyze security for businesses, protect head honchos from disgruntled employees. That sort of shit."

"Good cash?"

Matt laughed. "I'm doing okay." *I can afford to eat my dinner every night in the shit hole pub down the street from my one room apartment. I'm doing great,* he thought.

"So let me ask you something. You think that highfalutin firm'd have something for me?"

"You thinking about retiring, Vic?"

"Might be nice. I get awfully tired these days. Vice can really be a black hole."

Matt nodded. He'd never done any time in Vice but remembered his own dealings in Homicide, working in conjunction with the other department. You would never imagine there were some things worse than death, but there were.

"Hey, meet some detectives from my unit." For the first time, Matt realized there were people standing a few feet away, waiting for Vic. A man and a woman. *Jesus,* thought Matt, *how did I miss her? Must be slipping in my old age.* He flashed a ten-thousand-watt smile in her direction.

"Helena Abbot, Evan Cerelli, meet Matt Haight. He used to partner with Abe back in Homicide."

"Pleased to meet you," Matt said with a squeeze to Helena's hand.

She smiled back. Ho-ly Cow. Gorgeous smile. Violet eyes. Short, glossy black hair that looked more Fifth Avenue professional than Vice cop. He shook the guy's hand—Elvis?—and immediately turned his attention back to Helena.

He never got past opening his mouth. Helena moved past him and signaled the bartender.

"Evan, Captain, Matt, right? What do you guys want?"

"Club soda."

"Same."

"Aw c'mon, Evan, not even a beer?"

"Peer pressure notwithstanding, Helena, just club soda," he said.

"Uh, I'll take a beer," Matt piped up, resisting the urge to sniff himself or check his teeth for a plank of wood stuck in between the front two.

"Tap or bottle?"

"Tap's fine," Matt said, unable to come up with anything witty.

Her smile felt warm but her eyes indicated her mind was elsewhere. Matt wasn't getting any beeps on the interest meter. Uh…ouch.

The drinks came and Helena played hostess. Her main focus seemed to be Evan. She kept touching his arm and shining her bright smile in his direction. The conversation was light and full of Vic catching Matt up on old acquaintances, peppered with a few "remember that time" stories thrown in. He listened with half an ear—Helena was a distraction. He couldn't for the life of him figure out what she seemed to see in her partner. This guy was no player, that was for damn sure, and seemed on the stiff side. He obviously didn't know how to respond to Helena's flirting.

Vic excused himself when he saw a friend enter the bar, leaving Matt to officially become The Third Wheel.

Fuck. Maybe it was time to find Abe.

"Hey, I'm gonna check out the party in the back room. You guys coming?" He sounded idiotic. It felt like high school.

Helena smiled at him. "Thanks—we'll be in soon."

Thank you. I'm dismissed, thought Matt. He picked up his beer—and the dark cloud over his head—and walked into the back room.

About seventy-five of Abe's closest friends were toasting his health and, apparently, the size of his penis. Classy crowd. God, but he missed them. Matt scanned the crowd and spotted his old friend chatting with a few suits in the corner. Trying to avoid eye contact with anyone, Matt moved across the room.

He had almost made it when a hand snaked out of the crowd and grabbed his arm. "Matt Haight!" a voice bellowed. Matt turned and looked down into the red and bloated face of Rick Hanlon, a former Academy classmate. Last he'd heard, Rick was on the fast track to being a captain. If he didn't drink himself to death first.

Oh great, thought Matt, *exactly who I want to see right now.*

"Matty, baby! How the fuck are you? Jesus, they let you off foot patrol for this!" The Rick clones sitting around his table laughed obediently. "What are you doing on the big island?"

Matt flashed his most charming smile and counted backward from ten. "Hey, Rick. No, no foot patrol for me. I'm outta the blue uniform these days. Working private security—"

Rick cut him off. "Security guard—niiice. Do ya have a spiffy outfit?" More inane laughter.

"Yeah, whatever. See ya, Rick." Matt turned on his heel, heading blindly out the way he came. Jesus fucking Christ. How did he think this was a good idea?

He could feel all the eyes burning into his back. He felt like "America's Most Wanted." Brothers in blue—what a crock of shit. Brothers until you turned one of them in for being no better than the people they arrested. Brothers who had your back, your life in their hands, until you decided that the truth mattered more than their crap codes. Then all bets were apparently off.

The anger and frustration washed over him like a wave.

This was where he always got himself in trouble, and he was determined to keep a lid on it. He'd paid the ultimate price—his career—for the temporary gratification of letting the anger escape in one punch.

Never again.

Matt stopped, took a deep breath, and found himself back at the bar. He signaled the bartender, got his prompt attention by waving a twenty, and ordered another beer. Turning his head he saw that the Vice detectives had moved to a table in the corner. Wolkowski was gone—probably in the main room—but an attractive woman had joined Helena and Evan. Jeeze, didn't any ugly girls work at Vice? He considered going over to say hello but thought again. Did he want to be ignored by two women?

Without anything else to do—well, besides the obvious option of getting drunk—a tired and resigned Matt watched the three detectives at the corner table, still trying to figure out what this Evan guy had going to make two such hot women fawn over him.

But when Matt took a closer look, he realized that the detective barely reacted to their teasing. He smiled automatically but kept looking into the distance, as if engaged in an entirely different scene playing out in his head. After a few moments, Matt watched as he excused himself and got up, grabbing a cell phone from his coat pocket as he walked outside. When Matt looked back toward the table, he saw the two women frowning, whispering.

Something screwy going on in Vice. *Wow, what a brilliant detective you were, Matt. Stunning they let you get away.*

The door opened again and Evan returned, followed by another man. Round and balding, in a cheap suit, looked ten years older than he actually was—definitely a cop. There was general chatting as Evan grabbed another chair to add to the table and a friendly wave of conversation filled the air.

Evan settled down, glad to have Moses there to soak up some of the attention from his fellow detectives. Ducking out of the conversation mentally, he looked up to see Matt Haight watching the table with a hangdog expression on his face. Evan gave him a smile. He felt a little bad about what happened earlier at the bar. He could see Matt was interested in Helena and she hadn't seemed to notice.

He knew why; he was there and Helena was sweetly transparent. She'd been working so hard at keeping an eye on him over the past year that their once equal relationship had become more of a nurse/patient one. Every morning she brought him breakfast and watched him eat it. Every afternoon she nagged him about lunch. She told jokes and kept herself so perkily "up" that sometimes he worried she was going to hurt herself. Before they took leave of each other at night, she'd remind him about his dinner. The woman was obsessed with his eating habits. Sometimes she'd call him at home over the weekend, just to chat, pretending she needed his expert help on something.

Evan missed just being Helena's friend and partner.

Evan knew the story of Matt Haight. After a year of spending time in the "Vic Wolkowski's Widower/Divorced Guy Outreach Program" (as fellow participant Moses had christened it), he'd gotten the dirt. Matt Haight's legendary temper, his pissing off the wrong politicians with his also legendary opinions, and having his career offered up as a sacrificial lamb when he'd stumbled on a string of dirty cops while investigating a junkie's murder. Bringing down a corrupt but well-liked cop to put a "solved" sticker on the case of a dead heroin dealer didn't exactly get you a ticker tape parade. NYC homicide detective to Staten Island beat cop, a hell of a fall from grace. It was probably a cop's worst nightmare outside of death or injury. Or maybe not. Death most likely meant honor. What happened to Haight stained a man, inside and out, forever.

He motioned for him to join them at the table. Haight hesitated so he waved at him again. The former cop made like he was going to refuse but Evan could see the loneliness in his face. After a small pause, the tall man got off his bar stool and headed over.

"Hi, Matt. Come and join us?" Evan said politely.

Everyone at the table looked up expectantly. Helena seemed to realize her faux pas before at the bar because she started nodding enthusiastically.

"I didn't see you over there or I would have waved you over myself!"

Matt smiled wanly and pulled a chair over. They all scooted over until the chairs fit.

"Matt Haight, Kalee Jensen and Jonah Moses, Vice." Handshakes and nods all around.

Kalee flashed a flirty smile in Matt's direction and he gave her one in return before she launched into a rant against the Public Defender who'd cross-examined her at a trial the previous day. Things quickly turned into a "you think that's bad?" contest, with even Matt joining in to tell a few stories of his own. Helena signaled the bartender to keep the pitchers of beer coming as this was obviously warming up into something big.

After a while the conversation degraded into Kalee and Moses getting into a fake fight over which was a tougher department—Vice or Narcotics, where Moses had spent most of his career. It slid dangerously close to a Mighty Mouse vs. Superman sort of thing and everyone else just sat back and watched the two go at it. Evan spared a glance across the table at Matt, who hadn't said a word in quite some time. His rugged face reflected a weary acceptance of life that Evan recognized quite easily—he'd spent nearly a full year avoiding it in his own mirror.

Missing Sherri had turned out to be a full-time job. Add in raising his kids and working at Vice and he had simply given up a few things to get by. Like sleeping. Like eating (except when Helena or Miranda were around and forced him to sit down and swallow some food). Like conscious thought outside of what automatically needed to be done. This zombie-like existence seemed to be working fine. His work hadn't suffered—concentrating on the pain and misery of others proved to be a helpful distraction from his own looming grief. No one was really the wiser. They knew he was sad, figured that he was lonely.

But they didn't realize he'd become, for all intents and purposes, removed from life. He felt love for his children and friends, but it pretty much ended there. He couldn't feel what they gave in return, didn't respond when Elizabeth threw her arms around his neck or Danny curled up next to him on the couch after dinner. Every time Helena touched him he'd have to stare at her hand, to make the connection between his arm and brain. He knew at some point he'd have to seek help—this couldn't go on because frankly sooner or later he was going to end up eating his gun. And he couldn't do that to his children.

Over the din of conversation Evan caught Matt's eye and shrugged at his friends' nonsense, smiled again. He wasn't exactly sure why he was reaching out to this man—maybe force of habit. You see someone sitting that far down in the gutter, you lend him a hand.

Matt Haight let the conversational buzz and beer settle into his bones; it'd been a long time since he'd been drinking with anyone else around. While the conversation didn't actually include him, it was nice not to be completely invisible for awhile. And Evan Cerelli—well, there was something in his expression that Matt recognized. Neither one of them was entirely comfortable here, but, in the same breath, where else were they supposed to be?

So Matt smiled back.

The friends at the table continued their raucous banter. Matt felt his brain wandering again. He'd lost count of how many beers he'd consumed but knew he was nowhere near being smashed. His tolerance had built up to a pretty high level. More cops in and out the front door. More casual glances in his direction. More faint whispers of his name here and there, getting louder as the time got later and volume control was shorted out by cheap liquor. Matt's back stiffened up slowly, his shoulders creeping up towards his ears with tension and discomfort.

"Hey, Matt," he heard from a distance.

Evan was calling him from across the table. He raised his voice to be heard over the enraged shrieks now emanating from Helena and Kalee—as Moses had said something particularly ridiculous. "I see Abe over there with Vic. Have you had a chance to talk to him yet?"

Matt shook his head no. "Then let's go over." Evan stood up promising the table they'd be back.

Abe and Vic were leaning on the bar, nursing club sodas and wiping their brows. Judging from the noise, no one in the back room had noticed the guest of honor had left to get some air.

Looking up, Abe broke into a huge smile when he saw Matt and moved to give him a big hug. Matt returned the sentiment and felt a lump well in his throat. He always forgot how much he missed the old coot. It was a relief to see him retiring in one piece, the only one of Matt's partners to be able to do that. He tried not to think of himself as the Harbinger of Death.

"I was hoping you'd grace us with your presence." He winked over at Vic. "Shoulda checked the table with the beautiful women as soon as I came in."

Everyone laughed.

Evan stood discreetly to one side, watching the warm reunion. Nice. It looked like Matt needed someone to be thrilled to see him. He remembered how many times—you know, *before*, as he thought of it—after the worse possible day, he'd come home to have one of the kids greet him with a simple smile or hug and suddenly he'd forget the ugliness. Sherri standing at the stove, turning to flash him a big smile, glad to see he'd made it home before midnight.

'Cause ya know, Evan, he told himself, *if you're going to have a memory, have a real one.* He'd made it hard on her, working so many hours, leaving her to manage the kids, the house, their life. She'd done it brilliantly, which had made it so much easier for him to stay that extra hour (or four), or take off to pursue something that could have honestly waited until morning. There'd been a million arguments over it. It was really the only thing they'd fought over which made it even more painful. A problem that he could have solved simply by leaving Vice. But he didn't, and if wishes were horses or however that saying went.

Vic was saying something about another drink and Evan looked down at his watch. It was almost nine, and he'd promised the kids he'd be home in time to say good night. Damn. Evan begged off then hesitantly interrupted Abe and Matt's conversation.

"Sorry guys. I need to get home. Abe—I just wanted to wish you the best."

"Hey, Evan! Thanks for coming. I'm sure you'll see me around. This leisure thing is probably going to get old real quick, and I'll be stopping by to bug Vic here on a regular basis. Maybe impart some of my senior wisdom."

Evan grinned. "And I know you don't want to miss any of Vic's meetings."

Abe cracked up. "Oh yeah. That would be a shame. Why go out and look for the next Ms. Right when I can spend Thursday nights with you, Moses, and Vic?"

"Exactly. Take care. I'll see you soon." They shook hands and Evan turned to go. He stopped and went back to shake Matt's hand.

"Good to meet you."

"Hey, thanks."

Evan understood the unspoken message. *Hey thanks for not treating me like a circus freak.* He felt exactly the same way.

"Uh, we should you know, get a drink or something sometime," Matt said casually. "Just hang out."

"Yeah. Give me a call at the station."

Matt nodded. "Great."

Evan gave Vic a small wave and headed for the table to collect his things. He said his good-byes and was gone quickly out the door, before anyone could protest too much.

Matt caught more frowns and whispers going on at the table, especially from Helena who rubbed her forehead, pushing off questions from the other two detectives with a wave of her hand. He turned to Abe and Vic, who was watching with worried eyes of his own.

"So what's the story?

"On Evan? Wife died about ten months ago—car accident. Left him with four kids. It's just all...heartbreaking." He shook his head.

"Shit."

"Yeah. He's holding it together, at least on the surface. I been there myself ya know, and frankly, I don't think he's doing as well as he claims to be."

Matt grunted, looking down into his glass of beer.

Maybe that was the connection then. You grieve with every fiber of your being when the thing you love most is ripped out of your life.

Chapter Two

Matt Haight found himself at yet another bar on yet another Friday night. Beer, check. Slight buzz going, check. No female company in sight, check. Yep, good to go. He watched his reflection in the warped mirror behind the bar. Jesus he looked like shit. Starting to get that puffy look. Time to go on a diet, get back in the gym. Something. Anything.

He needed to talk to someone, just to shoot the shit. Seeing his old friends a few weeks ago at Abe's made him wish he'd tried harder to stay in touch. He saw his ex-partner Phil O'Neill and his family on the holidays but that was it. He spent his time alone, in this bar (or one remarkably like it). He hadn't made a new friend in what...years? It was fucking depressing. He didn't know how to connect with anyone anymore—he was becoming a hermit. A drunk hermit. Matt started thinking about Abe's party and remembered the guy he'd met there. Evan Cerelli? The widower. Cop. Seemed nice. Vic Wolkowski and Abe both gave him high marks. Seemed like he would be cool to just hang out with.

Matt took a deep breath. *Resolve, Matty, resolve. Get off yer ass and do something about your sorry state.*

Checking his watch, he saw it was nearly nine. Evan was home by now but Matt thought he might leave a message. Maybe they could hook up next week. He walked over to the doorway to give himself some privacy and flipped open his cell before he lost his nerve and dialed up Vice from memory (mind like a steel fucking trap). Asked for Evan Cerelli. Absently looked around the nearly empty bar, wondering what loser picked a dump like this to get drunk in. Then he heard a voice pick up on the other line.

"Cerelli."

"Uh, hey. Evan. This is Matt Haight."

"Hey, Matt."

"Oh, you remember..."

"Well, yeah." Evan laughed softly into the phone. "Mind like a steel trap."

Momentarily distracted, Matt tried to put his thoughts together. "Kind of surprised you're still at work..."

"My kids are at their grandparents' for the weekend," Evan said, and Matt could hear the distinct deadening of his voice. "I'm just catching up on some paperwork."

"Well then I'll let you go."

"Wait. Where are you?"

And the lie came out without Matt even considering why he bothered. "Manhattan. You guys are on the West Side right?"

"Yeah—you wanna come by? We could get that drink tonight." A hollow laugh. "I could use it."

Amen, brother, thought Matt. "Give me an hour—I have, uh, an errand to take care of."

"Great. Come up to the third floor."

"I'll see you soon." And he hung up the phone.

He stared at the receiver for a long moment then walked back to the bar, threw down a twenty for his last three beers and a healthy tip, and headed out the door. He had an hour to get from Staten Island to Midtown. Drive or ferry? He decided on the ferry since he presumed he was legally drunk and crossed the street, heading for the station.

See, that was easy, thought Matt. Things were already looking up.

Evan hung up the phone and stared at the pin neat surface of his desk. The paperwork he'd finished an hour ago. Then he'd cleaned out his drawers, updated several files, sharpened some pencils. He was about to go clean the coffee machine—anything to keep him from having to go home—when Matt Haight provided him with an escape plan. A drink. Maybe a whole lot of drinks. Conversation with someone who didn't automatically affect the "poor Evan" expression when addressing him.

Haight was essentially a stranger. He wouldn't be searching for clues to Evan's mental state or checking on his eating habits. Or watching his hands to see if they shook. (Which they did, but maybe Haight wouldn't notice.)

The kids needed this break—the house was a living testament to Sherri's life and a constant reminder of her death, and he knew it got to them as much as it did him. He was exhausted keeping up a normal front and his in-laws had picked up on it last time they "dropped in" for a quick visit. How anyone "dropped in" to Queens from Long Island he had no idea, but these days he preferred to keep his relationship with Phil and Josie as politely distant as humanly possible. He had no interest in hearing another two voices comment on how they thought he was holding up.

They'd insisted on taking the kids for the weekend—picked them up from school and driven straight out to the Island. Promised to return them on Sunday night. That would give Evan "time to relax"—*oh yeah, 'cause you know, sleeping in an empty house, feeling the absence of your dead wife and your children, that just screamed relaxation.*

Evan sighed. He thought maybe, with a belly full of liquor, he might sleep for a few hours tonight. It was the best he could hope for.

Matt arrived at Vice in a record forty-two minutes. He'd spent the entire ferry and cab ride over sobering up and trying to comprehend the fluttery feeling in his chest. Staring up at the brick building, he swallowed back the rush of memories, the overwhelming sense of longing he felt. It was bittersweet—like seeing your ex happy in the arms of someone else.

He took the stairs up to the third floor and paused at the squad room's doorway. Evan was sitting at his desk, staring off into space, his head turned away from where Matt stood. He slumped in his chair, his hands lying limp on the surface of his desk. His posture spoke of exhaustion, defeat. Matt suddenly realized how gaunt the man was—pale skin, looked like he could stand to gain ten or fifteen pounds. A wave of sympathy pushed Matt through the door. He cleared his throat, giving Evan a chance to pull himself together.

Blinking, Evan turned to see who had entered the squad room. Except for the occasional uniform wandering through looking for leftovers, he had been alone all evening.

Matt Haight stood a few feet away, smiling broadly.

"Hey, you ready to get that drink?"

They ended up at a hole-in-the-wall Matt remembered called O'Malley's—one of about six hundred bars in the five boroughs with that name but this one had the distinction of being run by a guy who was Cuban on his mother's side and Jamaican on his father's.

The place was filled to capacity—ten people—mostly at the bar, a few at the tables and booths that haphazardly filled the place, one guy having a fight with someone on the pay phone near the bathrooms. The two men moved to the table furthest from the door, tucked into the far left corner, just far enough from the angry drunk at the phone to be able to talk.

Evan took off his overcoat and suit jacket, pulling his tie off as he sat down with a heavy sigh.

"You weren't kidding when you said you could use a drink."

Evan shrugged. "Long week. I think I just need to unwind for awhile."

"Beer okay, or you want something stronger?"

"Beer's fine."

Matt got up and walked over to the bartender, ordered them two pitchers. "Ya want food?" asked the burly man. His faded tattoos peeked out from under his shirtsleeves and collar. Matt spotted the USMC logo on his inner arm when he pointed out the short menu on the blackboard behind the bar.

"Give me one of everything," said Matt. That should cover them for the evening. Greasy bar food and beer. He was going to have to start jogging in the morning.

The bartender grunted and slid the pitchers across the bar to Matt. "Tab?"

"Oh yeah. You want a credit card?"

"Nah, I trust cops." He turned and went back to cleaning up some spills in front of a bleary-eyed businessman.

As he balanced the pitchers and two glasses and wove in and out of the small tables back to their spot, Matt absently wondered if it was a learned skill or natural inclination that made bartenders able to spot a cop at forty paces.

"Ta-da." He put everything down on the table, impressed he didn't spill a precious drop. "I ordered some food, too."

Evan was already pouring beer into the glasses. "Uh, great. Thanks."

Matt sat down and took his beer, raising it to toast his partner in drinking to oblivion. "Here's to bad food, flat beer, and good company."

Evan returned his smile. "Sounds perfect."

They clinked their glasses and started the trip to numbness.

* * *

That was the first time.

Within a month, they were meeting for drinks on a weekly basis, whenever Evan was free. Evan's kids were his number one priority and he spent every possible night home with them, but more and more his in-laws were pushing for overnight stays. Unable to say no, Evan watched as his kids piled into their grandparent's station wagon and waved good-bye. He didn't blame their craving for home-cooked meals and warm hugs. He was a ghost now, haunting his house with quiet desperation that grew larger and heavier every day. He didn't know how to make things special like Sherri had. He could barely manage the minimum. His only outlet besides work was the simple comfort of sitting across from Matt Haight and drinking until he saw double.

They kept going back to O'Malley's for the quiet and for the surprisingly good buffalo wings. Their table was kept available most of the time, the bartender knew them and their order by the third visit. The routine was comforting, they liked not having to think about anything but the beer and the conversation.

It started out with sports, cop shit, superficial things until the buzz turned into a roar and then the ugly truth came out in a rush.

Maybe it was the beer or the quiet intimacy of sitting so close together in the near dark. Whatever the combination, Evan found himself opening up to Matt like he'd done with no one else in his life. There were no soothing words or trite advice when Evan talked about his dead wife on the gurney, wishing he could have five minutes with the son of a bitch who killed her so he could crush his skull in the exact same manner.

They became good enough friends to politely forget the tears, the self-pity, and the bitter outpouring of emotion. Matt kindly ignored the wet tracks down Evan's face.

And Evan just nodded when Matt slurred out his hatred of his "brothers" for ruining his life, even though he knew it was his fault alone, his fault that he had lost everything. Evan agreed without judgment, reaching for the pitcher to refill both their glasses. He knew how that felt.

* * *

Matt didn't know about Evan but it was the highlight of his week, sitting in the near-dark, just talking, listening, drinking. They created a little cocoon of their misery, a safe haven in which to feel like a piece of garbage. To be tired and bitter and a failure, with no apologies.

How exactly that moved to daily "shoot the shit" phone calls, he couldn't exactly say.

"So I got Giants tickets for this weekend—you game?"

"Where the hell did you get those?"

"Grateful client with box seats. So?"

"Yeah. Kids are away again. My sister-in-law is taking them pumpkin picking."

"Why don't you go too?"

Matt could practically hear the shrug over the phone. "Can't seem to work up the energy I'd need."

"I'll pick you up at ten a.m. on Sunday then."

"You got it."

After hanging up the phone, Matt got back to making dinner (two Lean Cuisines in the microwave) and nursing a bottle of Coors.

He couldn't pinpoint when he'd started noticing the little things, like the odd silver-blue color of Evan's eyes, or the way he moved...in control. The way his body moved under his unassuming button-down shirts as he sprawled in his chair, tipping his head back to work out the kinks. He couldn't remember when he'd begun moving his chair a little closer during their weekly drink fests, catching the subtle scent of soap and cologne from his skin. Matt imagined one of his children bought it for him, for Christmas or Father's Day. In his mind's eye he could picture Evan standing in front of the bathroom mirror, splashing it on, rubbing his face with damp hands. He tried not to spend too much time dwelling on any of it, because it posed a much larger question than Matt was willing to ponder.

Of course the not pondering didn't help the situation once the dreams began.

The first one was just...strange. The only thing he remembered was the USMC tattoo. At first, Matt thought he was dreaming of the bartender at O'Malley's, which was frightening in and of itself. But they weren't in the bar, they were...in the squad room. Matt's old squad room at Homicide. He was at his desk, typing, and when he looked across to talk to Abe, he saw...it was Evan. Smiling.

He could see the USMC tattoo on the inside of Evan's arm, a reminder of his brief time in the military before marriage and fatherhood demanded he return home. And that was all Matt could remember.

The second dream—a few nights later—was pretty unforgettable and this time Matt didn't have to decipher its meaning. He woke up in a cold sweat, his heart thundering in his ears. The sheets were damp. But this wasn't a nightmare.

In this dream—and all the ones that followed—they were sitting somewhere dark and...soft. Side by side, almost touching. Matt whispered, because it almost felt like church. Almost. *What does your tattoo taste like?* Evan said nothing. He was barely more than a ghost, his eyes radiating some kind of light...and then he pushed himself against Matt, lifting his arm to just outside the reach of his lips. Without a second thought Matt ran his tongue from Evan's wrist to the crook of his elbow. Paused. Then kept going. Up his forearm, tasting muscle. Past his shoulder, into the dip of his collarbone. The taste was addictive. Oh and his mouth...

His mouth.

After the latest dream—the morning after he'd made the plans with Evan for the Giants game—Matt ended up with his hands buried in his hair, breathing deeply, nearly turning to check and make sure there wasn't anyone in bed with him. This dream was driving him crazy. Every fucking night for the past two weeks he'd wake up shaking—and rock hard—his mouth burning with a memory from his imagination. This had never happened to him before. He'd always been strictly into women, 100 percent. Lost his virginity at fourteen, for Christ's sake. Granted, the past few years had been less than successful, and he honestly could not remember the last real relationship he'd had.

Like the one you have with Evan, you idiot? His inner voice sounded like his late partner Tony, sort of a cross between a wise guy and a sitcom dad.

Oh no. Matt shook his head violently, tossing the covers back to get up. He tried to pretend the hard-on was the result of needing to take a piss, but he wasn't fooling himself and hey, he wasn't fooling his dick.

Peering into his bathroom mirror he got close enough for his nose to touch. The drinking was taking its toll. He'd seen it happen to his old man, knew the signs. Was he aging badly? Would he ever find someone who looked at him with anything more than pity? Or contempt? Or casual affection? He wanted what Evan had, what he talked about from the bottom of a pitcher of beer. He wanted to love someone enough to grieve for them.

He also wanted to stop dreaming of running his tongue all over Evan Cerelli's body—well hey, we could start there and work toward the rest later.

Facing him on Sunday was going to be tough. Hard. He groaned inwardly. *Don't remind me*, he thought, trying to ignore the throb located in his groin. It's just a fantasy; it didn't mean he was gay. Didn't mean anything as a matter of fact. He was spending a lot of time with Evan, the first person in a very long while who listened to Matt, who made him feel comfortable, calm. His subconscious was just equating sex—which he hadn't had in a very long time—with that comfort. Man, all that time spent around his friend Liz the Shrink had apparently made him a dream analyst. How impressive. Maybe he should give her a call and ask her opinion of a been-heterosexual-all-my-life guy having sex dreams about another guy who happened to be his closest friend. And also straight. No, he didn't actually want to hear what she had to say. It would probably just make him swan dive off a pier.

He poured a glass of orange juice down his throat, trying to scrub the tingle off his tongue. Crawled back under the covers repeating his theory about his subconscious doing a little creative writing. Pretended that he wasn't thinking of Evan when his hand finished the job his dream had started.

Christ.

Chapter Three

On the Friday before the Giants game, his day off, Matt Haight started jogging and hated it after about five minutes. He huffed and puffed around his block once, twice, three times, waving to the crossing guard as he went by.

"You want me to time you?" she called out on his second trip.

"God no," he wheezed.

Back at his apartment he stumbled into the shower and stood there, dazed and in pain. He used to be in shape—he vaguely remembered this. Didn't he run after criminals? Didn't he walk up many, many flights of stairs without having a heart attack? Were these figments of his imagination?

"I'm not an old man. I will get back into shape." He felt better announcing this fact to his shower stall. The echo made it sound like an important thing.

He ate lunch sitting in his recliner, pulled up so he could rest his feet on the windowsill and enjoy the stunning view of the neighboring building's rooftop garden. His whole apartment encompassed one large room with a tiny kitchenette and bathroom. He paid a pittance for it, and it was close enough to his office that he could walk in good weather. It also looked like shit. He hadn't painted it since he'd moved in, the furniture was Salvation Army reject, and, God forbid he actually clean it once in awhile.

After his delicious ham sandwich and glass of iced tea (no sugar—he really was trying), Matt wandered around the room, taking stock. Maybe he could get a sofa bed. Replace the recliner with something that didn't need electrical tape to keep the stuffing in. A table, some chairs. Dishes that matched. New towels. Oh yeah. That would be nice. He had the money, sitting in the bank, collecting shit interest and dust. Why not spend some of it? The first thing the apartment needed was a fresh coat of paint.

Maybe Evan could come over and help him out... Yeah, and maybe they could rent gladiator movies and make out on the couch.

Christ almighty. He was losing his grip on reality. Matt needed to get laid as soon as humanly possible. This unnatural celibacy had to be the reason for his...odd dreams.

And the fact that you know what another man smells like. And It Turns You On. Admit it Matthew. Another Man Turns You On.

Paint. Think about paint. Was yellow a good color? Cream? Did he even know the difference between the two?

Matt pulled on his shoes, grabbed his wallet and jacket, and headed out the door. Paint. He needed paint.

* * *

Evan's plans for the weekend were rapidly going south.

He'd committed to the game with Matt on Sunday because Elena was taking the kids for the day. But she called Saturday night, asking if it would be all right if she switched the outing to next week. A friend needed help moving...something or another. The kids were disappointed, and Evan wasn't sure what to do with the day. The Weather Channel mentioned snow so he lamely suggested a fun day of board games and dinner out at their favorite restaurant (an Italian place around the corner, casual and with the genius idea of having video games in a separate room). After some skeptical looks—because Daddy wasn't usually into having fun these days—they agreed it sounded good.

Then he realized he'd have to call Matt and let him know about the change of plans. He got the kids settled for the night and grabbed the phone. Let it ring and ring and ring. No answer. No machine. The cell went straight to voice mail, which declared itself full.

"Shit." Evan put the phone down and paced around the room. He had no idea how to get in touch with Matt. He didn't want the guy to get all the way out to Queens for nothing.

By midnight Evan gave up and lay down on the couch, where he regularly pretended to sleep. He'd try again in the morning.

Once Matt got started he found it hard to stop. Painting. And cleaning. And throwing shit out.

Thankfully, his only real neighbor—the guy downstairs—was stone deaf so Matt kept going well past eight o'clock. At first he was going to cover his furniture but it looked like shit so why bother. He left the mattress on the floor. Everything else he marched down to the dumpster behind the apartment. The paint he'd bought was called "eggshell" and looked like beige on the walls. Or maybe what he thought was beige actually turned out to be eggshell. He pondered this mystery of life as he painted his apartment.

At one a.m. he finished cleaning his bathroom. The apartment was freezing cold. He left the windows opened to help the paint dry, clear the fumes out. He was looking forward to putting nice furniture in, making the place a little homey. After five years it seemed about time.

An hour later he was curled up on his mattress, under every blanket he owned and two overcoats. Thankfully, exhaustion kept his more erotic of dreams at bay and he finally had a decent night's sleep.

By nine a.m. he was on the road and heading to Queens.

* * *

Evan made pancakes. Miranda discreetly pointed out the ones that weren't cooked all the way through and put them back on the stove. He made sausage patties, which seemed to pass muster. They had a nice breakfast, chatting and planning the day. Kathleen wanted Scrabble. Elizabeth and Danny voted for a video store run. Miranda shrugged—she didn't care as long as they did it together.

"Let's do it all," Evan said, trying to get into the spirit of the day. Movies, board games, dinner. Talk had turned to Thanksgiving break when the doorbell rang.

"Oh no." Evan knew exactly who would be standing at his front door. He'd completely forgotten to try calling Matt again.

"Hey."

Matt stood on his steps, smiling. "Hey. You about—" And then, glancing a bit father into the house, he caught sight of the breakfast table full of junior sized Cerellis over Evan's shoulder.

"Sorry—I tried to call you. The plans fell through." Evan felt terrible. "I'm sorry you had to drive all the way out here."

"No problem."

"The tickets…"

"They were free. Don't worry about it."

"Hi!" a voice called out from behind the two men. Elizabeth, ever the social director. "Want some pancakes?"

"Uh, sure."

Evan laughed. "My kids have better manners than I do. Come in."

Matt walked into the neat little house, taking in the homey touches. Pictures of the kids everywhere. Piano. The cozy couch and frilly curtains. It looked like the set of a television sitcom.

And Evan's kids sat around the kitchen table staring up at him.

"Well hi."

"This is my friend Matt Haight."

Matt tried to keep track of the kids as they were introduced. Miranda, the eldest, blonde and pretty, with Evan's eyes and a sharp air around her. Kathleen, also blonde, also pretty. She seemed shy, ducking her head when Matt smiled at her. Elizabeth—a real beauty with Evan's dark hair and features. She radiated warmth and enthusiastically greeted Matt. He knew he'd made an instant friend. And finally Danny, who was less forthcoming than his sisters. He sat on his hands, swinging his feet against his chair.

Evan pointed to a chair and Matt sat down, trying not to twitch under the children's unwavering gazes. He accepted a plate full of breakfast and a huge mug of coffee from Evan, who still had an apologetic look on his face.

"It's okay!"

"Are you going to the game anyway?"

Matt shrugged, remembering his table manners around the kids. He swallowed his pancakes. "Not much fun to go alone..."

"Hey, we're having a fun family day. You like Scrabble?" Elizabeth again. She had scooted onto her knees and rested her elbows on the table, peering at Matt with a detective's intensity. All she needed was a rubber hose and spotlight.

A bit taken aback, Matt nodded. "Haven't played in a while though. Smart kid like you could probably kick my butt."

Elizabeth considered this for a moment. "You wanna hang out with us?"

Matt glanced sideways at Evan. "Maybe some other time—sounds like fun family day is for the family only."

Evan took note of the wistfulness in Matt's voice and gave a quick look around the table. He didn't know what to do—as much as he wanted the time with his kids he would love to have some pressure off of him, have another adult around.

Saved by Miranda. "Well, yeah, but it would be okay if you wanted to hang around for a while. At least play a game of Scrabble. Maybe someone could finally beat Daddy."

Marveling over his eldest daughter's intuition, and kindness, Evan flashed her a smile. The selfish teenager who lived in this house one short year ago had been replaced by a mature and quiet young woman. He regretted that she'd had to grow up so fast, because seventeen was far too young to be taking on so much emotional responsibility in their family. But he knew from experience that it could also help you learn compassion and kindness at a much deeper level.

"Uh, thanks, Miranda."

Evan caught Matt's eye and winked. "You have been challenged, sir."

A game of Scrabble turned into two. Winner of both matches—Evan Cerelli. Matt threw his hands up in defeat.

"Can't we play something easier?"

"Operation!" Danny got excited and ran upstairs to his room.

Evan laughed out loud. "You're a dead man."

They didn't let Matt leave after Danny was crowned Operation champ. He was dragged to the video store where he won valuable points by arguing that the PG-13 movie that the kids had their heart set on wasn't particularly...PG-13ish.

They checked out with four movies.

"Hey Evan—what's that one?"

"One for the grown-ups, haven't seen this in years—*Gladiator.*"

Red-faced, Matt had to leave the store, wheezing so hard he thought he might lose a lung.

Then they headed back to the house.

"You aren't leaving yet are you, Matt?" asked Kathleen shyly.

"Guess not."

"Hey, it's snowing." Evan had gone to refill Matt's glass of iced tea (uncomfortably realizing that this was the first time they'd spent time together sober) and glanced out the kitchen window.

"Cool!" shrieked Elizabeth, running to the front window, with the other three close behind.

"Maybe school'll be closed!"

This brought a cheer all around.

Matt smiled up at Evan as he returned to the couch. "I remember sitting there with the radio under the covers with me, praying to every saint I could think of for my school to be called."

Evan sighed. "Poses a bit of a logistical problem for me. I can't really take a day off."

"If you need a quick sub, let me know. I got more than enough vacation time coming."

"You serious? They're being on their best behavior right now. But their true personalities could easily emerge being snowbound."

"Please, I used to work in Homicide. I can handle anything they throw at me. I'll just ply them with movies, games, junk food, vast quantities of sugar. If all that fails I'll just write each of 'em a check."

This cracked Evan up. "Whatever works."

The dinner plans were changed due to inclement weather. Evan dug through the pantry, trying to come up with something, while Matt and the kids sprawled out in the living room, laughing hysterically over the movie Matt had sworn wasn't too PG-13ish.

"What did he just say?"

"Dad, chill out," called Miranda. "It's nothing the kids haven't heard before."

"Who are you calling a kid?" yelled Kathleen, tossing a pillow at her sister, who quickly returned the favor.

"Hey, I'm trying to hear the curse words, learn a few new ones…if you don't mind," yelled Matt, sending Elizabeth and Danny into hysterics.

Evan set to work making pasta, smiling as he thought what a pleasure this day was turning out to be.

The snow piled up to the window by ten p.m.

"You're not going home in this." Matt joined Evan at the back door, surveying the blizzard in progress.

"Aw c'mon, I'm sure I could get home in like six or seven hours."

"There's no way they'll have school tomorrow—it doesn't look like its slowing down."

"I told you, it's not a problem for me to spend the day."

"Seriously?"

"Lord God, but you're slow!"

"Okay, okay. If they tie you up and take your credit cards, well, you were warned."

Danny and Elizabeth fell asleep on the floor, bookending Matt. Evan carried them up, one at a time, feeling strangely sentimental. The kids had all seemed so lighthearted today, laughing and teasing. He'd forgotten to feel desperate and empty, so filled with their sweet smiles. He loved the bantering. Loved the way they fell asleep so easily, cuddled against Matt.

He tucked his little ones in, herded Kathleen off a few minutes later—she claimed to just be resting her eyes but Evan gently pointed out that resting one's eyes for an hour is considered sleeping.

Miranda wanted to stay up and watch *Gladiator*, so the three "grown-ups" settled down and put the movie in.

"How are you getting up in the morning?"

Evan didn't meet Matt's eyes. "I'll be fine. I usually stay up this late anyway."

Sitting in the dark, watching the flickering of the television set, Matt Haight swallowed repeatedly, trying to keep his emotions in check. This day—this long, loud, crazy day—made his heart ache. For all their devastating hurts in the past year, the Cerellis were a beautiful family. They radiated love for one another. Even Evan, whom Matt knew was feeling despair and pain every single day. He wondered what it had been like with Sherri around. He assumed, given how much each of her survivors grieved her, that she'd been nothing like his own mother.

He'd grown up with so much anger and hate and neglect. He remembered the slaps, the vicious slams—verbal and physical. Couldn't recall a day like today in his whole childhood.

The other part of his anguish came from being around Evan. Being around a depressed Evan had been bad enough—inciting all sorts of feelings to begin with—but a happy Evan? Jesus Christ. Matt had spent the whole day trying desperately not to stare at his face. He glowed. He laughed heartily. And smiled. Truly smiled. His eyes—those silver-blue eyes that woke Matt up from a dead sleep—were something to behold when he was happy. Something was happening in Matt's solar plexus that he couldn't put a name to but it scared the ever-loving crap out of him.

"Night." Miranda yawned and pressed a kiss on her father's cheek. She reached and shook Matt's hand. "Glad you hung out with us today. It was fun."

"Thanks, Miranda." He couldn't have possibly expressed his gratitude to this young woman. "Next time we'll do video games and pizza." He gave her a wink. "I'm fairly sure I can kick your dad's butt at *Area 51.*"

At Evan's perplexed expression, Matt and Miranda shared a laugh. She gave both men a wave and headed up the stairs.

Leaving Matt and Evan alone.

Matt's stomach promptly dropped five or six stories.

"So…"

"You must be exhausted. I'm used to staying up this late."

Busying himself with putting the DVD in its case, Matt shrugged. "You're the one who has to go to work. I'm just gonna hang out here and let your kids run wild."

Evan filled the dishwasher, his back to Matt.

"Couch looks comfy."

"Uh, yeah."

"You sleep here don't you?"

"Every fucking night for a year."

"I can take the floor…"

"No, no…I'll sleep upstairs."

Matt hated the resigned note in Evan's voice. The day had been such a joy, he didn't want it to end this way.

Evan kept the lights off as he got undressed. He brushed his teeth with only the night-light on. In his shorts—and his USMC T-shirt he pretended still carried Sherri's scent—he crawled under the covers, shivering in terror. Scooting all the way over to the edge on "his" side, Evan buried his face into the pillow and prayed heartily that he would quickly fall asleep. He tried focusing on the day, the kids' happiness. Matt. He liked having him there. Liked hearing him laugh and joke with the kids. Liked the fact that he knew Evan slept on the couch and didn't act like it was a big deal.

He liked that someone understood him.

Matt lay on the couch, listening to snowplows go by every twenty minutes. He was wide-awake. The clock over the kitchen sink read 5:00 a.m. It was still dark outside; he could barely make out a moon.

He couldn't sleep because his body was humming and his mind raced miles ahead of his heart. He knew this feeling. It was a combination of lust and that giddy excitement you felt when a girl gave you her phone number and you just knew it was right and not a dry cleaner's on her block.

He rubbed his face with both hands, sighing. Things were getting out of hand. Now he was fantasizing about Evan while awake. And sober.

And then Matt heard the moaning. He held himself very still. It took only a second to realize it was a man's voice; it was Evan and the sound he was making...

Matt jumped up and went upstairs, following the sound to a room at the end of the hall.

He knocked softly, but got no response. Turning the handle he walked in, eyes adjusting to the pitch dark.

"Evan?" Matt whispered, moving toward the bed. "Evan? It's Matt. Are you okay?"

More moaning. Tossing and turning.

Matt got to the edge of the bed, and, before he could stop himself, he reached out and touched Evan's shoulder.

Cop's instinct worked even when one was asleep and Evan shot awake instantly, grabbing Matt's arm.

"Easy." Matt used the twenty or so pounds he had on the younger man to hold him steady. "You were just having a nightmare. Relax."

Evan was breathing heavily, and Matt felt the clamminess of his skin. Which he was feeling a lot of, suddenly realizing that he was holding Evan's forearms in his hands. And they were just inches from one another.

"Oh God." Evan was moaning now. He pulled away, wrapping his arms around his knees. "Oh God. Please make it stop."

Helplessly, Matt sat on the edge of the bed, tentatively reached for Evan's shoulder again.

Stroked his arm. It was like his dream.

"Don't leave me okay? I can't…I can't do this anymore," Evan babbled. "I can't sleep. When I sleep I remember how much blood there was. She's there and I see the blood."

"Easy. I'll stay right here. Don't worry."

His hand moved rhythmically up and down. Up and down.

"I can't, I can't, I can't…" Now he was crying.

Matt moved up Evan's arm to his shoulder. To the back of his head. Thank God it was dark because he didn't want to see what he was doing. He just wanted to pretend this was a dream.

"Shhh."

Matt touched his hair, soft under his fingers. The sobs slowed down to deep, wet breaths. He squeezed the back of Evan's neck softly, sweeping his thumb against the skin. Heard the sigh that Evan made, which sent a hot thrill through Matt's body.

This wasn't a dream. Matt's hand stilled. Oh God. This was going too far. Matt pulled away and the silence swallowed him up. He waited one beat, two. Ten.

"Thanks, Matt." Evan's voice came through the darkness. It sounded like a death rattle. "I'm just so fucking tired. I want to go to sleep."

"Lie down." Matt reached out and helped Evan back under the covers. "I'm going to sit here okay? Close your eyes."

More silence. Then a sigh. "Don't leave."

"I won't."

Matt settled onto the side of the bed where Evan wasn't. His chest hurt like hell. His fingers burned.

"I...I..."

"What Evan?"

"I don't mind that you touched me that way. I'm sorry."

Matt sighed. "Why would you have to be sorry?"

"I shouldn't feel that way."

Welcome to the fucking club.

"Evan, go to sleep. Let's not talk about this now."

"Why did you touch me like that?"

God. Please. Not. Now.

"Go to sleep, Evan. Please. I can't do this right now."

"Are we still friends, Matt?"

"Of course we are. Now go to sleep."

Evan took his advice and stopped talking, for which Matt was eternally grateful. He laid next to him, listening to him breathe. Listening to the snowplows. Wondering how the hell they were going to face one another in the morning.

And all Matt kept hearing in his head was Evan whispering, "I don't mind that you touched me that way." Over and over and over again.

Chapter Four

Evan woke up promptly at six o'clock; hadn't needed an alarm clock since the Marines. For a second he was disoriented. After not sleeping in his bed for almost a year, it felt odd to wake up on a mattress...and with someone next to him. Matt. Last night came flooding back, with a painful impact on Evan's chest as he remembered what had happened.

Well, shit.

He slid out of bed, giving a glance to where Matt lay sleeping, one arm thrown over his eyes. The weak light of a wintry morning cast a pale line across the bottom half of Matt's face, set in a slight frown.

Moving slowly, stiffly, Evan gathered his clothes from the closet and walked into the bathroom. He didn't want to wake Matt up, didn't want to have to face him. Things had gotten completely out of hand last night and Evan felt awful.

They'd never really discussed sex—strange, as men he'd think it'd be the first thing. But that was fine with Evan because his contribution was short and sweet. He'd heard about Matt's rep— hell, seen his reaction to women like Helena—it never crossed his mind that Matt also liked men. Liked him.

Suddenly so much made sense. The looks he'd caught out of the corner of his eye. The way Matt would pull his chair close during their weekly beer-and-bitch sessions. Last night. Evan's nightmare had drawn Matt into the room, his desperation and anguish had caused him to reach out.

Evan stepped into the shower and let the hot water scald his skin. He couldn't believe how things had gone wrong. His friendship with Matt had grown very important to him; he'd come to depend on it. And now it was all going to dissolve into awkwardness.

Awkward because Matt might be expecting their relationship to…progress. Awkward because Evan had told him he didn't mind the touching, which was the God's honest truth. It was a lifeline to feel Matt's hands on his arm, his shoulder, in his hair. A shiver raced over Evan's skin. The steam blinded him for a second and he leaned both hands against the tiles. He wanted—he wanted more. He wanted to have someone hold him and stroke his hair and say that everything was all right—even if he knew it wasn't.

His own sexuality had never been a question, he'd never really thought about it. He'd met Sherri at the tail end of puberty and fallen deeply in love with her—they lost their virginity together, at sixteen. And that was it. He could look at other women, acknowledge their beauty, their sex appeal, but it never crossed his mind to take it a step farther than that. Sherri turned him on. Sherri satisfied his sexual urges. So that made him straight, right?

Except this encounter with Matt had thrown him for a loop. How could he tell this man, *Yes, I felt something for you last night. No, I'm not sure what it is. I wish to God I could try and find out, but to feel this for another person is just too terrifying and overwhelming.*

Matt had rolled over, facedown, sprawled across the entire mattress. Toweled dry and dressed, Evan stopped at the edge, seeing the man in his bed as if for the first time. Solidly built body, thick brown hair. He liked the way Matt's eyes smiled at him all day yesterday. Liked the way Matt walked, powerful. Commanding. Liked the way Matt's hand had touched him last night, brushing away the pain with each stroke.

Come on, Evan. Say it. Like Sherri always did.

Abruptly, Evan turned and walked out of the bedroom. He headed for Miranda's room and knocked softly on the door.

She was awake, her clock radio playing softly. The school cancellations.

"Hey, Daddy," she said sleepily. "We're all home for the day. I just heard the elementary school announced."

"Yeah, I figured. Listen, Matt's going to stay here for the day, until I get home."

"Geeze—you think we need a babysitter? I'm sixteen!" Miranda came alive, sitting straight up in her bed.

"I know, I know, but humor me, okay? What if there's trouble with the furnace or the electricity? What if you need to get somewhere? You can't drive alone yet—and certainly not in this kind of weather."

Miranda sighed her displeasure, but Evan could see she wasn't going to argue.

"Besides, he'll keep the kids busy so you don't have to entertain them all day."

"See? Now that's a big plus—you should have mentioned that first."

Evan had to smile at that. He crossed the room to drop a kiss on her head. "Could you try and make sure they don't torment Matt too much?" he asked as he turned to go.

"Hey, Daddy—he's real nice. I'm glad you made a friend like him."

A pain was starting to form behind Evan's right eye. Guilt? Stress? Exhaustion? All of the above. "Yeah. And thanks for inviting him to stay yesterday. He had a good time I think."

Miranda curled back down under the covers. "He looked lonely."

"Yeah."

"Bye, Daddy."

"Bye, kiddo. I'll see you tonight."

He shut the door behind him and hurried downstairs. He needed to get out of the house as soon as possible. Before Matt woke up. He just couldn't do this right now.

Evan jotted a quick note for him and left it on the fridge. He promised to be home as early as possible. Told him to call if there was a problem. Thanked him again for this huge favor.

And oh, by the way, about last night…

He quickly bundled up and headed for the back door— shortest distance to the car—and pulled out the shovel he left inside the broom closet. It helped him work off some of his tension to dig a quick path to the driveway.

* * *

How he managed to beat Helena—from Queens no less—to the station was beyond him. He was at his desk by nine. So was Moses. And that was the squad.

"Just you and me, dear Evan. Hey, did you know that the government has been controlling our weather patterns for the last fifty years? They have these satellites… No kidding…"

He sighed. Couldn't he have ended up with someone less chatty?

An hour later a bedraggled Helena stomped in. She looked like someone had kicked her into a snow bank.

"It's not even Thanksgiving yet! What is this shit?" Angrily she kicked the snow off her boots and tore off her outer layers. She looked up at Evan. Calm, cool, collected. "When the hell did you get here?"

"Tsk, tsk, someone has a potty mouth."

"Oh shut up, Moses."

"Well?"

Evan casually checked his watch. "An hour ago."

"From Queens?"

"And you always make fun of me for living there. Don't you feel bad now?"

"Argh."

Evan knew Helena hated being cold and wet. She also typically hated Moses being snarky yet cheerful and pin neat every freaking day (at least before she had two cups of coffee, then she adored him). And Evan beating her in this morning was icing on the cake.

She got down to her heavy wool pants and turtleneck/sweater combination and sat down hard on her chair. She pulled off her boots and threw them into the corner.

"No one shoveled the sidewalks from my apartment to the station house and there wasn't a subway running—forget the buses. Cabs? Please. It took me almost two hours of trudging to get here and...grrr."

Moses snickered from his desk but wisely turned around.

Evan dropped a mug of coffee in front of her. "You okay?"

"Yeah, just crabby."

Evan sat back down at his desk and sighed.

She gave him the skunk eye. "What?"

He opened his mouth to say "nothing" but reconsidered when he saw her look. "Long story."

"I doubt the phones are going to ring today. All the perverts are snowed in."

Evan cast a look over at Moses. This obviously wasn't for his ears.

Helena pursed her lips. "Captain Wolkowski here?"

"Nah," called Moses, happily listening in. "He's still waiting for the snowplow to unblock his driveway."

"His office is free."

Evan nodded.

They went in and closed the door.

He was going to tell her the truth—really, honestly—but when the moment came, and she was perched expectantly on the chair, waiting, he just couldn't do it.

"Helena...uh, I met someone...recently..."

"Uh-huh."

"And we're good friends."

"Uh-huh."

"I think...I think that she's developed certain... sexual...feelings for me. And I'm pretty sure I'm starting to ah...feel the same way." Evan cleared his throat nervously, staring down at his hands. He couldn't look at Helena's face when he did this.

"Okaayy..."

"It's just very complicated." Oh my God, welcome to the understatement of the year.

"Evan, I know it's tough to imagine yourself with someone...after you know, losing Sherri. But you're young and it's okay to feel an attraction to someone else. It's natural."

Hey, Helena, there are several major religions and political organizations that disagree with that idea. Evan bit back a hysterical laugh that'd built up in his chest.

"I guess. But that's just part of it. A pretty big part. And the other part of it is pretty big too. It would be very, very difficult for us to...move this into an intimate relationship."

Helena didn't say anything. Evan looked out of the corner of his eye and saw her biting her lip.

He thought about Matt lying in his bed.

They sat in silence for a long time. His mind wandering away from the dangerous image of Matt. Evan thought about how long it'd been since he'd seen Helena cranky. And she hadn't yet asked him what he'd eaten for breakfast. It was nice. Normal.

"Can I just tell you how good it is to see you in a bad mood?" He finally spoke up.

"What?"

"I just meant you try so hard around me, Helena. Always up, always perky. I love you to death for trying but I really missed your crabby days. Like today."

"So you don't like the Stepford Helena I take it?"

"Nope. I miss the grouchy one who used to tell me off occasionally."

"You got her in spades today, partner."

"Can you just be my friend from now on? No kid gloves. No handling me. Please."

"Thank God. I don't think I could do perky today. My underwear is damp. And not in a good way."

Evan laughed. He laughed into his hands until he felt tears coming. Almost lost it and told Helena the truth. Almost.

"Helena, I don't know if I can give someone what they want in a relationship."

She reached over and gave his hand a squeeze.

"Sex?"

"Love."

Matt woke up at nine to the sound of giggling.

"Hi, Matt!" chirped Elizabeth.

He shifted and looked down at the foot of the bed. "Hey, kids."

Danny and Elizabeth, still in their pajamas, stood there beaming.

"There's no school today and the snow is piled up all the way past the front window! It's so cool! Can we go out and play?"

"Uh sure, Danny." Matt sat up, rubbing his eyes. "Your dad leave for work yet?"

"A couple of hours ago," said Miranda. Matt looked up to see her leaning against the doorjamb. Her eyes coolly surveyed the scene and he could read her confusion. What exactly was Matt doing in her parents' bed?

"Yeah. Hey, let's get something to eat, and then we'll go out and have some fun." Forced gaiety. *Excellent job, Matt. You fooled the junior set, but Miranda isn't going to let you off that easy. Quick. Lie.* "Your dad was a sport to give me the bed. Bad back." He did an exaggerated stretch.

Miranda's expression didn't change, and she turned to leave. "I'll start breakfast." And then she was gone.

Matt got up—his audience remained—and realized his clothes were downstairs. Great. "You need something to wear?" Elizabeth asked. She pointed to her father's bureau. "Daddy has clothes in there."

Matt didn't think he'd find anything that fit—he had at least twenty pounds and a few inches on Evan—but he pulled open the drawer and looked through the things.

Dear God, please don't let anything weird happen like me getting excited because I'm looking through Evan's underwear drawer. Amen.

He grabbed some sweats—XL—socks, and a stretched out T-shirt, and went into the bathroom. When he came out a few minutes later, Elizabeth and Danny were perched on the bed, waiting for him.

"Hey, Matt, what are we going to do all day?"

The kids kept him running. Miranda eventually thawed out but he could see something was gnawing at her. They headed outside after breakfast and Matt put them to work digging out the driveway and front walk. They made a snowman.

When he found himself flat on his back, out of breath, and being pelted with snowballs, he realized (a) this was better than jogging, and (b) he was going to miss these kids if Evan came home and told him to get out.

He kept replaying it over and over in his head. The touches, the sighs, and most importantly Evan telling him he didn't mind... Jesus. He wished he could raid the liquor cabinet like a teenage babysitter. But every time he thought he'd cave, Elizabeth or Danny, or even Kathleen would flash him a wonderful smile and giggle in his direction, and he'd get this warm rush over his body. And then he'd wish that Evan were here, enjoying the moment.

Five o'clock came quickly. There'd been no calls—the city was pretty much shut down by the freak storm.

"I'm going to leave now."

"Okay."

"You want a ride?"

"Duh."

Evan smiled. "Moses?"

"I'm going to stick around. Brownnose the boss for a bit."

Wolkowski sat in his office, his feet up, taking a nap.

"Have fun."

They left. The snow had stopped hours ago but the cleanup was still underway. Traffic crawled. A few people hurried along the sidewalks.

"I don't think I've ever driven in this much snow with you. You safe?"

"I'm a brilliant driver. Shut up and get in."

"So what's going to happen with your lady friend?"

"I guess we'll talk at some point. I'll ah, tell her the truth."

"Which is?"

"I'll let you know as soon as I figure it out."

As they crawled uptown following a snowplow, Helena suddenly asked, "Do I know this woman? You've never mentioned anyone before."

Evan gripped the steering wheel. "Friend of Matt's—he introduced us."

"Matt Haight? Oh yeah. He's cute. Hey, maybe you should give him my number."

Concentrating on driving and avoiding Helena's eyes, Evan didn't bother to analyze the defensiveness that statement brought up.

Matt and the kids made hamburgers and mac'n'cheese for dinner. He thought kids needed to have vegetables with every meal—especially green ones—so he made spinach. Boiling water he could do. As the clock inched toward seven, Matt's anxiety built to the point of an explosion. His heart raced. The moment of truth, right? Evan would walk through the door and Matt prayed he'd be able to read his face, understand what he wanted him to do. Stay or get out. Those were the only two choices.

Evan sat in the car, parked in his newly clean driveway. He saw the snowman—was that his hat?—and light spilling out of the front window. He had to go inside and face Matt. And say something. Like...*I want something I can't have that you want to give me. I think. Maybe*. He wanted to turn back the clock to when it was just about shared misery and not shared...affection. Desire. Evan was good at misery. Caring about someone required a lot more work—and it was very dangerous. He just wished to hell he understood this thing they were creating between them and how he was going to look Matt in the eye when he got into the house. He got out of the car and walked slowly up to the front door.

Matt heard the key and held his breath. Facing the music began now.

The little kids ran over and gave their father an enthusiastic hello. Matt watched the hugs and kisses. Watched Evan lose the overcoat and gloves, his boots left on the mat. Miranda called out a hello and one of those "dinner's almost ready" lines that you heard in all the old television shows. Where was the Beav to break the tension when you needed him?

Eventually Evan couldn't avoid Matt's eyes, and he walked into the kitchen where Matt stood. "Hi."

"Hi."

"Thanks for spending the day—I really appreciate it."

Matt shrugged, keeping his face neutral. "I had fun. Beats having to go into work. They didn't even open the office."

"Wish I could say the same. We just sat there all day."

Insert awkward pause here, thought Matt. He didn't want to misread the moment, but Evan didn't seem to be hostile or showing him the door. Maybe, just maybe he wanted to forget the whole thing. Then this would be behind them.

Then Evan brushed past and touched Matt's forearm with his fingers for a long, lingering moment.

What the hell? A bolt struck Matt a hundred places at once. Brain, heart, groin. There was no mistaking that for an accident.

"What's for dinner?" Evan moved into the kitchen, his voice shaky as he picked up various pot lids. "Smells good."

Matt was rooted to the spot. The kids had drifted into the living room and were sprawled all over, watching television. The sounds of Nickelodeon filled the house.

His back to the living room, Matt stared at Evan, willing him to turn around. He needed to see his face.

Sighing heavily—in defeat or acceptance, take your pick, Matt thought—Evan turned to face Matt. They stood for a long time, just staring, blue eyes on blue eyes. Silver on black. Both shivered with a weird sort of panic. Excitement. Utter terror. As it was from the beginning, neither said a word. They knew what the other was thinking.

Matt wasn't leaving. Evan wanted him to stay.

They let the kids do the talking through dinner, through the rest of the evening. All the outdoor activity took its toll and the little ones put up no protest when bedtime was announced at eight thirty. Miranda asked for permission to use the phone for awhile. Evan absently said yes—thinking he'd be paying for it later—and she disappeared with the cordless upstairs. Kathleen tried to keep her eyes open best she could but by nine she was a goner.

Yes, folks. The moment we've been waiting for and dreading for hours now.

They let the silence sit between them for almost thirty minutes. They listened to the dishwasher and the drone of a sitcom from the television set.

Matt finally couldn't stand it a second longer. "Evan."

"Yeah?" So soft, so far away. He sat on the couch, Matt a few feet away in the armchair.

"We need to talk about what happened."

"I know."

"I'm sorry I stepped over the line. When I heard you having that nightmare, I just kind of slipped into automatic pilot. I wasn't trying to...do...anything."

Evan said nothing. Matt flickered his glance over his friend. He stared straight ahead, eyes unseeing, face shuttered. He'd changed into a gray T-shirt—nice view of the tattoo, thank you very much—and black sweatpants when he got home, and somehow this was pushing Matt closer to the edge. An overwhelming wave of desire buffeted against forty-two years of machismo and a once solid understanding of who he was.

"I don't want to fuck this friendship up, Evan."

"It's okay. I told you...I didn't mind. I just don't want to lead you on. I had no idea..."

"Man, *you* don't understand it? It's my fucking head and *I* don't understand it."

That made Evan turn to look at him. "You mean...I assumed you were bisexual."

Taken aback, Matt shook his head. "No."

"Then what?"

Matt pinned Evan down with a stare. "My whole fucking life just got turned upside down, that's what fucking happened. I've spent the past twenty-eight years trying to fuck women, and now I'm having a hard-on for a guy."

Oh shit. That just flew out of his mouth and he'd have given anything to take it back. Stunned silence. Evan looked like the proverbial deer in headlights. "Why didn't you say anything?"

"'Cause, uh, we're straight? I didn't think of us in those terms."

"Us?"

"You know what I mean."

"I swear to God I don't."

"Listen, Evan. I don't know what to tell you." Matt pulled himself out of the chair. He couldn't do this. "I'm leaving."

"Why?"

"Why? Why do you think? I'm embarrassed and I'm freaked out okay? I don't know how the fuck to handle this."

He moved past the couch to get his shoes.

"Don't."

Matt kept moving. He tried not to hear anything but the blood pounding in his ears. This was getting dangerous.

"Don't leave, Matt." Emotion was finally starting to creep into Evan's voice. "I asked you not to leave last night and you stayed."

"Fuck this. I can't do this." Matt kept murmuring over and over. "We can't do this." He stared at his shoes, feeling helpless and terrified. Exposed. Needing something this badly...it was too dangerous.

He sensed Evan standing over him but he couldn't look up.

"Don't."

He felt the hand touch the side of his face.

"I want you to stay."

He shivered as fingers stroked his jaw.

"And do what?"

"I'm not exactly sure… Can we take it slow? I don't want you to think I'm easy."

Matt had to laugh. Just had to. He reached up and tentatively took Evan's hand. Stood up so they were standing an inch apart.

Breathe in. Breathe out.

Evan was shaking. The bravado in his voice—utter bullshit. He wanted to feel the comfort of the previous night, but he had no idea what would happen when he did.

Thank God Matt took the bull by the horns, so to speak.

Matt let his hands travel the same path as last night. Up the arms, the shoulders, the collarbone under the soft T-shirt. The strong neck, felt the corded muscles, the ragged breaths. He let his eyes scan Evan's face—hard planes and pale skin. His eyes were closed. He trembled.

Matt let out a shudder. His mouth hurt from denial. *Just do it, Matty*, something inside him whispered. *He doesn't want you to stop.*

So he did what he'd felt like doing for weeks. Pressed his mouth against Evan's.

Live wires connected. Just a simple pressing together of flesh, but the jolts shook them both to the core.

Matt pressed harder. Pressed his tongue forward, pressed his body forward.

Evan took the pressure and offered the resistance to keep them both upright. Oh God, it felt so good to have someone touching him. To have Matt touching him like this. His mind skittered over Sherri's face, but he was able to put it away for now because this felt so different. The rough skin and the slim lips. The hardness pushed against his thigh. A moan was building from deep within him and he opened his mouth out of pure reflex.

And Matt pressed harder still. He flicked his tongue into Evan's mouth on autopilot. He felt the strength of Evan's body, the automatic grind of his hips as they used their mouths to explore. He pressed their bodies together and thrilled inwardly when he felt Evan's arms tighten around his middle.

Tenderly, Evan moved his hands up and down Matt's strong, solid back. He shut his internal critics and moral monitors off. He let himself feel each surge of desire, every stroke of Matt's tongue. So strange, so erotic. A body like his own—but stronger, bigger. The large but gentle hands cupping his face, stroking his hair. He started to grind against the older man, quickly losing control.

Oh God. Too much. Shaking, Matt stilled Evan's hips with his own. It had been a long time for both of them—they were both wound tight. Matt pushed Evan away slightly.

Suddenly realizing his actions, Evan flushed bright red. "I'm sorry," he murmured. "Oh Christ. My kids…"

"Yeah. Let's slow down."

Evan moved away from Matt, shaking and trying to pull himself together. He sat down on the edge of the sofa, his elbows on his knees, breathing heavily. He felt the cushions dip—Matt sat down next to him.

"Ever had this happen before?"

"Make out with another guy—uh no. You?"

Evan snorted. "I've only kissed one other person in my whole life, Matt."

"It just happened, man. I wasn't thinking about it, wasn't expecting it. One day I woke up and realized this was more than just...being your friend."

Evan nodded. "I knew I felt comfortable with you. But I didn't understand the—possibility—until last night."

"I'm forty-two years old and I never even considered—" He broke off, shaking his head. "Never considered that I'd be kissing a man and feeling...this."

"Tell me something. Are you still attracted to women?"

"I'd jump on your partner in a New York minute. Does this make me fashionably bisexual?"

They laughed together quietly, not touching, not looking at one another. "What the hell are we going to do about this, Matt?"

"I haven't the faintest fucking idea."

Chapter Five

They sat together on the couch, side by side, in drowsy silence, listening to the house settle. Matt didn't know what else there was to say. At one point there was movement upstairs—Miranda getting ready for bed—and they moved farther away from each other, to a more respectable distance. A few moments later Evan's eyes drifted shut. Matt watched hungrily until he forced himself to check the clock on the wall. Shit. It was nearly eleven and he hadn't been home since yesterday morning. Thank God he didn't have any pets.

He stood up carefully as not to wake the other man and quietly collected his things, put on his shoes and coat. He went to the computer desk in the corner and wrote a note for Evan, leaving it on the coffee table where he would see it when he woke up. Tenderly picking up a blanket thrown over the easy chair and laying it over him. At least he was finally getting a little sleep.

Matt had to leave, had to go back to his real world. He walked to the door, concern niggling in the back of his head. Walking outside would break the little cocoon they had created. Hopefully in the light of day, this...thing...between them wouldn't evaporate.

Standing in the doorway he cast a look back toward Evan. Man, did he look good lying there under the blanket...leaning against the back of the couch, head resting on an out flung arm. He looked...mmm, warm and inviting; Matt thanked God the cold air was bracing because heat flushed through his body as he turned and went to his car. Before he did something stupid like wake Evan up and get him out of his clothes. Not that he knew exactly what he'd do after that. He shivered as he sat in the car, waiting for it to warm up.

There's no way I'm sleeping anytime soon with the feeling of him on my skin and, woo boy, in my mouth. I've never been so fucking scared in my whole entire life. This is a man and I want him and I think maybe I lo… Nope, not going there, and oh shit, what the hell am I supposed to do now?

He banged his head on the steering wheel. That felt a little bit better. Putting the car in reverse, he eased out of the Cerellis' driveway.

Evan opened his eyes once he knew Matt was gone. He was ashamed of himself for feigning sleep, but it was the only way he knew to end this evening without having to answer any more questions. The note on the coffee table caught his eye and he sat up to read it.

Evan,
Didn't want to wake you.
We need to talk.
When can you meet at O'Malley's?
Call me at home tomorrow night.
Matt

Stuffing the note in the pocket of his sweats, Evan got up to shut all the lights and then crawled back onto the couch. His skin ached and his head pounded with endless internal conversations about love, about sex and lust, about sexual preference, and about what responsibilities Evan was jeopardizing by even contemplating this relationship. He lay there, idly wondering if he really was catching the scent of Matt's skin from the cushions or if it had just burned into his brain.

He knew no sleep would come, so he fixed his eyes on the only picture of Sherri he'd kept in the living room, hidden on the corner of the console table, behind a lamp. His very favorite— Sherri in the green sweater that drove him crazy, posed on a blanket in Central Park, taken before he'd left for the Marines. She had wanted him to have a picture to remember her by, so he wouldn't forget how much they loved each other. As if he ever could. They didn't know it wouldn't be for long, that she was already pregnant with Miranda, that he'd be back and they would be married before the year was out. All their plans—his for a military career, hers of a college degree—waylaid. He'd thought that had been the turning point in his life. Trading glamorous plans for bills and parenthood and grown-up responsibility. It wasn't so bad for either of them. They'd realized through the years that as long as they had each other, things ultimately worked out the way they wanted.

But that life was past and this new one...well, it included things that Evan had never even imagined possible. He wondered what Matt would say when they talked tomorrow. Wondered what he wanted him to say.

So Evan passed the night staring at Sherri and thinking of Matt.

Matt couldn't sleep a wink. He got to work two hours early, scaring the shit out of the cleaning woman, and moved like a madman through his in-box and e-mail. Skipped lunch. Everyone commented on his Energizer Bunny state and asked what magic pill he'd found. *Uh, let's see...he's about six feet tall, muscular— with these silver-blue eyes that frankly make me harder than any rack I've ever laid eyes on. Go figure. I'm an eye man. And apparently a "man" man.*

Every once in awhile he'd stare at the phone, wonder what kind of day Evan was having. *Good Christ, Matt, you've suddenly wound up in a fucking romance novel.*

* * *

Evan got to work a few minutes after eight. The freak storm that had frozen the city for twenty-four hours was now melting under an unseasonably warm sun causing floods everywhere. Lovely. Helena was at her desk. She looked up and gave him a radiant smile before sticking out her tongue. Things were looking up—the Stepford Helena had not come back.

"Somebody's late."

"Five minutes?"

"It's late for you. I win. Shut up."

She waited until he took his coat off, sat down, rolled up his sleeves, and turned his computer on in typical Evan-is-anal-retentive fashion. The man was clockwork incarnate. A furtive look around told her that no one was close enough to hear so she leaned forward. "Well?" she whispered.

Evan leaned forward and whispered back, "Well what?"

Her eyes narrowed. "Don't even try that. What happened last night?"

Evan opened his mouth to say something but couldn't quite put the evening into words. He dropped his gaze to his blotter, didn't look up. He could feel her eyes burning into his forehead. "Nothing," he mumbled. "We're, uh, going to have drinks this week, talk it over."

"Oh. You didn't talk to her about it last night?"

"No."

"Because it seemed like you were all gung ho on getting it over with."

"I didn't get the chance," Evan said quietly, thinking that it was sort of impossible, what with Matt's tongue in his mouth.

"You okay? Something's really got you dragging."

"I'm fine."

"Yeah right!"

"Listen—I don't want to talk about it okay? I can handle it. I'll let you know if I need your input." It came out sharper than he meant it to and he winced at the look in Helena's eyes.

"Excuse me. You wanted to talk about it yesterday." She slammed around her desk for a moment, moving things that didn't need to be moved. "You don't want me to hover? Fine, I won't. I'm sorry if I'm concerned about you." Obviously hurt and annoyed, she turned her chair around and began attacking a pile of folders.

Her parting shot hurt the most because it was the dead on truth. "You're full of shit when you say you're handling it. And if I was the one going through something this…big, you'd be crawling up my ass trying to fix it."

They barely spoke for the rest of the day. Evan couldn't bring himself to say the words she wanted to hear.

* * *

At six o'clock, Matt cleaned up his desk and left the office. He thought about stopping for dinner but realized he wasn't hungry. He just wanted to go and sit next to the phone and wait.

At his apartment, he changed his clothes and lay down on the mattress. Stared up at the ceiling and thought, shit, I really do need furniture don't I? Waited, waited, waited.

And then the phone rang.

"Hey, it's me."

"Hi." Matt heard the kids in the background and ached to be there.

"Uh, sorry I fell asleep last night. I was exhausted."

"Not a problem. I'm just glad you got some rest. I worry about you."

Matt heard the pregnant pause through the line and held his breath; being the emotional one in this sort of situation was not his forte. He worried he'd crossed a line when Evan cleared his throat and started talking again.

"Listen, I think you're right. We should get together and talk."

"Yeah."

"So I talked to my sister-in-law and she's going to take the kids out on Saturday. She said she'd pick them up on Friday after school. So uh, does Friday work for you?"

Three fucking days. Matt thought he'd probably go crazy before then. "Friday's fine. I'll meet you at O'Malley's, eight o'clock?"

"Fine."

"Great. So say hi to the kids. I'll see you Friday."

"Yeah." Another long pause in Matt's ear. "See you then."

They breathed at one another for a long moment, then hung up.

Matt rolled over onto his stomach and tried to pretend he didn't care about how distant Evan seemed to be.

* * *

Evan and Helena maintained their cool attitudes for the rest of the week—they were all business. Everyone noticed and no one said a word to either of them. But it was the hot topic of conversation at lunch for the rest of the detectives. Good money said lover's spat—they'd assumed for months that Evan and Helena were—you know—Evan and Helena.

* * *

Matt realized on Thursday night that he hadn't had a drink in over a week. That seemed odd. He jogged every night when he got home from work because it made his body hurt so much his mind was blank when he went to sleep. The dreams of Evan had stopped—maybe because now he could spend all his waking hours tasting him, feeling him...who the hell needed dreams?

Friday crawled. He watched the clock until his eyes went blurry. At seven he stood up and headed for the ferry, anxious to get this over with.

* * *

At O'Malley's, Evan sat alone at "their" table, halfway through the pitcher that magically appeared before he could even take his coat off. He'd purposely come a half hour early, so he could steel himself for what happened next. The beer tasted bitter and comforting as it slid down his throat. It pooled in his stomach and sent a warm numbness through his arms and legs. *Just enough to make me calm and rational.*

He sensed Matt before he saw him; his presence was unmistakable. He avoided looking up for as long as he could, but in the end he couldn't help himself.

The hunger in Matt's eyes made his stomach flip, and, without realizing it, he swiped his tongue over his upper lip...remembering.

It was Matt's turn to blush.

He slid into the other chair, not knowing what expression to lock his face into. He stretched his legs out, brushing them against Evan's, making them both jump.

"You been here long?" Matt finally said, pouring himself a beer with an unsteady hand.

"Nah."

They each drank, staring off into opposite sides of the bar.

The tension did nothing to dispel Matt's need. He felt that old familiar recklessness rearing its ugly head. He wanted to touch Evan so badly his hands shook. Wanted him to remember how good it felt when they kissed.

So what the fuck, he thought, and he slid his hand under the table and onto Evan's thigh.

He didn't jump. He just closed his eyes, swallowed hard.

"Matt..." His voice was low and ragged.

And all Matt's thoughts of rational conversation went right out the window.

"What are we going to do about this, Evan? What the hell do you want me to do? This whole thing is scaring the shit out of me, but I can't seem to stop..." He leaned over until he was inches from Evan's ear, whispering frantically. "I can't think about... us...logically. I can't explain this away."

His hand pressed down hard. He felt the tight muscles under the wool of Evan's pants. Felt the heat coming straight through his palm, burning a path to his groin. "I want you." He said it into Evan's ear, said it tightly, loved the shiver that he felt a second later.

They sat in this insane tableau—Matt's hand moving in small circles against Evan's thigh, inching closer and closer to where he wanted it to be—sitting so close that he was sure Matt could flick his tongue and touch him. Evan let the dizziness overwhelm him, closed his eyes and let the protests sit in his throat.

When he opened his eyes, he locked onto Matt's almost desperate stare. And from nowhere he could have named he said, "Let's go somewhere...private, okay?"

Matt said nothing. He removed his hand, grabbed his overcoat, and put it on without standing up. Good idea, Evan thought, dazed. He threw a twenty down on the table and silently followed Matt out the front door, ignoring the bartender's confused look.

Matt stood on the sidewalk, waiting for Evan to catch up. They gulped in the cold air, watched a few people walk by.

"Where's your car?" Matt said roughly, turning to him— hands in his pockets so they'd both be safe.

"The lot." He motioned across the street. "Should we, uh, drive to Queens?"

"No. My place." Matt knew that being at the house would just make things more difficult. Too many memories. They needed neutral ground. "That okay?"

Evan was relieved. "Yeah."

They walked across the street, waited for the car in silence. Didn't speak again until they were speeding toward the bridge. Matt cleared his throat.

"Are you sure about this?"

Evan let out a small, shaky laugh. "I wish to God I had an answer for you right now. All I know is that...I'm not turning this car around. I'm going home with you...and we'll see what happens from there."

"Good." Matt turned his head and watched the city turn into Staten Island.

Evan parked on the street. He grabbed his bag from the backseat and followed Matt up the stairs to his apartment. The building was small—a row house with four floors—old, but well kept. They walked all the way to the top, past the sounds of the evening news, the smell of something spicy and rich. At the top of the stairs, Matt unlocked his front door and stepped inside. He paused, flipping on the light, then waited for Evan to follow.

His look said it all—this was it. No turning back.

Without hesitation this time, Evan walked through the door.

"Studio Sweet Studio. Here's the tour. You're standing in the whole apartment. That door's the bathroom. That obviously is what passes for the kitchen. Tour over." Matt threw his jacket onto the counter that separated the kitchen and the main room. "You want something to drink?"

Evan stood there dumbly, his coat still on, bag in hand. "I think I need to be a little drunk right now," he said honestly.

Matt grunted and went to the fridge. "Throw your stuff anywhere."

Considering this, Evan glanced around the big room. It was freshly painted and the hardwood floor polished. And there was absolutely not one stick of furniture—just a mattress in the center of the room, Matt's phone perched next to it on a shoe box.

"You don't—"

"Have any furniture. I did some housecleaning last weekend."

"No shit." He took his coat off and put it over Matt's. The bag he dropped on the floor near the bathroom door.

"The new stuff is coming tomorrow. I'm sorry..."

"Don't worry about it." Evan didn't have a clue what to do next. He accepted the beer from Matt and stood in the center of the room, avoiding looking at Matt or the mattress.

Matt kicked his shoes off, threw his tie onto the growing counter pile. He was moving around almost angrily, taking long drags of his beer. He was also avoiding Evan completely, taking the long way around the room just to get to the bathroom.

Evan decided to follow suit. He got rid of everything but his shirt, pants, and socks, sitting down on the corner of the mattress to drink his beer and watch Matt move around the room.

"You want something to eat?"

"No."

"Take a shower…"

"Matt, please just sit down."

Matt stopped, standing a few feet from Evan with his dress shirt open and his eyes wild. "No."

"Why not?" Evan was growing weary of these repetitive conversations. "You wanted me here, didn't you?"

"I want you…here. I want you exactly where you are right now, but…I don't know what to do."

Evan smiled sadly. "Join the club. I probably have even less of a clue."

Matt clenched his fists at his side. "Finding myself turned on enough to cut glass and not knowing what the fuck to do about it is a new and unpleasant experience."

"Matt, please."

Matt waited for another moment, then pulled his shirt the rest of the way off, now in just his T-shirt and slacks. He watched Evan drain the rest of the beer—loved to see his mouth, his throat, moving, swallowing—then put it down next to the bed. Watched him slowly unbutton his own shirt.

"Come over here and sit down before I lose my nerve."

Matt finally moved. He sat down a few inches from Evan, brushed his shoulder against him. Slid his hand behind Evan's neck and pulled him forward.

"Tell me to stop," Matt whispered. "Last chance."

Evan said nothing. Leaned forward and pressed his mouth against Matt's, picking up where they had left off a week ago. He was tentative, kissing him softly, teasing him with his tongue, startling a bit when Matt opened his mouth to join in. He kept going, kept touching his tongue to Matt's, tasted like beer, tasted so goddamn good it made him dizzy.

The kisses became greedier. Matt sucked Evan's tongue into his mouth, tightened his grip on his neck. He pulled away, panting. "Is it okay...I want to touch you..."

Evan closed his eyes, swallowed hard. "Yesss...please."

Matt knew what he wanted, knew he wanted to feel Evan's body under his. He let his hands drop down to Evan's shoulders, squeezed softly, reached for the collar of his shirt and helped him pull it off. Let his fingers drift over his chest, felt every muscles' curve, felt his heart pounding through the white cotton T-shirt. Reached for the hem and without hesitation pulled the shirt over his head.

Oh yeah. Skin, that's what he wanted to feel...to taste...like his dreams, awake and asleep. He loved that part on a woman, that curve between the shoulder and neck. He leaned forward now and filled his mouth, moaning into the open kiss. Fuck yeah. He moved his mouth across Evan's throat, thinking this was different, this was rougher, saltier, sexier than anything he'd ever tasted. Like a man possessed he kept moving his mouth over Evan...

His solid jawline, his beautiful mouth—*yeah, Matt, fucking beautiful and you can't get enough*—all the while Matt registered Evan's hands frantically moving up and down his back, clasping his head as he moved back down his throat.

I wish he was a woman, Matt thought wildly, *wish I could rip his clothes off and fuck him with my mouth, with my dick...* He pressed more kisses down Evan's chest, pushing him down on the mattress, moving to kneel between his legs.

He couldn't ignore the massive, painful hard-on pushing against his pants. He needed to move against Evan, wanted to move inside him but he didn't know how to get to that point and the frustration made him crazy.

Matt moved to lie on top of Evan, supporting himself on trembling arms. Looked at his sweat-sheened face and haunting blue eyes. "Tell me to stop."

Evan reached up and ran his fingers across Matt's mouth. "Don't you fucking dare."

Permission granted. Matt moved until their lower bodies were touching. Cocks pressed together—Evan's legs scissored between Matt's. For a second neither one could move because it felt so good just to be touching...and then they just couldn't stop the inevitable.

The moans were impossible to tell apart. Matt's arms strained as he thrust against Evan, wishing he could do more, but God it felt so good, so good...

He knew it wouldn't be long; he couldn't stop his hips from slamming into Evan, pushing him into the mattress. He wanted to be inside him so badly, it was all he could think about, and then he felt himself losing control. Blinded by the tantalizing release of orgasm, Matt began grinding his hips, feeling the end coming.

"Ohhh!" He exploded, rocking himself into Evan's pelvis, hearing somewhere in the distance a moaning sob. His arms gave out and he fell slightly to the side, his face against the mattress.

Matt lay there, breathing his way back to reality.

Pulling himself on his elbows, Matt turned his head. Evan lay there, his arm thrown over his face, shaking. He was making these tiny gasping shuddering sounds that sounded like they were being torn from his chest.

Oh shit.

"Hey, hey…" Matt pulled himself completely off Evan, rolled onto his side. He didn't know what to do. Should he touch him? Would that make it worse?

Evan took a deep breath, moved his arm. He turned his head to face Matt.

"You okay?" Matt asked softly, worriedly scanning his face.

"Yeah. It just felt…"

Matt held his breath.

"Strange…to be touching someone…else." His voice broke, and Matt watched his eyes get bright. "I'm glad it was you though."

"Thanks." He didn't think he could say more with this enormous lump in his throat.

Evan scooted a little closer, so their bodies were touching. Matt smiled at that, rested his head near Evan's, an arm over his midsection. They lay there for a long time, silent but comfortable.

"Was it all you hoped for and more?" Matt finally said, trying to break the quiet.

That got a small laugh out of Evan.

Matt pulled up on one elbow.

"What now?" Evan asked, staring

"I'd say get cleaned up. And get some dinner. I'm starving."

"I meant long-term, but that all sounds pretty good."

"I thought we should start small."

Evan smiled up at Matt. "You're not going to let me be maudlin are you?"

"Nope, sorry. I just got rid of about eight weeks worth of tension. I feel great." He leaned down and they kissed again, long and slow. "Hmmm...I like kissing you."

"That part we seem to be pretty good at."

"We'll work at the rest of it, okay? I'm pretty sure with some practice I can convert some of my A material." With that, Matt got up and started to pull off his T-shirt. "I'm gonna use the shower first. Then I'll call the Italian place up the street and get us some food."

We're working at the rest? Converting A material—well, shit. This isn't a onetime thing is it, Evan thought. Then he laughed, amazed. "Does anything faze you?"

Matt shrugged. "I could have walked away from this about a hundred times, Evan. Could have lost your number the second I realized that I was attracted to you... Fuck yeah, I'm fazed. But I'd be a liar if I said I was sorry. Okay?"

"Okay."

Evan didn't move for a few more moments, watched as Matt stripped down to his shorts, then walked into the bathroom, with a backward grin at Evan. Listened to the water in the other room. He closed his eyes and let that wash over him.

"What?"

"Huh?"

"You were like on Mars or something. Everything all right?" Matt stood over Evan, hair wet from the shower and changed into a pair of black cotton shorts and blue T-shirt. He sounded suspicious and a little afraid.

Evan blinked up at him. He decided he wanted to just spend a few hours looking into Matt's face. "I'm fine."

"I thought we had an agreement on the maudlin shit."

"Yes, sir." Evan sat up, got off the mattress, bumped into Matt.

"Hmmm…" Matt didn't hesitate in taking Evan into his arms and kissing him. "Go take a shower," he whispered against his mouth. "We'll eat and then…"

"Practice?" Evan laughed, holding the other man close. Yeah, that felt nice. Matt's hands massaging his back, his skin hot against Evan's.

"Hmph. Practice sounds good." Smirking, Matt reluctantly let go. "Food choices?"

"Whatever. I don't care." Evan walked toward the bathroom, grabbing his bag on the way.

"You need clothes?"

"Brought some."

From the kitchen, menu in one hand, phone in the other, Matt whistled. "It's always the quiet ones. You slut—you knew we were coming back here."

Laughing, Evan went into the bathroom and shut the door.

He stood under the spray, washing away the tension, sweat, and…fluids…trying not to think too much. Matt was right. He was freaked but he wasn't sorry.

The door to the tiny room opened and Matt peaked his head in. "Uh hello? I pay for my water."

"Sorry!" Evan called, going along with the joke, rinsing off the rest of the soap. The little stall smelled good—exactly like Matt—and a tiny voice in Evan begged him to invite the other man in. He turned the water off, pulled aside the curtain part way.

"Jesus. I'm glad I went first. Is there any hot water left?" Matt was smiling, leaning his hands against the sides of the stall. He gave Evan a hard stare. "Remind me that I need a bigger shower stall."

"And why is that?" Evan asked, playing along.

"Only room for one."

"Hand me a towel?"

Matt moved to a small hamper next to the toilet, pulled out an oversized navy towel. He threw it to Evan, then stood close, watching him emerge with it tied around his waist. "Being a little modest I see."

"I'm playing hard to get."

Evan dried off and went to grab his clothes off the toilet. Caught Matt's now frowning face.

"What?"

"How much weight have you lost?" Matt asked harshly. He reached out to trace the hip bones that jutted out above the low slung towel. "You should be what? One ninety? Two hundred?"

Evan bristled a bit. "One ninety-five. I've been lifting a lot, trying to get into shape."

"Get into shape? As opposed to what? You're in great shape and you're also fucking underweight. You must be down twenty pounds. You're lucky you haven't hurt yourself."

"Matt, I appreciate your concern…"

"But you're fine? Right? No. You bitch that everyone hounds you about your eating habits and now I can see why. This isn't healthy."

Evan looked away. His face burned. "It happened after the…funeral. I just couldn't seem to keep anything down. The weight came off—and I just haven't put it back on. I *am* fine, I swear."

Matt didn't look convinced. He roughly moved his hands over Evan's arms and chest, as if taking inventory of each protruding rib and edge of bone. His touch gentled as he reached Evan's face, soothing away the furrow in his brow. "You need to eat more. And I need to eat less. Deal?"

Leaning forward, Evan touched his forehead to Matt's cheek. He let his hands mimic Matt's, stroking his torso with needy hands. "You feel fine to me."

"Oh yeah. Your spindly little arms could barely reach around me."

They stood there for a moment. Matt hated the way Evan treated himself—as less than an afterthought.

"You should take care of yourself for Christ's sake. Your job is dangerous—you need to be 100 percent."

"Yes, sir."

"I'm not joking."

Evan pulled away and went back to getting his clothes. "I'll be fine."

Matt squeezed his mouth shut, headed for the door. "Uh, I'm going to put some music on. You got any preferences?"

"Nah." Evan didn't look up. Pulled on sweats and a long-sleeved T-shirt. "Whatever you want."

"Look—I'm sorry if I went a little overboard…"

"Stop. It's not that. I had a stupid fight with Helena this week. She told me how full of shit I was, when I said I was fine. She's right. I don't eat or sleep enough. I've let my kids down…"

"Now hold on—you're the best father I've ever seen. Those kids adore you."

"Loving my kids isn't enough, Matt. What you saw last weekend was the first time in a year that we spent that kind of time together."

"Hey, Evan—what the fuck are you beating yourself in the ground for? Your wife died. You and your kids are in mourning. It takes a while to get over a blow like that."

"I used to be better—"

"Stop."

Evan sighed. "I would have made a fantastic martyr right?"

"Jesus would've given you a medal himself."

Evan walked out the bathroom, past Matt. Threw his bag back by the door. "When are you getting a couch?"

"Tomorrow. It's a pullout. Leather—very sexy."

"Why do I get the feeling like you're going to kick my ass every time I get like this?"

"You are a perceptive, perceptive man."

Smiling, Evan threw himself down on the mattress and stretched out. "And what's my job in this relationship?"

Matt walked over, dropped next to Evan, slid his hand under the black shirt. This time he wasn't feeling for ribs. This time it was personal business.

"You're going to keep me from drinking too much by giving me something else to do with my time. And mouth."

"Ahh."

"Deal?"

"Ah—deal."

Chapter Six

Since kissing was what they did best, Matt pinned Evan to the mattress—hands on Evan's wrists held over his head, leaning between his legs, teasing him with gentle brushes, pelvis to pelvis—and used every oral trick and tip he'd ever been privy to. He'd kissed a whole lotta girls in his lifetime, and Evan was on the receiving end of his wealth of knowledge. Sucked Evan's tongue into his mouth. Bit his lips, then licked away the sting. Moaned his own desire back into the other's man mouth. Matt could feel himself getting hard again, could feel that same frenzy from before seizing his brain.

Evan broke their kiss, smiled up at Matt. Apparently he wasn't alone in his excitement. "I take it this is A material," Evan said.

"Tip of the iceberg." Matt didn't wait for the crack he assumed would follow; he went back to work. Enjoying the taste, the freedom of kissing Evan and not being tentative. Tentative wasn't something that Matt Haight was good at.

Then the doorbell rang.

Reluctantly, Matt separated their mouths. "Uh, food's here."

Evan started laughing. "Are you going to make it down in your condition?"

"Shit." A few minutes later, with a sweatshirt tied artistically around his waist, Matt headed down the stairs, whistling. He paid the shivering delivery guy—healthy tip—and went back to the apartment with the bag of food. He walked up slowly, thinking suddenly of how long it'd been since he'd had a woman here. How long it'd been since he'd made love to someone, enjoyed their company, shared a meal? Months, maybe a year? A few women here and there, pickups at the bar. A couple of hours of drunken screwing at her place or a motel. No exchange of last names. No future.

His last long-term relationship (in Mattspeak that meant, what? Six months?) went back even further. He had a stunning knack for getting involved with the wrong women—married women, needy women, women who wanted the suburban husband/baby package that Matt had no interest in. Women who were destined to fail at keeping Matt entertained, amused, and aroused for longer than a few months.

At the door, he paused. Evan had so many qualities that appealed to Matt. Smart, funny, honest. He always said what he meant. He didn't judge. Matt snickered. And he was a cop. Yeah, he just couldn't seem to stay away from that world. The attraction had frightened Matt. But giving in to it made the fear small, made it less important. When they were together, he forgot that this wasn't anything he'd known before.

Evan lay quietly on the mattress, watching the ceiling, counting the tiles. His mouth and jaw stung from Matt's aggressive kisses, his rough skin. Evan was ready to go again. Matt had unleashed something dormant, something that had come roaring back after thirteen months of silence. Evan's sex drive had disappeared after Sherri's death. Nothing aroused him, nothing drove him to touch himself under the cover of night. He thought about her all the time, kissing her, making love to her. But his body didn't respond.

It felt strange to be feeling that lust again. The burning need for someone to touch and caress and kiss him. When Matt had him down on the mattress...Evan moaned quietly, covering his face with his arm. Each kiss seemed to be building on the back of the last. He knew they were going to keep having to go further. To increase the physical act until... Until what? Evan may have had only one partner in his life but he certainly wasn't naive. He knew what could eventually happen between them. It scared him.

It excited him.

Blowing out a deep breath, Evan tried to wrap his brain around the fact that he was responding so ardently to Matt sexually. He liked looking at Matt, liked watching him move. Liked his eyes, his laugh, his sense of humor. But the desire, the want that overwhelmed him, that came when he felt Matt's concern and tenderness. When he made Evan feel like he wasn't alone, that it was okay to be tired and scared.

Matt equaled comfort.

This is what love feels like, he thought to himself. *I remember this feeling. I want this feeling again.*

He heard the door rattle and looked over to see Matt walking back into the apartment, bag in hand. His thoughtful expression took about ten years off his age. "Hey, no maudlin shit, remember?" Evan called from the mattress.

Matt's face lit up in a smile. "Right. Come and eat. And don't think you're getting away with anything. I'm going to watch you."

A little kick of panic landed in Evan's solar plexus but he grinned through it. He got up and stretched, watched Matt walk into the tiny kitchen.

"I got chicken, pasta, bread. There's beer in the fridge," Matt said, emptying the bag. "Throw our clothes onto the bed." He started setting things up on the counter.

"I don't think there's much of a choice." Evan said drily, looking around at the empty apartment. "Where are we eating?"

"The fucking formal dining room. Christ, what are you the Queen of England?" Matt rolled his eyes. He pointed to the counter. "Stand there."

Evan dropped their suits and jackets onto the mattress, grabbed some beers out of the refrigerator and took his place on the living room side of the counter, while Matt rummaged around the drawers and cabinets for plates, forks, napkins.

"So what kind of furniture did you get?"

"Sofa...one of those pullout beds. Big beautiful recliner. Didn't want to get out of it at the showroom. Some other shit—the basics."

Evan looked over his shoulder. "Did you get rid of everything? There's no TV or stereo. No pictures."

Matt shrugged, shoveling pasta and chicken onto one of the plates. "Not much in the way of mementos. Got some stuff in a box—that's in the closet. Stereo and TV are small—they're in the closet too for the time being."

"No collections of porcelain animals or clown banks?"

Matt snorted. "Your house—it's really nice. I meant to tell you that. Real comfortable, you know?"

Evan accepted the plate of food, his stomach doing flip after flip. "Thanks. Uh...Sherri...she worked hard to make it that way."

Matt said nothing, opened a bottle of beer and took a very long drag. They had just entered dangerous territory. Evan was staring at his dinner like it was a foreign concept. And the break in his voice when he said his wife's name. Matt was about to tell a joke when Evan started talking again. Evan pushed the food around, dropped his fork to drink some of his beer. He kept his eyes moving, not settling on any one thing. "I haven't really talked about her much, have I?"

"No. I didn't think it was any of my business to ask. Too personal."

Flicking his eyes over the mattress in the middle of the apartment, Evan drily observed, "I'd say we're pretty much past anything being too personal."

"Good point."

Evan took a piece of bread, ripped it into a dozen pieces, as Matt nonchalantly watched him.

"Growing up, ah, it was pretty shitty at home. My dad died when I was four. Don't really remember much about him. He was a career marine, stationed in Germany. Me and my mom moved back to the states to live in Albany afterward. She remarried about a year later, some guy she met at church." He paused, picking up his fork to stir the pasta around for a moment. "He uh—left—four years later. We moved to Long Island after that. Another marriage. Ed was cool though. Good guy."

"Lot of moving around."

"Yeah. Lots of changes. Stability was never one of my mother's strong points." He ate a small piece of the bread. Chewed for a long time, washed it down with almost half the bottle of beer. "I met Sherri in high school. First day of football practice."

"Mmmm...cheerleader?"

"Equipment manager." Evan smiled. "Love at first sight is an understatement. I couldn't stop looking at her. When I finally got up the courage to walk over it was like...it was like she had always been waiting for me."

Matt swallowed a mouthful of food. Looking at Evan's face, he caught a glimpse of the man he was thirteen months ago.

"No other girlfriends, huh?"

"Never even crossed my mind. She was it—the one. I never had a doubt."

"Never? Amazing...I can't even imagine feeling that way..." Matt's words trailed off. "How do you like the chicken?" Matt asked. "I order from this place all the time—it's good, right?"

Evan sighed. Busted. Without a word, he took a small piece of chicken and put it in his mouth. Chewed. Looked at Matt defiantly.

"What? Do I look stupid? A molecule of chicken? Eat some fucking food please. Thank you."

"You curse a lot."

"Fuck you—I hardly curse at all."

They continued their meal in companionable silence. Matt cleaned his plate—sex made him hungry. Evan, on the other hand, pushed his food around and ate a bite here and there. When he got through about a quarter of the plate, Matt gave up. He started cleaning, putting the leftovers away and tossing his plate and fork into the sink.

"You done?"

"Yeah. More beer?"

"Nah. I'm good." *Hey, who said that?* Matt thought. He began washing the few things in the sink...and felt a warm body pressing up against his side. "Can I help you?"

"Just helping to clean up. Being a good houseguest."

Matt smirked. "If you wanna be a good houseguest..."

"Yeah?" Turning off the water, Matt turned to face Evan. They were standing close, and Evan leaned in for a kiss, which Matt artfully dodged, a smile twisting his mouth. Evan got a bit more aggressive this time, pressing his palms against the front of Matt's thighs, dragging them up—getting dangerously close to the straining fly of his shorts—stroking Matt's chest in grasping circles. He moved his hands to circle Matt's neck, roughly, tenderly...ended up tangled in his hair. Tightened his grip and pulled Matt close, pressing a light kiss on his mouth. Pulled back. Mirrored Matt's smile.

Matt blew out a long breath. He slid his arms around the other man, moved them to his lower back, fingers gently stroking. They kissed slowly, easily. Matt felt his hands sliding farther down, heard the groan it elicited from Evan. The heat between them grew with each touch, each kiss, and Matt's brain nearly exploded from the impact. He released Evan's mouth, pressed their foreheads together.

"Let's go to bed," he whispered.

Evan nodded, his breath ragged. He stepped away, moving toward the mattress. Picked up the clothes they'd left there, threw them on the floor. He turned to Matt, still standing in the kitchen, watching his every move.

Matt crossed the room in two strides. He grabbed the front of Evan's shirt, pulling it up over his head in one move. Bit that curve between his neck and shoulder, hard. He felt himself shaking with need. He slid his hands across the waistband of Evan's shorts, brushed his fingers underneath. Pushed the fabric away to feel the flesh—hot, tight. Moved his mouth across Evan's jaw, throat. Biting.

The roar in his ears built on the sounds Evan was making…raw, anxious moans and sighs. "Lie down," Matt rasped. He was using both hands to push Evan's shorts down, frantic to feel more of his flesh.

Evan let Matt take his clothes off. Let him manhandle him. It excited him to be overwhelmed, to be free of control for a brief moment. But he wanted the power back. He stood up, and when Matt tried to push him down on the mattress, Evan grasped his wrists.

"Mmmm…wait. Your turn." Matt's eyes were wild as he waited. With gentle hands, Evan began to remove Matt's clothes. T-shirt over his head, shorts and underwear pushed down. Matt stepped out of his clothes and kicked them aside.

They stood, touching, naked and trembling. For a second Evan hesitated, unsure of how to touch Matt, how exactly to please him. He reached out, touched Matt's face gently. Stroked his jaw, down his throat, his chest. His hand shook but he slid slower, to touch Matt—really touch him this time. Listened to the moan as he stroked the hot flesh in his hand. It made him shiver.

Matt pressed against Evan's hand—Christ it felt so good to have someone touching him. These strong hands holding him, lightly pulling on his cock until he thought he might lose his mind. He let himself be selfish for a moment, eyes closed, giving himself over to the feelings, but he couldn't keep his hands off Evan.

Opening his eyes, Matt gave him a hard stare. "God—that feels so good."

And Jesus that blush across the younger man's face.

Evan's hand didn't stop moving. He leaned forward and pressed an opened mouth kiss against the base of Matt's throat.

Sucked the skin so hard that Matt thought he might pass out. Matt brought his hands up to stroke the sides of Evan's face. Tightened his grip as that wet mouth trailed down a bit lower. Bit him. And that hand never stopped moving.

"Fuck," Matt breathed. He pulled Evan's mouth away from his body, bringing their lips together in a crushing kiss. They kissed passionately, tongues fighting for dominance. Matt let go of Evan's face, grabbed his shoulders. Squeezed tightly, feeling his fingers leaving bruises.

This time Evan pulled away, breathlessly. "Lie down," he whispered softly. He gave Matt's cock one last tight stroke, let his hand fall away.

Matt dropped down onto the mattress, lying on his back, knees apart. His look up at Evan was challenging.

Shakily, Evan stood over him, staring at Matt's body, feeling an overwhelming need to please him, to draw his own pleasure from this man.

Matt made the first move—reached up and touched Evan's leg, brushing his fingers up his thigh, teasingly touching him until Evan relented. He lay down on top of Matt, easing their bodies together with a maddeningly light touch. Matt moaned raggedly. They were both burning, the heat generated between them something he could taste.

Evan resisted the urge to rub against Matt. He wanted to make it last. He pulled himself up to kneel over Matt, reached down to clasp his hard-on again, sliding his hand slowly until the moans began. The sound made Evan almost sob with pleasure. It echoed in his ears until he couldn't stand it, until he had to suck Matt's tongue into his mouth to stop the torture. He thought he would go insane.

Evan could almost pinpoint the moment Matt gave himself over to the animal need and thrust his hips again and again. He moved his hands blindly until he clasped Evan's cock in his hand. Moved his hands in tandem.

Evan broke the kiss, practically weeping in thanks. So long, so long, his mind chanted. Too long since he'd felt this incredible rush of heat through his body. Matt was whispering to him and the words finally penetrated the fog around Evan's head.

"God, you feel so fucking good. I want to feel you come against me, I want to hear you lose your fucking mind." Matt groaned, arching his back. He wasn't going to last much longer. "You make me so hard. You make me want to do everything to you." He increased his hand motions until Evan's hips were grinding frantically. "I want to fuck you. I want to feel you in my mouth."

The flash image in his mind of Matt's mouth on his cock sent Evan over the edge.

He felt himself sliding out of control, pounding hard into Matt's hand, falling forward, desperately trying to connect their mouths. "Matt...God, please..." Evan came hard, spilling into Matt's hand, biting Matt's lips. Collapsing as his arms gave way.

Matt didn't need anything more than the feel of Evan's hard body against his to come. He slid his hands down to clasp his ass— *Oh yes,* he thought. *Oh God.* He arched up against the heat and wetness and pounded their bodies together until he couldn't think.

When he could move, Matt tightened his limp arms around Evan, sprawled across his body. "Hey," he whispered. "You okay?"

He felt the answer rumbled against his chest. "Yeah."

They lay there for a long time, until the dampness became cold and sticky. Matt rolled to his side, depositing Evan next to him. They kissed lazily, exhausted, sated. Dozed for a little while, their hands moving almost involuntarily across each other's chests, arms, backs.

* * *

Evan woke up, the overhead light harsh on his eyes. There was no clock and he couldn't remember where he'd put his wristwatch. He closed his eyes again, exhaustion pulling him down into the mattress. He should get up, clean himself off...but he couldn't seem to move.

He woke up again later to Matt's hand stroking his thigh. Evan started to laugh. He opened one eye to find Matt leaning over him, a suggestive grin on his face.

"Jesus Christ—more? Aren't you tired yet?"

Matt shrugged. "I recover quickly."

"I'm old, leave me alone."

"Yeah? I'm older—stop being such a baby." He leaned down to slide his tongue across Evan's lips. "This is the best part—the beginning. Where you're so turned on you can barely stop fucking to think."

Evan's mouth went dry. The low growl of Matt's words sent a wave over his damp skin. "You're sure you've never done this before?"

"What can I tell you—I'm a quick study." Matt pulled himself up, swung one leg over Evan's body, straddling him. "And pretty much from the beginning there's been something about you—something that makes me want you."

Evan felt the desire rise up again. "Which is?"

Matt grinned wickedly. He slid his hand to grab Evan's forearm, brought it up over Evan's head. The tattoo. He leaned forward and ran his tongue along the black edges of the design. When he reached the bottom, right above the wrist, he sank his teeth in and sucked until Evan was writhing underneath him.

And he didn't stop there.

Matt got up to turn the overhead light off and lock his door. He slid back under the covers and relaxed against Evan's warm body. They were "spooned"—a position Matt usually hated, but he was reluctant to let go of Evan. Wanted to run his hands over the man breathing quietly beside him. Pressed his mouth into his shoulder, sighing.

"So I guess I should let you go to sleep," he said softly. He ran his palm gently from Evan's shoulder to his knee.

"We have furniture to move in what? Five hours?"

"Mmm...yeah. Don't worry about it—we can take a nap on the new mattress after the delivery guys leave." Matt didn't bother to leave the leer out of his voice.

"I highly doubt I'd get any sleep in that case." Evan's voice sounded sleepy, and realizing what a precious commodity sleep was for him, Matt kissed him on the back of the neck.

"Go to sleep. I'm gonna make you carry all the heavy stuff," Matt whispered. He pulled him close against his body, one arm resting on the pillow above his head, the other draped over Evan's midsection.

Evan chuckled and leaned back comfortably. He sighed, rooting down into the pillow, under the blankets.

In just a few minutes, Matt felt Evan growing heavy against him. Heard the change in his breathing and realized he was asleep. *Well, if I'm not going to get him to eat enough at least I can make sure he's tired enough to sleep*, Matt thought drily.

Suddenly it wasn't the sexual feelings this man aroused in him crowding Matt's brain—it was the tenderness, the concern. He wanted to take care of Evan, ease his burden a bit. At the same time, Evan gave him a safe place to be—like he'd felt with Tony, with Phil—but with the added bonus of an addictive surge of lust that seemed to have obliterated any doubts Matt might have had about getting involved with a man.

He kept thinking about his old partners, about how he missed their company, their friendship, their concern. Having a partner back when he was on the force anchored him somehow. It was more than work, more than solving the cases. It was Matt's home, Matt's family, and goddamnit he missed it still.

But not as much as a few months ago, he thought. Not as much since Evan and he started this friendship. Their relationship brought back that old familiar sense of security cradling Matt as he went about his life. No worries, because in the end he could wind up here, in safe silence.

Matt laid his head on Evan's pillow, practically touching his mouth to the back of the sleeping man's head. He inhaled the male scent—Matt's soap on new skin, the smell of sex—and closed his eyes. Hushed his overactive brain and let himself fall under the seductive sound of Evan's rhythmic breathing until he felt himself drifting off.

The dream was always the same. *He walked down the corridor behind his stepfather Buddy—his first stepfather, the one who taught him about being too afraid to breath—numbly listening to the recitation about Sherri being dead. Evan was too frightened to speak. He just wanted to find his wife and take her home because she shouldn't be here with Buddy and she couldn't be dead...no, no, no.*

They turned a corner and Evan gagged—the smell of death overwhelmed him. He grabbed his throat, unable to breathe through the stench. Suddenly she was there in front of him on the gurney, the wound on her head so vicious, so cruel...so clean.

It enraged him because he knew it was a lie. Death wasn't so neat and tidy, so politely civil. He'd seen it enough to know that. He turned to Buddy, that disgusting leer permanently etched onto his face.

"Where did you put her blood?" he screamed. "Where is it all? Why are you hiding it?"

And then it was there—all of it—all the blood he could have ever imagined on his hands, on his clothes, in his eyes, and he started to shriek in terror because he thought he might drown. He could hear Buddy laughing, telling him to be a good boy or else...

He clawed his way back to consciousness, moaning and flailing desperately. He had to escape Buddy...had to escape the blood. Had to escape the look of his wife's corpse. Evan fought off the covers which were weighed down much heavier than usual. And he heard someone calling his name.

"Hey, hey, easy, I'm here—calm down." Matt.

Evan gasped, sitting straight up, shivering with nausea and fear. He felt Matt's hands soothing him gently, like that first night.

Felt his mouth close, whispering in his ear, "It's okay. I'm here."

Oh thank God, Evan thought.

"Sorry," he managed to get out. But Matt stopped him immediately.

"Come here." He pulled him back into his arms, lowering them both back onto the mattress. "Are you okay?"

Evan shivered. "Yeah." He buried his face into the pillow, unable to look Matt in the eye. Always the same goddamn dream. Always about the two things that Evan hated most in the world— Buddy, the predator that stalked his childhood, and Sherri, dead, taken away from him too soon.

"You want to talk about it?" Matt asked softly, stroking the back of Evan's head and neck, comforting him.

"No." Evan swallowed hard. "Talk to me, just talk about anything for a few minutes okay?" He needed a few moments to pull himself together.

"'Kay." Matt felt like sharing something with Evan, to make him feel less alone. "I used to have nightmares all the time—after Tony died."

"Your first partner?"

"Yeah. I heard the shot, turned my head and he was on his knees. Already dead. After his funeral, every time I closed my eyes I'd hear the gunshots. Knowing over and over again there wasn't anything I could do but watch Tony die." Matt sighed. "You become a cop and they teach you about protecting people and keeping them safe. But they don't tell you how it rips your heart out when you realize you can't do it. You can't save everybody."

Evan said nothing but leaned a bit closer to Matt.

"I couldn't protect Tony. I tried to but I couldn't."

"I know how you feel."

"It was a car accident, Evan. There was nothing you could have done."

Evan started to protest so Matt leaned over and kissed him, hard. "I know you loved her. I know you would have done anything for her, but it was the asshole in the other car—not you. You don't have to feel guilty. I blamed myself every day for years for Tony's death but I realized—I didn't do anything wrong. I didn't cause his death. Just like you didn't cause Sherri's death."

"I know." Evan's voice was barely audible. "But I...I just wanted to protect her. That's what you do when you love someone. You protect them."

"Yeah. That's what you try to do." Evan thought about Buddy and shook. He thought about his mother and how much he still hated her. He had never said anything to anyone but Sherri—she alone knew the source of his nightmares, the reason he worked so diligently as a cop. And now he wanted Matt to know. "My stepfather—the first one—ah...he was a piece of shit. He conned my mother though—treated her like a princess. But when she wasn't around, he...he said things to me...disgusting things... followed me around, watched me all the time. When I threatened to tell my mother he'd laugh, find some reason to slam me into a wall."

Matt held himself very still as the words poured out of Evan's mouth. He remembered his childhood, remembered the priest whose poison reach had only just missed Matt. "Did he ever...?"

"No. To this day I don't know why. When I was nine, two federal marshals showed up on our doorstep. Turns out good old Buddy had escaped from a state pen. In for child molestation."

Matt let out a harsh breath. "Jesus. You were lucky he never... Jesus. Your mother must've been devastated."

Evan made the strangest sound—somewhere between a laugh and a moan. "My mother? My fucking mother knew. She knew what he was, knew he was a rapist and a convict and she let him into our home anyway. Let him be around me, let him terrorize me for four years. She knew and she didn't care." By the end, Evan was breathing heavily, his voice breaking.

Matt said nothing. He just wrapped his arms around the other man tightly, sliding his legs in between his, until there wasn't any part of their bodies that wasn't touching. He couldn't think of anything to say.

Trembling with rage, Evan buried his face against Matt's shoulder, trying to control himself. It had been almost fifteen years since he'd said those words aloud, and he'd buried the memories as far down as he could. Sometimes they slipped out, in the dead of night, when a case hit too close to home. It would make Evan wild with anger, desperate to avenge those children who had no one in their corner. Up until tonight, it had been

Sherri to hold him like this, to let him rage and hate, then quietly remind him that he was loved.

Evan shifted, brought his mouth to Matt's ear. "There's so much I want to say to you...but it's just too soon."

Matt's heart clenched. "I'll be here when you're ready," he whispered shakily.

The other man nodded and they lay there in silence, until Evan once again succumbed to his exhaustion. Matt held him tightly still, refusing to let go. He had never known such peace...or such terror. He knew what Evan wanted to say, could hear it in the gentle tone of his voice, could feel the emotion pulsing through his body. He wanted to hear it, wanted to know it was true. But he didn't know how to say it back and mean it. He didn't know how to make it last, or how to make it beautiful. He only knew how to run like a coward and hide in a pitcher of beer, or behind a cheap fuck.

He didn't know if he deserved to hear those words from someone like Evan.

Chapter Seven

The phone woke them a few hours later, at eight a.m. The delivery men were lost and Matt sleepily gave them better directions. Hanging up the phone, he fell back down on the mattress and pressed against Evan's back.

"We have about forty-five minutes before they get here," Matt said, giving him a hard bite on the shoulder.

Evan pulled the covers over his head. "I'm sleeping. Keep your hands to yourself."

Matt smiled, following Evan under the blanket. A little levity after last night was good. A little kissing would be even better.

The moving men arrived and in short order the four men had nearly all the pieces up the stairs and into the apartment. When the two deliverymen went downstairs for the last box, Matt cornered Evan against the wall next to the front door.

"Let's get the couch set up first," he said, flicking his eyes across Evan's face.

Returning the stare, Evan said "You have me for another," he checked his watch, "seven hours. Use your time wisely."

Matt smirked and moved away, hearing the men coming up the stairs, banging his chest of drawers against the walls and the railing. He was feeling a certain swagger in his step this morning, drunk on this attraction, this feeling of affection that flowed like a circuit between them. He figured it would hit him later that Matthew Haight, Ladies Man Extraordinaire, was now fixated on getting Evan Cerelli, Poster Boy for Suburban Normalcy, naked and on his back as often as possible.

He should probably be freaked out, like he was before, but it was a natural high being alone with Evan and he didn't want to spoil it by thinking too hard.

A few hours later Matt was regaining his equilibrium, blinking up at the ceiling. He felt Evan stir next to him, the mattress dipping slightly as he got up.

"Hey, where you headed?"

Evan stretched, rolling out the kinks in his back and arms. "Shower. I have to get going soon. Traffic's going to be a bitch out to the Island—I have to pick my kids up by eight."

"Shower, huh?"

Smiling, Evan shook his head. "God you have a one-track mind... Stall's too small remember? I'll be out in a few minutes. We need to talk about some things."

The bottom fell out of Matt's stomach. It sounded as bad coming from Evan as it did from the countless women who'd uttered those words to Matt over the years. "You okay?"

"Fine." Evan wasn't looking at Matt while he talked. "I mean, this..." He motioned to the bed. "This is...good...but what about the real world? We both have a lot at stake."

Matt didn't think that was true—Evan's risks were much higher. He blinked a few times, trying to organize his thoughts. His chest felt heavy with fear, fully aware that he was the least important thing in Evan's life and the first thing to go if there was trouble.

"Well, to be honest, I thought we would keep this to ourselves as much as possible...at least for right now. Til we... uh...figure out what this...is."

Evan nodded, kept his eyes fixed on the floor. "I...don't know what to say to you except...this is important to me...for a lot of different reasons. I'm not ready...to give it up."

Matt said nothing, struggling. Nodded just to do something. "Did you want to tell someone?"

"Yeah. Actually, I thought I might let Helena know. It might help her to understand why I've been such a lunatic over the past week."

"I know she's your partner..."

"And friend."

"And friend...but do you think she'll...ah...be okay with it?"

"I think so. Helena isn't a judgmental person. She'll want me to be happy."

Matt swallowed. "And this...makes you happy?"

Evan smirked, finally locking eyes with Matt. "Yeah. And crazy and confused and..."

"Tired?"

"How about you?" Evan asked with a laugh.

"Shit, I'm exhausted. You wore me out."

"Thank you. I'm taking a shower."

Evan turned and walked toward the bathroom. Matt found himself doing something he'd never expected—checking out another man's body. Liking what he saw.

"Hey."

"What?" Evan called, not turning around. He waited in the doorway.

"Yeah. Makes me happy."

Evan's head dropped. Matt wanted to believe he was smiling.

"Good." His voice was slightly muffled, as he went into the bathroom and shut the door.

Matt got up, busied himself with folding the blankets, closing the couch. He pulled on his shorts, lying on the floor near the window—wondered how the hell they got there, recalled a lot of urgency in getting out of his clothes and touching Evan.

There were still some pieces in their shipping materials...only the couch and recliner were unpacked and sitting in their proper spots. With a sigh, Matt sat down in the chair, stared out the window to watch the garden across the street. The steam heat pushed its way through the radiator, taking the chill off of Matt's skin.

It felt so right to be here, to be listening to his shower run, knowing Evan was standing under the stream of water. He wanted to figure out when they'd be together again. Wanted to know when he could spend time with the whole family...didn't want to think about having this end.

"What are you doing for Thanksgiving?"

"Eating the turkey special at Ed's."

"I have to go to my in-laws..."

"And what? You need a date or something?"

"Oh God. I don't even want to think about my in-laws finding out about us."

Matt clutched the phone tighter, partially because of the fear of discovery, partially because Evan said us. "What about Thanksgiving?"

"We should be home by five. I was thinking of inviting some people over."

"Who?"

"Vic, Helena…"

"You going to talk to Helena tomorrow?"

"No, I was going to wait for Thursday. I don't want to do it while we're working."

"And Vic?"

"I'm thinking that maybe he should know…in case something gets around…"

Deep breath, Matt thought. Take a deep breath. He knew Vic Wolkowski to be an open-minded and decent guy but the thought of telling him…telling anyone. "Uh…could we wait a little bit? Let's just start with Helena, okay?"

"Yeah, fine. Whatever. I'm still going to have him over on Thursday."

"Great. I'll…uh…bring something. Dessert or something. See you at five then?"

"Okay."

Back to silence, Matt thought. What the hell do you say to the man you spent the weekend with—in bed?

As if reading his thoughts, Evan said, "I had a good weekend, Matt. Thanks."

"Thanks?" Matt snorted. "Believe me when I say I got as good as I gave."

"And on that note…" Evan was laughing and that sounded good to Matt.

"Say hi to the kids."

"Yeah. They told me to tell you hello. Wanted to know when they were going to see you again."

Matt smiled. "Tell them they won't be able to get rid of me on Thursday."

Evan cleared his throat. "You should…uh…bring some clothes with you…"

"Sure...okay...you sure?" Matt stammered. "Your kids..."

"What are you talking about, you're still sleeping on the couch."

"Oh...yeah...of course."

"But be prepared for a visit or two. See you Thursday."

And Matt heard a click. Waiting until Thursday was going to be torture.

Fighting through torrential rains, Evan got to work on Monday at eight thirty a.m. He whistled a little bit as he got his coffee, which elicited an odd look from Moses, who was rooting around in the donut box.

"Morning."

"Yeah—Morning." Moses watched Evan go back to his desk. "You're awfully upbeat on this hellacious Monday. What put the snap in your step?"

With a shrug, Evan sat down at his desk. "Nothing in particular. Just a good weekend that's all." He felt Moses's narrow gaze, heard him sniffing the air at the whiff of a secret. Evan tried to relax into his seat, busying himself with his daily routine.

He was praying he'd strategically hidden the bite marks on his neck, that no one would notice his shirtsleeves were staying down for the day (Matt's little tattoo fetish had left quite a reminder on the inside of his forearm). It was strange...and a little exciting...to be carrying around—evidence.

Deep in his remembrance, he almost missed Helena walking through the station house door. They exchanged wary glances across the floor, then she busied herself with hanging up her wet things. Evan sighed. This couldn't go any longer. He got up and met her at the coffee machine.

"Hi."

"Morning. Any calls yet?"

"Uh no. Helena?"

"I went over the files for the McCrory case. I think I'm ready to testify."

"Helena, could we talk for a minute?"

"This is talking," she said coolly.

"Please. Come out in the hallway for a second."

With obvious reluctance she followed him out into the hall. Standing against the wall with her arms crossed she waited for him to speak.

"Helena, I'm sorry for what I said to you last week—or actually, I'm sorry for what I didn't say. You're right. I wasn't handling things well at all and I snapped at you because...because I was an idiot."

He got a small smile from her. "Go on. I'm enjoying this."

"I'm a really big idiot?"

"Evan—you can't have it both ways. Either we're friends and we talk or we have nothing to say to one another outside of our work. I can't shut off being concerned about you. Any more than you could do it for me."

"I'm scum."

"Stop it. I'm worried about you—I won't lie and say I'm not. I promised not to hover but you have got to stop dismissing me. It's pissing me off."

"See, that I noticed." Evan took a deep breath. "I'm sorry."

"Are you going to tell me what's going on? Why you're acting so weird?"

"I'm just confused...about this potential relationship...it's a difficult situation. Extenuating circumstances if you will..." Actually it was probably misleading to say potential since Evan had spent almost thirty-six hours intermittently naked in Matt's bed, but…whatever. He just needed to get through this conversation. "Listen, why don't you stop by on Thanksgiving, at night. After you drop your grandmother off. Vic's coming by and a…a few other people probably. We can talk then…I… uh…I have a lot to talk to you about."

She didn't say anything.

"I…uh…the person is going to be there. The person I've been talking about. So you can meet." Again. But this time, the circumstances were very different. Evan tried not to turn red but it was impossible. He felt his whole body clench at the thought of anyone knowing about he and Matt. But he couldn't keep Helena in the dark forever. It wasn't fair.

Still solemn, Helena nodded. "All right. I'll come by. I don't understand why we can't talk before then."

Evan shifted, uncomfortable. "Well this just isn't the place to say…certain things."

He watched her swallow, move nervously from foot to foot.

"Okay."

There was a long uncomfortable silence that Evan didn't quite understand…Helena seemed to pull herself out of it and she smiled.

And then Helena punched Evan in the arm. "Stop being such an ass okay? Answer my questions and no one will get hurt."

"So this is settled? 'Cause we spent a whole week in a fight that I didn't quite understand."

"Yeah. I overreacted just a tad I think. If I come on Thanksgiving I meet the mystery girl who's causing you to act crazy?"

"Yeah." Sort of kind of. The crazy part was definite.

"I'll be there at seven. Can I bring my mom?"

"Sure, the more the merrier." Oh Jesus, Evan thought. Matt was going to lose his mind. The crowd kept growing.

"Great." Helena seemed back to normal and that made Evan relax. She reached out and squeezed his forearms. "I'm planning on continuing to ask you personal questions but without hovering, and I expect straight answers. 'Kay?"

Evan nodded, smiling.

Helena smiled back and turned back down the hallway, past where Moses was obviously faking an intent study of a folder. She rolled her eyes at Evan and went to sit down.

Evan sagged against the wall. That took a lot out of him and shit, they hadn't even gotten to the part where he said the words, I'm involved with Matt Haight. He rubbed his face and headed back toward his desk. Moses hadn't moved.

"Can I help you?" he asked wearily. There was a little gleam in Moses's eyes that was making him nervous.

"Nope. Just reading my file." He gave Evan the skunk eye and turned on his heel to go back in the squad room.

Evan counted to fifty and tried to look as calm as humanly possible as he sat down at his desk. He had three days until his little secret started to make its way into the light of day.

Three days.

* * *

On Thanksgiving morning, Evan found himself standing in his bedroom, staring at the bed, the dresser, the walls. He hadn't spent much time here in the past thirteen months. Couldn't bear to see Sherri's things—her perfume and makeup on the dressing table, jewelry box on the dresser. Nothing had been moved or put away. He couldn't bear to take that final step, to fully acknowledge that she wasn't coming back. Her life was over, but his still existed.

He pulled a heavy black sweater over his head, knew his jeans would annoy his mother-in-law and knew he would enjoy that. He could hear the kids banging around downstairs, as the Macy's Day Parade blared in the background. Oh good. Another marching band playing "Jingle Bells." The hint of Christmas made his stomach hurt. Last year they had pretty much let it slide—a small tree, a few toys for the kids. They'd spent most of the time at Sherri's parents, subdued. Evan had still been in a daze—it was only about two months after they'd buried Sherri—and couldn't do much more than sit on the couch and stare at the fireplace. Avoiding the mantel, so he wouldn't have to see Sherri, from birth through adulthood, her smiling face burning his eyes.

This year though...he wanted it to better. He wanted his kids to keep having good times, so they'd remember happy moments of their childhood. As hard as it would be, he would do it all—the big tree, the trimmings, the decorations, the flood of presents. Evan desperately wanted to hear his children laughing and shrieking with delight, opening their gifts on Christmas morning.

And he realized that in his mind's eye, imagining that happy moment, he could see Matt Haight sitting there, amid the chaos, smiling.

It made him a little dizzy.

"Hey Dad!" Kathleen's shouting woke him from his little reverie. "Dad?"

"Coming," he called.

Evan grabbed his watch and wedding ring off the dresser and moved toward the stairs. He wanted a beautiful family Christmas. And he wanted to share that with Matt.

* * *

Six hours of the MacGregors tested every molecule of Evan's patience and stoic nature. Phil smoked at least nine cigars, complained about everything from the mayor to the subways (which he hadn't been on in seventeen years) to the goddamn Jets. Every time Evan tried to participate in the conversation, Phil would change the subject and launch into another tirade. This Evan was used to—used to the rambles—but the steady stream of scotch that Phil was consuming was something new. He knew that Phil had been devastated by Sherri's death—she was his favorite—but he hadn't realized he was drinking his pain away. It made Evan tense up, because he knew he had been doing the same thing.

Elena spent most of her time on the phone in her old room. She occasionally came out to help her mother, but to Evan she seemed distant and worn out. He wanted to ask her what was wrong but she never seemed to sit still long enough for them to talk.

Josie fussed over the children nonstop. She fed them from the moment they walked through the door, right up until dinner. He could see they were practically drunk on food and knew it would be a quiet ride home—they'd all be unconscious. When she had all the kids chewing at the same time, she turned her attention to Evan.

He was offered every kind of food known to man, twice, and the third time Josie came out with a plate of fruit, cheese, and bread Evan caved and took it from her. She seemed relieved, as if she couldn't imagine what to do with someone who wouldn't eat.

It took him almost an hour to get through the whole plate. He chewed mechanically, listening to Phil's slurred litany of complaints, heard Josie's endless fussing from the kitchen. A football game played on the big screen TV. His stomach clenched hard. He wanted some of Phil's scotch.

The children eased the tension during dinner. They all competed to tell their grandparents stories about school, about sports; they threw out ideas for Christmas presents, charming and adorable, knowing they'd get whatever they mentioned.

Evan was able to keep quiet, choke down his plate full of food. Trying to figure out if this was hell because Sherri wasn't here or if he just hadn't noticed before. He'd thought her family was perfect, simply because he had nothing to measure it against.

As the meal wound down, the kids got fidgety and Evan couldn't keep his eyes off the clock.

"Uh, guys—are you almost done? Remember, we have to get home. There's company coming."

Josie began clearing the table. "I can't believe you have to leave so early!"

Evan gave his kids the "father look" and they got up, started stacking plates and putting things in the kitchen for cleaning. He did the same.

"Josie, I have a few friends from work who don't have families in town—I wanted to give them a place to be today."

Josie made a sniffing sound and carried a stack of plates into the kitchen. Phil reached for the bottle of scotch, ever present at his side; Elena murmured an excuse and disappeared again. Sighing, Evan stole another glance at the clock. It was three thirty—if he could just get out of there by four... He didn't want Matt standing on his doorstep alone.

They were on the road by four and Evan was only partially right—Danny and Kathleen dozed off, leaving Miranda to fiddle with the radio stations nonstop and Elizabeth to chatter happily about the next few days they'd have together, Christmas. Evan felt such overwhelming pleasure at hearing her sweet little voice, planning and enthusing...and he realized that Sherri wasn't gone completely. Elizabeth was her echo. It comforted him.

They pulled into the driveway at quarter past five. As the headlights swept across the front of the house, Evan saw a figure standing on the stoop and he smiled. There was no mistaking the tall, broad-shouldered form, weighed down with bags.

"Hey! It's Matt!" Elizabeth squealed from the backseat, waking Danny and Kathleen up from their naps.

Evan barely had time to put the car in park before the doors opened and the kids spilled out. He watched Elizabeth and Danny race over to slam into Matt's legs, nearly knocking him over with the force of their hugs. Evan watched him drop his bags, reach down to pick up both kids at the same time, swing them around until they shrieked.

Evan just wanted to sit there for hours and watch them all together, but he shut off the engine and got out of the car. As he walked up the driveway, he caught Matt's eye.

"Hey."

"Hey," Matt said breathlessly, giving the twins one last shake, dropping them on the stoop.

There was nothing to say...nothing they could say with the kids milling around, shoving one another toward the front door. Evan elbowed his way through the crowd, got his keys out. Herded his brood into the house. Matt brought up the rear, picking up his bags. Evan paused in the doorway, let Matt bump into him. He heard the quick intake of breath, let it warm him.

"I missed you."

The words were so softly spoken that Evan could barely make them out. But he knew the feeling. He felt it too.

Evan kept walking, let Matt in and shut the door.

Vic Wolkowski showed up twenty minutes later. His kids were off on a trip to Europe with his late wife's sister and he'd spent the day with an elderly aunt. He walked in with enough bakery cookies to feed all of Queens.

Seeing Matt he lit up. "Hey, Matty! Had no idea you were going to be here." Vic dropped his coat over a chair. "I didn't realize you guys were that close."

Evan turned on his heel and walked into the kitchen where Matt saw he was pretending to check the coffee machine. Like it was a nuclear warhead that needed his attention.

Bastard.

Chicken.

"Since we...uh...met at Abe's retirement party, we just started...you know...hanging out..." Matt knew he was sweating. And he was fully aware he sounded like he was hiding something. Which he was.

Vic pursed his lips. Nodded thoughtfully. Turned to Evan, who continued to stare at the Mr. Coffee. "Hey, how long till the coffee's done? I want to crack open those cookies."

Vic was on his third cup of coffee and unknown number cookie. He, Evan, and Matt sat at the table, relaxing, shooting the shit. Matt felt so comfortable, in this kitchen, with these men. The kids were in the living room, laughing uproariously at something on television. Occasionally Elizabeth or Danny would wander in and lean against Matt's chair, ask him some silly question, steal a cookie from his plate. Kathleen came in for more sodas, casually asked Matt how long he was staying.

Matt did his very best to keep his eyes locked on the plate of cookies. After what he felt was an appropriate amount of time, he looked up, caught Evan's eye—shit—and said, "Uh, we'll see... what, you kicking me out already?"

The doorbell rang at that moment and Matt said a prayer of heartfelt thanksgiving.

Helena and Serena Abbot stood on the doorstep, bearing even more food.

"Well, at least I don't have to shop for awhile," Evan quipped, taking the filled-to-the-top shopping bags from them.

Introductions were made all around. Matt flashed a smile at Helena and a bigger one at her mother. He was good at charming the moms. Serena shook everyone's hand then asked where the kitchen was so she "could get some food on the table," like they were all starving to death. Matt smirked at Evan as a suddenly flustered Vic Wolkowski offered "to help her out."

They went into the kitchen, leaving Matt, Helena, and Evan standing in a half circle in the entryway. Matt felt slightly nauseous. Helena was smiling so brightly it hurt his eyes.

After some genial small talk, she turned and winked. "Sooo...Evan..." Helena said, elbowing her partner. "Is she here yet?"

Matt's eyes narrowed. Evan look at the ceiling, refused to meet Matt's stare.

"Uh, no. Not here." Evan cleared his throat. "Yet. Not here yet."

Helena, eyebrows raised, cast a glance at Matt, who was trying to relax his facial muscles.

"Okaayy. Is she coming?"

"Yeah." With that Evan turned and walked into the kitchen, where Matt presumed he was going to monitor the coffee machine again.

Helena turned to Matt, her eyes narrowed. "What's up with him?"

Matt shrugged and quickly followed. He was never going to make it through this evening without dropping dead.

Helena didn't say much for the rest of the evening. Her detective radar was pinging like crazy. She listened to Vic and Matt tell funny stories about old cases, entertaining her mother—who played the wide-eyed civilian to her flirty best. Evan laughed along and Helena realized this was the most relaxed she'd seem him in ages (his weirdness when she showed up aside).

She checked the clock and realized that it was edging toward ten o'clock and she very much doubted the "mystery girl" was showing up...thus reinforcing her underlying terror that *she*, Helena Abbot, was said mystery girl, that her partner, her dearest friend, her model for the "ideal man"—he was like her freaking brother for God's sake—was developing romantic feelings for.

Oh God, she didn't want to go there. Didn't want to have the conversation she sensed was coming. Yes, she fully appreciated the fact that Evan Cerelli was a beautiful, beautiful man—inside and out (especially the out because she was not blind). Yes, finding a straight, single, non-sociopathic man in New York City was akin to locating shoes in your size during a sale at Bloomies—frankly impossible. But, while this was the rational Helena understanding these points, emotional Helena couldn't get past the fact that this was Evan. The guy who teased her about her slavish devotion to street vendor hot dogs and her spider fears and calmed her down during her more crazed moments and who taught her how to be a great detective. He was...he was her mentor and her brother and she just could not move from friends to lovers with him. Couldn't.

She saw Evan glance at the clock and thought he would make some excuse about the "mystery girl" but instead he gave Matt a smile and got up to announce bedtime to the kids in the other room.

"Hey, Danny, Elizabeth, Kathleen—let's go. Bedtime."

Groans met the pronouncement but Helena heard shuffling. The kids filed in to say their good nights and Helena watched with interest as all three ran over to give Matt hugs and kisses. She had no idea Matt had spent time with the kids. Strange that Evan had never mentioned that.

And then Helena heard Danny say, "Hey Matt—you gonna be here when we wake up like last time?"

It wasn't so much the words that made her take notice, Helena realized—it was Matt and Evan's reaction. The furtive glances, the "quick" recovery and non-answer.

"Well...it's not snowing again is it? Like last time?" Matt croaked.

And then Evan shepherded the kids upstairs. Miranda came in soon after and said her good nights, then followed the rest of the family upstairs. Matt made some vague comment about more coffee and got up.

Helena blinked. *What the hell was that?*

Wolkowski and her mom were still chatting, and seemed to have missed...whatever...just happened. Helena just sat there, rubbing her hands against her coffee mug. She let her attention drift to the conversation at the other end of the table—her mother was describing a recent trip to France with some college friends—dimly aware of Matt returning to the table.

She gave him a smile and watched him try to respond. He could barely meet her eyes.

"Everything okay?"

"Oh yeah. Just tired...long day...yeah so, last time I was here was when we had that big storm—two weeks ago was it, and uh, got snowed in, had to stay here...babysat the kids the next day for Evan ..." Matt rambled, gesturing with his hands.

Something clicked in Helena's head but before she could process the information Evan returned to the kitchen and sat down between Helena and Matt.

His eyes darted back and forth between the two, then he cleared his throat. "So, Serena...Paris...how was that?" he said, in such a blatant attempt to turn attention away from himself that Helena did a double take.

"Oh it was wonderful..." And with that Serena launched into an entertaining story about getting lost in the city and running into an old kindergarten friend—literally. Helena had heard this story about forty times so she cast her eyes around the room. Captain Wolkowski was staring at her mother like she invented oxygen and that was a little...icky. Matt and Evan were listening, nodding, smiling—perfect charmers those two boys. Knew how to impress the moms.

And then the smoke alarm went off.

They all jumped and Evan was out of his chair in a second. He made a motion for everyone to relax. "No, no, it's fine. I'm having some trouble with the alarm downstairs in the basement. I'll be right back." He quickly ran down the basement steps.

The alarm stopped a few seconds later and Serena resumed her story.

"Uh, hey, Matt? Could you give me a hand down here?" Evan called from downstairs. Helena watched Matt get up and hustle over. She turned her attention to her mother's story.

Minutes passed and Serena and Captain Wolkowski were laughing merrily. Then Serena looked at the wall clock—it was just turning eleven and her eyes widened. "Oh no—look how late it got. Helena, darling, I really must get home. It's been a long day." She patted Wolkowski's hand. "Although it's a terrible shame to tear myself away from such wonderful company."

Helena saw her captain blush at her mother's flirting and couldn't get out of her chair quickly enough. Oh great. It was like your mother dating your teacher.

"I'll go down and tell Evan. I need a few minutes to talk to him, okay?"

Serena nodded. "Fine, honey."

Helena walked down the basement steps, hearing more shared laughter behind her. She would really have to talk to her mother about this; it didn't seem like the best idea, for her to be flirting with Helena's boss. Lost in thought, she got to the bottom step and turned right, following the light in the far corner of the room.

She saw two shadows...Matt and Evan...and began processing. Two shadows...awfully close together. Two bodies, standing close together...Matt and Evan, with their arms around one another...holding one another...Evan had one hand on the back of Matt's neck, and they were...kissing.

Helena came to a dead halt. Evan and Matt were kissing. Passionately, erotically kissing. She saw tongues.

Lightning fast, the pieces fell into place. Evan had never actually mentioned dating a woman before his big admission about the mystery woman's developing feelings., just hanging out a lot with Matt...the big snow storm...the person he had feelings for, the complicated relationship...going home to talk to the person... Danny said Matt had been there when they woke up...spent the day...Thanksgiving—she'd meet the...

"Oh my God." Helena couldn't help the gasp. "Oh my God."

She watched as the two men pulled apart, turned and saw her. Saw their panic, and began sputtering—

"No, no...sorry...Oh God...I didn't realize. I didn't *realize*..." she choked out. "You two?"

Evan moved toward her, his face white. "Helena..." He couldn't get the words out. His mouth moved but nothing came out. "I...I was going to tell you...tonight..."

Helena managed to clamp her jaw shut. She could see they were both flipping out—Matt looked like he was eight seconds away from heart failure—and she made a calming gesture with her hands.

"Oh listen...it's fine...it's fine... I just had no idea...I thought..." Suddenly the hilarity of it hit her—believing that Evan was in love with her—and she started to giggle. "Oh God."

Evan blinked at her. "What...?"

Helena laughed so hard she had to hold her side. "I thought... When you said it was complicated...and you wouldn't tell me who she was...I thought...oh God...I thought it was me!"

"You? Jesus, Helena—that's like incest or something," Evan managed to say.

"I know!" She gestured toward Matt. "This is...great. Really. It's just a big surprise."

"Welcome to the club," Matt said drily, finally speaking.

Evan threw up his hands. "This isn't the way I wanted this to come out...I wanted us to really talk, Helena, to explain that this..." he gestured toward Matt and Helena caught a tender look on his face that did a funny thing to her stomach. "This is why I've been so crazy."

"Gee, thanks."

"You know what I mean."

Matt rolled his eyes at Helena.

Helena wiped her eyes. "So this...this is a thing? Like a dating thing?"

Matt and Evan exchanged shy looks.

"Uh, yeah...yeah. Right now, it's...this thing that we're uh...having."

"A thing we're having? So eloquent Detective Cerelli. Really. I'm getting fucking choked up over here." Matt groused.

Evan shook his head then gave Helena the skunk eye. "You thought I meant you? In the hallway?"

Helena nodded.

"I didn't."

"I know."

"I haven't given you signals because I don't think of you...in that way... We're friends..."

"I know. And I'm not disappointed or anything. I like my men stupid and dangerous, Evan. You're way too straight for me."

Matt snorted.

"What?" Evan asked, turning to look at him.

"Nothing," Matt said innocently.

"Does anyone else know?"

"No. Just you. You sure you're okay with this?"

"Evan, jeeze—I'm not homophobic or anything like that. It's a big shock—quite unexpected, but all I want is for you to be happy. That's all. There are no strings attached to that sentiment." She paused, shrugged. "Well, one string. You can't ever think lustful thoughts about me."

Evan smiled and walked over to her, gave her a big hug. "Thanks, Helena—and deal. No lustful thoughts."

They hugged for a long time and Helena felt herself welling up. Evan's face had gone through about fifty different emotions since she'd come down those stairs but the ones standing out in her mind were the tender ones he sent in Matt's direction. The teasing smile. The shy glance when she mentioned "dating." She wasn't sure if he realized it, but she knew...he was in love, it was written all over his face in big block letters. She squeezed him tighter.

"I'm happy for you," she whispered. "Truly happy."

He pulled away slightly and gave her a kiss on the cheek. "Thanks, Helena. We uh...we kind of want to keep this quiet for right now."

"Oh, of course—absolutely. You can trust me." She sniffed back the emotion that was threatening to pour out. "This is great. For both of you." She saw Matt standing awkwardly to the side and slipped out of Evan's arms to give him a tight hug. "Really."

Matt returned the hug. "Thanks, Helena. I don't think we're sure how to do this...kind of a new experience for both of us."

"New but...good," Evan said, shaking his head. "A good thing." Helena caught the look that passed between the two men and it was...beautiful...the only word she could think of was beautiful. It was love and lust and such a tender expression of care she wondered if they had any clue how lovely it was to see...

"So we better get upstairs before the captain asks my mother out," Helena said, pulling herself together. There were a thousand and one questions she wanted to ask Evan—like, *why didn't you ever mention to me you liked men*, that was on the top of the list—but this wasn't the time, the place, or the circumstances. For all she knew Captain Wolkowski had already gotten her mother's phone number.

"Oh yeah—Vic's working the mojo up there, Helena. You better watch out—could end up with a stepfather..." Matt warned.

"Oh God. Let's go. Quickly." The thought of it made her queasy and she practically ran toward the stairs. "Coming?"

"One sec," Matt said and watched her smile, nod, and head up the staircase. He took the two steps he needed to reach Evan and reached out to touch his face.

"Not so bad…" Evan said, closing his eyes to lean against Matt's hand.

"Nope," Matt replied and drew him closer, pulling him against his body, until they were touching the same way as before Helena had come downstairs.

"She took it well."

"Yeah." Matt just let his hands stroke Evan's face, then torso. Gentle strokes, nothing demanding or overtly sexual. Soothing him. He felt the tremors running over Evan's skin, knew he had been terrified of what Helena's reaction was going to be. Probably as scared as Matt was.

But she was fine, apparently, and they were fine, at least for another day.

It felt so good to be standing here together, holding each other. The four days they'd spent apart had been hell for Matt—sleeping every night on the new mattress, Evan's scent on the sheets—and then all the people…he couldn't touch him, couldn't kiss him. When he'd been called downstairs he was pleasantly surprised to find Evan leaning against the far wall, a small sexy smile on his face, beckoning Matt over. He hadn't needed to ask twice. And then the kissing…the feel of Evan's mouth—it had taken every shred of Matt's self-control not to tear his clothes off.

"We should go upstairs," Evan whispered against Matt's neck, his voice soft with pleasure.

"Mmmm…yeah…kick these people out of your house so you can…uh…visit me on the couch."

Matt felt the vibration of Evan's laugh and almost moaned. If Vic Wolkowski wasn't upstairs putting his overcoat on, Matt was going to lose it completely.

Evan pulled away, his blue eyes bright and almost…feverish. Matt could read the desire on his face. Oh yeah—it was going to be a good visit.

They didn't say another word, and Matt followed Evan up the stairs, back into the kitchen. It amazed him he could still walk.

It was another forty-five minutes before everyone was finally packed up and out the door. Matt stood as far away from Evan as possible at all times, afraid that his face would betray what he was feeling. What he needed so desperately he could barely keep a smile on his face.

He said good-bye to Serena and Helena, who hugged him extra long and made several comments about them all having lunch together. He said good night to Vic Wolkowski, made tentative plans for dinner in a few weeks. He watched them all walk out the front door, with Evan calling his good nights and drive carefullies to them. Evan shut the door and turned, leaning against it, smiling.

The house was silent. The kids were asleep. The company was gone.

Evan moved off the door and walked to where Matt was standing at the foot of the stairs. Matt watched him with hungry eyes, moistened his dry lips with his tongue—and saw the flare of heat across Evan's face.

Evan stopped a foot away from Matt, teasing him with a sexy smile, with his mere presence.

"C'mere," Matt rasped, reaching out. But Evan shook his head.

"Get changed. I'll meet you on the couch in ten minutes okay?"

"Don't be a fucking tease." Matt was hard as a rock and getting pissed off. He was three seconds away from pushing Evan to the floor.

Evan took a step forward, brushed his body against Matt's, silencing him. "I need to check on the kids, make sure we have our privacy. I need to get out of these jeans 'cause frankly I may be doing serious harm to myself right now." he punctuated the remark by pressing himself against Matt's thigh.

"Jesus," Matt breathed. He couldn't resist a kiss, angling his mouth against Evan, sliding his tongue in to explore.

Breathless and with an almost painful moan, Evan pulled away. "Okay, five minutes. Use the downstairs bathroom." And he practically ran up the stairs.

Matt counted to fifty, just to calm himself down to the "walking, changing clothes" point. His heart was hammering in his chest. A few weeks ago he would have never imagined being in this state, being aroused and emotional and so...*go ahead Matty*, he thought wildly, *admit it...* So fucking in love he could barely function. And in his entire life, he could never, never have imagined feeling this way toward a man. He got his bag from where it was sitting in the living room, under a table next to the fireplace.

And he saw the picture.

It was tucked behind a lamp, almost completely hidden, but when he leaned down he saw it clear as day. He pulled it out with a shaky hand, staring at Sherri Cerelli's radiant face. She was young—maybe high school? College? She looked gorgeous and sexy, blonde and fresh and...shining. Glowing. He had a pretty good idea who was on the receiving end of the radiance.

This was who Evan had planned to spend the rest of his life with. This was the person whom he loved and cherished. They had made a family together, a home. And if some asshole hadn't killed her, she'd be here right now, probably sitting on the couch with Evan. Talking, kissing, holding one another—the way it was supposed to be. Man, woman, children. Not two men fumbling in the dark, touching each other...

Oh God. Something speared through Matt, something part pain and part desire. He was too selfish to walk away, but this was wrong…wrong…wrong… It was all crashing down on his head.

He didn't realize how long he'd been standing there until he heard a sound behind him. With a sigh he turned, saw Evan standing there in black sweatpants and a tight black shirt. He was barely visible in the darkness. Matt couldn't read his expression.

Matt put the picture down, grabbed his bag and went to go to the bathroom. He wouldn't look Evan in the eye. As he passed, Evan reached out and took his arm.

"Hey. What's wrong?"

Sighed. "Nothing."

Evan's grip tightened. "The no maudlin shit rule applies to right this second, okay? Tell me."

Matt's head hurt. His heart hurt. "Your wife was beautiful."

There was a long, painful silence that Matt hated. He was being a fucking masochist, bringing her up at this moment. Then Evan sighed and Matt was forced to look at his face.

Those incredible eyes were focused on him, intently watching his face—and Evan smiled.

He relaxed his grip on Matt's arm, began caressing him through his shirt. "Beautiful, yeah. Inside and out. You know how much I loved her." His voice was soft, serious.

Matt felt tired. "Yeah."

"She's gone and I'll miss her every day for the rest of my life."

Matt said nothing. All he could feel was the sensation of Evan's fingers, moving up to massage his biceps, his shoulder.

"But I'm here, you know. I'm here and I need to be alive for… for my kids. For me." His hand moved to stroke the side of Matt's neck. "For…for you."

It was so still that Matt wasn't sure he was breathing. If either of them were breathing. He couldn't find his voice. The air around them was vibrating with Matt's fear and a shared desire that he swore seemed to get wilder and wilder every time they were near each other.

Evan moved closer, until they were leaning against one another, Matt's head on Evan's shoulder. Evan's voice was barely a whisper again his cheek. "I can't explain my feelings for you. I've only loved, and wanted, one other person in my life. I don't know what's going to happen. Don't know what I can give you... I have so many people depending on me Matt, I don't know what I can risk... But...I wanted you to know this...wanted to tell you...I love you."

That spasm of pleasure/pain burst inside Matt again, so intense this time he could barely see, breath, hear...in forty-two years he'd never felt this way, never heard those words said with so much emotion, so much truth. All he could do was wrap his arms around Evan's body and pull him close. He was shaking with need. Trembling with unspoken emotion.

"I...I understand if you don't feel the same way..." Evan's voice was panicked, thick and it broke Matt's heart.

He shook his head against Evan's shoulder. "No," he croaked out. "No...stop." He pulled away just enough to move his face, put his mouth against Evan's ear. He traced it with his tongue, sucked his skin. "Tell me why."

"What?" Evan moaned, his hands clutching at Matt's shoulders.

"Why do you love me?" Matt knew he sounded desperate and childish but he couldn't help it. He wanted to hear why. Wanted to understand how he—Matt Haight—could ever be the person whom Evan would love.

"Why? Because...because you make me feel like the world isn't so fucked up, and you make my kids smile... Because you're the best friend I've ever fucking had...because I want you in a way I never imagined..."

"Shut up." Matt's face was hot, burning. "Shut up."

Evan pulled away to look him in the eye.

"Shut up. I love you too," he breathed, and then he was kissing Evan as hard as he could, wanting to show him what those words meant. Wanted to please him...

He moved toward the general direction of the couch, disengaging their mouths just to make sure. Evan wasn't being passive this time—he was tugging at Matt's clothes, unbuttoning his shirt halfway then reaching for his belt.

Matt saw the couch was near, pushed Evan down on it. Felt himself harden even more, as Evan looked up at him, surprised, sprawled on his back...reached for Matt but Matt shook him off.

"No," Matt muttered, hearing the pound of his heartbeat. "No...this is for you... Want you to know...how much..." He couldn't go on, he didn't have the words. He reached down to stroke Evan's strong jaw, trace his fingers over that beautiful mouth. Trailed his hand down the front of his tight black shirt. Rubbed his flat stomach, the waistband of his sweats. Evan was watching him silently, those silver-blue eyes burning into Matt's face.

He knew what he wanted to do and it frightened him. Frightened him because he'd never had these thoughts before, never craved it. Shaking, Matt pulled the cushions off the couch so they'd have more room...straddled Evan's body, one knee on either side of his thighs. They stared at one another for a long time, then Matt couldn't wait and he leaned down, bracing his arms on the sofa, pinning Evan's arms.

"Trust me." And then Matt kissed him, hard and frantic, biting his lips. He felt Evan moving underneath him, trying to get free, to touch him.

"No." He moved his mouth down Evan's throat roughly, hearing his inarticulate groans, wanting more. Matt reached the top of the T-shirt, moaned in frustration.

"I'm going to move my hands," he whispered hotly in Evan's ear, "but I don't want you to move…"

Evan let out a rush of air. "Why am I not surprised you're giving orders in bed…"

Matt laughed hoarsely. "We're on the couch you idiot. And believe me, you're going to enjoy letting me take control right now…"

He was rewarded with a bite on the patch of skin right below his ear. "You call me a tease," Evan said.

"Shhhh…you talk way too fucking much, Cerelli." Matt kissed him again, sucking Evan's tongue into his mouth. He sat up, grabbing the bottom of Evan's shirt and pulling it off. "Move up."

Smiling, Evan moved back on his elbows, shifted up on the couch. Matt grabbed the waistband of his pants, pulled them down as far as they could. He crooked an eyebrow at his lover.

"You are a boy scout. Nice of you to come prepared."

"Your turn." Evan smirked. But Matt shook his head.

"Nope, sorry. Weren't you supposed to be shutting up?" His bantering tone warred with the pounding of his heart. He could taste the desire he had for this man on the tip of his tongue. "I told you not to move—and I meant it."

Evan nodded, laid back down on the couch, his eyes dark with want.

Matt took a long deep breath. He resumed the kissing, the biting, the claiming of Evan's mouth, neck…moved lower… across his chest, for the first time letting his tongue touch the hard brown nipples—Matt's brain almost exploded at the near-sob Evan choked out.

More...more...more... Matt chanted in his head. He kept moving, sucking skin. He slid down farther, pushing Evan up, pulling his sweats off at the same time.

Their eyes met again. Evan swallowed hard, shook his head. "You don't have—"

"Shut up. I want you. I want to do this." Matt's voice sounded foreign to his own ears.

Evan was still, then he scooted up, until he was resting against the arm of the couch, his eyes never leaving Matt's face. Matt leaned forward to take his first taste, moving his lips to the side of Evan's cock, caressing it carefully with his tongue. He pulled back and applied his mouth to the shaft, kissing it, listening to the sounds Evan was making—the soft hisses of air that told him he'd hit the right spot. Evan sank back into the cushions, his hands pulling at Matt's shirt "You okay?" Matt whispered.

"Yeah," came the breathless answer. "Are you?"

"Yeah..."

"You don't have to..." Evan moaned softly.

"Want to," Matt whispered, with authority this time, and then bent his head again to Evan's cock, covering it with slow, wet kisses. Evan gasped, made a halfhearted, inarticulate attempt to beg Matt off, but he didn't listen. He took his time, making his movements gentle and easy. Frankly he had no idea what he was doing, 'cause getting this *done to you* didn't really prepare you for *doing it* to someone, but ego and love demanded he do this right. Finally, he slipped the tip of Evan's cock into his mouth and the taste exploded across his tongue. Evan was breathing hard and moaning softly, his head thrown back against the arm of the couch. This was fucking terrifying and amazing and oh God, he could barely keep his brain from splintering listening to Evan sob and moan above him. This may be for Evan, but Matt had never been so turned on in his entire life. Matt moved his mouth, trying not to gag, not wanting to spoil it, taking more, and desperately thinking *this isn't enough...more...* Matt closed his eyes and let his mouth make love to Evan, let himself go without thinking about anything but pleasing this man.

The emotion of it all made his body ache, and knowledge that he, Matt Haight, was drawing these sobs of pleasure out of Evan, that he loved Matt as much as Matt loved him...it spurred him on. He dug his fingers into the sharp bones of Evan's pelvis, held him down on the couch and sucked harder, harder... Evan choked out a gasp of surprise and came abruptly, filling Matt's mouth with bitter fluid. Matt swallowed—choking, surprised, and overwhelmed.

He waited until the vibrations strumming through Evan's body stopped, then let him go. Shifted his weight. He laid his head against Evan's muscled thigh, shuddering as if he had been the one to come so hard. He felt Evan's hands softly stroking his hair, digging deeper, touching his scalp with strong fingers. He wondered if this had been a part of him all along and Evan had merely brought it into the open. He wondered if this was just love, not a lifestyle choice, not biology.

"Hey," Evan croaked, rubbing his hand against the back of Matt's neck. "C'mere. Up here."

Matt pressed his mouth against Evan's thigh, bit the skin gently, then pulled himself up. They maneuvered themselves to lay side by side, Evan still naked and flushed, Matt fully dressed and throbbing against his zipper so painfully he was starting to see stars.

"Would it be tacky to say 'oh shit, thanks—that was incredible'?" Evan asked, kissing Matt before he could answer. "And by the way, I think you're a liar."

"Wha?"

"A liar. 'Cause if you're telling me that's the first time you've done that…"

"First time. Boy Scouts honor. Or whatever you call that shit."

"You weren't kidding when you said you have A material."

Matt buried his mouth against the side of Evan's neck. Laughed. Felt Evan's hands moving over his back, touching him gently.

"You're seriously overdressed," Evan whispered. "I want to touch you."

Matt shivered so hard he thought he might come apart. He didn't move.

"Get up, Matt."

"You don't have to…"

Matt suddenly found himself being manhandled and divested of his clothes. "Hey, Evan," he protested. "Come on."

His shirt was pulled over his head, and he felt shaky hands on his zipper. He lay there a little dazed, feeling more and more of his skin being exposed to the cool air.

Finally naked, staring up at the ceiling, he felt Evan slide on top of him, felt the air leave his lungs. "You know," he rasped, trying to keep some coherency, "I didn't do it just to get something in return."

Evan smirked, moved his body in a slow grind against Matt's. "Then you're an idiot. Shut up, Mr. Haight—you talk too fucking much."

Danny Cerelli got his wish because when he padded downstairs the next morning—trying to gain custody of the remote control before his sisters got up—he found Matt Haight sprawled on the couch, tangled in an afghan. He was delighted, because Matt was cool and fun, and when he was around Danny's dad was happy.

He went into the kitchen and dug out the box of granola bars he'd hidden under the sink. His stupid twin sister Elizabeth liked the peanut butter ones too and she'd hog them up if he let her. The milk was a bit trickier, but Danny managed to pour himself a glass without spilling (much) and went back into the living room.

Matt was sitting up, his hair going all crazy, rubbing his eyes. He had a NYPD T-shirt just like Danny's dad.

"Hey, Matt," Danny enthused. "You're here!"

Matt smiled at him. "Yeah, kid, I'm here." He checked the mantel clock. "What the heck are you doing up at...at seven forty? Jeez kid."

Danny shrugged. "Not tired anymore. Want some of my granola bar? It's peanut butter."

"Nah. I'll wait for breakfast. You wanna watch TV, don't you?"

The eight-year-old nodded enthusiastically.

Matt sighed. "Fine. C'mere. You can sit on the couch with me." He swung his legs over, put them on the coffee table. "What are we watching?"

Danny gave another shrug as he settled next to Matt. "Don't care. But this means I get to pick before stupid Elizabeth gets up."

"Elizabeth isn't stupid. That's not, uh, nice."

Danny rolled his eyes. He stuffed some of the granola bar in his mouth, knowing it was crazy to argue with adults about his stupid sister. He grabbed the remote and turned the TV on, flicked through the channels until he found an old black-and-white Tarzan movie. He usually didn't like these sort of things, but hey! They were tying guys to trees and ripping them in half. Excellent!

He and Matt sat there for almost two hours, watching the natives kill more hunters, until the rest of the family came downstairs.

It turned out to be a great day, a great weekend, in Danny's opinion. Matt stayed until Sunday night—and in between there was pizza and a trip to the movies and a couple of hours at the arcade and more pizza. And Danny's dad was in a great mood, he laughed and smiled and told jokes. It was almost like when Mommy was alive, because everyone was happy and they were all together. But now Mommy lived in Heaven with God, and instead Matt was there, and Danny thought that was just fine.

Another Monday morning, another big smile plastered on the face of Evan Cerelli. Helena was waiting for him on the steps of the station house. She waved a piece of paper in his face.

"Morning!" she said enthusiastically. "We have an address on Robin Phelps—suspected rapist, con man, and slipperiest son of a bitch in the five boroughs."

"Good, good. Does this mean I can't get coffee?"

She pulled a bag from behind her back. "Don't say I never do nice things for you, 'kay?" They walked toward their car. "Did you have a good weekend?"

"It was fine, thank you for asking. And yours?"

"Keen. I cleaned out my closets then went shopping and filled them up again." She gave him a grin and leaned closer. "Soooo…?"

Evan raised his eyebrows. "No."

"Aw c'mon, Evan." She laughed. "Dish. Your boyfriend is *cute.*" She laughed harder as he blushed crimson. They settled into the car—Evan driving.

"That'll be enough of that, Detective Abbot," he croaked, pulling into the rush hour traffic.

"Seriously, Evan, tell me…what the hell happened? I mean, is this like something you've always known?"

He sighed heavily. "Could we talk about something else?"

"No."

"I'll let you tell me all about the clothes you bought…"

"No. I think you should talk about this, Evan—it's a lot more complicated than you just entering the dating field again! And if I'm the only one who knows…"

"Helena…please…I don't know the answers to half the questions I think you're going to ask…"

"Just answer me this—when did you know?"

"I met Matt in September. I didn't really realize what was going on until…"

"No, no…I mean…you liking men."

"Helena…"

"Evan, you can be totally open with me."

"I don't like men, Helena."

"Hi, hello. Saw you kissing Matt Haight, who is most certainly a guy."

"Yeah, but…it's not like this has happened before…" Evan's voice trailed off, he had a sudden flash of this weekend, remembered being in the shower late Saturday night, Matt on his knees…and Evan snapped his attention back to driving, before he killed someone. "What he and I…have…it isn't anything I've felt…experienced."

"Wow."

"Yeah."

"And him?"

"A newcomer much like myself," he said drily.

"Wow. I mean, wow. You never had any interest in men… but you're in love with Matt?"

"I never said the word love," he choked.

"What kind of greenhorn detective do you think I am? It was written all over both your faces in the basement on Thanksgiving."

Evan swallowed hard. "That obvious?"

"Neon would have been subtle in comparison."

They drove along in silence until they came to the Upper West Side apartment building where their suspect was apparently hanging out. Evan parked the car slightly down the block and turned to Helena.

"Like, really obvious?"

"What?"

"We're not ready to…make this public… It's still really new and…"

"Evan, honey, before I saw you kissing him I had no idea. Afterward, it was impossible to miss. Okay?"

He sighed. Oh this was getting complicated. "Okay."

They got out of the car and walked into the building—no doorman, old and unkempt lobby. 5G was what they were looking for. No elevator. They exchanged exasperated looks and headed up the stairs.

Evan's brain was nowhere in this building—it was anxiously processing what Helena said. Thinking about the kiss in the basement. And all the ones that followed it between Thursday and Sunday night, when Matt had finally forced himself out the door, his tongue in Evan's mouth up until the last second. They were like horny teenagers the entire time—and only the presence of the kids had forced them to stop. He'd gotten about eight minutes of sleep the whole weekend.

"5G," Helena announced, breathing a little heavily.

Evan nodded, motioned toward the door. "You knocking or am I?" She was constantly riding him for taking the "macho lead" as she called it, so he practiced letting her take the front role as often as possible.

She shrugged. "Boys first today."

Smiling, Evan shook his head, knocked on the door. "Robin Phelps?" he called loudly. "Police. We need to speak to you for a moment. Robin Phelps?" They heard some movement on the other side and both took a small step back. Then nothing.

"This is the police Mr.—" Evan raised his fist to knock again, started to call out the suspect's name, then suddenly a force threw him backward. The blow stunned him for a second then the pain hit so quickly he lost his ability to breath.

Instinct took over. He tried to sit up, grab his gun, but realized he couldn't move, couldn't move anything... He could feel the cold tile against his cheek but he couldn't see, couldn't hear... There was a buzz in his head like a swarm of angry bees...

He remembered Helena had been standing next to him and he tried desperately to move his head, to see where she was, but he couldn't. It was like he didn't have control of his body. The pain in his chest was crushing him and each breath grew a little harder to draw. He needed to find Helena, wanted to ask if she was all right, ask her why it was so cold and so loud and did they get the guy?

And why was it so dark he couldn't see a thing...

* * *

"Captain Victor Wolkowski. They told me you were taking care of my two officers."

The young doctor nodded, extended his hand. "Dr. Waresa, Chief Resident. Captain, the female detective..."

"Abbot."

"Yes. She has a dislocated shoulder and mild concussion. She's been sedated and will be moved to a room shortly."

"So she'll be fine?"

"Yes. She's in a lot of pain but not in any danger."

Wolkowski nodded—that took half the weight off his chest. "And Detective Cerelli?"

Dr. Waresa's expression got slightly more serious. "The shotgun blast sent pieces of the door—slivers of metal and wood—into his chest. He's in surgery now."

Vic felt his jaw clench. "And? What are we looking at here, Dr. Waresa?"

The doctor gave a small shake of his head. "Surgery of any kind is risky, Captain. He has shards of material embedded in his chest—we're not sure if there's any damage to his lungs, heart... Part of the operation will be to assess any damage. I suggest you contact their families as soon as possible." A nurse came up quietly beside them and whispered something Dr. Waresa.

"Excuse me, Captain. I need to go to another patient. You can either wait here or upstairs in the surgical waiting room."

With that, Dr. Waresa turned and walked away, leaving Wolkowski standing bleakly in the hallway of St. Vincent's hospital. He had been in this moment so many times over the years that he pushed the fear and anger and walked outside to use his cell.

Their suspect, Robin Phelps, was long gone. At the scene they found an old shotgun—improperly loaded—and enough drugs to open a pharmacy. They assumed that the drugs had led to the nonworking gun—and those were the two reasons Evan Cerelli was still alive. Moses stood grimly in front of Vic, delivering his update.

Wolkowski nodded, checked his watch. Evan had now been in surgery for almost two hours and he had yet to reach the MacGregors. He knew Evan had no other family aside from his in-laws and he didn't know what to do next.

"Still no word on the in-laws?"

"Nah. Got a uniform on the house, one on the sister-in-law's apartment. But nothing yet."

"The kids?"

"Jensen is standing by—you want her at the house when they get home, right?"

Vic felt his temples begin to pound. Jesus Christ, how much more did these kids have to go through? "Shit, Moses. I don't know what to do about that. Jensen should grab a social worker or someone from family services to go with her. I wish I knew someone else..." Matt Haight's face suddenly flashed in his mind. He'd seemed pretty comfortable with the kids on Thanksgiving...

"You going back to the station?"

"Yeah—Roarke's waiting for me. I have testimony tomorrow..."

"Fine. Listen, Moses, do me a favor. I need a number from my Rolodex—Matt Haight."

* * *

"Matthew Haight."

"Matty? Vic Wolkowski."

"Hey, Vic. What's going on?"

"Uh, listen... I'm down at St. Vincent's Hospital. Evan and Helena, uh...here...both of 'em... Evan got—"

Vic heard Matt's breathing change on the other end.

"Shot?" He asked in a chilled tone, and suddenly Vic was remembering the sound of Matt's voice after Tony was murdered. "How is he?"

"Matty...listen... Evan's okay. Well I mean, he's in surgery but he's alive."

"Shot?" Matt said again, his voice was shaking.

"Yeah...but the damage is from fragments—lousy shot with a poorly loaded shotgun through a door..."

"The kids..."

"That's the main reason I'm calling. I can't find the grand-parents anywhere—any of them—and those kids are going to need someone they know."

"I'm going to the house, to be there when they get home from school... I'll get to the hospital as soon as I can."

And the phone went dead.

Vic's phone call propelled Matt into a frantic state. He listened to the words as calmly as he could—*Evan...shot... surgery*—then hung up the phone and darted into his boss's office. He kept his cool, his voice neutral. Spilled out a perfectly reasonable story about a close friend—a widower with four small children and no immediate family—in the hospital, with no one to look after the children. He needed to go, had no idea when he would be back in and could he just take the time as vacation (seeing as he had almost two full years' worth sitting idly on the books)?

Once he had a yes, Matt flew out the door. He ran back to his apartment, changed, put some clothes in a bag, and grabbed his car keys. The drive to Queens took him a painfully long amount of time—lunch hour traffic on the bridge—and it was then, in his car, in the middle of a parking lot's worth of cars, listening to a news station prattle about the unseasonably warm weather, that

Matt started to shake. Started to shiver and feel his throat closing up.

Evan...shot...surgery...Evan...shot...surgery.

Shot like Tony.

He pounded his hand on the steering wheel until he felt the pain all the way up his arm.

The traffic crawled and Matt grieved, and raged, and was kept company by his fear. He wanted to skip right past the responsible adult shit and go to St. Vincent's, yell at every goddamn doctor he could find until he was sure Evan would be all right. And then he'd go sit in his room and wait until he opened his eyes.

* * *

Vic was alone. He sat in a hard plastic chair, one of the many lining the hallway, staring at his shoes. Serena Abbot, red-eyed and frantic, had been here for a short time. Vic did his best to calm her down, then walked her to the wing where Helena was sleeping peacefully in her private room. He regretted having to see her under these circumstances.

It had been almost six hours since he'd arrived.

There had been a dozen or so people in and out of this hallway to talk to him—the officers investigating the shooting, his own officers coming to check on their wounded comrades. Someone from the mayor's office had phoned about handling the press. Vic handled them all efficiently, calmly. He held his tongue when necessary and patted quite a few shoulders as cops wandered in and out with that slightly terrified look that said thank God it wasn't me.

His head hurt, pounded from the pressure of the day. Both his officers were alive and doing well—Evan had finally been wheeled out of the surgical recovery room two hours ago, taken up to ICU for the night. Dr. Waresa assured Vic that he'd be fine, no permanent damage, nothing wrong with his heart or lungs—but he had a substantial recovery period ahead.

Vic had nodded, said his thanks, followed a nurse's directions to the ICU floor, and went to wait on yet another hard, cold plastic chair. He didn't think it was right to leave Evan alone.

So he waited.

At four o'clock, he was dozing when he felt a squeeze on his forearm and jumped awake.

"Captain Wolkowski? There's a Mr. Haight downstairs."

Vic nodded, tried to shake the fuzziness out of his brain. He needed to go downstairs, see how the kids were doing...and thought maybe he should see how Matty was doing 'cause he'd sounded like shit when they talked this morning.

Matt Haight stood in the lobby of St. Vincent's hospital, holding Danny and Elizabeth's small sweaty hands tightly, feeling the throb of their fear keeping time with his own. Watched Miranda as she paced restlessly around the chairs and carts; watched Kathleen as she fidgeted with her jacket zipper, her eyes darting back and forth.

He wanted to throw up, he wanted to be drunk, he wanted to be anywhere in the world but in yet another hospital, waiting for yet another doctor to tell him that someone he loved was dead. Or just not coming back.

And he wanted to see Evan so badly it literally hurt.

Vic Wolkowski took one look at Matt Haight's face and felt something tighten in his chest. For a second he couldn't remember which time this was...morgue or ICU? And then he saw the white, panicked faces of Evan Cerelli's kids and sighed.

"Hey, Matty," he said, moving toward the small group in the lobby. "Hi, kids."

He watched Matt pull himself together. "Vic. How...uh... how is he?"

Vic put the brightest smile he could on his face. "Your dad is doing just fine. He's out of surgery, and now he's in ICU. After we get the okay from the doctor, you can go see him." He'd done his homework pretty well—talked to everyone he could find until he had the answers he wanted.

None of the panic on the children's face receded—he assumed that after what they had been through with their mother, they weren't going to believe anything or anyone until they saw their dad with their own eyes.

Vic understood. "I'm going to go check with the doctor again—find out exactly when you can see your dad."

The oldest girl, Miranda (the names were slowly coming to him), nodded and stepped forward. "Can the twins go up? They're only eight. Usually they don't let little kids in."

"I...ah...worked it out. They can go up." Vic didn't mention that he'd launched into a heavy-handed speech about the kids nearly being orphans, keeping Dr. Waresa verbally pinned to a wall until the young doctor swore he'd arrange it so that all four of the kids would be let into ICU. He wasn't going to look into the faces of those little kids and tell them, *Gee—could you wait awhile before you saw your dad? Just a few days...*

They all relaxed a little bit after Vic's assurance. The little ones weren't releasing their grips on Matt's hands and Vic didn't think he wanted them to. Matt looked terrible—maybe a few steps past terrible. Vic kept seeing little flashes of Matt—Tony's funeral, the trial...those had been bad. This seemed somehow...worse.

"Hey, Matty. Let's bring the kids upstairs—there's a waiting room on the second floor. I'll go check with the doctors, find out when their dad's ready for a visit."

Matt nodded woodenly and guided the small children along to follow Vic, giving a nod to both the older girls, who fell in behind him. Vic kept sparing little glances over his shoulder, watching the subdued little family behind him.

Well. Family and Matt.

"Vic—I didn't even ask. How's Helena?" Matt asked in a somber tone.

"She's fine. Dislocated shoulder. She's resting—her mom's with her."

Matt nodded. They stepped into an empty elevator and Vic pushed the button for the second level.

"Good—I'm glad she's all right."

Vic knew he wanted to ask more, wanted the details of the shooting, wanted to know if the son of a bitch was in custody. But he also knew that Matt wouldn't bring it up in front of the kids.

The elevator crawled and Vic did a quick visual check on the other passengers. The kids were still radiating fear and misery; the littlest girl had wound herself around Matt's leg, and it didn't look like she was letting go anytime soon.

"Hey, hey, Elizabeth. It's okay, honey. Really. Daddy's okay." Matt, still holding the little boy's hand, leaned down and spoke softly to the child. "You heard Captain Wolkowski right? He's resting and we're going to go see him now."

Elizabeth said nothing, just buried her face in the seam of Matt's jeans and shook her head.

Vic watched Matt stroke the girl's hair, coaxing her face up to meet his—and never letting go of the boy.

"Elizabeth. I promise. Daddy's okay and you're going to see him."

She sniffled wetly and gave him a tiny nod.

The elevator lurched to a stop on the second level and the whole group shuffled out. Vic led them to the little waiting room at the end of the quiet floor—giving a wave to the desk nurse, Pam. She had been very kind to him, and she knew to expect the kids.

Pam followed them to the waiting room, waited quietly at the door next to Vic as Matt helped the twins out of their coats, settled them down into chairs. Kathleen and Miranda took care of themselves, but both chose chairs closest to where Matt stood.

Matt turned to Vic, his mouth set in a grim line. "So Vic, where's this doctor? Maybe I can talk to him for a few minutes?"

Vic couldn't do anything but nod because the look on Matt's face, the utter weariness of his voice, was making him nervous. This was Tony's funeral all over again and there was very little—aside from a cop being shot—that connected the two.

"Yeah. Sure. Pam, do you know where Dr. Waresa is?"

"I'll go page him," she said soothingly. "Would you kids like something to drink? Some soda or juice?"

None of them moved. Matt answered for them. "Thanks a lot. Maybe some juice and a few bottles of water—that would be nice."

Pam nodded and walked out of the room. Vic leaned against the doorframe, his eyes never leaving Matt's face.

Matt wouldn't meet his eyes.

Oh shit. That was bad. What was he missing in this picture?

A few minutes of silence passed. The kids fidgeted, Matt paced a little, and Vic just…leaned.

Pam came back to the door, bottles of juice and water balanced in her arms.

Vic turned and saw her precarious hold, took some of the drinks to ease her load.

"Dr. Waresa is waiting for you gentlemen in the hall. I got someone to cover the desk, so I can sit here with the youngsters while you're gone."

Vic put the drinks on the small side table closest to the kids. Matt gave Pam a small smile.

"Thanks." He turned to face the children. "You guys wait here. I'm just going to go check on things, then I'll come back and hopefully you can go right in and see your dad."

Miranda nodded. "Okay. If you get to see him first, tell him we're here, okay? 'Cause he's going to start worrying about us."

"I'll do that. I promise. But don't worry about it, you can tell him for yourself."

Matt walked out the door, barely sparing Pam or Vic a glance—Vic could see he was in a hurry to talk to the doctor. Vic patted Pam's arm, then followed his friend into the hallway.

"Hey, Matty—wait up."

Matt stopped his long, anxious strides and impatiently waited for Vic to catch up. Fuck, he knew he was blowing this, totally losing it in front of Vic—Vic, who knew him so well, who knew the very distinct look of Matthew Haight melting down.

Vic reached his side and Matt took off again, not wanting to risk a moment alone with his friend. Because if he asked...well, Matt was about six seconds away from spilling his guts, and he wasn't quite ready to do that.

"That's Dr. Waresa," Vic huffed, trying to keep up. The young doctor was standing at the end of the hall at the nurses' station, reading a chart. He looked up and nodded in Vic's general direction.

Evan Cerelli figured there was a safe—one of those big steel ones that fell on people's heads in old movies—sitting on his chest. He could barely take a breath in...*whoa, that hurt way too much.* Actually, every part of his body hurt way too much.

His eyes fluttered open and he saw ceiling, white acoustical tiles. He wasn't home, in his bed. This was a strange ceiling...

He tried to remember what had happened last... Had he been at work? Home? He struggled to connect to something, anything...

He had flashes of his kids...of Matt...Helena talking... walking up the stairs...

Helena. Something had happened to her. He didn't know where she was...

He didn't realize he was struggling until a firm hand held him down against the bed.

"Mr. Cerelli? Sir, just relax. You're fine, but you have sutures in your chest and we don't want you to pull them out."

What? He wanted to ask questions but his mouth wasn't working at all. He couldn't even move his lips.

"You're in St. Vincent's Hospital. I'm Dr. Waresa. You were shot—do you remember that?"

Shot? Oh Jesus—Helena.

"Mr. Cerelli, you're going to be fine. We performed surgery to remove fragments from your chest. The slight paralysis you feel is a normal aftereffect of the anesthesia."

Helena, I just want to know she's okay...

"There are some people here to see you..."

The doctor's face swam away. And Vic Wolkowski's replaced it.

"Hey, Evan. How you doin'? Oh shit, that's right, you can't talk..." Vic spoke in a hushed tone. "Well don't worry. We've got your kids here and they're okay... Matt's here..."

At Matt's name Evan shut his eyes tightly. *Thank God*, he thought. *He's taking care of my kids, I know he is.*

"Uh...hey, Matty, come here and talk to Evan. I'm...uh... going to go talk to the doctor, see when the kids can come in."

When Evan opened his eyes, Matt was there.

Matt fidgeted like a child, waiting near the door of Evan's room. He watched the doctor and Vic talk to Evan, reassure him that everything was going to be all right. He took deep breaths, tightened his hands into fists that could probably punch through concrete at this moment.

Go away, he thought desperately. *Just leave and let us talk... let me talk to him. I have to make sure he's okay.*

When Vic called him over, his heart turned over. He mustered as much calm as he could and stood next to Vic. Struggling, he raised his eyes to meet Vic's—suddenly avoiding the man in the bed, the one with all the bandages on his chest—and saw...something. Vic nodded, patted Matt's arm, and walked toward the door. He didn't look back.

Matt let his eyes drift down to Evan—pale and drawn, hooked up to monitors and IV's. He shivered. Shit. His vision got a little hazy.

When it cleared, he saw that Evan had opened his eyes, was staring right at him.

Matt forced his voice past the lump in his throat. "Hey."

Evan blinked weakly.

Matt released the tension in his hands, let them stroke the back of Evan's hand, around the IV needle. It felt good.

He whispered, "You're fine... So is Helena. She didn't get shot, just a dislocated shoulder. They pumped her full of drugs, stuck her in a room... Her mom's with her. I thought you'd want to know she was okay."

He saw Evan's eyes fill up a bit. Matt knew exactly what had been running through his mind. Knew the relief of someone telling you your partner was alive and all right. He squeezed his hand gently. The lump in his throat swelled.

"The kids are here—Miranda wanted me to tell you not to worry. She's great, man, just great. Holding herself together, helping me with the little ones. Kathleen's quiet, but I think she's okay. The twins, they're holding on tight. They're scared...but I think once they see you they'll be fine." Shaking, Matt felt the words rush from his mouth. His vision blurred again. "And by the way, if you ever pull this shit again I'm going to throw you out a fucking window. I had to take off work, asshole."

He felt the hand under his move slightly, felt Evan's fingers work to touch him. He focused his eyes as best he could.

There was the ghost of a smile on Evan's face.

"Yeah—funny for you," he choked out. He took Evan's hand into his. "Jesus."

They stayed that way for a long minute, holding hands and watching one another. Evan's eyes started to flicker. Matt could see he wasn't going to be awake much longer.

"Hey, I'm going to go get the kids, okay? Then you can sleep as much as you want."

Evan managed to move his head in a tiny up and down motion. Matt felt pressure against his hand.

"I'll be right back." Matt was loath to let go of his hand but he knew how important it would be to all of them to see one another. He leaned down and pressed his mouth again Evan's, tasted the metallic tang of blood and anesthesia...the pressure against his lips was barely there but he knew… "I'll be right back," he whispered again. "I love you."

That small affirmative head move. That hint of a smile.

Matt managed to tear himself away and walk to the door. His face was burning hot. He knew he had to pull his shit together right this second because walking out that door meant walking back into reality, where he was just a nice guy, a friend of the family, and not…

And not Evan Cerelli's lover.

Vic checked on the kids while Matt was in with Evan. Serena had joined them and was holding the twins, an arm curled protectively around each of them, when Vic walked in.

"How's Helena?" Vic asked softly, sitting next to Serena.

"Fine. She's still asleep. They were taking her vital signs, changing her IVs… I thought I'd come and find you. They told me you were here." She smiled at the children. "And then I found my young friends and decided we'd keep each other company."

"Well, their dad is fine—very tired after the surgery but doing really well." Vic tried to sound as positive as humanly possible. "He looked better than I expected."

And then Vic thought about the look on his face when he said Matt's name. And the look on Matt's face, well shit, since he had gotten there… Vic felt uncomfortable all of a sudden, didn't know why, and decided he needed to talk to Matt now…and privately.

He patted Serena's arm and stood back up. "I'm going to go see if Matt's finished in there—get you guys in to see your dad."

He walked out, in search of Matt.

And found him, leaning against the wall outside of Evan's room. Sucking in air like it was his last chance.

Vic approached quietly, afraid to spook his friend. "Matty?"

Matt looked up at him, eyes red and damp.

"You okay, man?"

He opened his mouth but snapped it shut half a second later. And shook his head.

They stood in silence.

"Is it because of Tony?" Vic finally asked, because he burned with curiosity. "Is that what's going on here?"

Matt sighed heavily. "I can't do this right now, okay, Vic? But later...we'll talk."

Vic said nothing.

"I'm going to go get the kids. He's about to fall asleep and I know he wants to see them." Matt pushed away from the wall, moved away from Vic before he could speak.

Left alone in the hall, Vic stuck his hands in his pockets and waited.

They crept into the room as a group, with Matt standing guard. Evan's eyes fluttered opened as if he sensed his kids. Matt picked up the twins so they could lean over and kiss their father. Elizabeth began to weep afterward, little tiny sounds of relief and fear and exhaustion. Matt let her wrap her arms around his neck and carried her over to the door, whispering to her, assuring her that everything would be fine. He watched Miranda holding Danny's hand. They talked softly to their father and Matt could see Evan's frame relaxing, sinking farther into the mattress. He would be able to sleep peacefully, knowing the kids were okay.

Matt brought Elizabeth back over to the bed, to stand with the other three.

"I think your dad's ready to get some sleep. Let's say good-bye for now. We'll come back tomorrow, okay?"

"Okay," Miranda agreed, leaning over to kiss her father on the forehead. "We're going to come back tomorrow, Daddy. Promise." She lifted her younger brother up, so he could say good-bye.

The kids seemed a little less tense, but Matt could see their exhaustion. He waited for them each to take a turn, saying good-bye and giving their dad kisses. By the time Elizabeth had her turn, Evan was asleep, his face serene. Matt used all his willpower not to follow the kid's lead and put his mouth on Evan's.

"Okay, let's go," he whispered. "I guess I'm going to take you home."

They walked out the door and Elizabeth picked her head up.

"Grandma!"

Matt Haight looked up and saw a trio of tense people standing with Dr. Waresa.

"Oh, you poor babies!" the older woman crooned, stepping forward to pull Elizabeth from Matt's arms. She flicked a glance over his face, a little suspicious.

An older man, built like a bulldog, stood next to a very attractive brunette. Their expressions matched the woman Elizabeth identified as her grandmother.

Everyone was looking at him wondering—who the hell are you?

Forty-five minutes later, Vic Wolkowski was standing next to the nurses' station, gripping a cup of coffee so tightly he could feel the black oily crap sloshing up over the sides. He was waiting for Matt to come meet him here, so they could talk.

After the ten initial agonizingly painful minutes of introductions, explanations, and tension that made Vic's eyes ache, the MacGregors took charge of the children—effectively moving them away from Matt, who they kept glaring at like he was a convicted child molester. Vic watched Matt turn to steel, watched him gently say goodnight to the children, watched him practically tear up as they were led away by their grandparents and aunt.

They had barely managed "polite" with Matt, pretty much dismissing him after he introduced himself as a friend of Evan's. They spoke to Vic directly, inquiring about Evan and mentioning that they would take the children with them until Evan recovered. Vic couldn't challenge them—it was their right. And Matt couldn't challenge them—Vic saw it was taking all his self-control not to. The kids looked a little stunned, but the family was pretty overwhelming, smothering them with hugs and comforting baby talk. At the last moment, Elizabeth and Danny had some kind of weird twin moment and started getting hysterical at the same time. No amount of comforting by their relatives would help, and then things got even stranger because both started wailing for Matt.

And that produced more raised eyebrows and weird vibes. Matt announced he was going to walk down to the car with them, in that no-uncertain-terms voice that Vic knew well, and this calmed the twins down, and the other girls looked relieved as well.

The MacGregor's, on the other hand, looked like someone had stepped on their collective family feet.

So Matt, the kids, and the MacGregor family went en masse down to the parking lot and Vic was left standing there, thinking—*when Matty comes back, we're having a freaking conversation.*

Matt hugged the kids each in turn—even Miranda, who waited until the last possible second, made like she was going to get in the car before wrapping her arms around his middle—and promised that he would talk to them soon.

He saw four beautiful faces staring at him bleakly through the glass of the MacGregors' monster Oldsmobile and wanted to kick the door down and rescue them.

"I'll talk to you tomorrow, okay?" Matt mouthed to them. It was probably bullshit because Evan's in-laws didn't seem inclined to be helpful. But he smiled encouragingly and saw the kids respond. And that was all that mattered.

The car pulled away, followed quickly by the sister-in-law's shiny Volvo. Matt watched for a moment, then suddenly realized it was freezing and his coat was somewhere upstairs.

He hurried back inside, wanting to get warm and wanting to see Evan one last time before he left.

And then there was Vic, who he just knew was waiting expectantly for some answers.

He was actually tapping his foot.

Matt walked up to where Vic was leaning, coffee cup in hand, lips set in a straight line. He took a deep breath—*Steady, Matty, steady.*

"So, Vic—you ready for us to have that talk?"

"Uh, yeah. I think it might be nice to know what the hell is going on here."

In the cafeteria, they found a table in the corner and brought some more coffees along.

For a few minutes Vic just watched as Matt fiddled with the sugar packets and little cups of cream and two stirrers. He made it look like a chemical experiment.

Vic cleared his throat.

"Matty?"

Matt sighed, put the stirrers down, and finally peeked up at Vic. "Yeah?"

"I've been here for almost ten hours now. This coffee is wearing a hole in my intestines the size of freaking Canada. Talk to me, please."

"This isn't easy for me…" He rubbed his face with both hands, sighing heavily. "It's…" His voice drifted off.

"We've been friends a long time. You can say anything to me, Matty."

Matt nodded. After a long pause, he murmured, "I think you've seen…well, how I've reacted to this…uh…whole thing…"

Vic nodded. "Yeah, but I feel like it's more than this reminding you of Tony. Am I right?"

"What happened to Tony, yeah…it's a part of it but…"

They sat in silence for a long moment.

"We're…Evan and I…he's…we're very…uh…close."

"Close friends?"

"Friends, yeah. But…" Matt locked eyes with Vic, his face drawn and somber. "We're more than that."

His tone, his emphasis on the word… After a flair of shock— as he thought, *Matt just told me he's gay*—Vic felt the weight of the revelation settle heavily into his stomach. He had no idea how to respond.

Vic took a sip of his coffee, nodded at Matt. "Okay, Matty. I think I understand. I'm a little surprised, 'cause you never mentioned this to me before and we've been friends a long time…"

Matt smiled thinly. "Recent life-changing event. I'm still working out the whole thing in my head."

"Really?"

"Yeah."

"You okay with it?"

Matt shrugged. "I think so. I'm not sure. No."

"Does anyone…"

"You and Helena. That's it."

"The kids don't…"

"Jesus, no. We're just coasting right now…not thinking too far ahead."

They sat in silence. Vic felt uncomfortable because he didn't know what to say. He wanted to tell Matt it didn't change anything about how he felt for him, about their friendship. He wanted to tell him that their secret was safe, and that he would help Evan with whatever he needed at work…but he was just so fucking floored right now.

So he just sat there, sipped his coffee, and nodded. Watched Matt grow more and more restless in his seat.

"I'm going upstairs, see if I can say good-bye to Evan." Matt sounded tired and a little sad. And that made Vic feel worse.

Matt stood up, gathered up his garbage.

"Hey, Matty. Listen, I'm okay with this. I want you to know that."

Matt nodded.

"If you need anything…"

"Thanks. I'll talk to you tomorrow."

"I'll call you at work."

"No. I'll be here first thing in the morning. I took vacation time." His voice was flat.

"All right. I'll see you here then."

"'Night, Vic." And he walked away.

Vic felt like he had just blown a very important moment in his friend's life.

Matt relied on charm and blarney to get past the nurse on the ICU floor. He flashed his most persuasive smile until the young nurse sighed—with a tiny smirk on her face—and let him go see Evan one last time.

In the room, Evan was fast asleep, his chest moving up and down so slowly that Matt nearly lost his breath watching. He moved to stand next to the bed, letting greedy hands stroke Evan's face and shoulder.

He thought it had been a knife in the heart when Tony died. Watching your partner suffer was one thing... Watching someone you loved so much it hurt—Matt had a new definition of hell.

He leaned down to whisper, "I'm here—I wanted you to know... I love you...and I'm going to be here every day... I'll take care of you."

Matt kissed Evan's cold cheek, pressed his face into the curve of his neck. He didn't want to leave. He wanted to curl up in this bed and make sure that Evan had a peaceful night. Protect him from the nightmares.

He heard the door creak open and prayed to God that it was Vic. He looked up.

It was the nurse, Pam.

Shit.

But she smiled softly, her eyes warm. "I suspected as much. Do you need a few more minutes, honey?"

All the air rushed out of Matt's lungs. At first he thought—*oh God someone knows*—and then he realized—*hey, she knows and she's okay*, and a sympathetic person could help him see Evan whenever he wanted.

He smiled very shyly, feeling the blush burn across his face. Straightening up, he said, "He's sound asleep. I'm going now—I'll be back in the morning, though."

"I'm here at six a.m.—you'd best come after eight. I'll make sure you get in."

Matt nodded, his throat suddenly tight. "Thanks."

Without another word, Pam left.

Matt took a big breath, kissed Evan again (wanted desperately to feel him kissing back, wanted to feel his body in his arms, wanted to hear his voice), and forced himself out the door.

Chapter Eight

Evan swam up through the blackness, through flashes of sound and light. A gunshot. Shouting. His children. Matt.

He started to feel a swirl of panic in his chest when his eyes wouldn't open on demand. It took long frustrating minutes to budge his eyelids, until he could make out a sliver of light. It hurt when he took a breath—his chest, his throat, his head.

He was in the hospital. He remembered the ceiling. Talking to the kids and Vic and the doctor.

Helena was all right. Matt told him that.

Matt.

He took another painful breath. Opened his eyes a little more. The light was different. Maybe it was morning.

He turned his head slightly, looking around the room. Private. Not ICU. Fewer machines than last time he was awake.

That probably meant he was going to live.

The door past the foot of his bed creaked open and the smiling face of a woman peeked through.

"I thought so! Good morning, Mr. Cerelli. I'm Pam, your nurse." She bustled in the room carrying a small plastic basket. "I'm just going to take your vitals real quick before the doctor gets here."

Evan opened his mouth to respond but all he could manage was a raspy sigh.

Shit.

Pam seemed to sense his annoyance.

"Don't worry about it just yet, Mr. Cerelli. You're still recovering from surgery. There was a tube down your throat for several hours. Your voice will be back soon enough."

She went through her routine with practiced ease as Evan stared at the ceiling, frustrated and exhausted already. He wanted to ask questions, to find out where his kids were, where Helena was... He wanted someone to call Matt and tell him to get the hell down here so he wouldn't be alone.

There was a tiny knock at the door as Pam replaced his chart at the end of the bed.

"Come in," Pam called as she rearranged the sheet and blanket over Evan's body.

A doctor, chart in hand, walked in—Evan sluggishly searched his brain for his name—and stood next to his bed.

"I'm Dr. Waresa—do you remember me from yesterday?"

Evan tried his voice again, managing a weak "Yesss."

The man looked very pleased. He scanned the chart a few moments more, nodding. "Well, Mr. Cerelli, you are one lucky man. No major organ damage. No nerve damage. At worst, you have the next few weeks to read that list of books you've been meaning to—bed rest is your future."

Evan rolled his eyes. It took some effort but it was worth it. Both Dr. Waresa and Pam laughed.

"It'll be worth it. I can pretty much guarantee your return to work—*if* you follow my instructions."

Evan nodded. "Voice?" he rasped.

"Give it another few hours, keep the talking down to the minimum. It'll be back on line before you know it."

He nodded again. "Kids?" he managed, coughing slightly at the effort.

Dr. Waresa looked at Pam, obviously unaware.

Pam smiled brightly at Evan. "Some older folks came and got them from your friend right after they saw you. Your parents?"

Evan swallowed painfully. Of course. Sherri's parents were still his emergency notification. They must've come to the hospital and taken the kids home with them. *Shit. Shit.* Rationally he thought it was the best place for them, but in his heart he wanted them close. He wanted them home.

"In-laws," he murmured to Pam's question. He watched her eyebrows go up. Probably wondering where his wife was.

His head was aching.

"Wife...passed away...last year."

The harsh sounding rasp made the words even more painful. Both Dr. Waresa and Pam adopted identical expressions of sympathy. Evan hated that look.

"My...partner...Helena...?" he asked, trying to divert their attention.

Dr. Waresa smiled. "She's fine. I just spoke with her. I'm sure she can come and see you later this afternoon."

Evan sighed. The kids were fine. Helena was fine. He would have to wait until Vic or one of the other detectives showed up to find out about the suspect.

That just left Matt.

* * *

Evan started when Dr. Waresa snapped the chart back on the end of the bed. "I'm going to let Pam get you comfortable—you've got some visitors, I hear. I'll be back to talk to you later this afternoon."

Visitors?

Evan nodded, watched the doctor walk out the door. He turned his attention back to Pam. She was still staring at him, with that sad, sympathetic smile.

"Who?" he asked, hoping she'd get the idea. His throat was aching.

"The visitors? I saw your captain out there—the one who was here last night? And another man I didn't recognize."

Evan nodded. He didn't know if that meant Matt was out there. He felt a little ache in his chest thinking of Matt. Last night it'd been so comforting to have the other man there. Easy to relax knowing that Matt was looking after his kids, and checking on Helena. He closed his eyes as a wave of heavy grief washed over him, unexpected and unwanted. Matt doing Sherri's job. Again.

Pam was patting his arm. "I'm gonna send your captain in first. Is that all right?"

Evan clenched his jaw. He wanted to ask about the other man, ask her if he was in his forties, pacing like a lunatic and cursing at doctors—then he'd know it was Matt. Then he'd ask to see him first...but a stab of shame and fear made him nod. He was ashamed of himself.

He heard the door open and close. He waited.

A few seconds later, Vic Wolkowski ducked his head through the opening door. "Hey!" he called, walking in. He looked rumpled and exhausted—not too different from every day at the station.

Evan nodded. "Hi."

Vic moved to the side of Evan's bed. "Well shit, Detective Cerelli. That was a hell of a way to spend the Monday after Thanksgiving."

"Sssorry." But Evan smiled a little bit.

Vic made a snorting noise. He nodded a little bit, as if considering something. Opened his mouth but shut it quickly. His eyes suddenly began to track everything in the room—except Evan.

"Everything okay, sir?" Evan managed to ground out. "Doctor said Helena…"

"She's fine. I saw her a little while ago. They'll probably have her out of here by lunchtime." Vic was looking over Evan's shoulder.

Helena wasn't the reason for the crease in the center of his forehead.

"Suspect? We get 'im?"

"Took a few hours, but yeah—found him at the Port Authority, waiting for a bus. You know, I have to say…I'm pretty shocked we didn't catch this guy sooner. He's a freaking idiot."

Evan smiled. But Vic didn't.

"Sir?"

Vic sighed heavily. He bit his lip and then forced his eyes down to meet Evan's.

"Did I do something…"

"No, no." Vic blew out a breath. "I…uh…Evan, I talked to Matt last night."

Oh fuck.

Evan felt the burn on his face as if someone had dumped scalding water on it. A little hitch caught in his chest. *He knows,* Evan thought wildly. *He knows.*

Vic seemed to be waiting for Evan to say something, but nothing that resembled sound pushed its way through Evan's throat.

He ran a hand over his bald head, pursed his lips, and nodded. "I...just wanted you to know that I'm okay with this. Really. Was I surprised? Fuck yes. I've known Matt for over a decade and I never...I just had no idea."

Evan wanted to point out that Matt hadn't known either, but he pushed that random thought away for a moment. He desperately needed to know where his captain stood.

"Your business is your own, Evan. And whatever makes you happy at the end of the day—provided it doesn't eventually cause liver damage or cancer—is fine by me." He paused, waving his arms around a little. "I just wanted you to know—I'm fine. And I'll keep it to myself—whatever you guys say goes."

Evan nodded, his throat tight. His moment of shame returned—he was so afraid of what people would think, and so far, they'd responded with nothing but kindness.

"And, for what it's worth...Matt's a great guy." The last part was ground out gruffly. Vic's hands were back in his pockets.

There was a long silence. Neither man could seem to find a point to focus their vision on.

Suddenly, Evan realized he could ask the question now.

"Is...is Matt outside?" He whispered. "The nurse...said... someone else..."

Vic smiled tightly. "Sorry—he's not here yet. Douglasson from IA is here. He needs to talk to you for a second..."

"IA?"

"Procedure...don't worry about it. They just want to clarify what happened. He's already talked to Helena... I can't imagine it's going to take long."

Evan nodded.

"I think Matt went back to your place to sleep. Your in-laws..."

"Took the kids. I know." Evan felt that irrational annoyance flair in his chest. He wondered if the MacGregors were planning to bring the kids back here today.

"Is there anything I can get you? From the gift shop or wherever? I can call Matt, ask him to bring you stuff from home..."

"Yeah...phone book from my desk...clothes." He wanted to ask for the picture of Sherri but the thought of asking Matt to do that...it didn't feel right.

"No problem. I'm going to get Douglasson now. So you can get it over with."

"Fine."

An awkward silence descended again. Vic fussed a bit with his tie then said softly, "Uh...I'm really okay with you and Matty—you know... Really. I wish you all the happiness in the world 'cause...I know...when you lose the person you're supposed to spend the rest of your life with..." He stopped, looking a little lost.

The room spun around Evan for a long, painful moment. He managed to spread a thin smile on his face, look Vic in the eye, and nod. His teeth ground together in an effort not to speak.

Vic sighed and gave Evan an answering smile, equally as thin and strained. "I'll send Douglasson in, give Matt a call about that stuff you wanted. And I'll stop by later, see how you're doing."

More nodding. More direct eye contact. More pain lancing through Evan's jaw.

And then Vic was gone and Evan let a rush of air escape his lungs—and the pain that he felt in response made his vision gray around the edges.

He knew Vic was trying to be kind. And supportive. But Evan just didn't need to hear...he felt tired and weak and scared and he wanted Matt—here and now. But that wasn't right...he should want Sherri, but Sherri was dead and he knew that. He knew he was going on but...shit. He was really going on.

Evan closed his eyes tightly, counted to twenty, then thirty, then fifty, waiting for his heartbeat and breath come back to a point that didn't make his chest feel like it was going to implode. *It's the medicine*, he thought. *It's making me freak out for no reason*.

But that was a lie—he wasn't fooling himself at all. There were a hundred reasons to freak out and his original stress over being attracted to a man was just scratching at the surface of a much larger issue. Telling Helena didn't count—she was his best friend. She loved him unequivocally. She would never turn her back. And he knew Vic Wolkowski to be an open-minded person. But he and Matt were fast running out of compassionate, loving friends who would stand by them no matter what. Because if this was a relationship, with a capital R...

The door opened before he could complete the thought. Detective Douglasson from IA was calling his name softly and Evan suddenly had to stop the freight train in his head and be a cop.

He answered the questions, in his raspy voice, nodded and shook his head as much as possible to save the thin sound that he was able to make. Detective Douglasson was efficient and tight in his questioning. He didn't appear to think Evan and Helena had done something wrong, he just needed to get all the information. No difficult questions were posed—and Evan assumed he gave the same answers as Helena because the detective just nodded and grunted and scribbled things down in a little leather notebook. In a few minutes it was over and his hand was being shook. Douglasson left and Evan felt himself drifting off. He felt himself swimming in too much emotion, too many thoughts. He wanted to talk to his children but there was no phone on his bedside table. He'd have to ask the nurse...

When the door creaked open again, Evan awoke with a start.

He had been dreaming of his last vacation with Sherri and the kids...five days in Diamond Head, South Carolina, where Sherri's cousin ran a small golf resort. The best part of the trip had been the drive down—anticipation heightening with each mile, each revised itinerary. In actuality it turned out to be three days of rain, and two days of trying to relax after spending the previously mentioned three days in five rooms with six people. On the way back, while the kids slept, he and Sherri had talked about the far off days of his retirement...where they'd live, what they'd do. They talked of someplace warm, someplace from the crowd but in the end Sherri just laughed merrily and made him admit that (a) he'd lose his mind anywhere without sidewalks, and (b) they'd never move too far away from the children. 'Cause they were saps, and if there were grandchildren...

They laughed the rest of the way home.

That's what he was dreaming of. All that laughing.

In the hospital room, now in this moment, he blinked his eyes clear and glanced at the doorway. Matt stood there, a shopping bag in one hand and the world's ugliest fern in the other.

"Hey," Matt said, brightening when he saw Evan was awake.

Evan smiled, confused for a moment that it wasn't Sherri standing there—but she would have known where his gym bag was and used that instead of the Macy's bag that Matt had dug out of the pantry closet.

"Hi." His voice sounded a little worse. Too much use from the morning.

Matt's grin nearly split his face. "You sound as bad as you look." He dropped the bag on the floor, put the fern on the tray next to the bed.

"Bad?"

"Like shit." Matt came to stand right next to the bed. His hands tightened on the railing and for a second Evan was distracted by his hands. Men's hands, strong and dark, with swirls of hair and calluses and scars. He remembered what those hands had done to him.

"Hey. You okay? You want me to come back later?"

Back in the moment, Evan looked up and shook his head. "Stay."

Matt nodded happily. He leaned down after hesitating for the smallest second and pressed a kiss against Evan's mouth. It made him shiver. His lips were so dry they hurt, but the kiss made the ache worth it.

"You want some water?" Matt was asking. His hand had somehow found Evan's, and he was stroking his wrist.

"Huh?" Water. Yeah. Evan nodded. He felt so foggy. So fucking tired he could sleep forever.

Matt released Evan's hand and poured him a cup of water from the pitcher on the tray. There was a straw—thank God—because Evan was sure he was never going to be able to lift his head.

But Matt helped with that too, one strong hand under his neck, one holding the straw steady against his lips. He took a small drag on the straw, the effort pulling at the stitches in his chest, but it was worth it. His mouth felt so much better.

Gently, Matt laid him back down on the pillow, put the glass on the tray.

"Thanks."

"No problem. Anything else?

"The kids…"

Evan watched a weird cloud pass over Matt's face, a split second of time. He thought he might have imagined it.

"Your in-laws showed up and took them home. I called this morning before I came here. They're okay. I think they're going to be here tonight."

"Think?"

Matt looked uncomfortable. "Couldn't get a firm answer."

Evan didn't like the sound of that one bit. He understood the kids were upset—they had every reason to be—but that just meant they should be with him as much as possible.

"I'll call…myself…later." Evan spit out, his voice tight.

"Mr. Tough Guy."

"Thanks."

"No problem."

"Where did you stay last night?"

"The house. Kathleen gave me her spare key when I brought them here to the hospital."

"Thanks again, for that."

"No big deal. Shit—I was just working, you know. Making a living."

Evan chuckled, the action causing more tightness in his chest.

"I owe you one."

"One? The list is easily on its second page…"

"Second page?"

"I had to take your garbage out. Fuck. I'm charging you double for that."

And just like that, the cloud over Evan lifted. He just felt…lighter. Still sore, still tired, still worried about his kids. But lighter.

"Cash or check?"

Matt leered. "I'll make you work it off."

Evan laughed lightly. Then winced in pain.

Instantly Matt's face showed concern and fear. He touched Evan's face gently with his fingertips. "You okay? You want a nurse?"

Shaking his head, Evan took a calming breath.

"Don't...make...me...laugh."

The smirk returned. But Matt didn't stop touching him. "Damn. I got pages of good material just waiting..."

"Save...for later." The touch of Matt's fingers relaxed him, made him feel warm. Evan tried to give Matt a sexy look but given the way Matt rolled his eyes, he wasn't very convincing. "Make it up to you. I promise."

"Good." Matt bent down to kiss him again and this time it didn't hurt. It felt like the most natural thing in the world.

Matt stayed until the nurse came back to check his vitals. They kissed, held hands, talked of what the doctor had said. Evan worried about taking care of the kids and Matt reassured him that everything would be fine. Between him, and the in-laws, the kids would be taken care of.

And then Matt announced he would be taking care of Evan until he got back on his feet.

"No."

"Shut up."

"Matt!"

"Evan! What the hell are you going to do otherwise? It's me or your in-laws, and since they're better equipped to take care of four kids, guess what, you're shit out of luck. I'm your fucking nursemaid."

Evan sighed, frustrated. He hated feeling so helpless and out of control. He hated that Matt was right.

"I'm not telling you you're right."

"Whatever. I already know I am. I don't need your two cents." Matt crossed his arms and glared down at him. "So we're clear? I'm going home with you. I'm staying at the house. I'm taking care of things until you're on your feet and you and the kids are okay on your own."

"Fine." Evan had the sudden urge to stick his tongue out at Matt.

The fake glaring was cut off by Pam's arrival. She bustled in and started her routine.

"Hello, Mr. Haight. How are you?"

Matt shot her a dazzling smile. "Fine, Pam. How are you?"

"Good, good. Sorry to break up your private time, but I needed to get this done. How are we doing, Detective Cerelli?"

Gee, nice to finally get around to me, Evan thought sourly. "Okay. Throat's sore."

"Didn't the doctor tell you to slow down the chatter? I bet you ignored that completely."

Matt threw himself in the pleather brown chair in the corner. Evan could see his face but Pam couldn't. He was smirking openly.

Pam went about her business, chatting the whole time. Maybe it was a nurse thing, but she acted like Evan was seven and needed help navigating his feet under the covers, which was really irritating considering he guessed them to be around the same age. She seemed to be sharing a lot about her brother, who lived in the Florida Keys with his "friend" Maurice, and Matt was now laughing in his hands, silently. Evan used all his strength not to roll his eyes. When Pam went into the small bathroom to grab a new sheet, Evan shot daggers at Matt, who was gasping for air.

"She knows?" Evan whispered.

Matt nodded.

"How?"

Matt rolled his eyes. Made a kissy face. Winked.

Evan groaned.

Pam walked out of the bathroom, still chatting.

Matt excused himself and walked out the door.

Pam watched him go and smiled sweetly at Evan. "Your boyfriend is a real doll, honey."

* * *

The phone was hooked up shortly after Matt left—he needed to make some phone calls for work—and Pam came back in to dial the MacGregor's number for Evan. Some Percocets had Evan feeling like he'd spent a long day in the sun sipping beer—but he didn't hurt anymore.

He wanted to know how his kids were. His voice still sounded like shit but he had more control over it.

Two rings and Josie picked up—her chirpy voice hitting Evan right between the eyes.

"Josie?"

"Evan! How are you? You're talking on the phone! That's wonderful."

"I'm fine. How're the kids?"

"Oh dear—they're just exhausted. I kept them home from school—they need their rest. They need someone to take care of them. This has been quite hard on them, Evan."

Evan counted to fifty by fives, concentrated on the thin water damage mark that ran across two tiles over his bed.

"Thank you, Josie, for coming to get them and taking care of them for me. It shouldn't be too long, I promise."

"Oh, it's no bother, dear! I just love having the children here. It reminds me of when my girls were small." She sniffled softly.

"Can I talk to Miranda please?"

"She's resting."

"Is she asleep?"

"Noooo..."

"Then please put her on."

He heard the small sound of disapproval and didn't give a shit. Then Josie called out to the other room and he heard answering shouts of "Daddy!" A second later, Miranda voice was saying breathlessly...

"Daddy!"

"Hey, honey. You okay?"

"Me? I'm fine—how are you? Are you all right? You were so out of it yesterday..."

"I'm feeling much better honey. My voice sounds bad but that's pretty much it. I should be out of the hospital in a few days."

"That's great!"

"I still have some recovery time ahead but it'll be better for me when I'm home."

"Are we staying here?" The tension in her voice made his whole body tighten.

"Yeah, honey—I'm sorry. I know you'd rather be home. But I'm going to be out of it for at least a week. I want you guys to be with people who can take care of you—"

"Daddy, I'm not a kid. I can take care of things until you feel better—"

"Miranda, listen. I know you're not a kid and you've done an amazing job helping me since...last year. But midterms are coming up and you have a lot on your plate. I want you to concentrate on school, okay?"

Miranda sighed heavily. "Just until midterms are over, okay? Once I finish the tests, we'll come home. So we can get ready for Christmas."

Oh shit, Evan thought. Four weeks away. He coughed, feeling uncomfortable.

"It's a deal, kiddo."

"Who's going to take care of you?"

"Uh...Matt is going to stay with me for awhile, until I can get around on my own."

"Oh."

Evan squirmed. "Yeah, he has some vacation time."

"That's nice of him," she said politely.

"Yeah. He's a good friend."

"He took real good care of us till Grandma and Grandpa came to the hospital... Tell him thanks, okay? I think I forgot in all the excitement."

"I'll do that, honey. Let me talk to Grandma again—I want to find out when she's bringing you guys by."

"Uh...sure. I'll talk to you later, Daddy."

"Love you."

"Love you too."

Evan's eyes stung. He hated, *hated* not being able to take care of his kids. Hated they were so far away and—as far as he was concerned—alone.

"Yes, Evan?"

With a deep breath, Evan tried to get hold of himself—a stern voice was going to be mandatory in dealing with his mother-in-law. "Josie—I was wondering when you and Phil were planning on bringing the children by? Visiting hours..."

Josie cut him off, her voice honey and steel. "Phil and I have discussed this Evan, and we feel it's best for the children if they have a little break from the whole...hospital thing. When you're released and home, then we'll talk about bringing them..."

"Josie," Evan spit out, his voice dangerous, "They are my children and quite frankly, I don't give a shit what you and Phil discussed. I am their father and they need me. I want them here tomorrow. If it's a problem for you to drive them into the city, I'm more than happy to send a friend to pick them up."

There was dead silence from the other end of the phone. Evan's entire body hurt like hell and his throat felt raw. He fairly shook with rage at Josie's...presumption...that she was in charge of his children.

Josie cleared her throat. "I'll speak to Phil. I'm not sure when we can get out there," she forced out.

Just barely civil, Evan replied, "Visiting hours are until seven p.m. If possible, I'd like to have at least an hour with the children."

"Fine."

Then nothing but Josie's breathing. Through her nose— which meant she was furious. Quietly furious.

"Thank you. I'll speak with you tomorrow."

"Fine."

"Good night."

Josie said nothing. Evan heard the phone click on the other end.

"Fuck!" he raged at the ceiling. He threw the phone receiver to the floor. The effort of the day, the conversation, everything sent pain shooting through his body. Shaking, he closed his eyes, trying to calm himself. It didn't work. Long, painful moments that Evan sweated out, clutching the bedcovers and dazedly staring at the watermark on the ceiling, trying to remember when Matt said he'd be back. He hadn't felt this out of control since Sherri's death and it scared the hell out of him.

He tried not to think about the conversation with his mother-in-law. It only fueled his greatest nightmare, the terror that had lurked in the back of his mind since Sherri's death...

What if someone tried to take his children away from him?

Chapter Nine

Evan stared out his hospital room window as dusk settled outside, hazy from the sedative they'd been forced to pump into him a few hours earlier. After the phone call with his mother-in-law, Pam had found him tense and trembling in bed, grinding his teeth in frustration. She soothed him for a few moments with her gentle voice then called the doctor. Evan got a stern talking to about relaxing and giving his body a chance to heal, followed by a shot in the arm. He spent the rest of the morning drifting in and out, barely able to acknowledge his visitors.

Vic dropped in for a few with Moses and Kalee. He couldn't remember a word of the conversation. Serena came by wondering if he was up to seeing Helena but midway through the visit he'd drifted off and when he woke up, Matt was sitting in the pleather chair, reading the *Daily News.*

Then he fell asleep again.

Now it was almost dinnertime. He wasn't expecting any visitors for a few hours, with Matt running home to shower and his kids not expected for at least two hours. So that meant he had entirely too much time to worry. He played the conversation with Josie over and over in his head, until he could feel his blood churning.

How dare she? How fucking dare she?

He couldn't even form a coherent thought. Couldn't feel sympathy—she had lost her daughter. But hell, he'd lost his wife.

And he was raising his kids alone. That wasn't easy. But he was doing a fine job and she could just mind her own business.

His heart was pounding. What if... No, he couldn't even think of the possibility.

A gentle knock on the door distracted him from his morbid thoughts.

"Come in," he croaked, not at all sure the person on the other side could hear him.

He heard little bangs on the other side of the door, then it pushed open. He strained to see who it was...

Helena.

In a wheelchair, wearing a hospital gown, what looked to be half a straitjacket, and a really ugly robe.

"Shit."

Evan couldn't help but smile.

She banged into the door as she maneuvered into the room with her left arm. "Goddamnit."

"Need some help there?"

"Shut up."

"Shouldn't a nurse..."

"I'm AWOL. They said I should stay in bed."

"Ah."

She managed to get through the door, blowing a wayward strand of hair out of her eyes. Evan could see they were a little glassy, and she was holding her right side gingerly in the seat.

With a triumphant sigh she rolled her wheelchair one-handed up to Evan's bed, bumping into the rails.

"Hey partner," she said with a wide smile. "How are you doing?"

Evan answered her with an even bigger grin, reaching down with his hand to grab hers. "Better. It's great to see you, Helena. You okay? How's your shoulder?"

He could see her go to shrug but then think better of it. "Formerly dislocated. Currently...uh...located? You'll have to excuse me, I'm very, very high on some fluidy stuff they've been pumping into my arm."

Ahhh. He could relate.

"So you're legally high and your shoulder's okay. That much I'm clear on."

She nodded happily. "And you? Mom said you were okay—no permanent damage."

"That door amounted to a bunch of splinters in my chest. I'm okay."

Helena's eyes suddenly filled with tears and she laid her head down on their clasped hands.

Ignoring the rapid mood swing—chalking it up to the drugs—Evan spoke soothingly. "Helena, I'm fine. Really. So are you. And that asshole's in jail. Everything is okay." He spoke soothingly, squeezing her hand in his.

"I thought...I thought he killed you. I just heard...this...explosion. I knew it was a shotgun..." She shuddered against the side of the bed. "You went down and I drew my weapon..."

"Shhh..."

"No, it's okay." She looked up at him, her face wet and splotchy. "He blew out of that door like he was possessed or something. Slammed into me as I was yelling for him to freeze and then...we went right down the stairs... I don't remember everything—I whacked my head pretty well on the way down."

Evan managed to reach over with his other hand and pat her face tenderly. "Good thing you have such a hard head."

Helena's face contorted for a moment, trying to stay serious but a smirk wormed its way out.

"Jerk."

He pinched her cheek. "How long you in here for?"

"I get out tomorrow. How about you?" She sniffled loudly.

"End of the week? I'm going to be out on leave for four weeks. Uhhh. I can't imagine just lying around for all that time."

"Are you going home? How are you going to take care of yourself? I can't imagine they want you running all over the place."

Evan felt that old familiar blush creeping up his face. "Uh...Matt's taking some time..."

Helena bit her lip, a sly twinkle in her eyes. "Hmmm..."

"Stop it. He's just helping me out..."

"Oh, I'm sure."

Evan roasted in embarrassment. Helena chuckled.

"You really are high."

"And you are the color of a tomato, Evan. Calm down before they run in here with a crash cart!"

Staring at the ceiling Evan realized he was being ridiculous. Of all the people in his life, Helena knew about him and Matt, she was fine with it. Why couldn't he just relax?

He sighed. "He insisted. And I'm really thankful because I don't know what else I'd do..."

He gave her a stern look. "Don't tell him I said that."

"Macho stubborn pride in play here?"

"Yes."

"Hmmmm..." She smiled at him. "You two have it in spades." Helena readjusted herself in the chair, suddenly looking a little tired. "It's going to be crazy around that house with the kids..."

Evan felt himself tense up. "My in-laws have the kids. They insisted." His voice was flat.

"Oh." Helena squeezed Evan's hand. "You okay?"

"Yeah, yeah. My mother-in-law pissed me off yesterday. I hate not being able to take care of my kids right now. They don't need this sort of thing in their lives, not when it was just starting to feel...." He let out a shaky breath. "Starting to feel slightly normal, like we had it under control."

"Hey, hey. This is just a little setback. Your kids are going to be okay. They're with their grandparents, they'll get a little spoiled, they'll come home in what—a week or two? In the meantime, you rest and do everything the doctor's tell you so you'll be 100 percent for them when they do come home."

Evan nodded, shot her a tender smile. "Thanks, Helena. And I'm so glad you're okay. I don't know what I would've done..."

She wiggled her eyebrows at him. "No problem, guy. I'm hardheaded remember? And you have...a very strong chest. Like Superman."

For some reason that struck them both as funny and they started to laugh quietly. Helena snorted and it was pretty much over after that. *Too many drugs*, Evan thought. Too many drugs and too much stress and pain and worry and this is what happens. Two rational adults with tears streaming down their faces for absolutely no reason.

Helena was holding her arm. "Oh ow!" she cried out, then giggled harder. "Ow, ow, ow!"

Evan had his hand on his chest. He felt the same way—it hurt like hell but man, he needed to laugh.

The door opened at that very moment and Matt peeked his head in.

"What the hell?"

Neither one could get a word out. Another snort from Helena and both were off again.

Helena was rolled back into her room after she and Evan became somewhat coherent and realized just how sore they were. Matt helped a nurse deposit her into bed—she was asleep before he walked out the door—then headed back to Evan.

Matt pushed his way into the room, smiling at the memory of the two partners, red-faced and teary-eyed, giggling helplessly over what he determined to be absolutely nothing even slightly amusing.

* * *

Vic Wolkowski was standing next to Evan's bed.

Matt stopped in the doorway. Vic and Evan looked toward him—both seemed a bit wary.

Me too, thought Matt.

"Hey, Vic." He nodded to his friend, ducked into the room. His eyes darted around, finally rested on Evan.

"Hey, Matty. How you doing?"

"Good, thanks," was his quick response, feeling slightly uncomfortable in Vic's presence.

Vic cleared his throat awkwardly. "Just wanted to check on you guys before I headed home. You're...ah...looking better already, Evan."

"Thanks, Vic."

"Is there anything you two need? I could stop at the store or something before I leave..."

Silence. Matt couldn't think of what to say.

Evan shook his head, saying, "Thanks, Vic. I can't think of anything."

"Okay then, I'm off. You fellas have a good night."

"Thanks for coming," Evan said.

"Night." Matt spoke quietly, feeling like a moron. Vic's shoulders were hunched a bit and he obviously felt terrible. "Can I walk you out?"

"Uh—sure. That would be…great."

Matt paused to give Evan's blanket covered leg a quick squeeze.

"I'll be right back, okay?"

Evan winked. "Go on. I'll wait here."

Matt laughed, his tension easing. "Good man." He caught Vic's eye and pushed open the door.

Vic walked out, giving Matt a little nod. "I'll stop by tomorrow, Evan. Night."

"Night, Vic. Thanks."

Giving Evan a little wave, Matt let the door close. He and Vic stood there for a moment, looking everywhere but at each other. Matt cleared his throat. Vic looked up, then away.

"So, uh…Evan's looking much better. Even since yesterday," Vic said awkwardly.

Matt nodded in agreement.

"When is he going home?"

"End of the week."

"Hmm." Vic stuck his hands in his pockets. "You let me know if he needs anything."

"Thanks."

Matt's insides hurt. He couldn't believe that after more than fifteen years of friendship, he and Vic were standing here with nothing of substance to say. The worst part was that they couldn't even look each other in the eye.

Finally, Vic sighed. "Listen, Matty, I'm sorry if I did or said something wrong the other day. If I reacted the wrong way...all I can say is I was shocked...I..."

Matt held up his hand. Jesus, this was ridiculous.

"You didn't do anything wrong, Vic... It's just a weird situation."

That could apparently be agreed on, because Vic nodded heartily.

"I don't want things to be like this," he said, making sweeping motions with his hands.

"They won't be, Vic. Really. We just need to get...used to things. Right? It's weird, it's different, we're both a little freaked... it'll be okay. We're fine."

Matt let out a long held breath. Vic looked like a weight had been lifted.

"I'll see you tomorrow, okay? I'll come by, see if you need anything."

Nodding, Matt smiled, trying to convey to Vic that they were "okay."

"Night, Vic."

Happy now, Vic extended his hand, shaking Matt's heartily. "Night, Matty."

Matt watched him walk down the hallway. Okay. This was good. Fine. Being mature, talking to people about his... relationship. With a man. Everything was good.

Just fine.

He felt the tight pull of tension between his shoulder blades, but shrugged it off. Then he turned and went back to Evan.

* * *

Helena left the hospital on Wednesday, headed for the guest room of her mother's house. She didn't look thrilled when she visited Evan to say good-bye. Much as she loved her mother…

"It'll be fine," Evan whispered as Matt and Serena chatted in the doorway. "She'll make you big meals, fuss over you a lot, and it'll make her feel good."

Helena stuck her tongue out at him. "You can be magnanimous—you're going home with your cute boyfriend."

Evan blushed. "Helena…"

"You get takeout…sex…action movies… I'm going to have to watch Rogers and Hammerstein musicals and eat broccoli."

"Good-bye, Helena," Evan said loudly.

Serena came over to the bed with a smile. "Ready to go, dear?"

Evan grinned. "Have fun, Helena."

They said their good-byes, Helena shooting daggers at Evan until the door closed.

"What was all that about?" Matt asked, sitting on the edge of Evan's bed, his eyes warm.

Evan chuckled. "Helena thinks I lucked out with my recovery situation."

Matt stroked his fingers along Evan's arm, eliciting little shivers from his lover, stilling his laughter.

"And why is that?" he asked smoothly.

"She's jealous I'm going home with you… Thinks it'll be more fun than hanging out with her mother." Evan said softly.

"Mmmm…"

"I think she's right."

Evan felt that roller-coaster feeling come over him, that same feeling he'd been having around Matt for weeks. He knew the kiss was coming and it still shocked him, how much he wanted it.

He didn't wait long.

Matt pressed his mouth against Evan's, at first just brushing their lips, then dipping down again to taste him deeply.

The sense memories flooded through Evan's body. Every kiss, every touch. The rush of emotion, of lust, overtook any small fearful part of him. Evan reached his hand up to touch the back of Matt's head. He threaded his fingers through the soft hair, pulled his mouth closer.

Matt responded immediately, groaning his approval into Evan's mouth.

He pulled away, taking in a big breath and leaning his forehead against Evan's.

"When do you get the fuck out of here?"

"Friday morning," Evan managed to get out.

Matt moaned.

With a small laugh, Evan tightened his grip on the back of Matt's neck. He tilted his head, angling his lips to tease Matt. "I need my rest."

"Right now?"

"No, you idiot…"

Matt made a sound, halfway between a snort and a sigh, and leaned back into the kiss.

* * *

Evan saw his kids twice before he left the hospital. They arrived precisely at the time he told his mother-in-law and seemed tearfully relieved to crawl into bed and give him hugs. Josie waited in the hallway, which was fine with Evan. He had absolutely nothing to say to her at this point.

The kids were still miserable about not being able to come home—Miranda being the most vocal. Evan swore they'd be home in just one week, and then they'd start preparing for Christmas.

Temporarily mollified, they left the room when visiting hours ended, making him promise he'd call them every night.

Choking back unwelcome tears, Evan watched the door close. He stared up at the ceiling and counted the hours until morning, when Matt was coming to get him. Home, then seven days recuperating and finally the kids would be home.

He could do this.

* * *

Matt drove them back to Queens, Evan dozing in the front seat of the sedan. Getting dressed and signing paperwork took far more energy than he'd expected; his eyes drooped closed before they got through the Queens-Midtown Tunnel. He was vaguely aware of Matt humming along with a rock station, too low to make out the tune. Relaxed, Evan drifted into a light slumber, grateful to be out of the hospital, grateful to be alive.

"Hey." A hand was gently stroking his shoulder, calling to him.

Evan's eyes flew open. He blinked for a moment, then recognized his garage door.

He looked over at Matt.

"Hey, we're home. You okay?"

Nodding, Evan moved stiffly to undo his seat belt. His body didn't respond as quickly as usual, he felt like he was moving in quicksand doing the simplest tasks.

"I'll get the bags."

Matt got out and Evan heard him rooting around in the trunk for Evan's bag and, of course, the world's ugliest fern that Matt had insisted he bring home. The rest of the flowers were sent down to pediatrics.

Evan sighed. The act of unbuckling himself made him wish for a nap. He heard a rap on the glass next to him. Matt was smiling, his hands full.

"You need help?"

Shaking his head, Evan pulled the handle and opened his door. Matt hovered a bit as he swung his legs out and gingerly lifted himself out of the car. He leaned against the side of the car to catch his breath.

Matt shifted the bags to one hand, using the other to clasp Evan's forearm.

"Let's get you into the house, okay? You can lie down."

"Yeah."

Slowly the two men walked to the house, Evan shuffling his lead-weight body toward the front door. He leaned against Matt out of sheer desperation—his legs just weren't working properly.

A little fumbling and Matt got the door open. Evan watched him dumbly, thinking, *Shouldn't I be letting him in? I live here, don't I?*

Dropping the bags in the foyer, Matt's arms immediately encircled Evan's body and pulled him closer.

Evan sagged. Yeah, that felt good.

The door shut behind them—Matt probably kicked it closed, he thought, letting himself be led to the couch.

In five seconds flat, Evan found himself lying down, his shoes and jacket off, a warm blanket thrown over him.

"Pillows?" asked Matt. "Something to drink?"

Evan nodded.

With that sparkling smile that turned Evan to mush, Matt hurried off to play nursemaid.

Evan didn't see him come back, he was already asleep.

Matt puttered around the house, trying to be quiet while Evan slept. They'd been back at the house for almost five hours—the sun was down, the December wind rattling the windows. He straightened what little was out of place. Thought about dinner (Soup? Wasn't that what you fed sick people? Did injured count as sick?), thought about the past week and a half and got the shakes.

If he stopped to think...*really* think, Matt surmised he would probably need to drink his way through a fully stocked bar. The whole thing with Evan (Relationship. Love. That thing.). Vic and Helena knowing. The shooting.

Matt sighed. He needed to talk to someone. Vic obviously wasn't that person. Abe—do you call your ex-partner out of the blue and go, *Hey. How are you? Wanna have lunch 'cause I might be gay or something and need an objective opinion about what the hell is going on 'cause I'm in love with a guy?* Leaving only one person on Matt's ever-shortening list of friends.

Liz.

Yeah, he really needed to talk to Liz. Level-headed, straight-shooting Liz who Matt knew he loved a little more than a friend but not as much as a lover. He would call her in the morning because if there was anyone who could help him make heads or tails of this, it was her.

He heard a rustling on the couch and walked into the living room to check on Evan.

"Hi."

Evan blinked, trying to adjust his eyes in the darkened room. The only light was coming from the kitchen behind Matt.

"Hi. What time is it?"

"Almost six. You feel up to dinner?"

Evan slowly stretched his body, moving each limb and muscle as if it were made of glass. The pain pills had come and gone, he was feeling everything.

"Yeah," he gasped. "Could you...would you mind..."

"Pain pills?"

"Christ, yes."

Matt returned a few seconds later with a bottle of cool water and his pills. Evan smiled gratefully, swallowing the two huge capsules, praying they worked quickly. He gulped the water down, finishing half the bottle before he fell back against the pillows.

"Thanks."

Matt sat on the edge of the coffee table, leaning forward on his knees.

"How are you doing?"

Evan shrugged. "Okay. Sleeping helps. I'm just stiff."

"Would upstairs be more comfortable?"

In a sudden flash, Evan saw the bed upstairs, with Sherri snuggled in his arms. And then with Matt, holding him that first night when everything had started with them.

Shit.

"Nah. I'll just stay here."

Matt nodded, reaching out his hand to touch Evan's face. "I'll go get you soup. Anything else?"

"No. That's fine. Thanks, Matt." He meant that. He wanted to convey that in his words.

Matt got the message. He leaned forward, pressing his fingers firmly against Evan's jaw.

"Jesus I was worried about you," he whispered. "I was so scared..."

"Shhh..." Evan said. "I'm fine..."

He didn't get the rest of it out because suddenly Matt's mouth took his, hot and a little desperate. The room swam a bit around his head as he tasted the fear. And the love.

It had been more than a week since they'd really touched like this. In the hospital they were always waiting for the door to open. But here...here they were alone.

Matt dropped to his knees, leaning over Evan's body on the couch. It gave them both the leverage they craved—Evan's arms went slowly around Matt's neck and shoulders. Matt's hands gently cradled his face.

Nice, so nice. Tongues softly stroking lips, tasting. Getting hungrier.

Evan came up for air first, twisting his head to the side, gasping in a lungful of air as Matt moved to bite and suck on his neck.

Yeah. Very nice.

A hot wave washed over Evan's body, easing every ache and pain he could remember. He wasn't sure he could go any further than this, but while it lasted...

Matt deepened his demanding kisses, moving again, running his tongue under the edge of Evan's T-shirt. Evan shivered, arched under the pleasure, and then crashed with a burst of pain.

Matt felt Evan tense up slightly in his arms and suddenly remembered why Evan was lying on the couch.

He pulled back to stare into his lover's face. "Jesus, I'm sorry..."

Evan shook his head. "It's okay..."

"No, it's not! I got fucking carried away—I'm sorry. Are you all right?"

"Yeah." Evan reached up to touch Matt's jaw. His touch felt hot...but tentative. "I wish..." That bright embarrassed flush worked its way across his face. "I guess the spirit is willing, but the body still feels like shit."

Matt smiled. "Sorry."

"Stop." The fingers moved down the side of his face, circling Matt's lips. "Give me a little recoup time and talk to me in the morning."

"Sounds good to me," Matt said, a little breathless. "The talking part."

Evan's hand seemed obsessed with the face in front of him. Matt leaned in, mesmerized by the slow movements feather-light on his face.

"I missed you," Evan murmured.

"I'm here now."

"Yeah."

"Yeah. I'm not going anywhere." Matt felt Evan shiver. The words slipped out, soft and reverent.

Evan nodded slowly, his fingers stalled on Matt's forehead.

They stayed that way for a seemingly endless stretch of time...until Evan's hand dropped and he smiled.

"I think you promised soup..."

Matt blinked a few times, coming back down to earth. "Right...yeah..."

"It'll help my recovery process I'm sure."

Laughing, Matt leaned back on his haunches. "Blackmail. Nice...very nice, Detective."

They spent another few minutes smiling, their hands touching lightly.

Eventually Matt forced himself to stand, giving Evan's hand a gentle squeeze before letting it go. "Soup, rest, recuperating."

"Right."

They ate soup, they watched some TV—sports recap program after sports recap program—until the eleven o'clock news started. Evan lay on the sofa, his legs across Matt's lap, their hands loosely intertwined under the blanket. They didn't speak—they didn't have to, Matt thought randomly. This silence was comforting, easy. Their friendship still existed.

Even with the…new developments.

Matt watched Evan drift off yet again, waking with little jerks every few moments.

"Hey, man," he called softly. "Why don't you go upstairs to bed?"

Evan came totally awake with a start. "What?"

"Why don't you go upstairs? It's late and you had a big day."

"I'm going to sleep down here."

"Evan…"

"I'm fine." His tone was sleepy but stubborn. "This is fine. I'd rather stay down here. You can sleep upstairs."

Matt opened his mouth to protest but he remembered the terrible nightmares that had awoken Evan that first night…

He decided not to push it.

"Sure, man. Whatever you want. I'm going to head up then. If you need anything, just holler. I'll hear you."

Tenderly he lifted Evan's legs and got up, rearranging the blanket that covered him. Evan wasn't looking at him, he'd burrowed down into the pillows, his face half-hidden by the blanket.

"I'll be fine. Those pills knock me out."

"Right." Matt leaned down. Pressed a kiss on Evan's forehead. "But I'll leave the door open, okay?"

Evan nodded. Matt stood and stared down at him. He still wouldn't look him in the eye.

"Good night."

"Night." The blanket muffled the soft answer.

Matt climbed the stairs slowly and alone.

Chapter Ten

Matt trudged up the stairs, not looking back. He felt a heavy weight pressing against his chest. The upstairs hallway was dark and quiet. He'd been staying in Evan's bedroom since that first night, feeling both awkward and comforted by the big queen bed and dark oak furniture. When Evan had been in the hospital, Matt would wait until he could barely keep his eyes open before dragging himself upstairs to sleep. He didn't want to lie in the dark in "their room"…in "their bed" and think about…them.

Quickly, he stripped down to his shorts and pulled out a T-shirt from his overnight bag. Before he'd gone to pick Evan up from the hospital he'd changed the sheets and fixed the bed, neatened up as much as he could, under the apparent delusion that they would be spending the night up here. Idiot. Lying there in the dark, Matt thought about Evan downstairs, alone. He thought about how deftly Evan had dodged spending the night upstairs with Matt. That was understandable he supposed—not feeling comfortable about sleeping in his old room with his new… whatever.

And maybe he didn't feel up to having company all night— maybe that was why he didn't ask Matt to stay with him. But all the logic in the world wasn't quite working right this second. What hurt the most, what created that terrible pressure against Matt's chest, was the blossoming fear that he wanted this way more than Evan did.

Evan lay on the couch, staring into the darkness of the living room. He listened to Matt moving around upstairs and felt like shit. The sounds eventually tapered off and soon the house settled into silence. Evan didn't fall asleep for a long time, too busy replaying a thousand scenes in his head.

It was Sherri first, from the prom to cooking breakfast, from tucking one of the kids into bed to rolling over and smiling at him so beautifully he thought his heart would break. And then he was back in the bar, sitting across from Matt in those first days, crying and complaining and falling in love even though he didn't know it. He squeezed his eyes shut, trying to still the images. He didn't want to see himself in the arms of either one of them. Or their eyes. Why was it so hard to let himself go, to act on what he felt? Why couldn't he go upstairs—or even have asked Matt to stay?

Not one of his visions could give him an answer.

He finally fell asleep hours later, with his questions still lingering.

Matt crept downstairs at eight-thirty, in desperate need of coffee. He hoped Evan was sleeping but a quick glance to the couch proved him wrong. It was empty. "Hey," called a voice from the kitchen. Evan was sitting on a kitchen stool, looking pale but smiling. Matt walked over to the full pot of coffee sitting in the coffee maker.

"This is a wonderful thing."

"I thought you might appreciate it."

"What are you doing up so early?"

"Couldn't sleep anymore." Evan didn't say anything else. He toyed idly with the glass of water in front of him.

"You take your pain pills?

"Yes, Dad."

Matt laughed, taking his mug of coffee to lean on the counter next to Evan.

"Hey," he said softly.

Evan leaned over and kissed him. Hard.

Matt pulled away and crooked an eyebrow at him. "Feeling better?"

"Yeah." It came out a little fiercely. Evan pressed his shoulder against Matt's. "Much."

Matt wanted to believe that this was renewed passion but it smelled a bit like guilt and he wasn't interested in that. Tenderly, he kissed Evan, making it slow and soft, not inciting anything. When he pulled away, Evan could barely meet his gaze.

Right.

"Is there anything you need to get done today? Laundry or phone calls or anything? I should go out food shopping..." Matt walked over to the fridge, placing his cup on the top while he looked inside. "And I wanted to call my friend Liz, maybe drive out to see her." He kept his tone neutral. It hurt.

Evan blinked a few times, clearly a bit unsettled by the rapid change in mood.

"I want to give the kids a call."

"Sure. Good idea." Matt leaned on the door of the refrigerator, searching for breakfast and making a mental list of things they might need. Plus, he really didn't think it was a good idea to look over at Evan right now.

A blanket of silence lay over the room.

"You hungry?

"I'm fine..."

"You should eat. The prescription bottle says you have to take the pills with food. I'll make eggs." Matt realized he was talking too fast, his tone growing gruffer with each word. He pulled out a carton of eggs and a loaf of bread, gripping them tightly.

Evan must have realized it too because in a few seconds he was across the room and standing an inch away from Matt.

"Hey," Evan said softly.

Matt sighed. "Yeah?"

"I'm...sorry...about what happened last night..." Evan spoke hesitantly. He reached out with a tentative hand and caught the sleeve of Matt's shirt. "I feel like an idiot."

Without saying anything Matt closed the refrigerator door, maneuvering around Evan, and put the eggs and bread on the counter. He kept his back to Evan for a second to collect his thoughts. When he turned around, the wounded look on Evan's face nearly made him wince.

"Listen—this is just...crazy shit going on. You're still recuperating and we weren't exactly on solid ground before this happened..."

"I said I was sor—"

"I don't want to hear your apologies." *Fuck*, Matt thought. *That didn't come out right at all.* "I'm not blaming you for anything... I'm just...trying my best here, just like you are."

Matt took a deep breath. "I suck at relationships, Evan."

"Considering I've only been in one other...I'm not sure I know much more than you do," Evan murmured.

"I didn't mean to push you last night."

"You didn't...I just... It's weird, being here together, alone... being intimate..."

"We were together in my apartment and over Thanksgiving. We...we were...intimate...then."

Evan sighed heavily, leaning against the counter like all the fight had gone out of him. He seemed to be thinking aloud and

Matt just happened to be in the room. "It just seemed strange all of a sudden…just us…in this house…"

"And the possibility of making love with me in the bed you used to share with your wife doesn't appeal to you?" Annoyed, Matt's tone was harsh. "And you couldn't just fucking say that to me? Like I'm some sort of idiot who wouldn't understand why that would be painful for you? I could have stayed downstairs…"

"Why didn't you?" Evan asked, his voice suddenly just as angry.

Matt stalked out of the kitchen and threw himself down on the couch, staring blankly into space.

Evan followed silently, moving to stand directly in front of him.

"Why?" Matt's eyes—sad and tired—met Evan's. "Maybe I need to you ask me. Maybe I need you to tell me…"

"You know I love you."

"Evan, I don't fucking know what that means, okay? I've never been here before. Never had someone…never gave a shit…" He threw his hands up in exasperation. "It sounds good, and I can say it back, but the bottom line is—I don't know. I don't know how much I can fuck this up.

"I don't know how to do this. I don't know what you want from me." There he'd said it.

"I never realized we had so much in common."

Matt glanced up, caught Evan's small wry grin. He couldn't help but laugh a little. "Good Christ, we're fucked up."

"When you're right you're right, Haight."

"Come here and sit down before you collapse."

"Sounds like a plan." Evan folded himself gently in Matt's arms. They sat in silence, holding each other tightly, hands stroking absently.

The flare was over just as quickly as it had started.

"I am sorry about last night," Evan said softly. "I just...got a little lost."

"Just tell me next time, okay? You can say whatever you need to man, more than anything else, we're friends."

"Friends in a beer commercial sort of way?"

Matt laughed. He moved gently until they were both on their sides and facing one another.

"That's exactly what I was thinking. Wanna go out and rebuild your engine block?"

They laughed, moved their bodies in tiny increments, until the right parts were aligned. Matt watched Evan's eyes darken with arousal—this was better. This didn't feel like guilt. No, this felt like—a hard-on.

Matt made a noise that expressed affection, agreement, and intent. He slid his hands under Evan's T-shirt, stroked the skin not covered by a white bandage, unsure if the incredible heat was coming from his flesh or Evan's. Suddenly all the fears and the pure terror that Matt had lived with the previous week came flooding back and he moaned in need, in anguish.

He just wanted...wanted this release, this communication. He wanted Evan to know how much he loved him. And he desperately needed to feel Evan loved him back.

"Shhh, shhh," Evan murmured. "God, you feel so good...your hands..." Evan burrowed his head into the curve between Matt's shoulder and neck. He breathed in the masculine smell of sleep and coffee and sweat. Feeling a slight twinge in his chest, he ignored it, concentrating on the sharp pain/pleasure of grinding himself against Matt's leg, which was sliding between his.

He followed suit and felt the softness of Matt's back, biting gently on the roughly stubbled skin above his shirt collar. The jerk

of Matt's entire body, the sound that was pulled out of his throat…
Evan bit again and felt Matt go wild.

"God," Matt muttered, pulling slightly away and up so he
could pull Evan more fully onto his back. Evan suddenly
remembered

Thanksgiving, lying here on the sofa, Matt's mouth on…he
moaned, letting his legs fall open in a blatant invitation.

It didn't take Matt long to get Evan's message. He got to his
knees and pulled his shirt off, tossing it to the floor. With a shaky
hand he reached down and touched the small patch of Evan's skin,
between his shirt and pants.

Evan bucked up.

"You all right?" Matt asked desperately, hoarsely. "Does it
hurt?"

Evan laughed darkly. "If we're talking about my chest—no.
Everything else though…" He extended his hand, touching the
exact spot on Matt's stomach. "I'm fine. Come here. Touch me," he
said hotly, and for a second he didn't recognize his own voice.

Those big, hot hands Evan craved suddenly came alive,
quickly divesting him of his clothes, leaving him panting and
shaking, splayed open and practically begging for more. "Please,"
he finally broke down and said the word, because Matt didn't seem
in a hurry to do anything but tease him senseless with soft kisses
and a well-placed caress.

Matt stood up and kicked off his shorts, dropping back down
to the sofa in a crouch over Evan's straining body. He leaned
forward to take another kiss from Evan's willing mouth, but this
time it was rougher, more demanding. His teeth took a tiny bite of
lip, soothed the spot with a flick of the tongue, then started over
again. A bite, a flick. Teasing. Mindlessly, Evan pulled Matt down,
the older man having at least the presence of mind to keep his
arms straight, to keep Evan from having to bear the brunt of his

weight. Their lower bodies touched, locked into place and suddenly it was an explosion, a frenzy of movement as they bucked against each another. Every tilt and thrust, every slick touch set them off and at the last second of sanity, Matt leaned down and grabbed Evan's mouth with his own. They came within seconds of one another, grunts and breathless sounds of pleasure in stereo.

For a long moment they kissed and breathed in air and waited until the room stopped spinning. Matt reached down for his T-shirt and cleaned them both off, enough to keep the sofa safe from stains.

Practically boneless, his whole body humming with pleasure (and protesting the vigorous exercise a bit), Evan let himself be maneuvered to his side, curling around Matt as they settled down again. There was nothing to say, Evan thought as his eyes grew heavy. Nothing would make this moment better. Words just confused things—when they held each other like this, it made so much more sense.

Evan fell asleep while they lay there, his head against Matt's shoulder. It made Matt remember the few nights so far they'd spent in each other's arms. For someone like Matt, who'd rarely spent the night with any of his previous lovers, it felt strange to want this so much.

He wished they were back at his place, if only for the fact that there would be no question as to where they'd spend the night. No bed with sad memories or ghosts. No wife. Matt sighed. He let himself just enjoy the moment a while longer, without complicating things by thinking too hard. Evan felt good and warm and solid in his arms, the sex they just had was, well fuck, it just kept getting better—and God help his central nervous system when Evan got back to 100 percent—and later he would talk to Liz and she would help him negotiate the minefield that was his brain right now. He closed his eyes and listened to Evan breathe, pretended that when they were both awake and alert, things would be this peaceful.

His telephone call to Liz took all of about ten minutes. He knew that the words were casual and friendly, but he was also sure his tone belied the true reason for his call.

"Come on over," she said sweetly. "I'll make you lunch, we'll talk."

"Should I bring my checkbook?"

"Don't be ridiculous. I take VISA."

He laughed, she laughed. They decided on one.

When he finished the call, he turned to find Evan awake on the sofa, watching him with curious eyes. He'd pulled his clothes on at some point and lay wrapped in the quilt.

"Liz Friedman?"

"Yeah."

"The one that got away?" He smiled when he said it.

"Hmmm...something like that. Kind of. Nothing ever happened but there was this...thing between us..."

"She's married now."

"Yeah—three kids."

"Should I be jealous?"

"Only if you're a moron." He stood over Evan, hands on hips, looking serious.

"I should go upstairs and take a shower... Wanna come?"

Evan pretended to be thinking, "So soon? Shouldn't I get a snack or something? Some recovery time?"

Matt groaned. "God, that was just awful. Was it the sex or the pain pills that made you such a goof this morning?"

"You did sort of rattle my brain a bit."

"Oh fine. Come upstairs, you idiot—I'll give you a sponge bath."

"This is starting to sound like a porn movie."

"Shut up."

Matt helped Evan off the couch, led him upstairs.

Evan faltered a tiny bit when they walked through the bedroom but Matt didn't let him stop to torture himself. Or Matt. He pulled him into the bathroom and shut the door.

"Sit down, take your shirt off," Matt said, and Evan would have thought this was just a medical necessity except Matt started stripping himself, in a few seconds standing naked in the small bathroom. The look he gave Evan as he turned on the shower was frank and hungry, like they hadn't just been humping each other like crazed animals on the couch a mere hour before.

Evan shivered. It seemed too bright in the room, the overhead light illuminating the broad and powerful shape of Matt's body.

Evan's skin started to twitch, like a thousand ants were racing under the surface.

He pulled his shirt off, then stood up to pull down his shorts but Matt beat him to it. He dropped to his knees, nuzzling Evan for a moment through the fabric, nipping and then biting harder at the growing evidence that Matt wasn't the only one with an amazing recovery period.

"God, God...yes..." Evan murmured. This wasn't right. He couldn't be this out of control already, but he was and it felt like pure heaven as Matt slid his hands under the waistband of the shorts and tugged them down.

He heard Matt say something and shook his head to stop the buzzing that filled his ears. "What?"

"What do you want me to do?" Matt whispered and Evan began to shake in earnest.

"God...uh," he lost his train of thought when the gentle feeling of Matt's cheek against his dick started again, this time skin against skin. Jesus.

"Your...your mouth..." Evan finally got out. "Please...oh yes..."

There it was again, that beautiful wet sensation of Matt's mouth, the tender movement of his tongue...his hands. God, they smoothed along the backs of his thighs, then upward to stroke his ass, to grip it tightly...

The top of Evan's skull threatened to explode at any moment. He gently slipped his fingers into Matt's dark hair, stroking his skull with caressing movements, moving along with the rhythm that Matt had set. *God, God, yes.* The chant repeated over and over in his mind but his voice had been reduced to a series of moans and gentle cries of pleasure.

He felt Matt's hands move again, suddenly stroking...stroking between, touching him...wait, touching him there....a teasing finger... No, no, he wanted to stop it because this...that was too far, too much...but protesting was impossible because speech was impossible and Matt's probing finger was teasing him gently and the wet hot heat surrounding his dick was getting tighter and tighter and moving faster and suddenly Evan just grayed out, clutching Matt's head and the nearby sink frantically as he exploded in long deep spurts, crying out inarticulately.

"Beautiful," he heard Matt mutter, feeling soft kisses along his thighs and stomach. "So beautiful...can't get enough..."

Evan's heart lurched. He took a breath and pulled Matt up, pulling him close, letting his hands stroke his burning skin from his neck, down his back...and when his hands hit the curve of his ass, he faltered for a moment, but then continued on, tightening his hold.

Matt was making small sounds into the crook of Evan's neck, shivers racing up and down his arms. When Evan squeezed his ass he gasped and groaned, rubbing his erection against Evan's body.

"Get in the shower," Evan whispered. "I'll make you feel good."

"Christ—better than this? You feel incredible." Matt's voice was raspy. "I...I missed you so much...missed feeling you like this..."

"Come on," Evan pushed Matt backward toward the shower, feeling bold and frightened at the same time. He opened the shower curtain, urging Matt inside, then reached up to adjust the spray so it only hit the front half of the tub. He climbed in behind Matt, mindful of his bandage.

Matt tried to turn around but Evan wouldn't let him. He ran his hands gently down Matt's back, the same path as before, no hesitation as his slipped down to stroke his ass. The groan that echoed through the bathroom assured him Matt was enjoying himself.

There was no way his nearly forty-year-old self was going to get it up anytime soon—Matt had, rather efficiently, gotten Evan's best performance in a long time—so he just enjoyed the feel and sound and smell of Matt.

Evan leaned forward, pressing his lips against Matt's back, running his tongue down the bumpy ridges of his spine. Matt's whole body stilled, then he moaned and pushed back, wordlessly begging for more. Feeling emboldened, Evan pressed against Matt's back, taking a bite of wet skin at the back of his neck.

"Fuck me," Matt whispered, and a bolt of fear knocked the lust right out of Evan's heart. No, he wasn't...couldn't...

"God, just touch me, please," he continued, unaware of his lover's reaction. "I need your hand...something...please..."

Evan snapped back into the moment and reached around blindly, sliding his hand from base to head in one smooth glide.

Remembering Matt's reaction, he bit down harder on the top of his spine and was rewarded with something resembling a sob from Matt's mouth. He moved his hand faster, tightening his grip until Matt began to thrash wildly, and Evan felt the moment he went over the edge, felt his orgasm in his palm.

They stood there until the water ran cool and Matt sighed, reached down to adjust the temperature.

He turned, smiling. "You're right; this is turning into a porno."

Evan laughed, leaning against the back of the shower. "Where's my sponge bath?"

"Hang on." Matt looked around for a washcloth, soaping it up.

"I'm going to do this clinically 'cause frankly, I'm not up for more sexual high jinks."

"High jinks? How old are you?"

"Shut up."

* * *

"Hi, Daddy!"

"Hi, Elizabeth, honey. How are you, sweetheart?"

"I'm fine. We miss you, Daddy. So much. When can we come home?"

"Soon, honey, I swear."

"Daddy!"

"Hey, Danny. How are you son?"

"Fine. It's boring here. Can we come home now?"

"In a few days, I promise."

"Hey, Daddy! Are you okay? Do you feel any better?"

"Yeah, Kathleen, I'm better. I miss you."

"We're coming home soon right? Next week?"

"Definitely."

"Daddy?"

"Miranda? How are you doing, honey?

"Um...it's fine, Daddy. How are you feeling? What did the doctor say?"

"Everything looks good. I'm coming to pick you up as soon as I can. Maybe this weekend."

"Is Matt still there?"

"Yeah, honey."

"Good—I'm glad you're not alone."

They talked a few more minutes—all the same thing: We miss you. We want to come home. We love you.

He hung up the phone, staring at it for a long moment. *I love you too, babies. And no one is going to take you away from me. Ever.* He listened to Matt puttering around upstairs, getting dressed for his visit with Liz. He felt something in his chest tighten and twist, hurting him worse than that exploding door.

Matt dressed in the upstairs bathroom, his hands a little shaky as he buttoned his shirt.

There were a shitload of butterflies doing battle in his gut right now—some left over from the brain-melting sex he just had on the sofa and in the shower, and some from anticipating explaining the circumstances of said brain-melting sex to Liz Friedman.

God, he couldn't wait to see Liz. Never in his life had he known such a desperate need to spill his guts to another human being.

Matt jogged down the stairs. Evan was sitting on the couch, staring out the picture window. He turned his head slowly toward Matt. Nervous smiles all around.

"Hey. I'm off."

"Have a great time. Say hi to Liz."

"Will do. How're the kids?"

Evan swallowed. "Bored, homesick."

"When do you want to bring them home?" Matt asked, pulling on his jacket. "I was thinking this weekend maybe."

Home. Evan blinked suddenly, listening to Matt use that word so casually. Was he talking about their home? His and Evan's? Were they now "their" children?

"Sounds like a good idea," he said absently.

"Evan?"

"Yeah?"

"You okay?"

"Yeah—sorry. I think you wore me out. I need a nap." Evan managed to deflect the awkward moment with a tender smile and an easy joke.

The little flush that crept across Matt's face did something to Evan's heart. Oh God.

"Well...you rest. Get some sleep—I won't be gone long. We'll do something nice for dinner." Matt walked over to the couch and leaned down.

There was a long moment where both men held their breath, then Evan closed his eyes and let Matt press their mouths together.

The kiss was chaste compared to what had gone on earlier that morning, but it didn't matter.

Matt broke the kiss, ran a hand over Evan's head in an affection gesture.

"See you later."

"Yeah."

Matt grabbed his keys and walked out the door, with a small backward wave before he disappeared from view.

Evan held his breath until the wounds on his chest began to ache. He felt hot and cold and tearful and fucking furious. He shook with a thousand emotions, a thousand conflicting thoughts. He wanted his kids. He wanted Matt. He wanted to go back to work. And he wanted…wanted…no. No.

Suddenly the rush disappeared and Evan was left panting and sweating. He laid weakly down on the sofa, pulling the blanket over his head. No. No. No.

A few hours later, Evan woke. He felt chilled, dirty almost.

He'd already washed up once this morning, after…Matt and he…

Abruptly, Evan got up, shaky and dizzy already but the fast movement just made it worse. He was going to go upstairs, shower, then try and get some things done. Maybe call Helena, do some Christmas planning. Something.

* * *

In blue jeans and a denim shirt, Liz met Matt at the door of her home, looking like an ad for long-distance or tissues or something really wholesome like that. The house sat on a perfectly rectangular lawn, with trees angled perfectly on either side. Perfect. Matt couldn't name the style, but it looked like a giant cottage. A cottage on steroids. He wrinkled his nose when he caught a glance of the SUV in the driveway.

"Jesus, Liz—is that mandatory or something?"

She flashed him that wide gorgeous smile that still made his heart pitter-patter a bit faster.

"I'm feeding you lunch and shrinking your head for free. Be nice."

Matt laughed. He reached the top of the stairs and looked down at Liz, giving her a mock once-over.

"You still look normal. I don't see any pearls."

Liz reached out and gave him a huge hug. "Hey, Haight—it's really good to see you."

"You have no idea how glad I am to see you, Dr. Friedman." Matt sighed a little as he felt her arms tight around him. It didn't trip his switch like it used to, but it felt nice just the same.

Breaking the embrace but keeping her arms around his, Liz looked up, giving his face a long hard look. "You okay, Haight?"

Matt smiled tightly. "I'll be fine. Let's go in—you don't have a coat on."

Liz frowned, obviously concerned, but she didn't protest.

Matt took off his coat and hung it on the rack near the door. He looked around, finding a warm, lived-in decor—books and toys dominated every corner. It looked smart and cozy—kind of like Liz. She led him into the family room, where a fire burned brightly. More books, more toys.

And two dark-haired five-year-old boys coloring furiously at a small table.

"Jeremy, Alex—this is my friend, Matt Haight."

Identical faces turned and gave Matt the quick once-over. The twin on the left gave him a small smile. The one on the right obviously couldn't care less and he quickly bent his head back down to the paper.

"Hi," said Left Twin.

"Hi," Matt replied. "Whatcha doing?"

"Coloring. Dinosaurs."

Matt nodded. Left Twin nodded. Coloring commenced.

Matt gave Liz a look and she smiled. "Let's go into the kitchen."

They walked down a small hallway into a huge kitchen, complete with one of those island things in the middle. There were windows on three walls and about a thousand pots on a rack above the island. Something smelled terrific.

"Hey—nice."

"Thanks." She motioned toward a rough wood table that looked like it seated thirty. Two places were set and Liz was approaching with a coffeepot.

"Beautiful."

"Me or the coffee?"

Matt threw her a wink as he dumped some sugar into his coffee.

"Both?"

After taking a long swallow, Matt turned in his chair to watch Liz at the stove, doing something with spices and a wooden spoon to a pot of stew.

"The boys look good."

"They're doing so much better. It's amazing."

Three years before, Liz and her husband Ray were expecting their first child and Liz was pretty much just working in private practice, occasionally doing some consulting for the PD and Children's Services.

Everyone knew what a compassionate champion of children she was—so when the twin two-year-old boys were taken from their drug addicted mother, a coworker at CS called Liz. She thought they needed representation, someone to be their champion, before they were separated or ended up in a home. Ray, a lawyer, took the case pro bono.

Liz testified as to what was in their best interest. The judge severed the mother's rights but that left two biracial identical twin boys with a host of already diagnosed and potential disabilities without a home. For about a week.

Ray and Liz adopted the boys and suddenly had a much bigger family than they had anticipated—their son Peter was born during the whole saga.

Matt had kept in close touch with Liz during this trying period—he knew she was doing ten times what she had time for because that was her way—and frequently called to insist she take care of herself. He knew she appreciated it, even if she did ignore him most of the time.

"Are they in school?"

"Two days a week—a special school for kid's with emotional problems. But their teachers think they may be mainstreamed as early as second grade." Liz fairly beamed. "I've gotten lucky with finding teachers and therapists who support the way we're handling the boys' problems."

Liz brought a covered dish to the table—Matt smelled warm bread—and smiled down at Matt. "They liked you."

"Really?"

"Yeah." She walked over to the stove again. "So, Haight..."

"So where's Ray and Peter?" Matt quickly asked, not quite ready to get to the heart of the matter.

"Ray took the day off to do some Christmas shopping for the boys. Peter's taking his nap upstairs." She gestured toward a baby monitor, sitting quietly on the counter. "The boys already ate—I thought we could have a little quiet grown-up time."

Matt nodded absently. Reached for his cup of coffee. He didn't know where to start, how to explain what was going on with his life to Liz. The first words were absolutely the hardest in this case. Liz brought the pot over and set it down, ladling up their meals quickly. She sat across from Matt and propped her head on firmly planted elbows.

"Spill."

"The stew looks great."

"Haight."

"I want to eat…"

"It's too hot; you'll burn your tongue. Tell me."

"You're very pushy for a shrink, Liz. Aren't you supposed to be gently leading me into the conversation?"

"Liz your friend wants you to start talking. Liz the shrink will show up when and if it's needed."

Matt sighed long and hard. He looked longingly at the stew, wishing he could chew rather than talk. He took a deep breath and said, "I've fallen in love with someone."

She didn't say anything, and he knew she was waiting for the second half of the announcement which was hovering heavily over the table.

"A man."

He managed to say the words, his voice suddenly thick. Liz, bless her dear heart, didn't blink or stutter or react in any other way but to reach out, take Matt's hand, and squeeze.

"Congratulations, Matt. He's a lucky person."

Things got very blurry for a long time.

212 of Tere Michaels

* * *

Managing to mostly ignore the bed—rumpled, the pillows bunched together in the middle...they probably smelled like Matt too—Evan grabbed some clothes and went into the bathroom. He awkwardly gave himself a sponge bath, avoiding the bandage on his chest, which was nowhere near as fun as the one he got from Matt that morning.

Matt.

He wished he could finish a thought about Matt and what went on between them without feeling slightly horrified...like he wanted it, desperately, passionately, and while it was going on...God, there wasn't anything he could imagine feeling that good but then...then there was this heavy veil that dropped over his head when it was all over. It scared the hell out of him, feeling this out of control. With a man. A man he craved and wanted with all his heart, and that was terrifying. And maybe deep down he was afraid it was wrong. Wrong for a man who had been married for seventeen years, wrong for a father. Wrong for him. Damn, he was tired of this.

He put on a pair of sweats and his robe and headed slowly back downstairs. He couldn't seem to get warm. Maybe some tea would help...

He heard the doorbell ring.

* * *

"Evan!"

Susannah Post stood on Evan's front stoop in a bright pink ski jacket, a foil-wrapped Bundt shape proffered.

"Hi, Susannah." Evan pulled his robe a little bit tighter. Even though he wore a sweat suit underneath, he felt a bit exposed to the perky blonde's brilliant smile.

"How are you feeling? We heard about your dreadful...accident," her voice lilting a bit at the end, as if she wasn't quite sure if that was the proper word. "I'm so glad to see you up and around!"

"Thanks. And uh...thanks for the..." he motioned toward the foil mass in her hands.

"Bundt cake!" she trilled. "Chocolate cream cheese. I hope you like it."

"I'm sure I will. Would you...like to come in?" He prayed the answer would be no, but he didn't appear to have that sort of luck these days.

"Oh, just for a sec! I have to pick Tyler and Jordan up at tumbling in a few."

Evan opened the door, letting Susannah and a gust of cold air into the foyer. Susannah shivered theatrically and Evan took the cake, instead of asking for her coat because he was afraid "a few" meant an hour.

Susannah followed him into the kitchen where he deposited the cake on the island.

"Sooo—when are the kids coming back?"

"Probably Saturday."

"Oh, you must be so relieved."

"Yes."

Susannah did her "poor, poor Evan" face which curdled his blood.

"It's been a hell of a year for you folks hasn't it?"

"Uh-huh." He looked at the floor, trying to seem more distressed than annoyed.

"At least you've had a bit of help. So tell me, who's your friend?"

The very air Evan was breathing froze in his lungs. He tried not make any sort of suspicious sound.

"Friend?" He got out, perfect in tone and inflection.

"Um—that handsome fellow with the dark hair who's been over here for the past week." Her perfect blonde eyebrows disappeared under her poufy bangs. "Is he a relative?"

The lie slid from his mouth so easily it horrified him as much as it made him feel safe.

"We went to college together. He's been a friend for years."

"Hmm…really? I don't recall seeing him around before."

"He just moved back into the area."

"Ah."

Silence dangled around them for several long moments. Susannah never stopped smiling. She suddenly looked at the kitchen clock and made a squealing sound. Evan winced.

"Gotta get the kids!" She fluttered her hand in a waving gesture and headed for the front door. "Enjoy the cake! There should be plenty for you and your friend!"

And with that, Susannah was gone, in a cloud of fruity perfume.

Evan trembled. His legs gave out and he sat down hard on one of the kitchen stools.

Shit.

Chapter Eleven

Matt and Liz sat silently for a few long minutes—a pot boiled on the stove, the clock ticked, and a slow static sound came from the baby monitor.

Breathing deeply, Matt felt some tension bleeding out of his skin. The words were still frightening but their power has lessened. Every time he confirmed and confessed his love for Evan, the rightness of it was reinforced. It didn't feel alien anymore to love this man, to imagine being with a man.

When he could trust his voice Matt went on. He found himself spilling out the familiar rap—a cop, his first time with a man, both of their first times, the fear and the confusion.

"He's a widower. With kids. That's why things are so difficult. Complicated."

Liz's forehead developed a tiny wrinkle. "But he returns your feelings..."

"Yeah. He...says he loves me too. And sometimes, things are just great. We're good friends; we can talk and laugh. And the rest..." He blushed, embarrassed. "That works pretty good too. But...but Liz, he's got a career. And just...a lot still going on in his head..."

"Has he been a widower for long, Matt?"

"Little more than a year." Matt squeezed Liz's hand a little tighter.

He didn't like to think about Sherri's death and he hated to think about Evan's grief.

The wrinkle got a bit deeper. "Matt, you don't have to answer my question, but might I know this person?"

Matt sighed. "Yeah, Liz. You know him. Evan Cerelli from Vice."

"Wow." She took a moment, and he could almost see the wheels turning in her head. "Is there something specific in this relationship that you're having trouble with?"

"You mean besides the fact that it's with a man?" He asked sarcastically. "Do I need another reason to be freaking out?"

"Come on, Matt. The first thing you said to me was that you were in love. Then you mentioned he was a man. So what scares you most?"

Matt wondered why he even bothered to try the dense act around Liz. He really could not bullshit this woman. He never could. "At first it was the fact that he was a guy but that kind of, I don't know, faded into the background. Now, you know, it sometimes pops up at me but most of the time...I just want to be with him, I want this to work out."

Matt mulled this over for a moment. In truth, as much as it frightened him in the beginning, now it just felt like something he worried about for Evan's sake.

He told this to Liz, and she nodded. For a second he watched her struggle with something then she asked, "Matt, can we talk about you specifically? How you're doing with this?"

"I thought we were."

"No, we've mostly gone over how Evan feels, and how this might affect him and his career. But what about you? What do you want out of this?"

Matt opened his mouth then shut it quickly. His brain tried to give a quick answer but nothing came out.

What did he want? He wanted...love. A relationship. With Evan. He wanted to be around the kids, do things together...as a family? He felt himself get very still, and suddenly he couldn't look anywhere but at the shiny pockmarked surface of Liz's wood table.

* * *

After Susannah left, Evan just sat at the kitchen counter, watching dust motes in the frail streaks of sun. He felt numb. The lie he'd told about Matt hovered in the air. He could almost see it, feel the betrayal.

I was just protecting my kids, he thought desperately. *I'm a father first. I have to remember that.*

What if it got out?

What if the neighbors heard he was...sleeping with Matt? What if the children found out? He tried to picture himself sitting the kids down, talking to them about their relationship. Shaking a little, Evan put his hands up to his head, as if to stop the tremors. He couldn't even fathom their reactions. Couldn't imagine what they would say, how they would feel. They might be ridiculed, ostracized.

It terrified him.

And suddenly, a wave of panic swamped over him. He saw spots explode in front of his eyes...

What if they rejected him?

A cold chill made his bones ache. For a moment, his breath froze up in his lungs; he fought off the panic and forced himself to exhale. His children...what if this drove them away?

The phone rang.

He jumped, nearly slid off the stool.

With a trembling hand, he reached for the portable on the counter.

"Hello?"

"Hi, Daddy!" It was Miranda.

Rattled, Evan tried to get a grip. "Hi, baby. How are you?"

"Fine. We're all fine. Are you okay? Your voice sounds funny..."

Evan took a deep breath, concentrating on keeping it together. "I just woke up from a nap, sweetie—it's nothing."

"Oh, okay. I just wanted to know if you were feeling better, if we could come home this weekend." He heard the tremor in her voice as the words rushed out and he knew she was trying to sound grown-up. But he knew his oldest girl—he knew how homesick she was.

"Actually, honey, I'm feeling much better. I think this weekend would be perfect for you kids to come home. We can go out and get a tree."

"Yeah! The kids are going to be really happy. They can't wait to come home."

Evan had to smile at that.

"Well, I can understand that. You know how little kids are." Miranda gave a nervous little giggle.

"I'll come and get you guys on Friday. I'll be there early— we'll go out for dinner."

"Cool!"

"Put your grandmother on okay?" Evan hated saying the words but he needed to make nice with his in-laws.

"She's not here. She's at church."

Evan held his tongue.

"Who's there with you?"

"Grampa."

"Let me talk to him, honey."

"'Kay, Daddy. See you Friday."

Evan felt his heart expand and contract suddenly. He loved his kids so much, so much. He couldn't bear to hurt them, and he refused to let more time pass when they weren't all together.

"Yeah?" A voice, gruff and edgy, barked in his ear.

"Phil? It's Evan."

"What did you want?"

Evan's eyes narrowed. The slight slur in Phil's voice was familiar to a cop—he'd been drinking and probably for quite some time.

"I just wanted to let you and Josie know I'm picking the children up tomorrow." He kept his own voice calm and rational.

"'Scuse me? I thought they were staying here till Christmas."

"I never said that."

"That's what Josie said." Phil's voice got louder.

Evan reigned in his growing anger. "Josie was mistaken. I'm feeling much better, and the kids want to be home."

"They are *fine* here, just fucking fine. This is a good home..."

"Phil!"

"Good enough for my girls..."

"*Phil!*" Evan lost it and let his fury fly across the line. The thought of this man, drunk in the middle of the afternoon, taking care of his kids, took all his self-control away. "Calm down!"

"Calm down? Listen, you asshole, my girls grew up here...my good girls...my Sherri grew up here and it was a perfectly..."

"*Phil*, I am picking my kids up tomorrow."

"Fuck you."

"What is your fucking problem, Phil?"

"My problem!? My fucking problem is that you took my girl away from her perfectly fine home and you let her die!"

All sound died, on both sides of the line. Evan felt his breath freeze in his throat; Phil's words were vibrating in his ears.

Phil let out a long sigh.

"Fuck you," he said softly. "Fuck you."

"I will be there," Evan managed to choke out, "tomorrow. After school. I want the kids packed up and ready to go."

"Yeah, take them away from us too. You gonna watch out for them? You gonna make sure they don't get smashed up?"

"Make sure they're ready when I get there." Evan turned the phone off with a jerk of his shaking fingers, barely able to hold onto the cordless. For one moment he stared at it in his hand, unable to process that the conversation with Phil had actually happened.

It was almost like looking down at himself; he watched his hand rear back, watched the phone go sailing across the room, hit the wall. Motherfucker.

They thought he was a murderer. They hated him.

Suddenly the shock drained away and the fury came back in a rush. The wounds on his chest felt freshly ripped open and he checked to make sure he wasn't bleeding to death, it hurt that badly. Vaguely he heard a car pull into his driveway and felt his body tense up. Matt was...home.

Matt. Oh Christ. If they knew...if they knew... They already hated him, already blamed him for Sherri... He didn't want Matt here right now. He didn't want to look into Matt's loving, concerned eyes and feel comforted. He didn't want to fall down under that strong body and let himself be obliterated by lust, erasing all his well-earned guilt.

Evan just couldn't handle being reminded how much he loved Matt at this moment. Did he really need another moment to acknowledge that his wife was dead, that he had let her die and now he spent his nights in the arms of...a man. He couldn't possibly imagine how this was going to work out. The day might come...would come...when someone would ask for a decision.

Matt or his kids and his memories...

Shaky, tired, Evan walked over to the door and stood, staring quietly. He wasn't sure what he was going to say.

* * *

Matt pulled into the driveway of Evan's house at seven o'clock. Traffic had been a bitch—although nothing compared to his stopover at Toys R Us. Jesus. He had always imagined that's what Armageddon would look like. At least he'd been able to fight his way through the teaming masses of angry commuters whose last nerve had been stomped on hours before.

In the truck and backseat were bags and bags of gifts for the Cerelli kids. He'd bribed a harried salesperson—with fifty bucks—to lead him around and suggest age-appropriate gifts. Miranda was the hardest—he couldn't find much that would appeal to a bright, seventeen going on thirty-year-old—but fortunately the young man who was his guide mentioned a clothing store in the shopping complex that targeted the hip crowd...and couldn't possibly make a mistake by telling a teenager, "Here's a gift certificate—free money—go shopping."

Matt went heavy on the electronics—he figured he couldn't go wrong with things that needed batteries. Handheld games, radio-controlled cars, and the centerpiece of his gift-giving efforts—a Wii—filled the cart. His clerk gave him a supportive thumbs-up. He guaranteed the kids would go nuts. Add to that a bunch of games, software for the computer, and he'd moved on.

The dolls were next—he remembered seeing lots of Barbie stuff in Elizabeth's room so he spent some time in that section as well. Now Elizabeth's blonde friend owned her own plane, a show horse, and a speedboat. Matt was amazed at how expensive this shit was—he might as well buy the kid a *real* horse. He whizzed through games—did kids still play board games?—and threw a few in the cart.

Candy was last. Lots and lots of candy. Fuck the dentist, Matt thought gleefully. He then gave himself a little talking to about setting a good example for the goods and decided on a compromise—candy till they barfed *then* they had to brush. *Matthew Haight, role model,* he thought, smirking.

Getting out of the car, Matt pulled out as many bags as he could carry in one trip. He whistled, thinking of how much the kids were going to love the gifts, thinking of how much he wanted to spend tonight wrapped around Evan.

He'd never had much use for the holidays; after his father died, hanging around his mother and watching her drink scotch for five hours wasn't his idea of holiday cheer. Once he left home, he seldom returned, other to drop off a check and a dry peck on his mother's cheek. He'd spend the holidays with buddies' families, or whatever woman he was in good standing with come the end of December.

At the door, he juggled his packages to knock; he worried that he would be waking Evan up—but he saw the lights on in the living room and hoped. He didn't have a chance, the door swung open and Evan stood framed in the doorway.

"Hey," Matt said happily, extending his bundles. "I did a little shopping."

Evan did a little double take at the piles of bags at Matt's feet. "No kidding."

Matt found himself grinning widely, staring at Evan's face as he took in all the packages. He licked his lips a bit...

"You gonna let me in or are the neighbors about to get a free show?" Matt joked, giving a pointed eyebrow raise in Evan's direction. His smile vanished as he watched Evan's face go slack. "What?"

"Nothing. Come in," Evan said quickly, moving aside so Matt could enter.

He dropped his bags on the couch and shrugged off his jacket, keeping his head turned away from Evan. Matt felt his nerves suddenly on edge; something felt weird.

"Everything okay today?"

"Yeah," Evan said absently, walking into the kitchen. "You want something to drink?"

"Sure." Matt waited a second, watching as Evan woodenly pulled two glasses from the cabinet. "What did you do?"

Evan's movements stopped for a moment, then resumed. "Slept, talked to the kids. I'm picking them up tomorrow."

"Great!" Matt said, genuinely enthused. "What time do you want to get out there?"

"I can—"

"No, actually, you can't. You're not allowed to drive for another two weeks."

Evan's mouth went into a tight line. He went to the fridge and pulled out a pitcher. Matt couldn't help but notice the stiff way Evan was holding himself.

"Hey—you all right? Have you taken your pills?"

"I'm fine," he said shortly.

A bit taken aback by his tone, Matt just nodded. He watched Evan pour them both a glass of iced tea, pushing Matt's over to where he sat.

"Thanks."

As he returned the pitcher to the refrigerator, Evan made a sound that could have been "you're welcome"—but Matt couldn't tell. He quietly sipped his iced tea...waiting... watching. Evan's eyes were darting all over the kitchen, anywhere but near where Matt sat. He wiped his damp hands repeatedly on his pants; Matt took a hard look at his lover, realizing that he looked disheveled and pale, like he had broken a sweat.

He sighed inwardly. Something was definitely up.

"Liz says hello, by the way."

Evan's head snapped up.

"What?"

"Liz...she sends her best. She was sorry to hear about you getting shot."

"She knows about...me?"

"What are you talking about?"

"You told her my name."

Matt saw immediately where this conversation was going and went from concerned to pissed off in five seconds flat.

"Why is that a problem?"

Evan looked at Matt, obviously stunned he'd have to ask. "Because she knows people I work with."

"Helena and Vic both know—"

"Yeah, but not everyone else! There are a lot of people at my precinct...and the DA's office. What if she says something..." Evan's voice escalated with each new concern.

"Whoa, wait a second. Calm down. This is Liz Friedman we're talking about. Aside from the fact that she's a shrink, she's one of my closest friends. She would *never* say a word about this; she wouldn't betray my confidence that way." Matt stood up and moved toward Evan, his hands making calming motions in the air even as his anger grew. "What is wrong here? A few days ago we were telling Helena and you were fine. A few fucking hours ago, we were making love. Now you're acting like this is some dirty little secret!" he shouted.

The room went silent.

Evan's hands stopped moving, clenching into fists which he plunged into his robe pockets. He slowly raised his face to meet Matt's gaze.

Matt blinked. "What the hell happened? When I left here…"

"I did a lot of thinking today, Matt—I had to spend a little time alone." Evan's voice was a nearly monotone calm, each logical thought flowing smoothly from his mouth. "I thought about my kids, I thought about my career. This can't…"

"*This?* What is *this,* Evan?"

Evan faltered for a moment. Matt watched him swallow, watched his eyes dart around the room. "This is something that neither one of us is prepared for. It's happened too fast, Matt. Way too fast."

He heard the words and understood what each one meant, but for the life of him, Matt couldn't comprehend this conversation. He'd left a lover behind this morning, shy but committed, and now this cool stranger with the wild eyes was giving him a speech that spelled the end of everything.

"What the hell happened?" His voice was low, barely registering in his own ears. "Who did you talk to? What happened?"

And he knew, from the way Evan's face just convulsed with a nanosecond of panic that someone had terrified his lover, had frightened him back into himself.

"My…my kids need me, Matt. They haven't gotten over Sherri's death and frankly, I don't know that I have either. You were there when I needed you and I'm grateful. I swear to God I'm grateful, but…" He shook his head sadly, for the first time in this whole conversation looking "real" to Matt's eyes.

"But I don't think I can do this."

The bottom dropped out for Matt.

"You need time?" Matt hated, *hated* the way his voice sounded.

Needy, desperate.

Evan's eyes were glued to the floor. "I don't…I just don't think I'm ever going to get past it, Matt."

Surreal. So fucking surreal he almost expected to wake up on the couch, having dreamed this entire day.

"This is ridiculous. Absolute fucking insanity."

"Matt…"

"Don't. Not a word. You stand there and tell me that it's over because you *thought* about things this afternoon while I was gone. What—six hours? Six hours for you to figure this all out? Six hours for you to decide that everything that's gone on between us isn't real?"

Evan refused to look at him.

"I'm going to ask you one more time, Evan. One more goddamn time. What the hell happened today?"

The long silence that enveloped the room was broken only by Matt's ragged breaths and the everyday sounds of the Cerellis' neighborhood, filtering in through cracks in the windowpanes. "I thought about everything," Evan whispered. "I thought about where this was going and I couldn't see a future, Matt. I'm sorry."

And that was it. Matt was so used to being in this place, in this sad, bitter place, that he nodded automatically. "I'll get my things, I'll leave tonight…"

Evan's head made the tiniest shaking movement. "Stay tonight...on the couch."

"How are you going to get the kids?"

"I can dr—"

"*No*, you can't." Matt winced at his harshness.

"I'll call Vic."

"Fine. Fine."

The quiet grew and grew. Matt couldn't hear anything but the pounding of his heart. What happened? What happened? It kept repeating in his head. What the hell happened? He felt like an idiot. After the talk with Liz, everything was so clear. Now it was even clearer. Perfectly. He had ended up exactly where he always did. Nothing had changed. Haight luck.

He heard a noise and realized Evan was speaking. "What?"

"I said I'm going upstairs to bed."

Matt nodded absently. He was about to remind Evan about dinner, about his pills, about his dressings but he savagely bit down any words of concern. He felt childish and embarrassed and furious. He didn't care if he wasn't playing nice.

"Night." He nearly missed the whisper as Evan walked by. He listened to the sounds of his footsteps until they were gone.

* * *

Evan walked around upstairs, going into each of the children's bedrooms to gently touch their belongings, their clothes. Every nerve was deadened, he could barely feel himself moving.

Everything that had come out of his mouth downstairs had been automatic, as if some small part of his brain had just started to supply him with a way out. A brutal way out. He hadn't been able to look into Matt's face but he heard the devastation, felt it eating away at Matt's heart.

He felt like a murderer for the second time today.

Moving out of the girls' room and into his own, Evan stripped out of his robe and sweats. He felt dirty, like the guilt was clinging to his skin. The bathroom was another reminder of what he had accomplished—hours earlier he and Matt had been here in this room, together in a way he'd never imagined and now...now he was a monster trying to get clean, trying to scrub away the blood.

"I'm not good at this," he whispered to the showerhead. "I'm not good at taking care of the people I love. But I won't let my kids down. I swear I won't."

A few minutes later he was dry and in another pair of sweats, climbing into his bed; he never even put on the light. That icy terror that had kept him from this room was back, teasing him from the edges of the shadows. He knew that even the light wouldn't make them go away, he knew that they lived inside him and would never leave.

Matt woke with a start—at some point he'd dozed off in front of the fireplace. Nothing was left but a few embers, a small orange glow in the center. Stiff from the cool floor, he pulled himself upright and stretched. Damn. He was definitely too old for this. Standing, he twisted and turned until the kinks worked themselves out. In the darkened room, he realized all his things were upstairs. And so was Evan, who apparently wasn't interested in seeing Matt anytime soon.

Well fuck me, Matt thought morosely. *This is pretty much exactly where I usually am. Frozen out.* For a split second he thought about grabbing his jacket and heading back to Staten Island but it was so brief he was already unbuttoning his shirt when he said "no, I'm not leaving" aloud. Sighing, he pulled his jeans off. A T-shirt and boxers would have to do. There was a blanket on the back of the couch—which should be enough.

Matt went into the kitchen, poured himself a glass of water from the pitcher in the fridge. The clock on the wall read 2:00 a.m. He heard a floorboard creak above him. He froze. He listened for another sound but there was nothing more.

With a heavy exhale, Matt walked back to the couch and settled down, pulling the blanket over his body. The unbidden thought came—Evan had slept here the night before, curled up under this quilt.

Matt bleakly thought that this was it. The end of the road. The creak came back. This time it didn't stop and suddenly Matt heard Evan coming down the stairs. He didn't turn around. With a cop's ear, he listened as Evan padded quietly to the couch. He still didn't turn. He couldn't. He was tired of making all the moves, all the overtures, and ending up with a kick in the gut in return.

Matt listened as the clock ticked each second by; he stopped counting at one hundred.

Evan stood over Matt, knowing he was awake, not comprehending why the hell he was standing there. At some point he'd drifted off but awoke in a blind panic, reaching desperately across the sheets as he'd done before. But this time...this time he wasn't reaching for Sherri.

His weakness made him angry. And weary.

With a shaky hand he reached out to touch Matt's shoulder. Ice. Tension. Disappointment. He could feel it all. *I'm a terrible person*, he thought, *I can't believe I've done this to him.* He turned the touch into a caress, unable and unwilling to stop. He knew that in the morning his speech would be the same, but right now...right now he wanted to say he was sorry and apologize for being a murderer and a bastard... He wanted things to be different, but there was nothing he could do.

"If this is a pity fuck, you can stop." The voice was low and furious, and it stopped Evan's explorations.

"It's not."

Matt sat up suddenly, facing Evan across the back of the sofa. "Then what the hell is it?"

"I...I just wanted..." Evan sighed deeply. His head ached. He just wanted to lie down.

With Matt.

"I know you're pissed off at me, Matt. And you have every right to be. I'm sorry I hurt you but...I just don't know how to do this. It's not going to work..."

"We can figure this out," Matt blurted out. "We can find a way..."

Evan shook his head. "I don't think..."

"Trust me." Evan heard the desperation. It just about killed him.

"Matt..."

"Please."

He opened his mouth to argue but nothing came out. Without thinking about the consequences, he moved to the other side of the couch, pushing Matt down flat in one swift move.

"Evan." It was a warning and a question and Evan ignored it. He pretended that the conversation in the kitchen never happened, that Phil hadn't reminded him of being a murderer, that Suzannah hadn't made him a liar. He pretended that this was still something new and beautiful.

He pressed his body down against Matt's, soaking up the heat, and the sounds of sad moans—because Matt wasn't stupid, he knew. He knew Evan too well to be able to pretend.

They knew one another too well.

Matt reached up and pulled Evan's face down to his; these kisses were like the first, on this very couch. Clumsy and afraid and a tiny bit desperate. Evan ignored the rush of pain in his chest—it could have been the stitches, it could have been his heart fragmenting a tiny bit more.

The pain centered him; it made him remember everything that had led up to this moment.

This had to be good-bye.

Chapter Twelve

Vic Wolkowski tightened his hands on the leather-covered steering wheel and steered the minivan toward the EZ Pass lane on the Triborough Bridge. Out of the corner of his eye he could see Evan scrunched down in the passenger seat, staring blanking out the windshield. His skin was sickly white, his eyes were flat. He hadn't said ten words since Vic had pulled out of the driveway of the Cerelli house twenty minutes ago.

The phone call had come yesterday—just a few mumbled words. Evan needed someone to drive him to his in-laws place, to pick up the kids. He wasn't allowed to drive yet—it would only take a few hours. Was Vic available?

Of course Vic said yes. He spent most of his weekends rattling around the house, trying not to plant himself in one place and get melancholy. All well and good to keep busy, but there were only so many times you could mow the lawn or rearrange a closet. The thought of getting out seemed like a good idea.

Except.

Except all he wanted to do was ask Evan—where was Matt? Why wasn't he going with Evan to get the kids? One look at his detective's face as he opened the front door told him everything he couldn't ask. Matt had to be gone.

He was itching to ask what happened, but the words "did you and Matt break up?" just couldn't seem to find their way out of his throat and into the air. It wasn't that Vic was homophobic in any way, shape, or form. He didn't care what people did in the privacy of their own homes—hell, he'd been a cop long enough to know what actual perversion looked like and it sure wasn't two guys—or two women—going out to dinner and holding hands. He admitted to being old-fashioned enough to not want to see anyone's tongue in anyone else's mouth in public—but that was really true for straight people too. The Matt/Evan situation, well, that was different. It was just a shock. It took some getting used to.

Didn't look like he even needed to bother.

Well shit, Vic thought as he eased the rental through traffic and headed toward the island. He had gotten general directions to Sherri's parent's place but was hoping that Evan would perk up enough to guide him through the neighborhood. If he'd known what the hell was going on (whatever that was), he'd have given Matty a call. Looking at Evan, he worried that Matt was worse off.

Evan stirred in the seat next to him. Vic took the opening—hell, it was now or never.

"So, where do I go after I take exit fifteen?"

Bewilderment in his eyes, Evan turned to stare at Vic.

"What?"

"Your in-laws place?"

There was a long pause. Evan blinked a few times. Vic waited patiently.

"Take Grayson Road to the end. They live off of it. It's a left at the light."

"Great." Vic cleared his throat, unsure what to do now. He thought the kids might be a safe bet. "I bet your kids are thrilled to be coming home." He detected a slight nod from the tall man beside him.

"Any plans for Christmas?"

Evan stiffened.

"Quiet. At home. They don't need any more excitement."

Right, thought Vic, *and neither do you*. The monotone of Evan's voice reminded Vic of countless shell-shocked victims he'd seen sitting across from him over the years. The frustration mounted. It seemed as if they had gone back in time to the days and weeks right after Sherri was killed.

"Sounds good."

Evan grunted softly.

Vic went back to driving. He resolved to call Matty as soon as he got home. Someone was going to tell him what the hell was going on.

* * *

The rest of the drive took only thirty minutes. Evan grunted out some instructions as they got closer to the house but that was all. He felt like cotton lined his head and mouth; he hadn't slept since... He hadn't slept and his chest ached. He took his medicine because the kids were coming home, finally, and they needed him. He needed to be better so he could take care of them. That endless chant kept him from flying apart into a thousand pieces.

Evan felt the minivan stop; Vic cleared his throat. He hated looking like this in front of his captain, knew he didn't have much more time. He could only plead pain and trauma from the shooting for a little bit longer. Maybe another week or so of sympathy would be spared him... He needed to pull it together.

"Uh, we're here," Vic said nervously.

Evan said nothing and slid awkwardly out of the car. He'd taken a pill before he left the house and the blanket of numbness that enveloped him kept the pain at bay. For that, he was grateful.

He mustered up the energy to smile as the children came bounding out of the house.

For a few moments Evan felt overwhelmed by their voices and the feeling of their arms winding around his neck. A slender crack formed in his heart; for a second he actually felt alive but then the babble ceased and clear as a bell he heard—

"Where's Matt?"

Of course it was Elizabeth, innocent and smiling, clinging to his leg.

Evan opened his mouth but nothing came out. How could he explain what he had done? Any of it.

From behind he heard Vic Wolkowski's voice boom out, "What am I? Chopped liver? Matt had to take care of something for work. I got chauffeur duties for the day."

Looking up, Evan locked eyes with Miranda, whose quizzical glance was more than he could stand. He jerked his head to take in Danny and Kathleen and Elizabeth who stared at him expectantly.

"Let's go," he choked out. "Let's get your stuff and say good-bye to your grandparents."

They moved awkwardly toward the house, Evan steeling himself for what would happen next.

* * *

Whatever Evan was expecting, he was not disappointed.

His sullen in-laws stood in the foyer, staring at him like he was social services, coming to rip their children out of the only home they'd ever known. Which was bullshit, of course, but Evan wasn't entirely sure that Phil and Josie knew that. Very little was said.

While the kids were in the other room gathering their bags, Vic tried; he said hello and how are you to the McGregors, but they didn't do much in way of responding. As the kids came into view with their things, Josie burst into inconsolable sobs, which in turn upset the kids, which in turn made Evan see the red-hot fire of his anger flicker up behind his eyes. He was curt and moved everyone out the door as quickly as possible.

"Kiss your grandparents," he said quietly, trying not to let his glower be turned on the children. "You'll see them next week for Christmas."

Josie made little hiccuping sounds as she snuffled into a tissue. It pushed Evan's last nerve. Some angry, mean, spiteful bit of him wanted to cancel the Christmas visit but he wouldn't hurt his kids that way.

There was a general confusion as everyone said their good-byes. Evan slipped out the door with a bag in each hand; the pain pulling at his chest was a great diversion. Vic brought up the rear with the rest of the stuff. He made some noise about Evan doing too much but the words didn't quite register. The haze was descending again.

It took another ten minutes but everyone was loaded into the van, strapped in, and they were on their way. The entire process hadn't lasted a half hour.

Unable to keep his eyes open another second, Evan leaned his head against the glass. He heard Vic and Miranda trying to engage the younger kids in talk about Christmas. Things got lively and Evan felt a little peace. Okay, so maybe it was going to be all right. Maybe he could get it together, give the kids a nice holiday and go on.

Danny piped up loudly, saying what he really, really wanted was the Wii and *bam*! There went Evan's improved mood and following right behind was his ability to breathe properly. His mind flew back to the house, back to the scene of just a few days ago. In the basement closet sat the bags and bags of toys and gifts that Matt had bought. He'd refused to take them when he left; told Evan to use them since he wasn't going to be able to go shopping.

Evan didn't say anything beyond a quiet "thanks," as he watched Matt pack up his bag. There was no look of longing, no tender good-bye. They simply moved around each other like the planets around a sun, Matt picking up his things, Evan watching him. Haunting him. He'd felt the energy draining out, pooling around him on the floor. There was nothing to say, nothing to change the inevitable. This was for the kids...this was for the kids...it was the thing that kept his mouth shut. So he simply watched as his lover took one last look around, spared him a quick, blank glance, and walked out the door.

And that was it.

Now they were heading home to the emptiness and the pile of gifts from the ghost of Matt, mingled in with the ever-present ghost of Sherri, who would always be there.

And don't forget the guilt, Evan thought to himself, *you couldn't forget that.*

* * *

"Merry Fucking Christmas," Matt said, saluting his dark apartment. He'd come home from cleaning out his office—with a quick stop at the liquor store for some holiday cheer—kept all the lights off and sat his ass down in the cozy chair by the window. He couldn't actually see anything of interest but around ten p.m. it started snowing. Of course by that time he was half blitzed so maybe it was imaginary snow.

He had quit his job; the boss seemed to understand. He hadn't really been happy for a long time. It was time for a new challenge. The security firm was the place for Matt to hide and lick his wounds. Now it was time to get his shit together and move on.

What a mature decision! That called for another drink! Matt poured himself another half glass of bourbon. He had planned his evening out quite carefully and was assured there was enough liquor to get him to "unconscious" which was where he wanted to be. Desperately.

The week since he'd walked out of Evan's home had been numb and cold and exhausting. If he'd thought being brought up on charges in the department and ending up a beat cop had sucked out loud, he would like the opportunity to revise that opinion.

The entire relationship was bullshit. Everything was a big sack of bullshit.

He'd ignored Vic Wolkowski's messages on his machine—he didn't answer his phone because he didn't care to respond to anything remotely attached to Evan and that seemed to be the only thing that people wanted to discuss.

Vic—he'd known the man long enough to interpret the slightly gentled tone.

Liz—she called to invite him and Evan over to the house, then had called back several times to confirm. And finally, the last call this morning announced an openly stated threat that after the holidays she was driving to Staten Island and kicking his ass. He waited until he knew she'd be gone to her in-laws then left a message back, sending his holiday regards and apologizing for his lack of response. He promised to talk to her in a few days.

He drained his glass in one long swallow and waited for the awful burn to squeeze his brain and lungs. His rationale was that the pain from the liquor would kill the pain from the hurt, but that wasn't working out too well. All he had to show for nearly an empty bottle of bourbon was a physical ache to go with the one that wracked his brain.

Why?

Why?

Why had he been so stupid? Why had he believed they could work things out? He *knew* it would never work! Knew that right from the very beginning but still, knowing very well how it would turn out, he kept pushing. Kept believing that on this night, he would be sitting on the floor of the Cerelli house, watching the kids tear open their presents, watching Evan watch his kids with shining eyes and a peaceful smile. Bullshit. Everything was bullshit.

* * *

On Christmas morning, Evan watched his kids tear open their presents with exhausted eyes and a heavy heart.

The week had been a rough one with everyone's moods flying off the charts. One second they were all laughing and relaxing, the next moment the twins dissolved into shrieking, shoving combatants. Or Miranda stomped off into her room when Evan merely asked her a question about finishing her homework. Evan himself could barely keep his mind focused on whatever the task at hand was; paying bills, cooking dinner, doing laundry.

Sleep was a joke. He dozed, sitting up in his bedroom's easy chair. The bed taunted him with memories; the couch downstairs did the same. He took sponge baths in the bathroom downstairs. It was too much.

Yesterday, the kids spent the day with their grandparents. Evan was not invited—and he wouldn't have gone if Phil or Josie had deigned to ask. They were barely on speaking terms as it was; a few hours sitting across from one another would have been the final nail in the coffin.

Instead, he'd spent the day wandering around the house in a near daze, hearing memories of Christmases past, wondering where Matt had gone then remembering. By the time the kids came home, Evan could barely muster enough the energy to look over their gifts and do the traditional Cerelli family "cookies for Santa" ritual. Miranda thankfully took the lead (sending a blade of shame through Evan again—when would he be man enough to stop leaning on a teenager?), placating Danny and Elizabeth so they'd go upstairs and get into bed.

By the time midnight rolled around, the kids were asleep, and Evan had used the last of his energy to haul all of Matt's gifts up from the basement. He snapped off all the lights then sat on the couch, staring into the darkness and trying to fade away.

Waiting for morning.

And here they were. The happy Cerelli family, opening gifts under a gaily-decorated tree, snow softly falling just beyond the picture window.

Evan made some enthusiastic noises as the gifts appeared one by one. Matt had unerringly chosen something appropriate for each of the kids—even Miranda cracked a real smile when she got to the gift certificates. When the Wii was revealed, the whoops of delight were deafening.

Fucking Norman Rockwell couldn't have done it better.

But a closer look revealed the fine hairline cracks forming in Dad's brain. The strained expressions on Miranda and Kathleen's faces, as they tried to be excited. The higher than normal pitches of the twin's voices as they competed for attention.

The big invisible hole where Sherri used to be.

The big invisible hole where Matt should be.

* * *

Matt woke up Christmas Day with a mouth full of cottony regret and an invisible spear lodged in his head.

Happy Holidays, Matthew Haight.

After a long time spent negotiating with his stomach—*I don't want to have to clean it up, I don't want to have to clean it up*—he rolled off the sofa bed and staggered to the bathroom. He avoided the mirror—*I don't want to see how bad I look, I don't want to see how bad I look*—and slid into the shower, hoping to either die or wake up.

He woke up.

By the time the cold water streamed down over his head, Matt was conscious and in full control of his gut. He dried off, shaved (still avoiding the mirror, no need to chance it), and walked back out into his apartment, a towel wrapped around his waist.

He surveyed his kingdom. It sucked. One room, okay the furniture was nice but still. He was quickly approaching forty-five and he lived in ONE room. He was currently unemployed. In a few short weeks he'd met and fallen in love with another man, started a relationship, and ended a relationship. Two careers, nothing to show for it. Lots of people in his bed, and now he was alone.

Time for a change. Time for a change or time to lay down and die, and frankly, that wasn't an option.

So...Matthew Haight. This is your life. It sucks. What are you going to do about it?

He dropped the towel over the counter and went to the closet to grab some clothes. There was no plan for today, no invitations were forthcoming, and no one expected him to show up for dinner and dessert. He put on an old pair of jeans and his beloved NYPD sweatshirt—he clung to it like a talisman, enjoying the memories of his life when it was new and fresh and full of expectations.

And hey—maybe that was a place to start.

Coming out of the academy, Matthew Haight thought he could fly, save damsels in distress, and earn the gratitude and love of the city—all before noon. His head had been full of codes and laws and procedures and he just could not *wait* to put it into action. That was a feeling he wanted again.

Back in his easy chair—this time with orange juice as opposed to bourbon—he watched the tops of the buildings, faintly covered in snow. He thought about the academy, thought about college before that...

College. Could he go back to school? Get another degree? Start over at forty-five?

Well, he thought drily, sipping his juice, he'd started over in the human sexuality department. How tough could it be to take a few classes?

Helena waited on the doorstop, trying to control her impatience to hit the doorbell again. It had been almost five weeks since she had seen Evan—when she had left the hospital—and she was anxious to see him again.

Particularly after their last phone call.

On Christmas Day she phoned to wish him and Matt a Merry Christmas and was stunned by the lackluster and frail sounding voice of her partner. In near monotone, he'd told her that Matt wasn't here, the kids were back, and he hoped she was feeling better. She hung up less than five minutes after dialing, her jaw scraping the floor.

The next day, she got a visit from Vic Wolkowski; well, partially there to see Helena, partially there to drink coffee and eat cookies in the kitchen with her mother. They spoke about Evan's condition—and Helena was frightened to hear about the noticeable change in his physical appearance. She resolved to go see him as soon as possible...unfortunately that was delayed by Evan's dodging of her phone calls, Helena's slow recovery, and a bout with the flu.

But now here she was. And she was determined to get to the bottom of this...descent of Evan's.

The door finally opened.

"Jesus Christ!" Helena exhaled, before she could catch herself.

Her partner could only be described as a figment of his former self. He'd lost even more weight, and the dark sunken circles under his eyes had taken over his face.

A tiny flare of fire—anger? embarrassment?—flickered through his stare. "Helena, I'm not in the mood..." He didn't get to finish.

Helena walked through the door, bumping into him lightly as she walked by. She stopped in the center of the living room and surveyed the mess. Piles of papers and magazines littered every surface, and toys, clothes, and books competed for the rest of the space.

She eyed Evan critically. Under the terrible fear and concern she had over her friend's condition, she was angry.

"You look like a sack of bones in sweatpants."

Evan bristled. "I'm recovering from—"

"Yes," she interrupted. "Yes, you are. You're recovering from a serious wound, and you look worse than when I saw you in the hospital!"

"Is that what you came here for? To tell me how I look?"

"No, I came here because I'm worried sick. Evan..." she gestured toward him helplessly. "What's wrong? Please talk to me."

He opened his mouth then glanced away, a flush spreading across his face. Sitting down heavily in a chair, he aimlessly gestured for her to do the same.

This is going to take some time, Helena thought as she dropped her jacket on the back of the couch and took a seat kitty-corner to Evan.

Leaning forward on her knees, Helena ignored the slight twinge in her shoulder. She was nearly 100 percent recovered, but a round of whatever flu was paralyzing the city currently had kept her in bed for ten days and the shoulder had stiffened slightly. Back at work—but still on desk duty—she was anxiously waiting her partner's return. But now...seeing him...she couldn't imagine him passing a physical let alone making it past Wolkowski.

"Evan..."

He sighed, refusing to meet her eyes.

"What's going on? What happened..." Her voice trailed off gently. The unspoken "with Matt" hung in the air for agonizing seconds.

Evan's gaze stayed on the rug between him and Helena. "It wouldn't have worked Helena," he whispered. "It was just... something that happened between two lonely people."

Helena blinked repeatedly, trying to reconcile this man speaking before her and the one she'd seen practically glowing with love back at Thanksgiving. "That wasn't what you told me a month ago."

"I was deluding myself."

"Evan—give me a break. Give yourself a break. *Talk* to me."

"I *am*!" The sudden flare of Evan's anger jerked Helena back in surprise. She was shocked to see the condition of his face as he stood up. That blank demeanor was now teeming with rage. "I am talking to you! I'm telling you it was a mistake! I'm telling you I don't want to discuss it! If Matt Haight was the only reason you came here today, you can just fucking leave!!"

With that, he turned quickly and stormed into the kitchen.

Stunned, Helena sat back against the sofa. She listened to Evan slam through the kitchen; glasses rattled and the faucet ran for several moments. What the hell should she say now? Evan was practically unhinged talking about Matt... The wild look in his eyes frightened her.

A few minutes later, Evan returned with two glasses of ice water.

He handed one to Helena, not meeting her eyes.

"Thanks," she said softly.

He grunted quietly in response and took his place back on the side chair.

They sat in silence.

She let him get away with it until she got halfway through her glass. As she swallowed, she cast him a sideways glance. The lost expression on his face as he stared into the dark shadows of the room broke her heart. She hadn't seen that look since Sherri's funeral.

"Evan," Helena said softly. "Please understand that I'm your friend—your partner—and I care about what is happening to you."

He nodded, still not meeting her earnest gaze.

"Honey, come on," she coaxed. "Talk to me."

"It…it just wouldn't have worked," he croaked finally. "I just couldn't do that…that…" His voice trailed off.

"That? Do you mean…sexually?" Helena asked awkwardly, thinking that this didn't seem to be a problem when she'd caught them kissing passionately on Thanksgiving.

Evan's red-hot blush could be seen through the dim light of the room.

"No…I mean…how would I have told my children, Helena? How would I have told people at the station? My…my neighbors? Just introduce Matt around as my what? Boyfriend? Lover? That isn't my lifestyle…"

"Whoa, whoa—who's talking about lifestyles here? I think all your concerns are valid but did you and Matt discuss everything? How you would handle things?"

Evan's eyes dropped down to his lap as he toyed with the moisture droplets on the side of the glass.

Helena's eyes widened. "Did you talk to him about this at all?"

A quick shake of his head was the only indication that Evan was listening to her at all.

"Jesus Christ, Evan. You just ended it without telling him why?"

"I told him it wouldn't work," Evan repeatedly wearily, still not looking up from the glass. "He...he wanted to try...but I already knew..." His voice trailed off, as if he'd lost his place in the conversation.

Helplessly Helena watched her partner drift away from the conversation, from the room itself. She caught the waves of despair roiling off of him; they were practically visible. Unable to think of anything else, she put her glass down and walked over to the chair.

"Hey," she murmured. "It's okay." She knelt down slowly, putting her hands on his knee and shoulder. "It's okay, Evan. I know you're in a lot of pain right now, but I'm here for you."

A soft sound, something akin to a denied and strangled sob, was wrenched from Evan's chest. Gently, Helena took the glass from his hands and placed it on the floor. As Evan started to fold in on himself, seeming to deflate with each shuddering sound of grief, Helena caught him, ignoring her shoulder, ignoring her own fatigue. If he wanted to cry, the least she could do was support him.

"It's okay, Evan. It's okay." She said it over and over again, hoping he would believe it.

* * *

Matthew Haight, dressed to kill and on the prowl.

He suppressed a snicker at his own line of bullshit.

It was a typical Friday night in January—icy cold, dead streets, Matt bored out of his skull. All the smart people were home camped out on their couches in pairs (if they were lucky), and all the drunks were already on their stools. Matt couldn't spend another five minutes in his apartment; he wanted to get out, he wanted to let loose.

He just wanted to forget for a little while.

The itch had taken time to return. For weeks all he could do was lie in bed and let his body relive every sensual second he'd spent with Evan. But soon he grew tired of his hand, grew tired of being cold and alone.

But all of a sudden, standing in the doorway of the bar, the enormity of the moment hit him. He hadn't done this in awhile *before* Evan and to be here now felt...stupid. And old. And pitiful. He thought what—he was going to get some action? He was on the steady decline to fifty. He'd just spent the past six weeks chasing another man only to be dumped, this coming after a drought of women, a string of failures that stretched back to the *seventies* for God's sake. Which one of the nubile chickies at the bar was going to leap at the chance to land him? Quick guess. Nada.

With a deflating sigh, Matt walked into the smoky Manhattan bar. At the very least, he was going to have to have several dozen beers. Keeping his eyes trained down—God forbid he make eye contact with someone and have to deal with the sting of rejection—he made his way to the bar and sat down on the stool farthest away from the door. It wedged him between the bar and a small sidewall; the jukebox was conveniently around the corner. Perfection. The crowd was minimal—well he assumed it was minimal. He hadn't been to this bar in years. It was a few blocks away from his old precinct, and had been among the many spots he'd divided his time among back in the day. He slid off his leather jacket, leaving it on the stool next to him.

The television was positioned so that he could flick his eyes up to check out the wrestling match in progress. A slender young woman with hair too black to be natural slid a napkin in front of him as he got settled.

"Hey," she said. "What can I get you?"

Matt returned her friendly—and most likely routine—smile. "Corona Light.

"Sure." She turned away and rummaged around in the cooler. Matt took the opportunity to admire her trim form, poured into leather pants and a black sparkly halter-top. The creamy expanse of skin on her back held his gaze. He readjusted himself on the stool as discreetly as possible.

The bartender returned with the bottle, shaking off a few drops of water that clung to the side. "You want to start a tab?"

Matt nodded, throwing down a five in her direction. "You want a credit card?"

"Nah, I trust cops," she replied with a grin. She pocketed the five and walked back to the other side of the bar.

What the fuck! Matt thought. *How do they* do *that?*

He swallowed down a long drag of beer, taking another look at the hockey score on the television. A young couple, already high on cheap beer, cigarette smoke, and promised sex, wandered over to the jukebox, giggling and whispering through the selections. Matt tried to ignore them. He didn't really want to think about anything tonight but sex. And seeing as all he was going to be doing *was* thinking, he didn't want to be reminded that other people were having sex with people they liked. Evan. He almost rolled his eyes when the name popped into his brain. Jesus, what was that—like a whole hour he didn't moon over the guy?

Now repeat after me Matt Haight, he told himself, downing the rest of his beer in three gulps—and signaling Halter Girl for another—it was a *mistake*. An experiment. It's *over.*

Fuck.

Matt started on his second beer. He hadn't eaten anything since a few slices at lunch and the buzz was blossoming nicely. *Oh yes. I remember this*, he thought. He remembered sitting alone in a roomful of people, feeling the slide of alcohol warm his blood and haze his brain...

By the time he hit his third, the joint was jumping. Large groups of thirty-somethings, eager to prove they were still hip enough to drink the night away, showed up at ten o'clock, and things began to escalate. There may have been someone dancing on the other end of the bar at one point, but Matt was on his fifth beer and it didn't quite register.

The man who sat down next to him when he was cracking open number six did. About the same height and build as Matt, but thinner, more defined. The way he sized up the room, and took a seat with the next best vantage point screamed "cop" or ex-military loud and clear. It was exactly what Matt would do...and did. He was wearing black jeans and a long-sleeved black sweater; his black leather jacket ended up spread across his lap as he settled down. A quick sidewise glance to Matt—and then he was hailing Halter Top.

"Hey," she said in her friendly way. "There a cop convention around here today?"

Aha, thought Matt. *I was right. I could be a bartender.*

The man laughed, the sound low and scratchy. Apparently there was something in the man's smile, because Halter Top almost oozed into a puddle. Matt tried not to stare.

"Good eye. I'll take a Corona."

"Sure," she purred, her demeanor quickly switching gears. "I'll start you a tab. You new here? I haven't seen you before."

Hey, Matt thought. *Am I chopped liver? I didn't get a questionnaire when I sat down.*

"Just visiting," the man replied. "I'm from the West Coast."

"LA?" She gave him the Corona and lounged in front of him, showing off her bared skin to the best advantage.

"Washington State."

"Oooo. Great music, man! Do you go to a lot of clubs?" Matt almost rolled his eyes. He reached the bottom of his bottle and put it down on the bar.

"S'cuse me, honey, but I'll take another." He motioned with the bottle.

Halter Top gave him a "can't you see I'm busy, loser" look, but he didn't care. He wanted a drink. As she walked away, working on a good "huff," the man next to Matt turned his way.

"Thanks. I was afraid I was going to have to have a discussion about Seattle music or the brilliance of Kurt Cobain."

"Who?"

"Exactly."

Matt laughed quietly. He swiveled a bit on his seat to get a better look. The guy was his age, maybe a little younger, and no stranger to a gym. Matt guessed he was still on the force, probably a detective.

"Matt."

"James. Nice to meet you." He extended a hand and they shook.

"Mind if I stick around for a bit? I don't feel like being holed up in my hotel room, and it's too cold to walk around."

Matt shrugged. "Not a problem. I could use the company. All the youthful exuberance in this place is starting to piss me off."

"When did people in their thirties become youthful? Better yet, when did I get so goddamn old?"

Halter Top slid the Corona to Matt and didn't bother to try and engage James in a conversation again. She gave them both a strange look, then smiled and walked away.

Well, what the fuck was that, Matt thought.

"Old? I'm practically dead. I'm the same age my father was when I realized he wasn't indestructible. That's a bad place to be."

James laughed. "I hear you, brother."

Matt sipped his beer. Okay, this was nice. This was cool. Nice guy, conversation, beer. Not too shabby.

If he knew he were going to get laid tonight, it would be a perfect evening.

* * *

They talked until the thirty-somethings gave up the ghost and went home to their overpriced and underfurnished apartments.

They talked until the next crowd of bar hoppers wandered in; a smaller group, subdued because they were already drunk. They started playing darts on the other side of the bar, ordering pitcher after pitcher from Halter Top.

They talked until Matt realized he hadn't had a seventh beer but he needed one because his throat was dry.

"So Matt, what the hell are you doing at this bar with me instead of being out on a date?"

The question, on the surface seemed pretty innocuous, but Matt Haight, former detective, heard the leading edge of it clear as a bell.

And he wasn't sure how he wanted to play it.

"Nobody on the radar right now to call. Truth is, I came there hoping to meet someone," he said carefully, trying to subtly get Halter Top's attention.

"A hookup?"

Matt laughed. "No, a meaningful relationship forged out of sharing a couple of beers in a bar."

"Ah. Definitely a hookup." James took a swig of his beer, turning slightly to face Matt. "That's not usually my thing, but it can work."

He sounded thoughtful.

"Yeah. It can. When both people know the score." Where the fuck did that come from, thought Matt. No more watching *Sex & the City* reruns on Sunday nights—it was starting to influence his mind.

"So do you have someone waiting for you back in Washington?"

It slipped out easily and Matt swore he no longer had control over his voice.

There was such a long silence that Matt turned his head to look at James's face. He looked like Matt had shot his dog.

"Hey, man, I'm sorry…"

"No, no," James said, recovering. "I don't date much…" He was stammering a bit, and Matt was bewildered by the sudden change.

James sighed. "The fucking truth of the matter is I'm crazy about…someone but they aren't interested in me like that. In fact, tomorrow I get to fly home and start planning a bachelor party."

As soon as he said "bachelor party," James stiffened up. He pulled subtly away from Matt and faced the opposite side of the bar again.

Matt felt bad for him.

"It's okay."

"I'm sorry. I…this was stupid…I have no idea if you're…I just thought you might be interested." His voice was low, as if he were afraid that someone would overhear him. "I came here because I'm lonely and tired and I don't know what to do to make it go away."

Well shit, Matt thought. *Thank you for verbalizing exactly how I feel.*

"Does he know?" Matt asked softly.

James shook his head. "No. He's straight. Up until about a year ago, he thought I was too. I was afraid…I was afraid to tell him about the men in my past. It's just always easier to mention the women."

Matt nodded. Would this be his plan going forward?

"How about you?"

"Me?" said Matt. "I uh…in a stroke of 'it could only happen in NY,' you sat down on a barstool next to an ex-cop going through the same shit you are."

"No shit. Straight guy break your heart?"

Matt laughed uproariously. "Something like that. I fell for someone who couldn't handle it. Not that I could—I mean…he was the first…you know. I didn't even know I was capable of feeling that way…"

James whistled. "You just figured this out recently?"

"Ever been hit by a garbage truck?"

"Um…almost."

"*That* is what I feel like. I meet this guy, I start feeling shit I had no idea was programmed into my fucking brain, we start…you know…trying to make something happen, and then boom! I start to feel comfortable and he bails." Matt almost cried out in relief when Halter Top graced them with her presence and two more beers. Matt sighed heavily.

"That's some serious shit you have to handle there, Matthew. I don't envy you. But if it helps any, I understand."

Matt heard all the pain in James's last statement. He sighed again.

"Yeah. It helps."

They sat in silence for a long time, drinking their beers and staring straight ahead.

Then Matt felt James's shoulder touch his.

Followed by his thigh.

And whoosh—there went racing heat from the top of his head down to his freaking shoes. Jesus, when did it get so hot in here?

But Matt didn't pull away. Without even consciously thinking about it, he leaned into the touch.

Neither man said a thing.

Finally, Matt felt compelled to speak.

"I think you're hitting on me."

"Score one for a cop's instincts," James said drily.

Matt snorted.

"It has nothing to do with being a cop and everything to do with what's nudging my leg."

He quickly drank his beer, feeling his face burning with embarrassment. Or something.

James looked down at his lap, then back up at Matt. "Thanks for the compliment, but that's just my knee."

A thinly veiled snicker exploded into hearty laughter when Matt saw the "innocent" look on James's face.

In a second, James joined in and it was a few minutes before either could speak or even take a proper breath. In the companionable quiet afterward—punctuated only by the moans of defeat from across the room, near the dartboard—neither man made eye contact.

Halter Top made another pass to their end of the bar, grabbing tips and cleaning up spills. She smirked a bit in Matt's direction, and he felt his ears singe with embarrassment. James seemed to pick up on it because when she walked away, he leaned close to Matt and spoke softly.

"Let's get out of here."

A rush of emotion and a tangle of thoughts swirled around Matt in a brief second. Evan was no small part of it all.

Without having any idea of what he was going to say, Matt opened his mouth and heard someone say,

"Good idea. Where are you staying?"

James smiled, keeping his body near Matt's.

"Lafayette Street. A quick cab ride."

Matt nodded because his voice had gotten stuck behind a mile of dry throat. He could smell James's aftershave and the smoke from the bar that had seeped into his black shirt. And there was no mistaking the flare of heat that their close proximity was creating. There was a moment of sheer panic when the reality of it all slammed into him—they were going back to James's hotel room to have sex, there was no mistake about it. And no virginal fumbling either; James had experience and know-how, and he was looking at Matt like he already knew the first ten things that were going to happen once they reached the room.

It was frightening.

It was sexy.

James seemed to read Matt's mind, because with a practiced hand, he touched the inside of the other man's thigh, gently. In invitation. In comfort.

"Let's go," he murmured again. "No pressure. We'll just talk unless you want something...else." His voice was low, gruff. Matt felt it seeping into his bones.

He stared at James's mouth. Yeah. Fuck yeah. He wanted more. He wanted to know what it was like—all of it, now that he had had a taste. And maybe it couldn't be compared. This wasn't love but it was comfort and that's what he wanted.

"We'll talk in the cab," Matt answered suddenly, finding his voice and a full reserve of Haight courage. "Let's get out of here." Nothing more was said as they gathered up their jackets. Halter Top slid over the credit card receipt for Matt to sign, so he scribbled something he hoped would pass muster. In less than three minutes they were standing on the sidewalk, feeling the biting cold press up from the concrete. Matt felt a rush of déjà vu so strong he could actually taste it but before he could process it, James was calling him and then he was in the cab.

And they were on their way.

Chapter Thirteen

The richly accented voice of Placido Domingo welcomed Matt and James into the cab and reminded them to buckle up for safety. Matt didn't bother since he was wedged in so tightly between James and the Plexiglas divider there was little chance of him going anywhere. James's body seemed to have grown since they got into the cab; his legs were tangled up in Matt's, his arm resting on the seat behind Matt's head.

James gave the address of the Holiday Inn off Canal Street and leaned even closer to Matt.

Jesus, was it hot in here or what?

"You okay?" James murmured in his ear.

Matt nodded dumbly. "Yeah. It's just a tight fit..."

James snorted politely.

Ah yes, Matt thought, *another double entendre. It was hard enough...shit!*

He snickered at his own joke.

"What?"

"Nothing." Matt turned his head.

"How are you doing?"

Matt had a pithy reply on the tip of his tongue, but when he saw the concern on James's face, it died a quick death. This wasn't a faceless bar pickup—this was a nice guy. A nice, lonely guy. Someone who Matt would easily buddy up with if they worked together. A guy who's heart was just as kicked around as his own… This wasn't what he was looking for. This was what he had been trying to forget.

"Okay. A little surprised. But okay," he finally said, trying to be honest.

"I didn't expect to meet you tonight."

James seemed taken aback by the comment. He turned to stare out the window as they made their way downtown.

"Maybe this wasn't a good idea," James murmured, still facing away. "I didn't mean for this to be complicated."

Matt gave a short laugh. "As opposed to being uncomplicated? Sorry that word doesn't have any place in my life. Everything is a shit storm with me, man—don't worry about it." Feeling a little brave, he reached out and ran his hand along James's outer thigh.

That got James's attention pretty quickly.

"I wouldn't have come with you if I wasn't interested." He spoke softly now, just for James's ears.

"I know you're interested," James sighed. "I just want to make sure this doesn't make things…worse for you."

"Thanks." Matt smiled at him gently. "You don't have to worry. Really. This is…good."

"Yeah?"

"Yeah." Emboldened, he deepened his touch. It was nice. It was sexy. He felt a little drunk on the hormones, way too comfortable with this big, strong man who seemed to understand exactly what he was saying. What he was not was afraid—afraid that this would grow into something, afraid he would get his insides shredded. James wasn't a threat.

He was…a comfort.

The thought had no sooner crossed his mind when he felt gentle fingers graze the nape of his neck, ruffling his hair. He didn't have time to prepare for the kiss, the warm dry lips, and the subtle hint of tongue. They kissed for a long minute, taking their time getting to know one another. As Matt had suspected, James was firmly in control, moving his hand slowly against the back of Matt's head, deepening their kiss, then pulling back to keep thing civilized.

No need to rut like animals in the cab.

When they came up for air, Matt kept his eyes closed. He needed a moment to get used to the idea that he, Matthew Haight, had just kissed yet another man. Maybe this was getting easier.

He looked over, saw James staring at him with weirdly pale blue eyes—filled with worry and lust and anxiousness. Then James licked his lips—dragged his tongue across and down and over— and Matt's brain barely stayed secured in his skull. Perhaps restraint from rutting in cabs was overrated.

* * *

The shadows had swallowed the room completely when Helena felt she could pull away from Evan's tense embrace. He'd wept quietly for a long time, then after a deep sigh, he'd just trembled. She wanted to let him drain himself of all the pent up grief—over Sherri, over the kids, over his injury, and, apparently, over Matt—without disruption. It was obvious from the way he'd let go that it had been a long time coming.

She gently disentangled herself, holding onto Evan's shoulders to look at his weary and damp face. He had that faraway look that spoke of too much worry and not enough sleep so she urged him up, murmuring assurances and encouragement.

"Let's go upstairs, Evan, just to take a little nap..." Helena whispered.

She felt him moving to protest. "The kids...dinner."

"I'll take care of it. You take a nap, I'll get some food started and wait for the kids to get back from Elena's."

Evan didn't bother to disagree with her and let himself be led upstairs.

That didn't seem like a good sign to Helena.

* * *

By the time Helena got Evan under the badly mussed covers and watched him close his eyes, it was very late. The kids were due back from their aunt's by six and she assumed they'd be expecting dinner.

Dinner was not exactly Helena's forte.

She grabbed the portable phone and dialed her mother as she moved around the house, throwing on lights and picking up some of the newspapers and toys scattered around the living room. The house needed cleaning. Screw it—the house needed cleansing with cock's blood and chanting.

The other line picked up.

"Mom? I need help. What are you doing right now?"

* * *

Helena wondered if her mother had been in the meat section of Food Emporium when she called because when Serena arrived a scant hour later, she had ten bags of groceries.

"Mom, I said dinner for the family, not Thanksgiving dinner for gen pop."

"Shush. I'm sure there's not a decent thing in this house. Poor babies."

Serena went into "sweeping busyness mode" and Helena ducked out of the kitchen. She was cleaning as much of the house as she could; a load of laundry was in the washer and another tumbling in the dryer. It made her nervous to see how disorganized things were. Evan would never, never let it get this out of hand unless he wasn't functioning normally. Wasn't this sort of thing a sign of depression?

Feeling antsy, Helena pulled out the vacuum. She felt she should be doing more but was unsure what the next step was. Beyond a housekeeper, Evan needed someone to talk to—and not just a friend. A professional. Too much had happened to him in the past year and he was obviously at the end of his rope.

Needing some guidance—and knowing her mother was better suited to cook and fuss over small children—Helena grabbed the phone yet again. She took a chance that Captain Wolkowski would still be at his desk.

* * *

Vic had his jacket on—well, an arm of it at least—and visions of take-out from Ming's Palace when his private line rang. He debated whether or not to answer it for about a minute but the reality was, sesame chicken and wonton soup just wasn't that much of a draw.

"Vic Wolkowski," he said, letting the jacket fall off and sitting back down.

"Sir? It's Helena...I'm over at Evan's..." her voice trailed off and Vic felt himself instantly go on alert. "I was wondering—could you come over?"

"Is everything all right?"

Helena sighed heavily. "No...I mean, it's nothing too dramatic but Evan's just—completely out of it. He's like a zombie. I'm not exactly sure what to do."

Vic remembered the trip out to pick up the children and felt immediately guilty for not following up with Evan afterward. It had been obvious then that things were hanging by a thread.

"Are the kids home?"

"I'm expecting them soon. They're with Sherri's sister. My mom is here—she's making dinner."

Great, thought Vic, perking up a bit. "I'll be there as soon as I can."

"Thank you, sir." His officer sounded relieved. "Maybe you can talk some sense into him…"

"Sure, we'll see what I can do."

He hung up the phone, put his hands over his face. The situation with Evan had spun out of control. Chicken soup and well-meaning words weren't going to solve the problem. He needed a professional.

Vic pulled out his personal phone book from his top drawer. He couldn't remember if it was still in there… Yes, yes it was. The name of the shrink he'd seen after his wife had been killed. He felt a sharp squeeze in his heart that would never go away, but Dr. Rueben had been an incredible amount of help to him. He jotted down the number on a piece of paper and tucked it into his pocket. He hoped that Evan would be receptive to his gesture. He didn't want to have to use his position as Evan's boss to get him to see a shrink—but that was rapidly becoming a possibility.

* * *

By the time Helena heard a key in the front door's lock, there was a pot roast in the oven and vegetables boiling on the stove top, and her mother was halfway into the refrigerator, cleaning out old food.

Steeling herself, Helena walked into the living room to greet Elena and the kids.

Miranda was the first one in and she visibly reacted to seeing her father's partner. "Is everything..." died on her lips when Helena plastered on a smile and nodded. Somehow she managed to convey "something's up but don't freak everyone out," because the teenager changed her question to "Hey, Helena!"

"Hey, guys!" she said brightly, watching as Kathleen, Elizabeth, and Danny walked in, with Sherri's dark-haired sister bringing up the rear.

Elena didn't hide her surprise in seeing Helena there. "What's going on? Where's Evan?"

The children, taking off their coats and boots, stopped in their tracks. Miranda sent Helena an anxious look.

"Oh nothing," Helena enthused. "Evan was tired and went upstairs to lie down."

She made a sweeping movement with her arms, indicating the clean living room. "You know how he is, he totally overdid the housework." She smiled. "He asked my mother and me over for dinner—so here we are!"

Serena popped into the room as if on cue. "Hello, kids."

There were smiles and polite "Hello, Ms. Abbot" greetings called out.

"Something smells great!" said Danny, grinning.

"Well, we have lots of somethings that taste great. I hope you're all hungry."

She clapped her hands together then motioned for them to follow her. "Would you like to start with some cheese and bread? I think there's some fruit too..." Like a Pied Piper, she led them out of the room and into the kitchen.

Miranda followed last and Helena gave her a reassuring wink as she passed by. The young woman relaxed a little and continued on. Helena turned to face a frowning Elena.

"Huh. He didn't mention that when I left with the kids…"

"It was a spur of the moment thing. We were in the area."

"Right."

The two women stood for a moment of awkward silence.

"Well, I guess I'll be going."

Helena nodded enthusiastically. *Yes, please*, she thought.

Elena fidgeted with her wool scarf for a moment, casting a look up the staircase.

"Should I give Evan a message from you?" Helena said, mentally willing the other woman out the door.

"Um…yeah. Tell him to call me at my office tomorrow. The number is in Sherri's phone book." She couldn't hide the sad look on her face as she said her sister's name.

Helena felt bad for Elena. She'd never had a sibling, but she could imagine losing one would be an unimaginable pain. "I'll tell him. It's not a problem," she said gently.

"Thanks."

She called out her good-byes to the children, who ran in to kiss her. She left, promising to call them the following day.

Helena let out a sigh of relief as Elena's car pulled out of the driveway. Okay, now she just had to keep the kids calm, get them some dinner while preventing her mother from overfeeding them…

And then…then she needed to figure out what to do with Evan…

* * *

By the time the cab dropped them off on Canal Street in front of the new—and bizarrely out of place—Holiday Inn, Matt was sweating, his shirt was halfway untucked from his pants and his face burning. Not to mention the fact that he had been forced to artfully arrange his jacket to hide what could only be deemed proof positive that Matthew Haight was indeed attracted to his own sex.

James looked like a GQ model. At best, there was a slight gleam in his eye, a little hint of dampness across his forehead and cheeks. Nothing else said debauched. Matt felt like the poster child for horny deviant.

They entered the tiny first-floor lobby (a generous overstatement—the vestibule of Matt's building was bigger) containing big plants, a bored-looking doorman, elevator, and escalator. The doorman gave James a polite nod, casting an odd glance in Matt's direction. Oh yeah. There was no hiding what was going on here.

Matt was starting to feel a little cheap.

They took the escalator, ending up in yet another lobby; this one was much larger. The Asian theme was done in typical hotel style—exotic plants in giant urns with a delicate floral pattern painted on, an Oriental rug, gold gilt on everything. The middle-aged woman behind the counter barely looked up as they walked to the small, mirrored elevators.

"I'm on the tenth floor," James murmured, trying valiantly to make conversation.

Matt nodded dumbly.

They didn't say another word until they reached James's room.

At the door, James fished his card key out of his wallet. He inserted it, waited for the green light, then gave the door a half shove.

Matt was just opening his mouth to say something—anything, but most likely "maybe this was a mistake"—but before a sound could come out, James's tongue was probing his with single-minded determination.

And any unspoken protestations flew completely out of Matt's brain. Blood pooled directly behind his zipper—not like it wasn't already bad enough down there, but James sucking on his lips was pretty much the end of the line for thinking, reasoning, and general higher thought.

He twisted his arms around James's neck, one hand pulling his mouth closer (if that was possible), the other sliding down his back until it came to rest at his waist. James kept the kiss up but managed to push the door all the way open at the same time, walking Matt through the doorway.

After that, lack of oxygen and a war between his zipper and his dick got him disoriented. He didn't realize what was happening until his knees hit the corner of the bed.

He managed to tear his mouth away and sucked in some breath.

"Small freaking room."

"How much space do we need? The bed's a king," murmured James, his hands moving everywhere over Matt's body, pulling clothes off with practiced ease.

"Right," Matt managed—more a moan than actual language. In ten seconds flat he was standing so close to James he thought they were sharing DNA.

With sure hands, James touched the top of Matt's jeans, hesitating for a moment.

"You sure?" he whispered.

Matt stopped and truly considered the question. His body had no problem with shouting a resounding "yes!" but his brain and heart took pause. A quick look to James's face and he saw a reflection of his own confusion. There was no deception in this moment. Neither man was seeking anything but comfort and satisfaction. It relaxed Matt to know that, eased his sudden grief that this wasn't Evan, that it would probably never be Evan again…

Before that thought could overwhelm him, James leaned in and softly kissed Matt's lips. It wasn't anything more than a "yeah, I know" confirmation, and James stepped away, as if to stop the progress of the evening.

"No," Matt said gently. "Come back here."

James hesitated, but Matt reached out his hand.

"Come here," he said again, a little more forcefully. James's eyes narrowed. His sky blue eyes glittered, and Matt watched them turn molten in a single second.

After a long pause, James whispered, "What do you want?"

"What?" That surprised Matt. Something in the low growl of James's voice told him this was a very simple…and loaded… question.

"What…do you want?"

Matt smiled, a small and (as reported by former lovers) sexy smile. He knew the game now.

"You. Back over here to start."

With a mild swagger—Matt just had to grin, wondering if James practiced that in the mirror a few hundred times—James moved closer, not stopping until his chest brushed up against Matt's bare arm. Bingo.

Their eyes locked, inches apart, sharing the heat of the moment. When James leaned in to kiss him, Matt had no hesitation.

They kissed, mouths open, tongues entwined, hands moving restlessly with halfhearted attempts to get each other undressed.

Finally James's exasperation seemed to get the better of him and he disentangled himself from Matt's two-fisted groping.

"Wait, wait."

"What?" murmured Matt.

"Get undressed."

No argument there. Matt took a step back and stripped down, his eyes downcast. Naked sounded great to the raging hormonal beast created by James's fine mouth and even finer body. But a small corner of his brain was having "almost fifty and getting naked with a great-looking stranger" fits of terror. Oh yeah, Matt Haight had fallen a long way from "Hey baby, I'm going to send you to the moon, moaning my name."

Now he was worrying about middle age, his sexual performance, and the emotional validity of sleeping with someone he didn't know that well. Shit. This was just sad.

When he looked up, mind a million places at once, body strumming in fits and starts, James was staring at him curiously, half a smile—a damn sexy smile—sitting across his face. He was also naked as the day he was born.

Whoa. Yeah. "Time to start doing sit-ups again," Matt sighed.

Flicking his glance across Matt's body, James snickered. "I'm not complaining."

"Nice guy."

"Can we please stop talking?"

"God, yes."

By the time they took the few steps that separated them, Matt's tongue was delving deeply into James's mouth. The swell of lust and hormones obliterated everything in his mind, every thought, every fear. Every sweep of James's lips, every movement of his strong confident hands moving with rough precision over his body sent Matt's brain into overdrive. They pushed together, moving slowly, a steady grind.

James didn't relinquish Matt's mouth but managed to get them both lowered onto the bed. It wasn't graceful, but it got them where they wanted to be. Finally. The (still) strange feeling of having another man's body (not Evan's, but he wasn't going to think about that) pressed intimately against his shocked Matt into a moment of stillness, but it was quickly obliterated by a slow roll of James's hips against his own. Matt felt his brain flicker into a hazy paradise while his body ignited.

Perfect.

They took a few minutes...hours...eternities...to grind lazily against one another, each shift of hips heightening the moment. The anticipation. Their eyes locked. Feeling singed, Matt managed to keep his eyes open for about one...two...three...rolls of James's pelvis before succumbing to the need to block out the ceiling of the hotel room.

James took the opportunity to move his mouth from Matt's jaw, a little nip...to his shoulder, a stronger bite. Matt moaned his approval. Excellent choices.

With another little...devastating...roll of his hips, James began to get more ambitious with his mouth. Sternum. Clavicle. Nipple—yeah, so good—stomach.

Unbidden, unwelcome, Evan reappeared in his mind's eye; for every move James made down Matt's body, Matt felt an echo of the other man. He tried to banish the image, but it was impossible. He felt himself growing more and more distracted. He felt James stop moving, felt him lean close to Matt's face.

"Go on...pretend I'm him. It's okay."

His eyes flew open at the unexpected words and met James's. He searched for...something. He searched for how James was feeling. Matt faltered, overwhelmed by his unselfish gesture.

Frantically his mind raced—it wasn't fair to James, he wouldn't do it—but unbidden, the ever-present thought of Evan crept into his mind's eye.

The feel of him, the taste…he missed it so much, and the very real possibility that it would never happen again pushed him over the edge.

"Let me," he murmured against James's cheek. "Let me…" his voice trailed off and he hoped that James would understand what he meant without forcing the words.

James nodded—thank God—without him having to say anything else. He pressed a tender kiss, chaste, against Matt's jaw and the simple act made Matt shudder. Moving carefully, James lifted up, allowing Matt to roll onto his side.

It felt strange to be able to move with common purpose without words. It made the roiling of Matt's stomach settle down, made him move his eyes from the garish bedspread where they'd ended up, moved his eyes up James's beautiful body and finally to his face. And his smile.

"It's okay."

"I know."

"This can be good for both of us."

"I know." Matt chuckled weakly. "Come here."

Scooting down, Matt put his arms out, drawing James's body closer. Drawing James's lower body closer. He didn't avert his eyes, didn't get shy. Licked his lips, felt the tiny shudder roll through James's body—*he must be watching*, Matt thought, and that felt…hot—pressed his mouth to the tip of James's cock, and this time James's shudder was matched by one of his own. *God. So good.*

A sense memory burned behind his eyes, somewhere between taste and scent; Matt's body churned with desire. Evan. He was remembering Evan. It gave him pause. It gave him a tight fist in his heart. The stroking hand in his hair was a surprise, but then again, James had done nothing but prove himself to be a veritable saint over the past few hours. Maybe he could make them both feel good. A memory relived, some shared pleasure...

After a moment's hesitation, he closed his eyes, drawing James's body closer, resuming the gentle movements of his mouth. He felt James's body tense so he ran his free hand up and down his flank, soothing him until he felt him relax.

Once the rhythm returned, Matt let his thoughts wander, back to his apartment, back to that first time. So hungry, so awkward... Matt moaned in the back of his throat, which set off a chain reaction in James. He struggled faintly for a moment, then quickly moved to lie down beside Matt, facing the opposite direction. A shot of raw lust dropped Matt's stomach three stories.

Easier to pretend, he thought wildly, easier to think about Evan. God.

He let himself go, threw himself into that abyss where he forgot about everything but how it felt to make love to someone with his heart and his mouth and his soul. The close walls of the Holiday Inn disappeared and he was back on the lumpy couch with Evan, caressing his body tenderly, listening to his muffled moans. He was touching Evan, teasing him with his mouth, moving on instinct and an ambitious need to please... Oh, but it was difficult to stay in that memory because Matt's body was being scalded by James's skilled tongue, hands restlessly searching the skin of his thighs...

Somewhere on the precipice of the memory—Evan, arched against the cushions, Evan in the shower, Evan in the basement tasting like nervous energy and love—and the here and now— palms pressing down tightly on the inside of his legs, aggressive mouth bobbing up and down, Matt's entire body arched, clenched, soared, and splintered. A second later, he felt a soft bite on his thigh, and James pulled out of his mouth, violently shuddering his own end against Matt's chest. Matt heard a name called out amid the moans and stroked James's back as he came.

He understood.

With the rest of his brain slowly returning to his skull, Matt tugged at James's arm, flopping over Matt's hip.

"Come here."

"Bossy," came the murmur.

Matt laughed. James turned around and dropped next to him, their shoulders touching, each quietly regaining his breath and deep in thought. The phone rang, shrilly interrupting their silence reverie. James started a bit; he obviously wasn't expecting a call.

"Go ahead," Matt said. "It might be important."

James nodded—obviously he was a cop who never went off duty, something that Matt understood and respected. He rolled over to snag the receiver.

"Hello?"

Matt tucked his hands behind his head, watching James's face go from concern to absolute bliss to pure pain in about ten seconds. It didn't take a brain surgeon to figure out who was on the other end of the line.

"Hey, man," James finally spit out. "Everything okay? Is the place still standing?"

He listened to the conversation at the other end, averting his eyes from Matt's side of the bed. "Yeah? Okay, not a problem. I'll be back on Sunday morning...my flight leaves New York at nine thirty."

There was a long silence on James's part. Matt could hear the chatter coming through the line. James still hadn't looked up so Matt scooted over until he was directly under his downcast eyes.

"You okay?" he mouthed.

James nodded, but the look he gave Matt wasn't all that convincing. After a second, Matt put his head in James's lap. That got a slight smile.

"Uh yeah. Yeah. That's fine."

James took his free hand and stroked Matt's shoulder. It seemed to calm him down, so Matt remained still.

After a few more moments of stroking and the chatter on the other end of the phone, James said, "Yeah. I'll see you then. Right. You too."

Sitting up, Matt grabbed the receiver and put it back in the cradle, then returned to sit hip-to-hip next to James, whose eyes were focused on the ugly floral pattern of the bedspread. He realized they hadn't even managed to pull it down.

"Everything all right?"

"Fine," James mumbled.

"Well gee, I know I don't have a detective's shield anymore but I'm going to go ahead and call bullshit."

James gave him a glare but it didn't last long. He broke into laughter, shaking his head. "You...you remind me of..."

"Your roommate?"

James snickered. "You make it sound like a sitcom. Or college."

"Did you lust after your roommate in college?"

"For about eight minutes." He winked.

"Ho, ho!" Matt laughed. "Big man on campus."

"Quarterback," James sniffed.

Matt fell back on the bed. "So basically I scored really well tonight—if I was eighteen."

James dropped down next to him, rolling to his side to face Matt. "Hey, I think you scored pretty damn well—for an old guy."

"Fuck you. And don't think I missed the fact you changed the subject."

James infused his words with fake awe. "God, you're good."

"Asshole."

"A lesser man would take advantage of that line."

Matt laughed. "Uh, still not backing down. I took my Geritol this morning and I remember I asked you a question."

James sighed heavily, put-upon. "Okay, okay. It was my roommate. I came to New York to avoid his wedding preparations. Now he's called to tell me they're having a little prenuptial ritual—some nonsense—at the loft the night I get back. He wanted to make sure I'd be back in time." Weary, James scrubbed at his eyes with the back of his hands. "So now I get to fly three thousand miles home to make a party I'd rather cut my arm off than attend."

Matt lay quietly, trying to think of something smart and supportive to say. In the end, he went with, "That fucking sucks."

"No shit."

"But you'll go back. And smile. And never say a word about how you really feel."

"Yeah."

"That sucks even harder, my friend."

"Yeah."

Chapter Fourteen

From deep under the cover of restless sleep, Evan began to climb into consciousness. His hearing picked up a gaggle of young voices—the kids were back—and some adult ones blending in to the dull roar that always accompanied his children during their waking hours. Helena was undoubtedly still here. He smelled something delicious, meaning his partner had invited someone who could cook. For a moment, Evan curled up under the heavy quilt and enjoyed it all. Family, friends, a moment of rare humor, anticipation of sitting down with all the people he loved, enjoying a good meal.

The doorbell interrupted his dreamy reverie and a male voice called out a greeting. For a heart-stopping moment, Evan thought, *Matt's here. He's back.* But reality, as it was wont to do, crashed down too quickly for him to savor the possibility. Matt wasn't back. He wouldn't be. Because Evan had sent him away, broken his heart.

A cold chill spread through his body like a shock. He burrowed under the covers. It had been so long since he'd ventured up here, into their bed. Sleeping—or rather, restlessly tossing and turning, pretending to sleep—on the sofa had worked for a while, but now even that place was haunted. Sherri lurked up here in the shadows, Matt waited for him downstairs. And in the shower.

If the actual experience of being with Matt in the shower had altered the shape and scope of Evan's brain, the memories of it threatened to burst a blood vessel. The sound of running water made him hard as stone, which certainly keep his mornings interesting. But it wasn't just the sex (and the sex was always on his mind), it was the intimacy, the touching, the very sight of Matt's warm and welcoming face he missed so much. Some mornings he doubled over from the sheer pain of it, hiding in the bathroom. Ashamed and quite suddenly aroused, Evan clenched the covers in his fists. In the days since he'd forced Matt out the door, Evan had gone from startlingly numb to a depth of pain he hadn't felt since...

Since...

Since Sherri's death.

Now the memory of Matt (his kindness, his smile, his hands, his mouth) sat side by side with Sherri's ghost (her eyes, her love, her faith), and both of them sat in judgment of Evan, every second of every day. He'd abandoned Sherri and let her die alone. He'd let panic and shame push Matt away.

He was alone.

The kids and his job were all that he was left with. As much as his children fed his soul and gave him a reason to get up in the morning, he knew it wasn't enough. Sometimes it was easy to ignore the emptiness, the man who needed more. The man who needed comfort, companionship. Passion. Love. Images flashed through his mind. Every one the internal movie of Matt and their time together. No matter what he did, no matter what thoughts he conjured up to fight it, Evan couldn't banish Matt from his mind.

His body burned.

He tightened his hands on the comforter, trying to quell the feelings of lust thrumming through his veins. It had been so long, so very long, since he'd given into it. Since he'd relieved the ache with his hand and a fantasy in his mind's eye instead of willing it away, being a martyr to the pain. But this time his control felt a little too thin, and the urge too sharp.

Eyes tightly shut, he eased one hand under the covers, trying to disassociate himself with each tiny incremental move. Too soon his hand grazed against the straining bulge between his legs. Evan blew out a breath he'd been holding far too long; little pinpricks of light flickered behind his eyes. Before he could change his mind, he squeezed his cock and just...arched...off the bed.

Biting his lip to mask the hungry sound fighting to escape his throat, he tightened his fingers slowly, letting the rush of pleasure flood his skin. It was easy to keep his hand moving once he began, once he gave himself permission to just feel for once.

The fantasy was always the same—no, not a fantasy. It was a minute-by-minute remembrance of every caress, every kiss, every...push...of his hips Matt had gifted him with. The first awkward night in Matt's apartment, when he felt like he was going to fly apart from the sheer joy of being touched and held. Kissing on the couch, bodies pressed together...then the shower.

His hand moved faster, tightening; his legs fell open and something at the base of his spine crackled with fiery heat. He could hear Matt gasping "Fuck me" and now his hand was moving at a painful pace, and then he shivered with agonizing and perfect completion, shuddering through the aftershocks, slowly coming down to rest on the bed.

His hand was wet with semen, his face damp with tears. It always ended the same—a flash of release and then the weight of his guilt pressing down until Evan gasped aloud. It wasn't guilt for the release; it was guilt at having to cheat with Matt's memory.

* * *

He took a quick shower—in the dark, cold—then dressed in jeans and a sweater, trying to look human, trying to warm up a bit. Evan's brain felt a bit less fuzzy, and in a way that wasn't an entirely good thing because self-realization hurt.

His list of victims—a list that included his own name as well—seemed far too long.

How long could he hide in the haze and pain, burying himself in avoidance?

He knew he was hiding from Sherri's death, from his feelings for Matt, from being the father he knew his kid's deserved. His job—he couldn't even go there. Everything he'd prided himself on had somehow ended up in a big ashy heap.

On shaky legs, Evan descended the staircase. The tribunal awaited.

Miranda spotted him first and let out a loud but guarded "Dad!" that was quickly echoed by Kathleen, Elizabeth, and Danny. Helena came around the corner to watch him warily. This was going to be fun.

He noticed Vic Wolkowski sitting on the sofa. Watching intently. Shit.

"Evan."

Nodding a greeting, he then spotted Serena Abbot, drying her hands on a dishtowel, and watching him speculatively from his kitchen.

"Hey," he croaked, cursing his weak voice. "Something smells great."

A few nods amongst the crowd; the rest were blank faces. Jesus, was he really that fragile these days? Even his little ones were watching him like the seams of his sanity were about to split and spill onto the floor.

Which wasn't very far from the truth.

He girded up his strength and plastered on something resembling a smile. Reaching out his arms, he walked over to the couch and gave the kids each a tight hug. His heart broke the way they minutely tensed.

Swallowing his bitterness, Evan kept smiling as reassuringly as he could, moved to stand near Vic, who had a look in his eyes that bespoke of reproach and suspicion. He didn't bother to meet Helena's gaze because she had already seen him fall apart and wouldn't believe any bullshit.

Serena flashed a look very similar to Vic's. They made a lovely couple.

Awkward silence.

Some more awkward silence.

Finally Helena apparently took pity on him because she clapped her hands together and said, "OK! Let's get the table set. We've got about a ton of food to work through tonight!"

Serena rolled her eyes, which made the little kids snicker as they moved into the kitchen. Helena caught Evan's glance and smiled gently; she seemed to understand he needed to ease into the evening.

Everyone clamored into the kitchen to "help" Serena but Evan held back. He could see Vic staring at him and he knew what was coming.

When the living room had cleared out of non-essential personnel, Evan faced his boss with squared shoulders.

Vic sighed. "Evan, I realize how tough things have been for you. And that's not bullshit, you know that," he said softly, intently. "You need help. And you need it now. No more pussyfooting around."

A huge lump settled in the middle of Evan's throat. He nodded.

"I have the name of someone, someone who helped me a lot after my wife...died. I'm going to give you his number, tonight. And tomorrow, first thing, I want you to call and make an appointment."

As he reached around to grab his wallet, Vic gave Evan a very stern look.

"After you make that appointment, you come and tell me the time and date. After that first appointment, you come and tell me how many sessions you're scheduled for. We'll work your schedule around so you don't have to miss a lot of time, all right?"

"Yeah, Vic... Thanks," Evan said quietly. He took the card and stared at it.

"Evan, this is an opportunity I'm giving you here. Frankly, it's only because I do understand your situation that I am giving it to you. Either work with this doctor and salvage your life or I'm putting you on leave."

Evan's head jerked up. "What?"

"This is your last chance, Evan. I've let a lot slide but it ends now. I can't trust you on the streets in your condition."

That made Evan bristle. "I'm a good cop."

"You're a brilliant cop. One of the best I ever worked with but you are depressed and lethargic and distracted and grieving on so many levels that I can't trust your instincts are at 100 percent."

Vic's voice raised slightly, and Evan could hear the emotion behind his words.

"You are a fortunate man, Evan. You have four beautiful kids who love you desperately. You have friends who want you to heal. And you have a chance to love someone pretty damn terrific..."

Evan tensed up, his face frozen. Jesus.

"I know that something went wrong, but I have to tell you, Evan, I hope it's something you can fix. I've known Matt for a long, long time and...he's a special person. He doesn't fall very easily, Evan."

He tried to move his mouth, tried to say something, but his throat was sealed closed. All he could do was nod and drop his eyes to the carpet.

When he found his voice, Evan whispered, "I'll call the doctor first thing in the morning. I'm due back on Monday morning—is that still a go?"

Vic shrugged. "You tell me."

"Desk duty for the first few weeks. I can do follow up calls, that sort of thing."

"That sounds workable."

"Okay."

They stood in silence for a few minutes, sounds of laughter and chatter coming from the kitchen.

"Hey, you guys almost done in there? We've got food on the table." Serena came to the edge of the room, a little tentative.

Vic shot her a smile. "Coming. It smells incredible."

Serena glowed her thanks and turned to go back into the kitchen.

"Let's go enjoy the meal and the company, okay?" Vic said kindly. "Tomorrow you start putting it together. Tonight, you get a reminder of why it's worth the work."

Evan nodded. "Thank you. For everything."

Vic reached out and gave Evan's arm a light punch. Evan couldn't suppress a grin.

"Yeah. Thanks, coach."

Vic rolled his eyes. They shared a quiet moment and then joined the rest of the family in the kitchen.

As Evan looked around at the smiles and let himself be filled with the sounds and smells and warmth of these people, he realized that someone was missing.

Matt was missing. And he couldn't deny that anymore.

* * *

Matt and James woke up early and decided to get breakfast before going their separate ways. James had to hop on a plane and go be a great (heartbroken) best friend. Matt had to go be...Matt and figure out what the holy fuck to do with his pathetic life.

They showered separately because Matt just couldn't go there. They found a hole-in-the-wall diner down a side street and ordered King Breakfasts—five ninety-nine for enough cholesterol to set off warning bells. It was delicious.

Somehow there was no awkwardness, considering they'd only know each other for about fifteen hours and had already both shared their deepest feelings. And had sex. They talked police, baseball, basketball, and traffic in New York versus traffic in Washington state. It was enlightening. Matt only had a few twinges of "I wish I were here with Evan."

And most of them were, "I wish I was here with Evan and James, because I think they would get along." And of course, "I wish I was here with Evan and James, but that I had had sex with Evan." He didn't let it interfere with the good time he had with James though.

They parted ways on the street. An airport farewell seemed a little...bold. They exchanged business cards and home numbers, promised to keep in touch.

"Call Evan," James suddenly said, apropos of nothing (they were discussing the best route to Queens). Matt started a bit. "I mean it," he said, a little more passionately. "Don't let too much time pass by, okay? Don't blow this."

Matt knew exactly where this was coming from so he just nodded, feeling an odd twinge in his throat.

"You should take your own advice," he said softly.

James shook his head. "I missed my shot. But you…the door's still open."

"I'm not so sure about that."

"Kick it in." James winked.

Matt laughed out loud. "Okay, okay. I promise."

"Good."

"I'll think about calling."

"Jerk."

They grinned at one another for a moment.

"Take care of yourself."

"You too."

And then, with a firm handshake and a gorgeous smile, James was gone, whisked away in a hastily hailed cab to LaGuardia. It was quite simply the oddest one night stand Matt had ever had—aside from the fact that James was a guy.

Matt watched, long after the vehicle had disappeared from view, then turned to hail his own cab.

And ran smack into Miranda Cerelli.

Blinking in surprise, Matt struggled to find his voice. He had no idea how Evan had explained his abrupt departure from their lives.

"Matt!" Miranda cried, with real delight in her voice. A second later, she seemed to retreat, as if she regretted her exuberance.

"Hi, Miranda," he said, going with sincere warmth as his safest bet.

"How are you doing?"

"Um...good." Her eyes seem to flicker everywhere but Matt's face. He tried not to notice how much the nervous mannerism reminded him of Evan.

"No school today?"

"We're off—teacher's conferences. I'm meeting some friends for lunch. Then we're gonna check out NYU."

"Hey, that's right—you're almost done with school."

She warmed to that. "I know! I can't believe it."

"NYU's a nice school I hear."

"Uh-huh. Totally awesome and it has everything I want. 'Cause I'm going to take communications, you know. To work in television. I so hope I get in."

Matt smiled warmly. "I'm sure you won't have a problem."

"Thanks."

Caught up in the moment, the words just slipped out. "I bet your dad is damn proud of you, Miranda."

They both froze, Matt cursing himself for venturing into that painful territory. Miranda's eyes went back to the ground and her shoulders clenched.

"Shit, Miranda. I'm sorry. I didn't mean...shit..." he babbled. "I don't want to put you in an awkward..."

Shit.

He also realized, quite suddenly and quite painfully, that he was seeing his ex-lover's daughter—and she was just seeing a friend of her dad's. He bit his tongue viciously.

"Matt, can I ask you a question?"

"Uh, sure."

"Why aren't you and my dad friends anymore?"

And there you go.

Matt took a deep breath and swallowed the knot in his throat.

Gee, Miranda, I don't know. We stopped being friends a few months ago when we started being lovers.

"I still care...about your dad, Miranda. And I wish him the best. He just needed...space...to deal with, you know...everything that's going on..."

That sounded fucking lame even to his own ears.

And then there was the confused twist to Miranda's face when she lifted her glance. "Why would he need space from his friend? He has hardly anyone but Helena and Mr. Wolkowski. And they're work people mostly, you know. You were like the first real friend he had in forever. He was happy. It was so nice." Now Miranda was starting to tear up, and that just stabbed a red-hot poker through his heart. "He's so sad now, even more than before."

She sniffled and Matt just about died.

"Aw, honey, please don't cry. I'm so sorry, I really am. But your dad knows what he's doing. He must've had his reasons. And I want you to know, I am here for you guys. You and your sisters and your brother *and* your dad. You just have to ask."

She sniffled a little more.

"Okay." Matt fumbled for his wallet and grabbed a business card (his second of the morning, the circumstances of which made him dizzy at this moment) then a pen, writing down every possible number he could think of where Miranda could find him. He thrust it toward her.

"Here you go, honey. You keep this with you. Anytime, *any*time you need something, you let me know. Anytime."

Her shining blue eyes pinned him with a piercing gaze.

Something in the air between them shifted and settled, like knowledge passed with molecules and not words.

"Thank you."

"I...I'm sorry, Miranda. You'll never know how much."

"I...thank you, Matt. I'm sorry too. I hope my dad wants to be friends with you again someday. I think he needs...I think he needs to be friends with you."

It was in her face, even he could read it—that mix of girlish innocence and "seen too much" wisdom. A little voice told her this was more than friendship but she didn't seem worldly enough to put all the pieces together. For that, Matt was grateful. Given Evan's reaction during their last...fight...his kid knowing about their relationship wasn't something to reveal on a street corner in Chinatown.

So finally Matt just said "Me too, Miranda" and tried to resist the urge to hug her. She didn't have the same impulse control, because a second later she was throwing her arms around him and giving him a hasty squeeze.

"Okay, I have to go."

Not trusting his voice, Matt just nodded.

"Uh...bye."

Deep breath, Matt, deep breath. "Take care, Miranda. Say hi...to your family."

"Yeah. Bye."

And then she ran. Literally.

Shaking, Matt lifted his arm to hail a cab.

* * *

Matt checked the map in his hands, trying to make heads or tails of which of the little boxes translated into the admissions building for NYU. In a bold, shockingly non-alcohol-induced decision, Matthew Haight had decided to Return To School.

Amazing. Nothing like giving yourself a second (or was this third?) start in life.

The NYU catalog was sitting with his mail the Morning After (he was beginning to think of many parts of his life as being in capital letters). The cab ride from the city to Staten Island had been a revelatory one for Matt.

Between James and his run-in with Miranda, he was simply rung out and ready for a lightning bolt. Either one bringing death or one bringing revelation; at that point, he didn't much care. He realized that his life had stalled, had been stalled for years. He needed to do something, needed a shake-up to get him moving. Anywhere. Just someplace better than "here." "Here" was waiting for his old job to come back (never gonna happen), waiting for Evan (Magic 8 Ball says "future is hazy"), waiting for his youth. He needed to stop waiting.

No pressure.

The NYU catalog, sitting there in complete innocence, was his thunderbolt. The conversation with Miranda? The catalog sitting there? The catalog he hadn't ordered? Matt didn't believe in a lot of things but he did acknowledge when the universe was bitch slapping him with a message.

After registering for the spring semester's classes at NYU (Psychology, Intro to Business, American Literature I, and Spanish II—'cause he felt like showing off), Matt hightailed it over to the West Side to meet with the real estate agent. The tiny studio was scarcely a size improvement over his place on Staten Island but at least it was a change. He signed the lease, got the keys, and— relieved of a large portion of his bank account—headed back to his soon-to-be-former pad.

Matt had a million things to occupy his mind during the ferry ride home. He needed to get a new phone number, with an extra line for the computer. He needed to buy a computer. And something to put the computer on… It went on and on. The packing was nearly done seeing as there wasn't much outside of clothes and furniture in the apartment. And the couch and the chair wouldn't be a problem since the delivery men hadn't…

Ouch.

One second Matt was thinking about moving and the next it was all about his weekend with Evan.

Shit.

* * *

As he trudged into his apartment's vestibule, he noticed a yellow sticky note on his mailbox. After pulling out his mail (bill, bill, flyer, bill), he read the note. USPS had kindly informed him that his neighbor in 1A held his package.

Mrs. Crimene was about two hundred years old and the size of a lawn gnome. Matt was always afraid he would break her should they pass too closely in the hall. She blinked myopically at him for a few minutes then scurried away to retrieve his package. It took her several moments to return; the box wasn't large but it apparently weighed far more than her stick arms could manage. Matt reached into the apartment—not stepping over the door rubber because Mrs. Crimene had been quite adamant about him staying on his side.

"Thank you, Mrs. Crimene," he practically shouted.

She nodded, blinked, and slammed the door without another word. Gee, Matt thought, she was really going to miss him, wasn't she?

* * *

Upstairs he dropped the box on the counter and tossed his jacket there as well. No messages on the machine, to match the boring mail in his box. Oh yes, Mr. Excitement. At least he'd gotten a package. He didn't recall ordering anything. One look at the return mailing label and he broke into a smile.

Washington.

He had no idea what James might be sending but the very reminder of his friend (lover? Nah, too weird.) brightened his mood as he tore off the paper.

Inside Matt found a neatly sealed box. A few quick swipes with his scissors and it was open. A small square of paper lay on the top.

In James's bold handwriting, he read:

Matt—

Here's a little research material. Have you called yet?

Don't be an idiot.

J.

Matt chuckled. He imagined the stern "tone" of James's voice as he wrote the words. Digging in, Matt pulled out three hardcover books and burst out laughing. "Research material" indeed—*The Gay Kama Sutra?*

Snickering, he flipped open the cover and saw James's neat script in the corner.

Call him was underlined several times, and beneath, in smaller letters, was written, *I recommend pages seventeen, thirty, and forty-one. Stretch first.*

Matt laughed until his gut hurt. Goddamn but he was sorry James lived three thousand miles away! The books were great for a laugh, but they also expressed the kindness and encouragement that James wanted to give him.

Call Evan.

Call him.

You idiot.

Matt sighed. Yeah, he wanted to call Evan. He truly did. But not right now. Right now, he was going to call James and bust his chops for sending pornography through the USPS.

Matt grabbed his wallet from the jacket he'd flung over a pile of boxes, rummaging through until he found what he was looking for. James's business card. He checked his wall clock and did a little math. Eight thirty on the West Coast. James would probably be home.

On the third ring, the phone picked up.

"Hello?"

Ah. The infamous roommate.

"Hi. Is James there?"

"James?" The voice sounded surprised. "Do you mean Jim?"

"Yeah." Matt smiled a little. The roommate seemed a bit off balance.

"Is he home?"

"No, he's…out. Running. Can I take a message?"

"Sure." In a burst of sudden inspiration, Matt decided to have a little fun. "You can tell him that Matt called. He'll know who it is. I just wanted to thank him for…everything."

"Uh…huh. Anything else—a number?'

Laughing, Matt dropped the pitch of his voice the tiniest bit.

"Oh, he has my number."

He could almost hear the imaginary rim shot.

"Riiiight."

"Thanks."

"No problem." With that, Matt hung up the phone. He wanted James's roommate to be boiling over with questions—and maybe a little jealousy—when James got home from his run.

* * *

A shower relaxed Matt after his busy day; he needed to do a bit more packing before the weekend. He had just finished changing into some sweats when the phone rang. Grinning, he picked up the receiver, expecting to hear James's rich voice on the other end. "Hello!" he boomed out. There was silence on the other end.

Okay—not James. "Hello?" Matt asked, quieter this time. He could hear breathing.

"Um...Matt? Hi. It's...it's Miranda. Miranda Cerelli."

Something broke in the center of Matt's chest.

"Hi, Miranda. Is everything all right?"

She made a shuddering sound into the phone and the fist tightened around Matt's heart.

"I'm...I'm in jail Matt," she blurted out, sobs taking over. "Please...please can you help me?"

Matt got dressed, grabbed his keys and wallet, and ran out of his building in a breathless panic. He was already on the bridge into Manhattan before he realized he was fucking panicking and took a deep breath.

The traffic was moderate and he sailed downtown, parking in a lot near the police station. Before he ran into the building Matt stopped, running his hands through his hair and cursing out a stream of blue that would make a marine blush. This was like a fucking minefield—him rushing down to help Evan's daughter without calling Evan. Part of it, hell a *lot* of it felt deceptive, and he just didn't want this to mushroom cloud into his face, like Evan thinking he'd use Miranda's situation to try and…

Something.

Faking calm, Matt headed into the precinct, ducking around boys in blue and their suspects/victims/witnesses to find the desk sergeant. He didn't recognize him, but the guy was clearly a vet with enough worry lines under his eyes to make Matt think he also had a mess of kids somewhere over the Queenborough Bridge.

"Hey, Matt Haight," he said, smiling and extending his hand. "Retired NYPD," he fibbed casually. "I got a call from the daughter of a family friend—she's being held down here."

The desk sergeant—his name tag identifying him as Sgt. Pollock—nodded cautiously and shook Matt's hand. "Name?"

"Miranda Cerelli," Matt said, sticking his hands in his pockets. "Picked up with some kids—vandalism or something." He tried to play it casual. "Her dad's out on a case right now so she called me."

Sgt. Pollock glanced up and then went back to his clipboard. "You have some ID?"

"Absolutely." He opened his wallet and leaned against the large desk. "You need some more backup you can call Captain Wolkowski up at Vice." Matt slid his wallet into his back pocket.

More nodding and Sgt. Pollock gave Matt a long hard look, using a cop bullshit detector with the laser beams coming directly out of his eyes.

There was a painful pause, lingering until a trickle of sweat ran between Matt's shoulder blades.

Then the sergeant picked up the phone and dialed down to holding.

* * *

Matt said a few prayers of gratitude on the way to the room where they'd stashed Miranda. He bumped into a detective outside the door, Joe Banyon, whom he knew in a very distant, very casual way. A tremor of panic but Detective Banyon clearly didn't remember old news like Matt Haight and he bought the line of bullshit with a weary nod.

"She was with some kids. The boys got mouthy with a shop owner, there was yelling and they threw a garbage can at the front window of the store. We picked up the girls as they were running away." The man shrugged and indicated the room with a tilt of his head. "She's clean, right? You know the family?"

"Her mom died last year," Matt said quietly, leaning forward a bit. "She's a great kid though, no problems. Dad's a detective up at Vice—it's all just peer pressure shit, I'm sure."

Banyon nodded. "Yeah, that was my gut. The girls seemed more scared than anything. You gonna take her home? The guy's not pressing charges against her or the other one. They might have to testify though."

Matt paused then reached into his pocket for his keys. "I'll drive her home. You need me to sign some stuff…"

"Yeah, I'll go get the file off my desk." Banyon shook his hand and wandered off, stopping at the coffee machine before he went any further.

Weak kneed at the level of bullshit he was fertilizing this place with, Matt ducked into the room.

* * *

Miranda had her head down on the desk, sniffling and shaking. She had to pee *so bad* and she wanted to take a shower because God, it was *so* disgusting down there in that room. She hadn't seen her friends since they were put in the squad car, and

God, her father was going to kill her. What if he didn't let her go to college now?

The panic flared in her chest as the door opened and she sat up, turned around, and there was...Matt.

And then she ran to him and cried all at the same time, throwing her arms around his middle because he was an adult and he would make things better and he wasn't her father.

"Hey, it's okay," Matt said, swallowing around a lump in his throat as he rubbed her back. "I'm springing you right now okay? We're going to get you home."

"No, no—can I go to your p-place? My f-father's going to kill me!" She wept, looking up at him imploringly.

"Miranda, come on. Your dad's a reasonable person. You just tell him the truth." Matt tried to look stern but failed miserably. "You're going to get grounded, we *both* know that. But your dad loves you more than anything in the world..."

"I swear, I didn't do anything. We were just standing there! I told the police that!"

"And they believe you, which is why you're getting out of here now, with me." He looked around and spotted a small box of tissues in the corner. "Here—wipe your eyes, okay? We'll stop somewhere so you can wash your face and...you need something to drink?" Matt untangled himself from Miranda's tightly held arms and grabbed the box. "I just have to sign some papers then I'll drive you home." Home, where he would have to explain to Evan why he brought his daughter home from jail...

As Miranda wiped her face, her expression of trepidation matched the one on Matt's face perfectly.

The drive to Queens was quiet, punctuated by a few sniffles and slurps on her Big Gulp from Miranda in the passenger seat. She got her bag back, washed her face, and combed her hair, and the caffeine seemed to be calming her down a bit. Matt tapped his fingers on the steering wheel as he practiced what he was going to say to Evan, how he was going to look at Evan, and whether this could all be done on the front steps, because walking into that house was going to make him throw the fuck up.

Fortunately, there was a truck breakdown before the tolls and Matt leaned back in his seat, glancing over at Miranda. She was lost in thought but eventually turned her head his way.

"Thanks, Matt. Sincerely. Just…I made such a stupid mistake and I didn't know who to call and I just couldn't call my dad, you know? And you were always so nice…" Her voice trailed off into a watery little sigh. "I don't understand why you don't come around anymore."

Suddenly the traffic was more nightmare than reprieve and Matt turned to stare out the windshield again. "Miranda," he began, his innards twisting up into knots. "I really can't go into this. It's…it's between your dad and me. But…just so you know—I really loved being around you kids." His throat hurt and he rolled down the window for some musty hot air to gulp into his lungs.

Miranda sniffled again and turned to look back out the passenger window. The traffic lurched ahead and Matt followed, every positive and rational thought he'd had about what happened shrinking into that same confused anger as the day Evan suddenly decided it was over.

* * *

Evan was caught in traffic himself, listening to the oldies station and absently humming here and there. Early day as Wolkowski was still keeping him on a light caseload and a close leash. A few cases were thrown his way and every week he had to sit down with Wolkowski and discuss his ongoing therapy. Sometimes it burned, sometimes he punched a wall or kicked a garbage can in fucking frustration, because Jesus, he didn't have much left in his life aside from his kids and his career.

Not that that was anyone's fault but his own, of course.

It was the highlight—and that was sarcasm—of therapy. Evan Cerelli's Guilt Complex. Guilt for Sherri's life and death. Guilt for Matt. Guilt for ending things with Matt. Guilt for starting things with Matt. Guilt for being happy. Guilt for World War Fucking II at this point—the list went on and on. And when the shrink asked him why he thought everything was his fault he didn't have an answer, not even a flippant one.

That was bugging him.

Because rationally—and he was still capable of being rational once in awhile—he knew he wasn't responsible for everything. Jesus. How many times had he explained to some grieving parent or spouse or witness that they couldn't have prevented something terrible happening to the person they loved? He gave himself the same speech in his head and wondered if the people he gave it to over those years wanted to smash his face in with a tire iron.

* * *

They pulled into the driveway; Miranda and Matt both made the same relieved sound.

Evan wasn't home yet.

"The kids are at the sitter," Miranda murmured, her hand gripped on the door rest. "Wanna...should we go inside and wait?"

No.

"Okay." Matt cleared his throat, turned off the car, and opened the door, the memories assailing him.

Miranda followed, dragging her feet as she pulled her key out of her bag. It was literally in the lock, the little cylinders clicking, when the sound of a car approaching made them both turn around.

Evan pulled into the driveway.

There was a car in his driveway, a familiar car, and his eyes went to the front door…

Evan slammed on the brakes. Then he parked in the driveway, behind Matt's car, his brain flying in every possible direction and coming up with nothing.

Matt. Here. With Miranda.

* * *

Matt's heart went *boom!* and *thud!* and his brain started cursing a mighty blue streak as he tried to do something other than jam his hands into his pockets and look uncomfortable. It didn't work. Miranda was practically vibrating herself into hysteria next to him.

"It's okay, Miranda. Just go talk to your dad," he murmured, putting his hand over hers and opening the door.

She just managed a nod, walking toward him with agonizing slowness.

Evan met her halfway, his mild freak out over Matt replaced with fear at the look on his daughter's face.

"What?" he said, running the rest of the way and putting his hands on her arms. "What's wrong?" One of the other kids…?

And Miranda just erupted in a flood of tears, huge choking sobs as she bowed her head. It was all so surreal and then Matt walked over, gingerly approaching them.

Evan looked up, his eyes wide with confusion but seeing Matt's calm expression he started thinking, *If he's not freaking out, maybe it's not so bad.*

"She, uh, got into some trouble. I picked her up and brought her home—she's okay, just freaked out," Matt rambled, gesturing toward the house. "You wanna uh…"

"Yeah," Evan agreed, quickly, automatically. He wrapped his arms around his still crying child and herded her into the house, his rational side wanting answers—his irrational side completely and uncomfortably aware of Matt following them into the house.

* * *

Matt shut the door and found the light automatically, watching as Evan led Miranda to the couch. There was a lot of murmuring and quiet conversation; he stood there like a piece of excess furniture until it felt intrusive. He headed for the kitchen.

Once there, the memories started popping up like targets at the firing range. Here they are, kissing. Bang! Here they are, fighting. Bang! Here they are, Evan splattering Matt's guts all over the floor. Bang! He went into the fridge and stared until Bang! the cold propelled him to move. Matt grabbed a pitcher of iced tea, continuing to make himself at home—ha—pouring three glasses and arranging them on the counter. And waiting for the other shoe to drop.

Bang.

* * *

The story came out in literal dribs and dabs; Evan used up the entire box of tissues as Miranda worked herself into a mild hysteria. He managed a bit of sternness and disappointment, but mostly he was just scared shitless at how scared she was. Like she thought he was going to fly into a rage instead of just holding her close and telling her that everyone makes mistakes.

Yeah.

* * *

Matt drank his iced tea. Then he drank Miranda's. Then he had to take a piss and fuck it all if he was going upstairs into that bathroom. Basement, he thought and then *fuck*—that one was aloud—he walked downstairs into Memory Central, grumbling the whole way.

He took a piss in the small half bath, flushing and avoiding the corner where Helena had caught them kissing. Matt stomped back up the stairs, his flight instinct kicking in. What the fuck was he doing here? He helped Miranda, he took her home to her father, and now he was done. Right? Evan broke things off, he didn't want him around. This was fucking masochistic.

And that carried him all the way upstairs and right into the kitchen where he surprised Evan, poised over the sink filling a glass with water.

"Hey," Evan said, awkward and tired and still wearing his suit jacket. "Uh…"

"Had to take a piss," answered Matt, snapping off the light, his tone just as hard. He looked around and didn't see Miranda.

"I sent her upstairs to wash her face and lie down. Listen…thank you. She told me that you rushed down to get her and I appreciate that," Evan murmured, leaning against the sink and staring in the vicinity of Matt's shoulder.

Matt shrugged, asshole behavior bubbling over. "No matter what happened between us, I don't have any ill will toward your kids."

Evan winced.

"Yeah…well, thanks. I'm going to bring this up to her, see if I can't get her to take a nap." He walked past Matt, fingers itching and brain burning.

"Right." And then Matt had a clear path to the door. Fuck this, whatever. "Tell Miranda to feel better."

"I will." Evan was on the stairs, hit with a wave of nostalgic memory so keen he nearly dropped the glass. He started to say thanks again, but as Matt reached the door, hand on the knob, what came out was, "Can you wait a few minutes? I have to move my car." And he disappeared upstairs.

Matt turned around to say something sharp and "hurry the fuck up"-ish but Evan was gone and he couldn't.

He kicked the door then went and sat on the couch. He had just decided it was a bad idea when the door opened and a gaggle of Cerellis fell through.

"Matt!"

The three younger Cerellis hadn't had a shitty day, complete with being arrested, and they weren't reliving the memories of what had happened in this house—good and bad—they were just happy to see an old friend.

Matt got hugs and questions and even a kiss from Elizabeth, and Jesus, when did these kids get so big—had he really been gone from this for so long?

"What the hell are you three eating? You're like weeds!" He managed to sound gruff and not emotional, but clearly his eyes gave something away because Kathleen grinned over her younger siblings' heads.

"It's a growing up thing, Matt. It happens to kids," she said cheekily and he could see she was going to be a handful in about…six weeks. "Where the heck have you been? We totally missed you."

"Totally," Danny echoed, throwing his bag in the direction of the umbrella stand. "Are you staying for dinner?"

Matt was at a loss. Totally at a loss, because anything was just a stab in the dark. "I have to move my car" isn't actually a "missed you, stay for dinner" offer.

"Uhhh, not sure." He ruffled Danny's hair and smiled.

"You're not sure where you've been?" Elizabeth looked a little confused.

"Maybe he was abducted by aliens." That was Kathleen again, disappearing into the kitchen with her brother on her heels.

Elizabeth laughed and Matt made his decision right then and there that Evan could just toss his ass out if he didn't want him here. He was staying for dinner.

* * *

Evan took his sweet time getting downstairs. He sat with Miranda until she drifted off, then watched her sleep. There was no way he could have missed the stampede of the rest of his kids and their voices mingling with Matt's.

It hurt. More than he ever thought possible.

All this lonely time, all the regrets—and now there was Matt, falling right back into place. Filling a space in their lives, all of their lives. And Jesus, that had been hard to miss what with Matt not looking anything like Sherri… It never occurred to him that a man could fit that role for him.

Drifting through his thoughts, Evan tried desperately to remember all the perfectly valid and reasonable reasons he'd pushed Matt away. Really—it made sense. For his kids (downstairs, laughing and talking, and did someone yell up something about pepperoni?), and his job (Helena and Vic, huge supporters of what he and Matt had together), and his reputation in the neighborhood.

Mother of God, was he doing this because of his reputation? Was he afraid to admit Matt made him happy, turned him on, filled a space in his life? The consequences of making a decision like this...when did he decide being miserable, and therefore making his kids miserable, was acceptable?

Miranda stirred in her sleep. The fact that she'd called Matt over him—he couldn't stop thinking about that. She was afraid of him. Afraid of Evan's reaction. The first person she thought of after that fear...Matt, even after all this time. It blew his mind and neatly ordered decision out of the water.

That's where his thoughts sat, his body still as he watched the shadows fall across the room. A little knock at the door caught his attention, finally, and Evan turned to see Elizabeth shyly hovering.

"Matt ordered pizza!" she whispered loudly, the most excited he'd seen her in a while.

And it wasn't because of the pepperoni.

Evan nodded, smiling back at her. "One minute, honey," he whispered back. She dashed back downstairs to the hub of activity. He tucked the blanket a little tighter around Miranda, took a deep breath, and headed toward the staircase.

* * *

"We have pizza, we have meat and meatless, we have sticks, we have a salad without olives, we have...what else do we have?" Matt asked, looking around at the ravenous faces clustering the box of food.

"A need for antacids?" Evan's voice cut through the babble and his kids managed to pry their attention away from the steaming tin foil-covered containers to say hello.

"Yeah, good idea." Blustering, Matt ducked his head and started opening everything; Kathleen passed paper plates and Danny was in charge of plastic silverware.

"Napkins," Elizabeth said. "And who wants milk?"

"Milk and pizza?" Matt looked up to shudder.

"Beer and pizza?" Evan ducked around the island, narrowly avoiding a collision with Matt as Danny leaned through to claim the last somethingoranother in the fridge.

"Much better." And Matt couldn't help himself, he looked up and caught Evan's eye, waiting. Challenging. This would be much easier if his chest wasn't tightening up so goddamn much.

"Thanks for taking care of dinner." Evan didn't back down from the stare; he grabbed the fridge door from Danny and got out two beers. "The kids are thrilled to see you."

"Duh, he knows that," Kathleen said, filling her plate over the grabs of her brother and sister. "Did you know he was abducted by aliens?"

Evan handed Matt the beer and just like in the movies their fingers touched, and just like in the movies Evan got a thought bubble over his head full of regret and want.

"It's the only reason they could think of that I'd not be here."

The gauntlet was thrown down; Matt turned away first, popped open his beer and reached for a slice.

* * *

Dinner was a hit, and afterward, no one gave Matt a chance to say good night. Danny was already putting *King Kong* into the DVD player. Evan fussed in the kitchen forever; he put together a plate for Miranda, put away the leftovers. Cleaned the counter. Ran the dishwasher. And then finally turned out the light.

At some point the movie would end, the kids would go to bed, and Evan knew as sure as he knew his name, that Matt would still be there.

The look the other man gave him as he sat down was all the confirmation he needed. They were going to talk.

King Kong might possibly have been the longest movie ever or maybe it seemed that way because Matt just wanted the goddamn thing to be over. So he could—or they could—talk or fight or something. Anything that wasn't sitting here in hazy domestic comfort with a room full of sprawled out kids and a sofa that suddenly seemed entirely too small.

Or cramped with memories, that might be it.

By the time the credits rolled he was wishing he still smoked so he could duck outside and suck down some nicotine, but the kids distracted him. There were good night hugs and Elizabeth gave him this look, like she was staring into his brain when she said, "See you soon." It wasn't a question and the air was suddenly very heavy.

"Night!" Danny yelled, tearing up the stairs and declaring he was first in the bathroom which brought up a sound of furied frustration from Kathleen as Elizabeth trailed up, reminding them both about Dad's bathroom and jeeeeeeeeeeeze what dorks.

Matt grabbed the remote and shut off the DVD as Evan unrolled from the couch with a stretch and a sigh.

"You need to go upstairs or anything?" Matt asked, his voice loud in the quiet absence of the family.

"Nah, not unless I hear bloodshed over bathroom time," Evan answered, a wry smile playing around his mouth as he turned and looked at Matt. "I, uh…you want a beer or something?"

"Beer, beer is good." *Cop wouldn't offer a drink if he was kicking me out in five minutes.*

Evan walked into the kitchen and Matt thought he heard the words "need fortitude" in the air.

* * *

Two beers in hand, Evan returned to the living room slowly. He had so much racing through his head, too much to articulate. And there was no way to hide in sex or fighting with the kids upstairs. Jesus, he had to communicate. It was giving him hives.

"Here," he said, handing one of the sweating bottles to Matt. Matt, who looked big and strangely comfortable on the sofa. Who looked like a man who remembered that sofa and what had happened on it—the good, the bad, and the fucking ugly.

"Thanks." Matt opened the bottle and took a swig. "Sitting down or ready to run?" he said after he swallowed, throwing Evan an expression he could only describe as challenging.

"I was going to pace actually." Evan opened his bottle—and paced a bit to the other side of the room and back. "I wanted to apologize to you."

Matt shrugged. "Hey, whatever. You had a change of heart. Understandable. Not like we made any promises to each other."

Evan was pretty sure he'd given this speech before, and inwardly, there was a pretty serious wince on his part.

"But we did. Or at least...I did, to myself. I made a lot of promises to myself and then I sort of got sidetracked by—by fucked-up thinking." Evan's voice was low as he looked down at the rug. Spied popcorn. Resisted the urge to vacuum. "And I made a huge mess of what was...the thing...with us."

"You make it sound so appealing," Matt laughed, deep and hollow.

"It was."

"Yeah, it was."

Silence wove through the air, punctuated by doors slamming and feet stomping above them. Evan took a breath, taking some comfort in the sound.

"I panicked and I'm sorry. Because you didn't deserve that—you didn't deserve me just kicking you out like a freak."

"No offense, but more used to that than...this." Matt did a wave that encompassed the room. Upstairs. Evan's life.

"But you miss it. You miss the kids." Evan was bold for a moment, moving into Matt's personal space, metaphorically at least.

Matt's eyes narrowed. "They're good kids. Course I miss them."

"They miss you."

"I'm a fucking amazing guy—who wouldn't?"

The air sizzled. The noises upstairs abated a little more as the house settled down.

"Who wouldn't—good point." Evan cleared his throat and sat down on the couch—the middle of the couch. He didn't look at Matt just yet, but he could feel the other man's heated gaze boring into the side of his head.

"Don't play me," Matt said finally, and the sound of his voice made Evan's head turn. If he didn't feel like a guilty piece of shit before, the look in Matt's eyes took care of that.

"I'm not. I had pretty much convinced myself I made the right decision but there's gotta be a reason...there's just gotta be a reason you're here right now."

"Your kids asked me to stay."

"Yeah—yeah they did. And if I ever needed a better blessing than that..." Evan's voice trailed off and softened. "I have to talk to them, I have to tell them everything, but I'm not so afraid of that anymore."

* * *

Matt coughed, like beer went down the wrong pipe when actually it was more like air went down the wrong way.

"Tell the kids—what happened with us before?" he managed eventually, wiping his forehead with the back of his hand.

"Tell the kids what might be happening with us down the road," Evan offered casually, his cool eyes flickering over Matt. "I mean—if you're not convinced I'm a fucking head case with enough baggage to take a plane down."

"I have a matching set of luggage." Matt laughed, his heart trying to batter out of his chest. *What? Wait? Huh?* rolls around his head like loose dice on a craps table. "So uh—you talk to the kids and then what?"

"I don't know."

"That answer should scare me more."

"They love you."

"They love me as Dad's friend. Not necessarily as Dad's uh…special friend."

Matt watched the shudder rattle Evan's frame and reached out instinctively, resting a hand at the back of his neck. And really, he was thinking of just backing out because no matter what his assload of anger and issues, the idea of messing up this beautiful family made him want to take a header off the Brooklyn Bridge. The words would have come out of his mouth—seriously—but the corded muscles of Evan's neck against the damp of his palm disconnected his thinking brain, and then they were just staring at each other…

If he thought about it later, the best part of all this was that Evan was the one who leaned toward him, grabbing his shirt to bring him closer and then—then their mouths met.

It wasn't easy for Evan to concentrate for the next twenty-four hours; he was working on adrenaline and emotion—not a new state of being for him, but for the first time in a long time it didn't manifest from work. It bloomed from Matt and seeing him and kissing him and thinking that maybe (just maybe) this could work out.

Hope felt like a strange cloak to wear at this point in his life.

He got up and showered the next morning, pretending he had slept, answering the kids' questions about whether or not Matt would be back soon with affirmative words. Miranda hovered on the edge of the commotion, warily eyeing her father as if waiting for the explosion.

Evan just grounded her instead.

He dropped them off at school, grabbed coffee for Helena on the way to work, and felt inordinately grateful for the slow-moving traffic into Manhattan. Because he could sink into his thoughts, the reality of last night, the reality of his own stupidity. Denial and fear were never going to let him find happiness, and not finding happiness would be counterintuitive to everything he'd built his life on. Everything he and Sherri had taught their children *not* to do.

The reality of his own stupidity—definitely something Sherri would agree with.

* * *

In the squad room, Evan moved on autopilot through the morning greetings and shift change, sitting down at his desk and shuffling through papers without seeing a thing.

Which of course was the very first thing Helena noticed as she sat down across from him.

"Where the heck are you?" she asked, sucking down half the tepid coffee he'd left on her blotter.

"Huh? Oh…just got a lot on my mind," he answered absently, but apparently there was something in his tone that piqued her interest because he suddenly felt like a bug under a microscope.

"Do share." It wasn't exactly a request.

Evan's eyes flickered up from the file in front of him and he did a quick sideways glance to see who might be paying attention and murmured, "Lunch, we'll talk."

Helena smirked.

"Ohhhhhhhh, we're taking an early one," she muttered.

And they dove into their day.

* * *

Lunch turned out to be a late afternoon hot dog and soda binge in the car—not that either of them was complaining. Helena let Evan have about four bites before she turned in her seat to give her partner an evil stare.

"What's going on?"

"Chewing," Evan pointed out, moving his jaw slowly.

"C'mon. I've been good all day. Spill before I start guessing."

Evan swallowed, wiped his mouth and tried not to smile—though a tiny bit leaked out.

"Actually I should really be freaking out. Miranda got into some trouble in the city with her friends…" He sighed, rubbing his palm against the knot in his forehead. "Luckily there aren't going to be any legal consequences. Matt straightened it out."

"Matt?" Helena's grin took up all the remaining oxygen in the car. "Seriously? Matt Haight?"

"No, Matt Jones. The other guy I was uh…seeing." He crumpled up his napkin and tossed it into the paper bag.

"So what—Miranda called Matt?"

"Yeah. And he went down there to get her, and then we…well, he stayed around for dinner because the kids missed him."

"Riiiiiight, the kids missed him."

"Keep it up and I'm going to stop talking, and I haven't gotten to the good part."

Helena took another bite of her hot dog, chewing and grinning, her eyes wide.

"So we talked a little bit and…you know." Evan made a hand motion that he hoped explained everything. "Maybe I was wrong with the way I ended things."

"Duh."

"Really not a vocabulary word for a woman of your professional level."

"Whatev, dude. Is there more? Anything follow the talking?" She even used quote fingers around talking and Evan blushed.

"No," he lied. "I'm not rushing things. I need to talk to the kids; I need to figure this out."

"You need to stop thinking so damn much and just get laid." Helena drained her soda can with an obnoxious slurp. "Matt is a great guy, and second chances with a great guy don't happen all that often. Take it from me."

"I'm going to try okay?"

"There is no try…"

"Oh God, you're quoting Yoda?"

"He's a wise little alien and you need all the help you can get."

* * *

Instead of Yoda, Evan went to Vic Wolkowski. There was a vague physical resemblance...but he didn't mention that.

"Hey, you got a few minutes?"

"Case stuff or personal?" Vic shoved some folders to one side and leaned his elbows on the desk.

"Personal."

"Shut the door and pull up a chair."

Evan settled in across from Wolkowski and fidgeted for a moment before he cleared his throat and began.

"I need to know if it will affect the department if...if I'm involved with someone...who's a man."

The words were strung together with tension wire, but when Evan got them all out, a bit of air seemed to creep into parts of his lungs that hadn't felt used in a while.

Vic's expression didn't change. He was like a statue. "Depends. Do I know this someone?"

Evan smiled. Half a smile. Maybe a quirk of his lips.

"Yeah, you do."

Now Vic's facade cracked. A little. Maybe a quarter of a smile.

"So long as you're doing the same job you've always done around here, I don't see where your personal relationships come into play." He shrugged, all casual like, but the grin was teasing at his eyes. "Could certainly liven up the holiday party though..."

"Yeah, that bridge we'll cross...later. Maybe." Evan shook his head. He didn't want to see Matt drown Moses in a bowl of dip.

"I'm just glad to hear things are…going another way, Evan. I mean that."

"Honestly? Nothing is settled, not really. I don't know if he's going to give me a second chance. And I don't want to put everything out there until…until I talk to some people."

"Like the kids?" Vic's eyebrows did a little rise and fall dance.

"Yeah, like the kids. Like my in-laws." The latter of which was comparable to having been shot in the chest at this point. He winced.

"The kids are crazy about Matt…and your in-laws' approval is not required, Evan."

"No, it's not. But they could fight for custody…"

"And if they do, they'll lose. There's nothing about the way you conduct your life that makes you a bad father."

"Can I count on you as a character witness?" Evan smiled ruefully.

Vic rolled his eyes. "C'mon—you'll have so many character witnesses they'll not only throw out a custody suit, they'll give you the key to the city."

"No need to go crazy." He wiped damp palms on his slacks and checked his watch. "Thanks, Vic. I have to get home, pick up the kids. We have some talking to do."

"Understood and good luck. But you know, I don't think you're going to need it. Those are some amazing kids you got there."

Evan stood and reached his hand out; Vic shook it, giving him an extra squeeze before letting go. "Go on, get out of here. I have a warm cream soda and two weeks of back reports to read. Wanna trade?"

"Come to think of it? No."

* * *

Matt sat at his kitchen table with the sports section of the *Daily News* and a plate of lasagna. And two beers. His knee jiggled with nerves that his placid face did not reveal.

He reread a trade article four times before he remembered he wasn't an Islanders fan and really didn't care.

He checked his watch. Checked the clock on the wall. Checked the digital time on the microwave. What he was waiting for he didn't quite know; did he think Evan would wave a magic wand and make everything terrific and get settled and call him over for some sex?

Okay—that was his ultimate fantasy. That was not even vaguely reality.

He finished dinner, the beers. Took out the recycling and read an ad on the tenant board about samba classes. And a parrot for sale. Neither interested him but he read them twice for something to do.

Then he went back to his apartment.

There was no message on his machine and Matt rubbed his face with both hands. Getting his hopes up seemed stupid but he couldn't help it. You'd have thought his life thus far would have taught him a few things about, you know, lying down and playing dead when reality kept taking potshots at your head.

Guess he was just a stubborn son of a bitch.

Matt shut off the light and headed for the bathroom; he figured he could jerk off in the shower, then go to bed and stare at the ceiling for a few hours. Perfect. At least that was familiar territory.

* * *

Evan sat on the floor of the living room, sucking down a beer like it was the last one he'd ever have. Two hours. Two torturous painful hours with some tears and some anger and a lot of Evan trying to find words for things he wasn't sure existed. In the end, the twins had enough information to be confused…but fixated on the point that Matt would be around more and that was good.

Kathleen understood a bit more; she seemed torn between wanting to please her father by accepting what he said and conflicted about what it all meant. She nodded a lot, her eyes wet and her smile confused.

Again—Matt being around more was a plus for her.

Miranda was another story entirely, but really, Evan wasn't surprised by that at all. She started out stone-faced and ended up wanting to talk to her father "alone," with a meaningful glance at the other children.

After they were tucked in, Miranda launched a full-out assault. Was he always gay? Was he going to tell people? Would he lose his job? Did he really love Mom or was that all a bunch of crap?

He kept his temper—barely, but he did. He understood her confusion because hell, he was still dealing with it. How did you go your whole life thinking one thing then have it turned on a dime?

Explaining wasn't easy because Miranda was too overwrought to hear. He tried to talk about Sherri and ended up choked up which didn't help his explanation. Finally—finally—Miranda made a sound of frustration and said, "I don't want to get attached to Matt again and then have him leave okay? The kids—it hurt them."

And then she went upstairs.

Don't give us someone else to love if they're going to leave.

He couldn't agree more.

When Evan was done with his beer he dropped the bottle in the recycling and spent a few minutes cleaning up the kitchen. He made school lunches and filled the dishwasher. It was all so incredibly normal after what could only be labeled UNnormal. A good reminder that life wasn't going to end because of how he felt.

The phone seemed to loom large; Evan itched to call Matt, tell him how things went. But he wanted to wait until the morning, see how the kids were when they woke up.

Plus there was the nervous factor.

He wanted Matt to come over.

He missed him more than he thought possible and now with it potentially becoming serious again? It was hard not to dial his number.

* * *

Seven days and it was growing tougher every day; Evan called and left a message, just to let Matt know that things were being discussed and things were okay and he would call soon.

The coward's way out, sure, but if they actually spoke and connected, Evan was pretty certain there would be an invitation made. Accepted.

Not yet.

* * *

Matt went through his daily grind, through the new grind of school. He jogged. He pondered buying a fish. He heard they lowered your blood pressure and his was starting to climb.

The message from Evan helped and hindered this thing he was doing wherein he pretended to have a life.

A few fleeting times he considered ducking into a local bar; just a few drinks. Maybe get his flirt on. Maybe get laid. And yeah, then he was back to the fish and watching movies on HBO like a boring old man waiting for the phone to ring.

Maybe he should get a cat.

* * *

Evan's next meeting was with his sister-in-law; Elena suggested they have coffee at her apartment and he agreed, nervous and tense and hopeful at once. If Elena was completely on his side…

The apartment was dark and a little grim—not that Elena was much different. Since Sherri's death, she'd seemed to sink further into her quiet self, speaking little unless she was around the children. Evan couldn't remember the last actual conversation they'd had.

Elena walked out of the kitchen with two mugs of coffee. Evan thanked her, took the cup and sat down on the soft green velvet sofa.

"So…Miranda mentioned to me that you'd met someone new." And Evan's entire plan of easing into this quagmire was shot to hell.

"Uh, yes actually." Evan tried to judge Elena's tone, tried to read her sallow neutral expression. "I didn't expect…honestly, Elena, I never expected to feel something for anyone after Sherri."

Elena nodded sadly. "I know. I know you loved her. But you have to move on, Evan. You don't want to end up like me."

That raised eyebrows. His. He didn't know…Elena had lost someone? Elena had been in love? She'd never even brought anyone over to family gatherings so long as he'd been around.

"I didn't realize…Sherri never mentioned…"

"Oh, she didn't know. It was while I was at college. It was very serious but...but I knew my parents would never approve." Her eyes dropped to her lap and Evan felt a surge of fear/hope that she would intimately understand his problem here. "I mean, he was..." Her voice dropped to a whisper. "Black. They never...I couldn't bring him home. He got upset and I ended it."

"Sherri and I would have loved to meet him, Elena, Jesus Christ." Evan's hands shook. "You never had to hide someone from us."

"Thank you." Her voice was small, her eyes damp. "He...he's called me a few times since he heard about Sherri."

"Call him back."

"Oh, Evan..."

"No, seriously. Is he married?"'

"N-no."

"Call him and get your second chance, because, Elena—you can't let that pass you by. You just can't." He was clearly passionate about this one.

Elena wiped at her eyes with her free hand. "We're here to talk about you."

"In a way, we are. I almost let someone out of my life for ridiculous reasons... I mean, ridiculous because it's other people's problems—not mine. Not...his."

Now he had Elena's attention. *All* her attention. The flabbergasted expression on her face produced a nervous damp laugh on his part.

"Yeah, so—bring a guy home who's a different race, Elena. I got you beat in the shocking department."

* * *

"So Dad, when is Matt coming over?" They were Kathleen's words but Evan got the distinct impression that there had been a discussion previous to her "innocent" question.

"I was thinking we'd have him over for dinner next Saturday." Evan tried to be nonchalant as he dished up chicken and potatoes for everyone.

"He should come over Friday and stay the whole weekend," Danny announced as Miranda elbowed him in the head.

"Shut up, Danny."

"Don't say shut up, Miranda."

"I think that's a good idea!" Elizabeth decided, racing for the phone. "I'll call and ask!!"

"I think we should vote," Miranda snapped and Kathleen tossed her ponytail triumphantly.

"We did vote, you lost. Ha."

Before Evan could put the plates down, Elizabeth had already started dialing.

* * *

Matt folded his laundry on kitchen counter, one eye on the Rangers game and one on the pot of boiling water on the stove. Another fabulous night at the Casa de Haight.

The phone rang and he reached out absently to get it, not bothering to check the caller ID. Maybe it was a nice telemarketer who wanted to chat for awhile.

"Hi, Matt!" a sweet little voice blared in his ear and Matt almost dropped the cordless in the middle of his socks and underwear.

"Hi...Elizabeth? Everything okay, honey?"

"Everything's great! Hey can you come over Friday night and sleep over? We're going to have dinner and rent some movies and we can go to the park and stuff!"

"Uh...wow, Elizabeth, that sounds great. Is your dad there?" he asked weakly.

"Yeah, hold on! See you Friday!" There was a muffled conversation, some phone wrangling and then Evan's embarrassed, amused, breathless voice.

"Hi. Sorry about that."

"No problem...especially if the offer was genuine," Matt said, trying to sound casual and most likely failing miserably.

"It was. It is." Evan laughed. "There was a vote."

"How did you vote?"

"I think that's obvious."

"So I should bring my toothbrush?"

"Yeah," he said slowly and Matt grinned ear to ear. "Bring your toothbrush."

* * *

So the week for Evan went like this—work, teasing from Helena, work, "looks" from Vic Wolkowski, work, "looks" from Miranda, work, Elizabeth asking if it was Friday yet, work. Sleeping fitfully and smiling unexpectedly. He called up the counselor at Danny and Elizabeth's school to make an appointment; he did the same at the high school. He talked to his therapist. He crossed his t's and dotted his i's.

He kept checking the calendar to see if it was Friday yet.

* * *

Matt showed up at seven on Friday night with ice cream, presents for the kids, and his overnight bag. He waited on the stoop, breathing deeply until he got the balls to press the bell.

When the door opened he was dive-bombed by the twins, both talking over each other like it was a competition. He got that they were glad to see him and they'd rented *Transformers*. There might also be pizza and was that ice cream in the bag and *oh, were those presents for them?*

He really couldn't love them more.

"Let the man *in*," Kathleen yelled, exasperated, grabbing a twin in each hand (by the collar) and pulling them off of Matt. "Sorry, they're like puppies. I'm asking Dad for a taser for Christmas."

Matt smiled and winked, stepping inside and kissing her on the cheek. "Thanks for the assist."

"I'm super glad you're here and...stuff." She blushed a little and looked down at her scrapping siblings. "It's just...good."

"I agree." Matt didn't push, just stepped over the kids and into the living room where Miranda sat on the couch, not looking at him.

"Oh, hi, Miranda," he said casually, passing the bags of gifts to Kathleen. "You can figure out who gets what. The pepper spray is yours."

Kathleen smirked then tossed her big sister a look. "I hope you got Miranda an orange jumpsuit."

"Shut up, Kathleen."

"Shut up, Miranda."

"God, enough with the shut ups, please," Evan said, walking down the stairs looking good enough to eat (at least to Matt).

"*Dad*, Matt *is here!*" Elizabeth announced, diving into the bags of goodies.

"Thanks, honey." Evan was rubbing the back of his neck, looking as shy and awkward as Matt felt. "Hi."

"Hi." Matt held up the bag of melting Ben & Jerry's. "I uh...this belongs in the fridge."

"I'll make room."

"I'll follow."

"I'll vomit," Miranda muttered but her mood was blown when Kathleen took great delight in asking "Why she's got that stupid smile on her face?"

Oh God, Matt had missed them so much.

Evan opened the fridge, moved one pack of Hot Pockets, and turned expectantly to Matt—who was standing there with a shit-eating grin on his face.

"Hi. I love your kids."

"Make me an offer."

"Yeah, no. I'll just visit in their natural habitat." Matt could feel his face getting stretched out of proportion.

He wanted to kiss Evan, but for all the warm welcomes, he didn't want to tip the scales into something weird, anything that messed up this new beginning.

The ice cream got tucked away and then the swarm of children came to the kitchen; there were presents to show off and pizza to beg for and even Miranda wandered in with an air of "whatever"—and sat next to Matt at the table.

"You're not gonna kick me under the table are you?" Matt whispered, passing garlic knots in her direction. Miranda snorted.

"You should have told me sooner. I'm practically an adult."

"Yeah, true. I mean—you already have a record..."

"Matt!"

"No whispering over there." Danny didn't like being left out. Especially if it might concern the divvying up of garlic knots.

"Sorry, Danny. Grown-up business," Matt said, without sarcasm.

Danny considered disputing this but instead reached for the aforementioned garlic knots. "Yeah, whatever."

There was limited conversation as they chowed down. Matt asked about school and sports and everyone contributed; his eyes drifted over to Evan's face now and again, both of them clearly enjoying this domestic moment.

Before had been wonderful, but this? This without a lie? This was perfect.

* * *

Transformers was loud and Matt enjoyed it, sandwiched between the twins, who had called dibs before the table was even cleaned off. Matt pretended to be exasperated for about twelve seconds and that was a stretch of his acting abilities.

Eleven o'clock came and went with Danny and Elizabeth sent up to bed. (Elizabeth declared tomorrow needed to be Pancakes by Matt for breakfast and he promised.) Kathleen followed a few minutes later and Evan had to remind her that "texting beyond midnight is against the law."

Miranda decided to bust some balls and lingered for a while, watching *The Daily Show* and *The Colbert Report* and flipping around in the TV Guide to see "what's on next."

"Yeah, okay. I'll give you twenty bucks to go upstairs," Matt said finally and Evan made a shocked sound. Possibly grateful, mostly shocked.

"Thirty.

"Twenty-five."

"Miranda!"

"Deal. Good night."

"Good night." Smugly she flounced up to Matt, hand held out.

"Yeah, you'll get it tomorrow after I'm sure there'll be no further interruptions."

"I'm vaguely grossed out."

"Now you know how I feel when you bring dates over," Evan threw in drily and now Miranda fake-gagged.

"Yeah, okay, going upstairs to write in my diary about how scarred I am," Miranda mumbled. She drifted upstairs, throwing a few concerned looks over the banister before she disappeared.

Matt looked over at Evan, sheepish. "Sorry, I didn't mean to go the bribery route but uh..."

"Yeah, it's okay." Evan unfolded himself from the armchair and gave the upstairs another glance. "I don't know if I should go up...make sure..."

Matt shrugged, amazingly calm. "Go ahead. I'm guessing you'll be a lot more relaxed once you do."

"You want me relaxed?" Matt liked that half smile.

"Yes, yes I do."

* * *

Matt cleaned up the living room while Evan was upstairs. He dug around in his overnight bag, pulled out some sweats and a T-shirt, changed in the downstairs bathroom. He was amazingly Zen or in shock, not quite sure which at that point. He just wanted Evan to find the kids in...whatever state he needed to find them...then come downstairs and see...see if it still worked between them.

* * *

Evan checked on the younger children; straightened Danny's covers, shut off Elizabeth's bedside lamp. Reminded Kathleen that at the stroke of midnight her phone turned into a pumpkin. He almost chickened out going into Miranda's room, but she was the one he was most concerned about so...

"Yeah come in, Dad. Jeeze," Miranda called. Evan could hear the eye roll in her voice. He ducked his head in.

"I just wanted to..." Evan's voice drifted off awkwardly as he straddled the doorway.

"It's fine, Dad, really. It's weird, but it's fine." She picked at her bedspread. "I like him. So it's okay if you do too."

"But?"

"But...what happens when people start noticing?"

"We're not...we're not going to be hanging out at PTA meetings, Miranda." Evan's face got warm, and he refused to trip down that dangerous road of "what-ifs" again.

"Maybe we should move."

"Miranda...I'm not taking you guys out of school. I'm not going to make you start over somewhere else so close to graduation. It wouldn't be fair."

"Okay. So when people start saying crap to you guys, when they start teasing Danny or Elizabeth or Kathleen—what then?"

"Then we'll deal with the bullies."

"You make it sound so easy."

"It isn't easy. Believe me when I tell you—I thought about this a lot. But then I have to think—why do they get to win? Why do people I don't care about have a say in my life? When I married your mother people said we were too young. They said we were crazy to have four kids. I can't imagine having let other people deprive me of that..."

Miranda rubbed her eyes on her sleeve and nodded. "Okay. Now um...go downstairs before Matt reneges on his twenty-five bucks."

"You okay?"

"I think so." She perked up, eyes damp. "Another twenty-five bucks might help though."

"Extortion is a felony. Good night."

"How about if I make sure the kids don't wake you guys up before ten?"

Evan blushed, closing the door as he muttered, "Deal."

* * *

Evan stopped in the bedroom to—God help him—make sure it was cleaned up. He changed the sheets.

He was a pervert.

Jogging downstairs, Evan found Matt on the couch with the television off and most of the lights off as well. The mood was clearly set, but then again at this point, he figured they'd end up making out on the platform of the A train during rush hour.

"What? No candles?" he laughed nervously as Matt leaned up to look over the couch.

"I was just about to light a few. Got any mood music?"

"If you press Play on the stereo you're going to hear Miley Cyrus."

"I don't know who that is."

"Count your blessings."

Evan stopped standing awkwardly at the bottom of the stairs and walked over to Matt's side of the couch.

"Hello sailor?"

"I'm not really up for role-play tonight…" Matt looked up, smiling and squinting, and Evan thought he might have missed that look most of all.

"Ah, taking it slow I guess." Evan got the words out then Matt had his hand on his arm and he was (very willingly) falling onto the couch next to him. And sort of on top of him.

"This slow enough?" Their faces were close and Evan expected to feel nerves or butterflies because this was it. If he started down this path, he was not stopping this time.

And Matt seemed to be waiting for him to make the next move. His hand was firm against Evan's forearm but that was all. He was holding his breath.

"Too slow," Evan said, quiet and urgent, leaning in to initiate the kiss. Because really, it was his turn to prove he had something invested in all this.

They had been here a few times, or at least a reasonable facsimile of "this"; kissing tentatively. They had been further than this and every single time Evan had been holding something back—out of fear, out of guilt. Now he was being quiet because the kids were upstairs, but screw it—he was totally invested in sliding his tongue into Matt's mouth.

* * *

Matt figured he was dreaming but his leg wouldn't be cramping if this were a dream, and Evan wouldn't be wearing jeans…so this must be real, them folded on top of each other and kissing, and Evan was really kissing him. Tongue and everything. And then Evan was moving and straddling him and Matt liked reality better than his dreams.

He ran his hands under Evan's T-shirt, up over his chest—the scars, his heart—around and down his back, dipping into the gap of his jeans.

Evan didn't tense up, he didn't stop moving. And Jesus, he was moving; grinding down on Matt's lap until Matt's eyes rolled back into his head with pleasure.

"Not going to last long," he pointed out with a moan when they came up for air; his hands pushed deeper into Evan's pants and Evan's hands came up to tangle in Matt's hair, and clearly Evan wasn't concerned about how quickly this was happening.

"We've got all night," Evan murmured, rocking forward.

"Uh…'kay." Matt exhaled roughly, yanked one hand off Evan's fine, fine ass to pull his T-shirt up. "This…this is good."

Understatement of the year.

Evan didn't hesitate; he slid his T-shirt off and threw it next to them. He didn't hesitate to reach between them to grab the hem of Matt's own T-shirt—and brushed against the massive erection Matt was sporting. Okay, he hesitated before sliding his hand down the front of Matt's pants, but it was brief enough to give them both a chance to breathe in…oxygen they both needed because about three seconds later Evan had his mouth clamped over Matt's and it was all over but the screaming.

Or the moaning.

Or the wetness all over Evan's hand as Matt stiffened and arched and Evan felt it everywhere—the want and the need and the pleasure he was giving and getting and it was all good. Every bit of it.

* * *

Matt blinked up at Evan—who looked as smug and pleased as Matt had ever seen him—and smirked.

"Well, my fears this wasn't going to work the same way are alleviated," Matt said, feeling like a nap. Or maybe he would just feel Evan's ass some more...

Evan shrugged, trying to look casual as he rocked against Matt—and used his T-shirt to wipe off his hand. "Practice makes perfect."

"I think this couch just makes me horny."

"How does the bed make you feel?"

Matt blinked. "I think it makes me feel...surprised."

"I want you to come upstairs with me."

"In a minute." Because Matt needed to take care of something first. He put his hand on Evan's chest—scars, heartbeat, muscles—pushed him back enough to reach the fly of his jeans. He held Evan's gaze and he liked what he saw; still some shyness, still some fear, but mostly—this time it was mostly lust.

And maybe something more.

"You break up with me again, I'm going to do something drastic...like move to New Jersey," Matt murmured, pulling open Evan's jeans and reveling in the sound it produced.

"Can't...have that," Evan said, breathless and raw.

"Then don't...

Matt had a tight grip on Evan's cock and then the talking was over.

* * *

Evan put his T-shirt at the bottom of the kitchen garbage.

He shut off all the lights and headed up the stairs to the bedroom. Matt had already gone up.

Matt in his bedroom.

Evan didn't freak out; he had a single moment of missing Sherri then gently pushed the thought to the side. Not out of the picture because she would never ever be completely gone from his mind, his life, but there was room now for both of them.

He put his hand on the door knob, inhaled, and pushed it open. Matt was standing at the side of the bed, stripped naked and looking slightly confused.

"You uh—changed the room?"

"Yeah, thought it was time." Evan shut the door, turned the lock.

"I like it."

"Thanks. Sheets are clean," he added, helpful and a little dorky at once.

Matt laughed, shaking his head. Climbed into the bed, punching the pillows like he was settling in for a long winter's nap. Like he was settling in, period.

"Not for long. Get in."

Evan's jeans hit the closet wall in record time.

THE END

Tere Michaels

Tere Michaels began her writing career at the age of four when her mother explained that people made their living by making up stories -- *and* they got paid. She got out her crayons and paper and never looked back. Many pages and crayons later -- she eventually graduated to typewriters and then computers -- Tere has article clips from major magazines, a thousand ideas still left to write and a family in the suburbs. She's exceedingly pleased every time someone reads her stories and cries, laughs or just feels happy.

Check out Tere's website at http://www.teremichaels.com to see what she's up to.

Breinigsville, PA USA
14 February 2011
255536BV00001B/89/P